DOOR

OF

BRUISES

SIERRA SIMONE

Cover Design: Hang Le
Cover Image: Vania Stoyanova
Cover Models: Austin Taylor Simon
Interior Layout: Caitlin Greer

Editing: Erica Russikoff of Erica Edits
Proofreading: Michele Ficht

Content Warning

This book contains themes of ritual murder and ritual suicide in a religious context.

This book also has a character who experienced sexual violence in the past; this violence happens off page, before the events of the story, but is referenced in Chapter Seventeen.

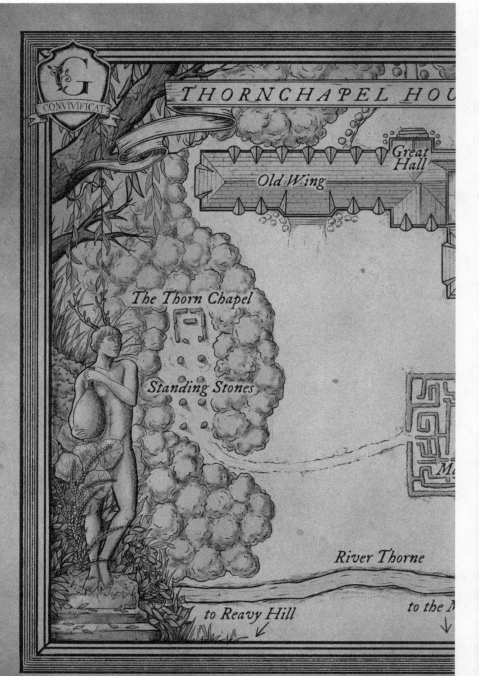

Here and there,
king and door,
cup and spear,
corn and war.

Proud and wild,
there he bleeds.
Thorn and rose,
tines and king.

—Thorne Valley folk rhyme
source unknown

Prologue

It took him a long time to find the chapel, coming from the wrong direction. A few hours at least, striking from the unnamed lane, which branched off an obscure B-road, and then straggling through open moorland until he found a pair of standing stones at the edge of the property, like an ancient stile.

Only when he walked through the stones did he see it properly— the manor house with its glinting windows, the trees in their autumnal riot of scarlet and orange and gold. The strangely dark roses that were crawling everywhere.

And the chapel. The chapel.

He hadn't been able to stop dreaming of it. Couldn't stop thinking of it. When he prayed, it curled in his mind like candle smoke.

He had to come back.

His parents would be furious with him, he knew, for taking his Nanna's car; even the famously indulgent Hesses drew the line at grand theft auto, especially when at home he only had a learner's permit, but he truly had no choice. It was either take the car and drive to Thornchapel, or burn alive with a yearning he didn't understand.

He was *called*.

And now here he was.

It took some time to work his way down to the heart of the valley, especially with the roses, which were guarded by razor-sharp thorns and which snagged at his pants and coat as he pushed his way to the chapel. He stopped between the trees before he got to the clearing, something like awe and alarm together filtering through his blood.

There was a door.

There was a door where there hadn't been a door before.

And it was open.

The zeal flared in him, making everything blurred and dreamlike.

The door.

The rest of your life is through that door.

He took a step forward—only to freeze as he realized he wasn't alone. There was someone else in the chapel—a man—a man who was on his knees in front of the altar. The man was wearing a torc around his neck, and while Becket watched, the man lowered his head and wept.

Becket knew who he was.

Dislike and fear ran cold fingers up his spine. He'd seen the man hurt Auden earlier this year—a backhanded strike right to the face— and he'd seen how the man controlled the other adults, sometimes with venom and sometimes with charm. He had no doubt the man would hurt him if he knew Becket was there—in fact, he had a knife dangling from one hand, a pale knife that looked to be very, very old. As if the man had come here to do violence anyway.

Becket swore softly to himself, his gaze going to the door. The zeal whispered to him, plucked at his sleeves, entreated him on.

The rest of your life is through that door.

Becket wondered if he could get to the door anyway.

But then a woman burst into the clearing, running, dark hair tousled from the wind and her clothes creased as if from travel. There was something small and white in her hand, like a folded piece of paper.

Her voice carried from the ruins as she called out to the man— she was relieved to have found him, but her distress was palpable. His voice raised to match hers, and though Becket couldn't hear what he said, he could hear the pain shaking in the man's voice.

It was the pain of someone with nothing left to lose, Becket thought, and he suddenly felt scared for the woman. He stepped closer to see, and both adults whirled at the noise—eyes scanning for him.

He ducked just in time, but then when he raised back up, he saw something horrifying, something that sent adrenaline flooding through him—a bright, chemical buzz to mingle with the beautiful blear of the zeal—

The man was trying to kill the woman.

The knife was between them, and she was trying to grapple the man away from her, she was desperately trying to keep him from stabbing her...

Becket didn't have to think, he didn't have to decide. Someone was in danger and he could help, he had to help. He would help.

He launched himself from the trees and over the wall, meaning to tackle the man to the ground, meaning to stun him long enough for the woman to run.

He would never know, in the years to come, what his mistake was. A mistake of trajectory, perhaps, or of speed. Or maybe it was the zeal, which always muffled his earthly senses at the expense of his spiritual ones. What Becket Hess would know—and remember—was the slam of his body into another's.

The sound of puncture.

And the slick crimson of blood spilling into the earth.

I

Eight Years Ago
Auden

Once upon a time, when I was seventeen and full of crimson misery and livid hurt, I came upon a flower in the thorn chapel.

It was a rose. A rose so darkly and deeply red that it looked black in the weak light of the frozen midwinter day. And all around it was stone rimed with frost and dead vines caught with small, cheerless snowflakes, and it shouldn't have been there, roses didn't bloom in midwinter outside, roses didn't bloom surrounded by ice and snow.

Certainly not roses that looked like that, like a freshly turned bruise.

We'd arrived at Thornchapel the previous night, and already my family was miserable without the necessary distractions of London. My mother was drinking, my father was at turns distant and beastly, and I missed St. Sebastian so much that it felt like someone had cinched my heart with razor wire and doused it in petrol. I burned alive for the boy who'd left me.

The boy who left me after I quite literally bled and broke for him.

So I hated him, and my parents, and I hated the world, the entire world, and everything in it, Thornchapel and St. Sebastian most of all. But hatred for me has never been simple, just as love has never been simple—not at least since I kissed two people in front of the grassy forest altar and grew a heart of thorns to replace my heart of flesh.

My hatred looked like this: a fervor that would have rivaled a saint's, an antipathy akin to worship. A reverence—a vengeful carnality that bordered on the sacred.

I hated most of all that he wasn't here.

With me.

Where he belonged.

I hadn't meant to go to the chapel that morning; I hadn't meant to go anywhere at all. I just knew I couldn't endure another moment inside the house with my unhappy parents, with my newly healed bones that still twinged sometimes, with the knowledge that there was no beautiful, dark-eyed boy waiting for me in the village. And so even though I despised Thornchapel in general, I put on a coat and scarf and a battered pair of boots and thought maybe I'd kick along the kitchen garden paths for a few minutes, just until I was too cold to remember how much I didn't want to be inside.

But once I stepped out onto the terrace, my choice was made for me. The maze, shrouded with snow and a hazy morning mist, beckoned, and then once I was in the maze, the center beckoned, and once I got to the center—once I saw Adonis and Aphrodite in their doomed embrace, dormant rose canes crawling over the base of the statue and twining over their feet—I knew I had to go to the chapel. I didn't want to, I didn't even *decide* to, truthfully. It simply happened. One minute I was staring up at Adonis, who seemed blissfully unaware that he'd soon be mangled by a boar and his death commemorated with broken pots and dead lettuce, and the next I was walking down the stairs and into the dark tunnel that led out to the woods.

The chapel looked much as it had when I was twelve and I was married by the altar. Although the grass was no longer emerald and the roses were no longer blooming on the walls, thorns still crawled everywhere. The altar still huddled at the far end of the ruins and the broken walls remained broken, remained home to blackthorn clumps and the lingering sloe berries caught in the frost and now quite dead.

But unlike then—when the clearing had been full of happy summer sounds, birds and bees and the distant chatter of the river— all was silent. The birds gone, the river choked with ice, the blooms for the bees long since withered and rotted away. If the thorn chapel was a flowering and a festival of life in summer, then in winter it was a tomb. A church of hush, a chancel of lack.

Mist clung to the standing stones and drifted through the arched opening where a window had once been. It gathered around the snow-powdered altar, and it swirled around my feet like water as I pushed deeper into the clearing.

I had the strangest feeling that the chapel *wanted* me to come inside, that I was meant to in some way. Like the mist and the snow and the silence had all been waiting for me, that it had all arrayed itself in solemn panoply for me, and now I was supposed to receive it and to participate. To take it into myself somehow.

Which was a translucently ridiculous idea.

And yet I couldn't seem to test my own scorn by stepping inside.

I wandered around the outside of the chapel instead, hearing only my own breaths and the crunch of my boots in the frozen grass, and heard nothing either to dispel or inflame my unease.

It wasn't that I was *afraid* to go inside, I told myself. It was only that I didn't want to. Why would I? The fallen walls of the chapel hid nothing of its insides from view, I already knew everything that was in there anyway. There was no point in standing in there and remembering the day I'd never forgotten in the first place, the day when I changed. When everything changed.

A heart of thorns to replace a heart of flesh.

That's when I saw the rose.

It was growing from inside the chapel, its vines twisting up from someplace right behind the altar and up the back wall. And here, where the stones had crumbled down enough to see over, the rose peeked above the edge, impossible and alive.

It was midwinter today, it was cold enough that even the hills seemed to shiver under the merciless December wind. All the other roses were dead—along with the flowers, the trees, the grass. Everything was dead. Everything except for this.

It was the most beautiful thing I'd seen since I last saw St. Sebastian's eyes.

I was curious. I was compelled.

Again, my feet moved without my willing them to, and again I found myself drawn onward, as if I'd been meant to take these very steps from birth. I walked around the walls and standing stones to the front of the chapel and—knowing both my resistance and my eagerness were equally contemptible—went inside.

It was not as if a veil had been drawn over the world outside the chapel. It wasn't as if I stepped inside the chapel and the silence deepened or the mist thickened. No, the chapel wasn't like that, it wasn't a discrete and bounded space the way it ought to have been. It was more like a cathedral, like a Levantine temple, with a diffusion of holy spaces branching and expanding from one central, sacred locus. The temple in Jerusalem had its Holy of Holies protected by an outer sanctuary, which was protected by courts, which were protected by chambers, which were protected by walls and gates, and so too did the thorn chapel have an altar protected by walls, which were gated by standing stones, which were guarded by the snow-dusted trees.

And so I cannot say that any one threshold made a difference to what happened next, and I cannot even claim to know what thresholds I crossed and what they meant. But I do know this: all of Thornchapel is a threshold of sorts, and when you are there, you are one too. I became a gate, a tabernacle, and an altar. A holiness of lanky limbs and angry lust, and a hallow of ink-stained fingers and unmet needs.

The mist seemed to part for me as I approached the altar and the impossible flower behind it, and I skirted around the spot where I once kissed Proserpina and St. Sebastian, I skirted around the snowy heap of the grass-covered altar, and I came before the wall. If it had been a proper chapel, a proper church, the entrance would be at the west and the altar to the east, but the thorn chapel was not a proper church, and so the entrance was at the south and the altar was to the north. Which meant this early in the morning, the rose was not only framed by the old stone but also by the morning-dark woods. The rose seemed to draw shadows to itself, seemed to be in a light all its own, which was not a light at all, but a sort of murky umbra that made me think of graves and thunder, of walking alone in the fog-laden dark and hearing something move behind me.

It was fear that I felt, but it was an awakening too, a recognition, like I'd been waiting for this, just as it had been waiting for me. Like I was about to complete something I'd started five years ago with flower petals stuck to my face and St. Sebastian and Proserpina's mouths on mine.

I tugged off my glove and reached for the rose.

There are many fairy tales that begin like this, with this moment right here, and perhaps I should have known better, perhaps I should have stopped myself. Perhaps I should have waited, come back on another day when the light was less strange and the mist had gone. Perhaps I should've understood that the need and hunger in me were only fed by this place, and nothing here could ever, ever soothe me— at least not until I had my St. Sebastian back.

But I was seventeen and I didn't want to be soothed. I wanted to hurt, and I wanted to throb, and I wanted every possibility in the world to lay itself bare to me, to come running and kneel at my feet, heads bowed and begging forgiveness for staying out of my reach.

It was not the first time I'd ever felt possessiveness—no, Proserpina and St. Sebastian had made sure of that—but it was the first time I'd ever felt *possession*.

Dominion. Imperium. Command.

I was entitled to whatever grew, crept, or slumbered at Thornchapel, and it *would* reveal itself to me. My fingers found the stem of the rose and followed its thorny tether up to the heavy, tightly furled head of the bloom itself. I pulled it, meaning to pluck only the bloom, but registered my mistake an instant too late. An unseen thorn sank into my thumb and bit into the skin, sending pain right down to the bone, up my wrist, up my entire arm.

I swore, but I didn't let go, twisting harder and tearing the bloom right off the plant, until it was mine.

I looked down at my prize—a whorl of bruise-colored petals, a scroll of silky impossibility. Blood from my pierced thumb—a bright and shocking red against the dark, shadow-scarlet of the rose—was smeared over the petals and sepals, over my palm and my wrist. It dripped onto the snow below.

The back of my neck crawled with awareness, a feeling of not-aloneness that superseded the usual watchfulness of the chapel. I turned with the rose still in my bloody hand and then took a step back.

A woman, beautiful and feral looking, with pale skin and eyes as green as a cat's, was staring at me from the other side of the altar. She wore a long dress—a near-white, with the kind of shapeless fussiness that spoke of Victorian origins—and a slender torc of gold around her neck, its terminals etched with interconnected spirals. She reminded me forcefully of Proserpina—those cat eyes—but also of Proserpina's mother, who'd gone missing here at Thornchapel five years ago.

I was reminded of something else. A painting. But that was an impossibility.

The woman didn't step forward, she didn't move. She only tilted her head. "You are a Guest," she said.

I suppose it was a testament to how thoroughly my manners had been bred into me that I answered a ghost. "Yes."

My bloody hand continued to cradle the rose. My thumb hurt.

"It was the Kernstows first," the woman said, "before the Guests. But it was always a king. It has to be a king."

Her voice was pure Devonshire, big vowels and bigger *r*s, and shockingly loud. Unnervingly present. I could have been talking to someone from Thorncombe, talking to one of the gardeners who came in to tend the grounds. That's how *here* she was.

But she couldn't be here, she couldn't. Either my conception of reality had to bend or I was finally succumbing to St. Sebastian-leaving-me-without-a-word-induced insanity.

"You're not real," I said, pointlessly.

"And you're not a king," she replied. "Yet."

I could only stare. I used to pretend to be a king as a little boy—and for a brief time last summer, I made myself the king of one St. Sebastian, and he would be mine to kiss whenever my royal heart desired. But I knew better now. I knew that boys like me didn't get to be kings—of pretend or kink or otherwise. Boys like me went to Oxford or Cambridge, they married girls like Delphine, they found respectable careers that had nothing to do with art and everything to do with being quality, with furthering the undefinable but all-important Guest-ness that had been assigned to me from birth.

The woman touched her cheek—a mirror to the place on my own where a cut had healed into a bright pink divot. "That is the scar of a king," she said, nodding to the healed wound. "A someday king."

She closed her eyes as her hand dropped, her fingertips settling on the curve of the torc around her neck. "You must remember," she said, "because it will happen again. Who is John Barleycorn, little Guest prince?"

John Barleycorn. It was a Burns poem, a folk song. I stared at her.

"John Barleycorn is a memory," she said, opening her eyes and answering her own question. "A memory of the kings who walked to the door."

I was utterly lost now. "The door."

"By dusk," she said softly, and there was something like a shudder in her voice. "If it's not done by dusk, it may be too late. It almost was for me, and through the door I saw—"

Another shudder.

"And it has to be a king," she went on, her voice firming slightly as she spoke. "A true king would never let anyone go in a king's place. That is the price, you see."

Fear, not cold but hot—hot and sticky like the blood dripping off my thumb—was all over me when I spoke. "The price of what?"

There was a kind of tender pity to her words when she finally answered.

"You will learn."

And then she nodded at my hand, as if all the answers were there.

I looked down too, and when I looked back up, she was gone, with only the swirl of the mist to testify that she'd ever been there in the first place.

With a sharp inhale, and long-delayed panic, I bolted from the chapel, and tore my way home as if every ghost in England was on my heels. And when I got home, I slammed the crumpled rose into the biggest book I could find, stripped off my clothes, and then stood in the shower for as long as it took for me to believe that I'd hallucinated the entire thing. I'd hallucinated Estamond because of my childhood games, I'd hallucinated the part about John Barleycorn because…well, because who knows why. So it hadn't been real. None of it had been real.

Except for the rose. The rose which later on I'd open the old, heavy book to stare at. The rose which grew brittle and dried but never, ever lost that distinctive, bruised hue.

If nothing else, the rose had been real.

It has to be a king. That is the price.

Years passed, and I never told anyone what happened that day. Why would I?

But if I had, maybe Proserpina and St. Sebastian would still be here at Thornchapel, maybe Delphine would be curled at Rebecca's feet. Maybe Becket wouldn't be enduring a sinner's exile in Argyll. Maybe we would all be together. Maybe all would be as it should be.

Then again, maybe not. I've learned caution when it comes to Thornchapel, to predicting how this place moves through people's minds and bodies.

I've learned caution about a lot of things.

But I've learned too late, it seems.

2

Auden

Ten days after the two loves of my life leave me, the phone rings.

"Guest," a voice says after I answer. "You should come down here."

I stand and go to one of the many windows in my home office. Out on the south lawn, my oldest friend stands in an emerald-green jumpsuit, facing the house and looking up at me. Behind her, the workers hired to demolish Thornchapel's maze have stopped working, and they've all gathered around something I can't see.

Something low. Something in the ground.

"Can it wait?" I ask, glancing back at my desk. I'm supposed to be finishing a proposal for Historic Environment Scotland—a visitors' center situated near the Ness of Brodgar in Orkney—and I've already told Isla I'd have it on her desk this afternoon. Earlier than she needs it, yes, but what else do I have to do? When St. Sebastian has left me and Proserpina has followed him?

"I'm afraid it can't wait," Rebecca says. "We found something." She pauses, and then adds, "Auden…"

"Yes?"

"We'll need to stop construction."

Worry kicks in my stomach. Any number of capricious variables can halt construction—bad weather, any weather at all, planning difficulties, parts delays, labor delays, labor disputes, protected birds roosting in the construction equipment—but there is only one variable that truly worries me. Only one that no amount of money can fix, that no force of will can bend into submission.

"Fuck," I mutter, already moving. "I'll be down straight away."

A charcoal sky hangs above the world. Broken slabs of stone litter the site.

"We knew there was rock," Rebecca Quartey says. She looks down at the exposed chasm before her feet, frowning at it like it's a badly trained submissive. "But there was no reason to think…"

She's right, there really had been no reason to think this was possible. This had been a maze for a century and a half, and a labyrinth before that. When Rebecca had asked if I wanted a ground survey when I'd first hired her, I'd waved her off, telling her I didn't need an overpriced map of hedge roots and dormice nests. I knew the maze's secrets already, I knew about the tunnel leading down to the woods. There was no reason to think this place was anything other than a Victorian diversion, an elaborate gate Estamond had erected to conceal her comings and goings to and from the chapel.

"How many of them are there?" I ask, squatting down to peer inside the pit. Now that all the hedges are gone—the statues removed, the gravel scraped away—the site is mostly damp, dark earth. The site is mostly as it should be.

Except for the squarish slabs of granite embedded right into the soil. Except for the chambers underneath them.

Those are not at all as they should be.

"We've found seven that would have been underneath the maze itself," Rebecca answers, and then points to the middle of the site, where the now-exposed tunnel opens like a hungry mouth. "And then the one by the tunnel makes eight."

She hands me a small torch and I click it on. The slab at our feet has been shifted enough to reveal the empty space underneath, lined with more stones to create a box. Like a granite chest that's been sunk into the earth and then lidded.

A kistvaen. A cist.

A Dartmoor grave.

When I shine the torch inside, I see more soil, and then the unmistakable shape of a mostly-buried axe head, which appears to be a dull greeny-brown. If there were any doubt that these could be some kind of naturally occurring coffins in the landscape, it's extinguished then.

What a fucking bind.

"It's bronze, Auden."

"So it is," I say, standing up. "We'll have to make the call."

"The planning authority first. Then they'll call the shovelbums."

The archaeologists. Neither Rebecca nor I are strangers to this particular roadblock. Like flooding or subsurface clays with unpleasantly high plasticities, archaeology is yet another construction hazard waiting to happen, and archaeologists are the natural, necessary evil that follows. Like plumbers after a broken pipe, or stumbling heiresses after a few hours in the tents at Henley. Cause and effect. Catalyst and reaction.

It's not that I *hate* archaeology—or archeologists. Of course not. Yay history, and all that. But I would rather it not interfere with the things I want to do…such as remake the face of my ancestral home into something that would horrify my very dead but no less loathsome father.

I run my free hand through my hair, trying to think. "We'll need to let the project manager know—a full excavation could take weeks, even if I'm leaning on them to go faster, and we'll have to furlough the workers until it's over. I'll also make sure the archaeology team knows the thorn chapel is off limits. I don't want to risk any curious excavators wandering back and seeing the door. At least not until we understand it better." I pull at my hair once more before dropping my hand. "I've a friend from school who does rescue archaeology. I'll see if his firm is available."

Rebecca nods. "If you can handle the authority and commissioning the excavation, I'll deal with the rest." Then she pulls her lower lip into her mouth and releases it with a decisive exhale. "There's one last thing I think you should see."

She leads me past a few more slabs, these still covering their chambers underneath, and together we walk to what used to be the center of the maze. There's no real pattern to the graves that I can discern—they seem dropped into the earth at random, as if a giant stood here and carelessly emptied his morbid pockets—but the one near the center is uncomfortably close to the tunnel entrance. Too close to be coincidental.

"This was the first stone we moved," Rebecca explains as we get closer. "We thought it was part of the tunnel entrance at first, but then..."

"Another grave?"

She shakes her head slowly. "I don't think so. But I don't know what it is either."

I click the torch on again and approach the cist—only to realize it's not a cist at all, but something much, much bigger. A space large enough for a person to stand in, to take a few steps in even. I get on my stomach, ignoring the damp kiss of the earth through the linen of my popover shirt, and shine the light farther inside. This chamber has fared better than the last one—I can still make out parts of the stone floor at the bottom—although I don't see anything else on the floor. No bronze axe heads, no beads or jewelry or burned bits of bone. There's only the stone. But that's more than enough, because—

"You see it?" Rebecca asks quietly.

"Yes," I say, shining the torch this way and that, trying to make sense of it. The walls are covered with carvings of double spirals—spirals just like the one Proserpina found at the Kernstow farmhouse, just like the ones that decorated the ends of Estamond's torc. A carved coil going clockwise, which then leads into another coil, this one carved in a counter-clockwise fashion.

And in between the spirals are other shapes—two other shapes, I realize—laid out sporadically and rather crookedly.

"I thought those could be antlers," Rebecca says. She doesn't get on her stomach, instead squatting very easily for someone in heeled boots, pointing to the angled tines carved between the double spirals.

"And those other shapes—what do they look like to you?"

I don't need to think about it long. "They look like roses."

Not roses like one sees in medieval heraldry or on the walls of Knossos, with flat petals and overzealous sepals poking out underneath. No, these roses are surfeits of silky petals unfolding into glory, practically spirals in their own right.

What color were the roses in their minds when they carved these walls, I wonder. Pink roses? White or red?

Black?

I get to my feet and turn off the torch, handing it back to Rebecca as I pivot to take in the scattered cists. "It's like a field of bones."

"It *was* a field of bones," Rebecca says, stepping forward to a cist that faces the chamber with the rose-and-spiral-etched walls. They are only a few steps apart, almost as if they are facing off against each other, almost as if this grave was meant to be within reaching distance of the spiral chamber. It reminds me of something, but the harder I try to think of what it is, the more it eludes me.

"…a handful of centuries," Rebecca is saying to me. She uses the side of an elegant ankle boot to nudge the soil around the grave. "The soil here might be too acidic for unburnt bone to last longer than that. The archaeologists may find some cremains, however."

"You're saying Thornchapel eats bones."

She gives me a look indicating I'm being dramatic, which is something I've never been able to help. "I'm saying *Dartmoor* eats bones. Most moors do. Because of the low—"

"If you say pH to me, I'm going to stop listening."

Rebecca gives me a stare that would singe the eyelashes off a lesser man. "Because of the low pH, you absolute dickhead."

I sigh.

"But," Rebecca goes on, "we are quite lower down here, in our valley. The soil is different. Who knows what they might find?"

I think of Adelina Markham, buried behind the altar by my father, and I squint at the trees under the dark sky, as if I could see through them to the chapel itself and the grave it once hid.

The chapel. The memory of kissing St. Sebastian there, of feeling that lip jewelry against my mouth as the rain streaked down around us, comes so abruptly that I have to close my eyes.

A hand touches my elbow, right above where my sleeve is rolled up. I open my eyes to see Rebecca looking at me with an expression of pure empathy.

"Are you okay?" she asks quietly.

"You know I'm not."

She nods.

She does know, just as I know that she's also not okay. We've spent the last ten days in the same loop of misery and work. Getting up early, staying up late. Working until our eyes hurt and until not even tea sounds good anymore, drifting through the house like wraiths with iPad Pros, sighing over emails like widows sighing over embroidery.

Because working is the closest we can come to forgetting, even just for a moment, that the people we love aren't here.

"Get inside and call the planning authority," she says. "I'll see you tonight."

I start to leave, and then I stop. "Quartey." On the edges of the lawn, the trees stretch and hiss and sigh. "Thank you," I tell her.

"Of course."

"No, not for the work. For coming back."

She stills, her face turned to the ground. Her braids are pulled into a high bun today, and so I can see the effort it takes for her to keep her face schooled and expressionless.

"You're the one who comes back, Bex. Always."

There's a quiver to her lips as she looks up at me, and I'm seeing what almost no one else has ever seen: Rebecca Quartey trying not to cry.

"Heeeey, hey, hey," I say gently, pulling her into my arms. She's tall, but I'm taller, and she can nestle her face into my neck, which she does. And soon I feel why, with the tears wetting my throat and her shuddering breaths coming in fast and hard against my wet skin. "It's okay, Bex. I'm here. I'm here."

As she cries, I carefully angle us away from the workers clustered around the excavators and backhoes on the other side of the site. I know Rebecca would be furious with herself if anyone in a professional setting saw her cry, and I understand why she can't afford to be seen as emotional, as anything less than perfectly composed.

But I also understand why she can't hold it inside any longer, I understand that sometimes it's a seemingly irrelevant remark or gesture or memory that brings reality crashing back in.

The woman she loved hurt her. The woman she loved embarrassed her in a way that's nigh impossible to forgive. And now all she has left is work and an equally broken-hearted—but useless—best friend.

Her wet eyelashes move against my throat. I hold her as tight as I can, kissing her temple, and murmuring, "*Hey*." I have little practice soothing people—only my mother soothed me as a child, and it only happened when I was too young to really remember it. But Rebecca herself has taught me over the last few months how to care for someone in pain. How to show love and concern when someone is vulnerable in your arms. It's the heart of kink, after all. Pain and concern. Vulnerability and safety. No reason it can't work with friends too.

I kiss her again, and then squeeze her into my chest as I rub my hands along her back. "It'll be okay," I murmur. "It'll be okay."

When she speaks, her voice is thick. "I want it to be okay. I want it to be okay *so badly*. I *hate* myself for feeling this."

After a minute, she says, ducking her face into my collarbone, "I never stood a chance, you know."

"Against what?" I'm thinking of Thornchapel, of the door, of the graves. Of my father's sins, of the prices we've all paid for those sins.

I never stood a chance against those things either.

"Not what—*who*," Rebecca sighs. "I never stood a chance against her."

The evening is cool, like the sky promised it would be.

A rumpled vista of yellow gorse and pinky-purple heather greets me as I reach the equinox stones, panting from my punishing run from the house. I stagger in uneven circles as I unscrew the cap of my water bottle and take an ill-advisedly long drink—gulping the water down and immediately feeling nauseous. I stop drinking and focus on pulling in precious air, very aware that the wind seems to be gasping with me. Aware that the grass and gorse around my feet are slowly tossing in agitation, as if trying to catch their breath too.

I thought a run would clear my head, but it didn't. Instead, I feel even fuller of everything: my missing Poe and my missing St.

Sebastian, Rebecca's grief, Delphine's seclusion, Becket's forced retreat. The graves. The chapel.

The roses.

The door.

I can nearly see the chapel from here, although not quite. The view from Reavy Hill would be better. Instead, I can see above the lip of the Thorne Valley, I can see out to the myriad villages, tors, farms, fields, hedges, rivers, and rocks that make Dartmoor the beautiful place it is. I can see nearly to the farthest north end of the valley, where the Kernstow farmhouse huddles against the wind, bleak and beleaguered.

It was the Kernstows first, before the Guests. But it was always a king.

For centuries and longer, it seems, people have been going to the door. The door which is now open.

And what's terrible is I don't even care.

I don't even care right now, because I turned into my father and St. Sebastian ran from me, and I made Proserpina run after him, because I'm a monster who should be alone and I'm a man who can't be trusted.

I'm the wrong kind of king.

I should go back to the house. I should go back and eat the supper Abby's prepared for Rebecca and me, and I should sit in the library with my friend and work in silence until one of us breaks down and gets the gin or the scotch or whatever our nightly poison will be.

I should go home and pretend I'm not checking my phone every five minutes, pretend I'm not miserable at the prospect of more and more days like this. Working at Thornchapel, working in London. Sleeping alone.

Regretting everything and yet not regretting enough.

Would I do it again? Would I tie antlers to my head and chase St. Sebastian through the forest knowing we shared a father? Would I make him vow to be mine forever and ever?

I don't even have to ask myself that. Of course I would. I won't absolve myself, I won't release myself from the utter wrongness of lying, but when it felt like the other option was saying goodbye…losing him once I'd finally gotten him back…

No, I would have held on to him with my teeth if I could have.

See? I told you.

The wrong kind of king.

I turn away from the moors—currently misting over with an effete evening rain—and make to go back down to the house below, and that's when I see it, tucked against the base of a standing stone. A small sheep…or a large lamb. I think it's asleep until I realize its eyes are open, and it's in fact quite dead.

I pull out my phone to call the Livestock Society—dead animals are common enough that I'm familiar with the reporting process—but the reception up here is shit. I'm going to have to wait until I get back to the house to report it. With a sigh that would definitely earn the label of dramatic if Rebecca were around, I get closer to take a quick picture in case the livestock people want it.

I see it on the screen of my phone before I see it on the sheep itself: a rope of thorns caught around one hoof. Strung along the thorns like fruit on a vine are several black roses, looking fresh and full and totally out of place up here in the open hills and the green grass.

The sheep must have wandered into the chapel and back out again. It's not uncommon for the sheep to find their way down there, not at all, but the sight of the roses gives me pause all the same.

I walk closer, approaching the carcass like it's a trap designed to snare lonely architects, and then crouch in front of the animal to examine it more closely. It must be recently dead—there's no bloating of the belly, no awkwardly jutting legs indicating rigor mortis. No flies, no nothing. It looks like it simply laid down to rest next to the standing stone and never got up again.

Unease crawls along the back of my neck and I stand up.

It's nothing, it's absolutely nothing at all. This is Dartmoor, sheep—alive and dead—are everywhere. That it could have been in the chapel is nothing. That the animal doesn't look sick or injured or anything other than half garlanded with the roses from near the door is nothing.

I'm just on edge because I miss the two other pieces of my heart, because I found eight graves within sight of my bedroom window today. It's nothing and perhaps if I keep telling myself it's nothing, I'll believe it.

I turn and jog down the hill as the rain finally comes, as listless and feeble as I feel.

3

Auden

I hadn't meant to keep it from him. Not at first.

I'd set the letter from my father down, and I'd stared at my desk—brand new, empty, the desk of a fresh start—and I'd let myself quietly bleed out onto the floor.

My father was a murderer, an abuser, an adulterer. During his life, he'd inflicted his strange combination of toxic charisma and cruelty on anyone within reach. That he fathered a child I hadn't known about shouldn't have surprised me; it shouldn't have counted among the worst of his sins.

In a way, it made a perfect kind of sense. The money my father gave Jennifer Martinez, the way Jennifer stayed here in Thorncombe long after her husband's death. My father's reaction to our assault in the graveyard: cold fury and possessive concern not only for me, but for St. Sebastian too.

The way St. Sebastian himself seemed drawn to this place, to its wild edges and lonely secrets. The way we seemed drawn together—to fight, to fuck, to love the same person—and the way that however we came together, we also always fit somehow. Even with fists and blood, even with bites and kisses, we fit.

In architecture, we talk about honesty. An honest structure is one that shows its history and its bones. Visible struts, rivets, trusses. You can walk into a building and see what holds it up and why; you can perceive the need of each and every element; you can see the fingerprints of its builders, the concessions to budget, the compromises and the mistakes.

It is a thing of beauty to walk into a space and see with such unvarnished clarity its purpose, its very existence.

I was not honest later, but in every other way, my love was an honest thing made even more honest by learning the truth. Yes, I could see the rivets and trusses now.

Yes, I could see the stains, the splinters, the scars.

I chose it anyway. My sin was not trusting that he would too; my vindication was knowing I was right, because I lied and in the end, it was for nothing.

In the end, he chose to be alone.

"Shh," I tell Sir James Frazer after a solid thirty seconds of growling. I'm typing my weekly email to Becket. While he's on his leave of absence, he's not supposed to have access to email and social media, so I don't expect a response, but I've grown used to having him around, to having him only a few miles away whenever I wanted company, and so the emails are a temporary balm.

I miss him. I miss him, and now is when I would need my priest the most, not only his conversations by the fire, but his blessings and his absolutions. The way he looked at you like he was going to lead you right to God himself and help you press your forehead to the top of God's presumably sandaled feet.

But now he's gone and Poe's gone and St. Sebastian is gone and Delphine is with her parents, and everything is hollow here, including me.

Sir James doesn't listen to my admonishments and continues to growl at the glass. He loves the new office because the windows offer vantages out to the lawn—where bunnies quite rudely nose for clover without his permission—and into the trees along the front of the house, where the even ruder birds flap around without giving him a chance to chase them. I assume he's growling at the birds now, until his growls abruptly change into happy puppy-barks and he's tearing across the length of the office and down the stairs.

I go to the window in time to see Proserpina locking the door of the car I lent her, a bag slung over her shoulder, her hair a waterfall of dark silk down her back. Even from here I can see the expression on her face—pensive, sad—and the short skirt she's wearing with no tights underneath.

My dick is hard in an instant, my heart is outside my body even faster than that, and then I'm tearing downstairs just like Sir James, desperate to see her, to see those green eyes I feel like I've known forever. Eyes as green as the trees around the chapel. Kernstow eyes.

Twice while she was with St. Sebastian, she called me. I didn't ask her to—in fact, when I told her to leave, I told her not to call, to spend all her time with him, to focus entirely on him. I didn't want her to feel like her loyalty was bifurcated or split—I didn't want her to be anything less than whole and happy with him, as much as wholeness and happiness were possible in the circumstances.

But even then she called me twice from the hotel room she was renting. Both times needing something only I could give her, and so I did, out of weakness or mercy—or both, because I needed it too.

The first time, I had her kneel alone on the floor, her skirt up and her cute little blouse unbuttoned, and then I had her prop her phone against the wall so I could watch as she slowly brought herself off. The second time, I had her pinch herself from the inside of each knee to the dip of her navel and then in one line across the soft stretch of her lower belly—making a long, skinny *A* of bright red blotches on her body.

And then she made herself come for me.

It was a relief—a small blessing in a time that seemed starved of them—but it wasn't enough. How could it be enough? I'd barely been satisfied having both Proserpina and St. Sebastian constantly available to me in my house. Two phone calls, however filthy, were never going to slake me.

And so when I reach Proserpina downstairs, when I see her in the Great Hall murmuring to Sir James as she scratches his ears and he wags his tail in big, excited tail-circles, I can't handle it, I can't stop myself. Even though I know there are workers in the old wing of the house, even though I know she's probably had a long drive. I love her and I want her, and the line between loving and wanting has always been thin for me.

As has the line between loving and taking.

I stalk over to her and thread a hand through her hair while my other hand moves her so she's pressed against me, her back to my front. I find the placket of her blouse, run my fingers up the buttons until I find the top one resting at the base of her throat. "You're not supposed to be here," I say, popping buttons open and reaching inside. Through the lace of the bra, her nipples are drawn into hard little points. "I sent you away."

"I couldn't *stay* away," she says, sounding miserable. "I missed you and I missed this place and I have a job to do and also I had this dream—ohhh."

I've found a nipple, and I roll it between my fingertips. "No, little bride. You promised."

"You know I think that promise was bullshit anyway—"

I've found her other nipple now, and I pull on her hair, not hard enough to hurt, only hard enough to tug her head to my shoulder and expose her throat. I can look down the front of her like this, down the path of skin and lace I've just exposed, down to where my hand is toying with her. Glimpses of berry-pink tease up at me through lace and between fingertips.

She shivers against me, and I'm shivering right back. It's been so long, too bloody long, and when I think of her with him—when I think of *him*—I'm burning with that feeling again, that feeling I felt in the thorn chapel as a youth, that feeling I felt during Beltane. Like I'm full of the entire world, like I'm full of leaves and sunlight and fire and doors that will go anywhere I want them to, absolutely anywhere.

Like a king. And not a king trimmed with ermine and jewels, but a king like how kings used to be. Stripped to the waist and panting, young, half reckless and sometimes-wild.

I wish it were Beltane. I wish I were running through the woods now, hunting the people I love, getting ready to claim them by the fire with ashes in the air and hunger in my heart.

Proserpina goes pliant against me, her body softening and molding against mine. "I know my safe word," she whispers. "You don't have to hold back. Not now."

There's a long table in the hall—old enough that I've never had the heart to throw it away, but ugly enough that I donated it to the renovation efforts—and I have Proserpina bent over the top of it in less than an instant, her hands braced next to a coil of wire and cans of paint, and her skirt flipped over her creamy bottom, which I quickly redden with a few judicious swats. Not as punishment, not as discipline. Not for any other reason than I like seeing her lips part as she gasps against the table. I like seeing the arch of her back and the reflexive kick of her feet. I like feeling her skin against my palm and knowing that here, right now in this moment, the gnaw of the thorns around my heart no longer hurts as it normally does. It feels right and necessary—and inevitable. Lightning finding the ground, rivers finding the sea…and my body against hers.

"You're not wearing anything under your skirt," I say, my knuckles brushing against her bare skin as I unzip my trousers. "Good."

"I hoped for this," she confesses, looking back at me as much as she can. "I missed this."

I was the one who told her to leave, I was the one who made her promise, and yet I'm squeezed all over by miseries and longings too numerous to name. "Did you miss this? While you were fucking him?"

I sound jealous. I am jealous. And I'm also not jealous at all. There's no explaining it, except to say that even jealousy can be exquisite sometimes. Who can account for all the ways we like to be bruised? The beautiful girl in front of me likes to be spanked and bitten. I instead have chosen to fall in love with two people who also love each other.

One of whom now hates me.

You're being selfish and you're trying to keep people who don't want to be kept…you're no better than him.

So that's the equation you're proposing. I'm not our father if I let you leave me.

He was right. And I was right to make Proserpina leave too, but I'm too selfish to make her leave again. I'm too selfish to let her go.

Maybe I am my father after all.

She's nodding against the table at my question, panting softly as I run my fingers up her thigh to see if she's ready to be fucked. "You know I did. You know *he* did. We can…try…with each other, but it's not the same, it's never the same."

She's mostly wet but not quite there. My aching cock surges in envy as I slide a finger inside her tight heat. "You try topping each other without me there?" It fires my blood to think about—both with hunger and with an irritated possession. "You let him, what? Spank you? Bite you? Fuck you rough?"

Her eyelashes are fluttering—I haven't let up on my exploration between her legs—and when she answers, her voice is breathy and low. "Sometimes. If I make him do things, it almost works."

Because she likes the pain, the roughness, the touch of it, and St. Sebastian needs the spirit of the thing, the subtextual anima that makes kink work. The compelling would almost be enough for him, and the pain would almost be enough for her.

Fuck me, I wish I could watch them do it. Not that I'd be able to stand it for very long. Within minutes I'd be on them both, my fingers in their hair, my mouth seeking theirs. Even imagining it has me crawling out of my skin.

"You know your safe word?" I confirm as I slide my fingers free. She's still not wet enough, but she told me once that she likes it that way. She likes the first few thrusts to walk that line between pleasure and pain. My organ is ready to oblige, throbbing painfully as I rub the dark, swollen cap against her skin, seeking out her entrance.

"Yes," she says, moaning impatiently. "I already told you—"

I push inside without any further warning, spreading my hand between her shoulder blades to keep her pinned to the table as I fuck. Quick, shallow, a little mean.

She comes almost immediately, keening into the table as her hands scratch at the surface of it. I curse as I feel it, that first sharp quiver, and my testicles draw up tight to my body, already aching to come too. My head drops to my chest, and I drag in a long breath, fighting for control. But I can't not look at her for too long. She's too wonderful like this, pinned under my hand and whispering my name as her body shivers around my erection.

Though I've been keeping a loose watch on our perimeter, I check the doorway joining the old wing to the hall to make sure her hardly-quiet climax hasn't brought us any voyeurs. The team is working on the top story this week, but workers on a site are like ants on an anthill, swarming everywhere, and so it's very possible we might have someone coming through the hall for something. Proserpina is an exhibitionist and probably wouldn't mind being seen so much, but "can the construction team watch me shag you over a table" is a conversation we haven't had yet, and I wouldn't cross that line until I was sure.

Satisfied we're alone for now, I pull out again, looking down so I can see how her body grips mine as I slide away. She's tight and warm and sweet, and her curvy bottom makes the perfect heart shape when she's bent over like this. A heart shape I get to fuck.

"Auden," she breathes. "Sir." A hand reaches back for me, and I catch her fingers in mine as I pierce her again, this time driving all the way in until every inch of me is squeezed and wet.

"*Fuck*," I say, because that's it, that's it, that's it. Who can get anything done when there's a Proserpina around?

But there's more—we both want more. So I press in, hard, harder, watching her face carefully as I do. I wait for her sharp intake of breath, the quick wince—I want the edge of the table to bite into her hips enough that she feels it, but I don't actually want to bruise her like that—and right *there*, there it is. The breath, the wince, the furrow in her forehead: the crest of the pain curling in over itself like a wave.

I ease up a little with my hips, keeping my hand firmly on her back, and then I fuck in earnest, I fuck her like I haven't fucked in ten years instead of almost ten days. I fuck and feel the moment her brain starts to unload endorphins into her bloodstream, the moment she starts sliding into a bliss beyond the usual gratification of sex, going loose and shivery with a small smile curved against the scarred wood of the old table.

And I follow her in.

I let the slick pleasure thrum along every nerve ending, run down the backs of my thighs and up my spine and down to the very fingertips that hold my little bride in place. I let every part of her overwhelm and conquer every part of me—her hair spilled onto the table like a Pre-Raphaelite muse's, her soft, needy moans, the hot heaven of her cunt. Those eyes—framed by dark lashes so long they rest against her cheek when she shuts them.

And when she opens them, gazing back at me with eyes like the color of life itself, I'm sawn wide open, like nothing of me will ever be held apart from her. How could it, when she is who she is? When it was always meant to be her? Even when we were children and playing children's games, somehow I knew. Proserpina Markham, the dreamer, the believer. Proserpina who kissed two boys as lightning cracked across the sky.

My feet have always been sunk deeper in the earth than I would like, even before I made it my job to think about footings and foundations. I used to blame this place for that, I used to blame my family, stuck as they were in a backwards-looking way of life, in what it meant to be a Guest. But now I know it's me, that I was somehow this way from the beginning, all on my own and apart from swollen bank accounts and ancient properties. And the problem with being so thoroughly planted in the ground is that it's almost impossible to drift or to dream, it's almost impossible to remember that sometimes the questions are more important than the answers. Which is why she is everything to me. I need her questions, her buoyancy and dreams and smiles.

Those smiles. Wide and dimpled and with that creased lower lip I love so much. She's smiling up at me now, her eyes bright and her pupils blown, as if she's drunk, drunk, drunk from me.

From only a handful of minutes with me.

Oh, that's a dangerous feeling *indeed*.

And it's that feeling that pushes me over the edge—more than the actual fucking. It's the warmth of her back under my hand, it's her shoulder blades moving like a bird's wings under my spread fingers. It's the sight of her lace-covered breasts pressed against the table, her unbuttoned shirt open and the plastic buttons shivering on the wood.

It's the giddy dent of her dimple as she smiles in subspacey bliss.

My thighs tighten and my belly clenches, and then I'm flooding her, pulse after jerking pulse, emptying myself into her body and already knowing it won't be enough, it's never enough with her or St. Sebastian. Like I could make it my job and my vocation to fuck them every day for the rest of my life and I'd still never be satisfied.

I finish with a soft exhale, reluctant to stop, deciding not to stop. I pull free—and with a final glance at the entrance to the old wing—tuck myself still hard and wet inside my trousers.

I scoop Proserpina into my arms. She's limp and loose and she nestles right into my arms like it's the only place in the world she belongs. I don't disagree.

"Where are we going?" she asks, in the hazy voice of the well-endorphined.

"Our room."

"For more?"

I kiss her hair as we walk to the stairs of the south wing, smelling flowers and leaves and sun. Her hand is toying with the hair at the nape of my neck, and with her blouse open and her skirt still around her hips, she looks like a debauched schoolgirl.

"For more," I confirm.

4

Auden

An hour later, and Proserpina Markham is stretched sideways across my bed on her stomach, her head pillowed on her arms and her eyes closed. I'm rubbing arnica gel onto my sub's bare bottom and thighs, admiring the geometric welts the crop has left on her skin and also keeping an eye on the usual things—her breathing, the goose bumps on her arms and legs, the expression on her face. I can still taste her on my lips from when I rewarded her for taking the cropping so well, and I consider tasting more straight from the source...but her contented sighs as I massage the soothing gel into her skin are almost as delicious.

I love those sighs. I love feeling like the whole world could be this. Us.

Sighs and welts and cum.

If only he were here too.

I finish with the gel and go to the en suite to wash my hands. When I'm finished and changed in a fresh pair of cotton drawstring pants, I come to lay next to her, propped on my side and toying with her hair. Her eyes are still closed, but she makes a purring sound as I sand my fingertips lightly over her scalp.

"You should have stayed with him."

I'm not angry. But I don't want St. Sebastian alone either.

"I told you I thought that promise was bullshit," she murmurs. "You're not your father."

I don't have the heart to argue with her. Not now, at least, when she's back in my bed and allowing me to run my fingers along the gel-slick welts I've just given her. Instead, I ask what I really want to know. "How is he?"

Poe sighs. "Sad. Stubborn."

My raw, moody Saint. "So he's St. Sebastian then."

"He misses you."

Bitter, defensive words press at the back of my lips. Words I would have said just a couple weeks ago, accusations I would have flung back at her, as if she were some kind of Saint lawyer, as if she were our messenger, our meditator.

How dare he miss me when he's the one who left? How dare he leave again when I was willing to do anything—anything—even if it killed me to do it?

She's not our mediator. She never wanted this separation, she never wanted to be caught between. She wanted all of us together, and it would be careless and cruel of me to press her into the role of referee.

Anyway, as soon as the words take shape, they dissolve right back onto my tongue. I'm not sure why—because it's not out of forgiveness, or not exactly—and I still feel as selfish and greedy as ever. But something's shifted inside of my selfishness, inside of the greed.

Or not shifted, but grown inside it.

"I miss him too," I finally say, and it's funny how ten days of misery can be flattened into a mere four words. Four dry and lifeless words, one prosaic phrase, and there you are, a torn and empty Auden.

Proserpina doesn't say anything, but not in a way like she's not paying attention or like she's slipping into sleep, but like she's waiting for me to say more, like she knows *I miss him too* isn't what I really want to say.

"I feel like half my heart is gone," I admit.

"And the other half?"

I roll her over. The bedspread has left lines and creases on her breasts and stomach like the veins of a leaf. I want to follow them with my tongue before they disappear.

But for now, I press my hand to her chest. "You carry it for me. You have for a long time." And it's the truth. The physical truth. When St. Sebastian left, I felt the incision on my chest, I felt my rib cage crack open. I felt it as one ventricle was excised away, then one atrium, the superior vena cava. I felt it as my body struggled to pump blood to the tips of my fingers and the ends of my toes, I felt it as my thoughts grew sluggish and muddy from lack of oxygen, as my organs began to shut down one by one.

And then when Proserpina left?

I was dead altogether.

My little librarian covers my hand with hers. Her eyes are wet when she looks up at me. "It wasn't supposed to be like this."

"I know."

"I don't know what happens next."

Ten days ago, I wouldn't have known how to say what I say next. I've gone from knowing everything to knowing nothing at all. "Neither do I."

Is that what heartbreak does? Is that what *love* does? Or is it only here at Thornchapel—

is it only us, only the fucked-up rich boy and the fucked-up poor boy and the reckless dreamer who loves them both?

I used to have every answer to any question I cared to ask; the answer was always what I wanted it to be. I should have learned my lesson the day I wrenched a midwinter rose from the chapel wall.

Real answers bite back.

Poe's hand tightens on mine. "Auden...I had a dream," she says softly. "Last night."

She's no longer a limp, leaf-veined woman. She's tense. Anxious.

I slide my arms around her and then move us so that I'm sitting against the headboard and she's curled against my chest. "Is that why you really came back?" I ask.

"Yes, although I wasn't lying about needing to get back to work," she mumbles into my chest.

I resist the urge to sigh, because I really want to tell her that *I don't care* how often she works in my library, because *I trust her* and also I really just *don't care*, but I know keeping our professional relationship separate from our personal one is important to her. "What was the dream about?"

Her hands find my forearms and wrap around them, as if it's not enough to be in my arms, she needs to hold on to me too.

There's a clammy bloom at the base of my neck as she starts talking.

"We were in the chapel," she whispers. "All of us. It was late afternoon, and we didn't have a fire burning yet, although the light was fading and the lanterns were already lit. Dark red roses were everywhere. Not just near the door, but all over the chapel, all over the standing stones outside. They'd twined through the trees, they covered the front of the house. They were in the village, Auden. Climbing through the gravestones and around people's doors.

"Someone had come to the house earlier. I don't know who. We were arguing about it in the chapel, arguing about what to do. You and St. Sebastian were arguing about who should—" Her voice gets thick, and I can feel the tears against my bare chest before I feel her shudder with them. She's trying not to cry and failing. "You were arguing about who should die to close the door. You said it had to be you, and Saint was refusing."

I remember being in the chapel on my birthday, the Lammas storm threatening overhead, and St. Sebastian's teeth on the skin over my heart. His fingers around my neck, his drugging kisses. Him sketching the act of sacrifice for me, but making it wonderful, so unbearably wonderful.

I remember the woman in the chapel, standing in the snow with bright green eyes.

A true king would never let anyone go in a king's place.

I press my lips into Poe's hair, making a soothing noise as I do. "A very discomposing dream. But I can assure you that I have no plans for self-slaughter, not now or at any point in the future. No matter where some roses are growing."

I mean the last part to be dismissive and blithe to allay her fears, but it doesn't come out blithely at all—in fact, I sound quite uncertain. I think of the chamber Rebecca's team found near the entrance to the maze, the walls covered in ancient, carved roses, and I think of the rose

I once plucked on a midwinter's day, growing eerie and alone among the ice and rock.

It's not as easy to dismiss as it should be. Not the self-slaughter, of course, that I can easily dismiss. But the idea that the roses would do things that roses shouldn't. That we would be driven to do *something*, anything, that we would be arguing in the chapel in the long, gray twilight with the door yawning in front of us...

That idea is much harder to dismiss.

Proserpina is shaking her head, tears still sliding off her face to pool against my chest. "You had changed your mind. Something had changed your mind a long time ago, and you were determined, desperate. We all were desperate, and yelling, and Becket's eyes were so strange...and night was coming and that meant something, I don't know what. I just know that the door was open and the roses were everywhere and when night came, we had to be ready."

I hold her close, but I don't placate her. I don't tell her that it was just a dream. I don't know that I could with any honesty anyway. Proserpina has a connection with Thornchapel, a deep one, and it's one that defies rational explanation, like so much else here in the Thorne Valley.

"At least the door isn't open yet," Proserpina says, with a sorry attempt at brightness. "So the dream can't happen any time soon."

I haven't told her about the door. I told myself it was because I didn't want to trouble her while she was with Saint, I told myself it was because the door could close on its own at any moment, and so there was no sense in making any kind of fuss about it.

But truthfully, I didn't tell her because I thought I could mend it before she came back. I thought I could light the right fire or sing the right songs to somehow make it close itself again. It was nonsense to think so, and I felt quite silly night after night burning logs and singing and dancing alone, but given that I'd seen the door after Beltane, it seemed reasonable to assume that the same things that made the door appear might make it disappear.

None of it worked. Plainly.

"Poe," I start, as gently as I can. "Staying away on Lammas, staying away from the chapel altogether—it didn't work. You were right all along. It was going to happen no matter what we did."

"What was going to happen?" she whispers, although I think she already knows.

"It's open," I tell her. "I don't know how, but the door opened during Lammas, and it hasn't shut itself since."

She chews on the inside of her lip. "And the roses?"

"They're there too. We can go down and look if you'd like."

"I don't suppose it will do me any good not to look. Oh, Auden, what are we going to do? About the door?"

I angle her in my arms so I can meet her eyes with my own. "I know what we are *not* going to do, and that's act out anything you saw in your dream. Understood? I am not letting anything hurt us, I am not letting anyone hurt themselves. We can get through this without death, without harm." I almost add *it's just a door*, but I don't. We both know it's not just a door, we both know it matters in some way that we don't entirely understand.

"My mother couldn't get through this," Poe says. "Estamond couldn't. Is it arrogant to think that we can?"

"Of course it's not arrogant," I say.

Okay, and maybe there is a *touch* of arrogance to my voice when I answer. But really. How hard can it be not to human-sacrifice myself? I think some confidence is warranted.

"In the dream, it was so necessary," she murmurs. "There was no other way."

"There's always another way," I say, and I may not know anything about myself or my own life anymore, but I do know this. "Always."

"But there wasn't. John Barleycorn is a memory," Poe says. "That's what Estamond said in my dream. You remember what I told you about what Dr. Davidson said. It's a memory of killing the Year King—a memory that keeps coming up when we learn more about Thornchapel."

John Barleycorn is a memory. I open my mouth to tell Proserpina about the midwinter in the chapel with the roses, but then I don't. I'm not sure why—most likely because it won't materially change anything vis-a-vis whether or not I'll one day kill myself in the thorn chapel—but also because something about that memory feels intensely troubling. I don't want to worry Proserpina with it.

Also—and I recognize this is beyond ridiculous given the circumstances—but I'm almost worried she won't believe me. That if I tell her I saw the ghost of Estamond Kernstow in the chapel along with an impossible rose, she'd smile and nod in a patient way, the same way someone might nod at a child's story of how their cat can secretly speak and read minds, and then tell me not to worry about it. That surely I imagined it or dreamt it up.

Proserpina wouldn't do that. Not only because of who she is and what she dreams, but because of the things we've seen in this place together. I know this deeply…and yet, the words still don't leave my lips. Instead, like a coward, I steer the subject toward less personal waters. "Rebecca found graves under the maze. Eight of them. They look to be quite old."

Proserpina's eyes widen. She's practically twitching against me, like a kitten who's just seen a length of abandoned yarn. "How old?" she asks.

"Bronze Age. We think."

She wriggles out of my arms and walks over to my window to peer out onto the south lawn. The rainy light from outside limns her form in a hazy silver glow, highlighting very faint notes of red in her dark, dark hair.

Like the roses, I think. *Such a dark red they're nearly black.*

"We had to stop construction," I continue, getting off the bed too. The whisper of my hands over her skin as I pull her into my arms is drowned out by the spatter of rain against the window. "There will be a team of archaeologists coming in Monday to assess the site and plan an excavation."

"Graves," she echoes, looking out onto the rainy expanse in front of us. The lids of the kistvaens are barely—and I mean just *barely*—visible at this distance, through the rain and the metal forest of fencing and digging equipment.

"When you were researching for Imbolc and Beltane, did you ever come across any mention of them?" I ask. "Rebecca thinks Estamond must have known of them when she built the maze, and if that's the case, then I'd think the medieval Guests who built the labyrinth predating the maze must have known about them too."

Proserpina shakes her head, her hair brushing against my shoulder and her eyes still on the graves outside. "No. I don't recall…" She thinks for a minute, as if to make completely sure. "No. No graves."

We stand there for a long minute, Proserpina looking outside while I hold her against my chest and draw circles around her exposed navel. My cock is fully hard again, aching against the top of her backside. After a while, she turns to me with a sigh.

"Well?" she prompts. "Are you going to ask me?"

"Ask you what?" Although I already suspect.

She sighs again. "Where he is."

"I don't want to know," I lie.

"That's what you said the first time you and I spoke on the phone too. But I'm not giving you his postcode and flat number, Auden. I thought you'd just like to know, as his Dominant and his half-brother, that he was safe somewhere."

"I don't want to know," I repeat, and she gives me a look like she sees right through it, although when she speaks, her voice is kind.

"You're not your father, Auden. You can trust yourself. You can trust yourself with this. The name of a city, nothing more."

I brush the hair away from Proserpina's face, marveling for the millionth time how lovely she is to me, how wonderful. The rise of her cheekbone, the corner of her eye. The slightly elfin peek of her ears between the waves of her hair. She cannot be sketched, she can only be drawn, and when I draw her, I need all of my pencils.

Leaf Green and Chrome Oxide Green and Viridian for her eyes. Browns 946 and 947 for the undertones of her hair, Espresso and Chocolate and a hint of Burnt Ochre for the rest. Blush Pink for the tips of her ears and her nose, Rose for her lips and cheeks, and Black for the sooty lashes that frame her summer eyes.

Even her imperfections are art—the asymmetrical widow's peak, the creases in her full upper lip—and I abruptly want to cancel the rest of my life, my job, my work, the renovation, eating meals, all of it, and spend the rest of my life drawing Proserpina Markham. I want to spend the rest of my life with her naked in the late summer light, stained and smudged with the marks and bruises I've given her, and I want the most important question I ever answer to be which shade of blue to use for the veins tracing their way along her throat and chest.

"Do you know how long I waited after the two of you left before I went to Thorncombe looking for him?" I ask her now.

"No."

"Three hours. I made it *three hours* before I decided I was dragging him—and you—back to me."

"But he didn't go to Thorncombe," she says. And then she understands. "*Oh.*"

"Exactly. He didn't go back to his house, because he knows me. He knows I can't be trusted. It's just better if I don't know anything about where he is, because even now, I still—"

I stop, too ashamed to continue.

Even now, I still want to chase him, catch him, pin him to the ground.

Make him swear that this time he'll stay.

Poe searches my eyes, and then she shakes her head. "I don't believe you," she says softly. "I think you're a better man than you think you are. Your father was a murderer, Auden. An asshole. You're not."

"I lied to St. Sebastian. I hid things. I pushed every boundary he set. I'm well on my way to being him, Poe."

She leans in, her breasts pressed against my chest, her lips against my throat. "So you fucked up," she murmurs. I can feel the vibration of her words against my throat, humming right down into my chest. "We all do, every single one of us. The important thing is doing better now."

"I don't know if I can," I admit, holding her close. Outside the rain sweeps even harder across the lawn, like the Hyades are personally weeping over my valley, and somewhere in the house I hear Sir James bark. "Doing better means letting him go. For real. And I just—I don't know if I can."

"You held on to him all these years," she says. "Not with your hands or your words, but inside your thoughts, inside your heart. You don't have to stop loving him, Auden. All you have to do is give him the space to choose that love or not."

She's right, of course, she's right.

But.

"He's already chosen," I say, and then I pull her away from the window. "Let's get dressed. We can go see the door now, if you'd like."

She makes a face. "In the rain?"

"Unless there's something else you'd like to do while we wait for the rain to pass?"

She gives me a wicked smile and then lowers herself to her knees in front of me. "I can think of a few things."

I'm deeply indebted to the inventor of drawstring pants because I have my cock past those rose-hued lips in seconds. I let out a long, relieved sigh at the feel of her tongue against the underside of my erection, and then my hands are in her hair as she looks up at me. I go slowly, so slowly, letting myself skate along the edge of restraint and release, until I can't take it any longer and tie her to the bed. I fuck her until she comes, and then I allow myself a long, trembling release, the kind that feels never-ending.

After I come, I keep her tied to the bed for a little while after, just because it makes her happy and it makes me happy, and when I untie her, she curls into my arms and falls into a sleep that seems thankfully dreamless.

Wise, curious, dreamy girl.

And I lied earlier, I now realize. Because there is one thing I would sacrifice my own life for, there is one thing that could make Poe's dream come true.

If something ever threatened her or St. Sebastian—or even Rebecca or Delphine or Becket—and if my life was the only price that could be paid for their safety...

Then yes.

Yes, I would walk to the door without ever having to look back.

Rebecca

"It's your mother's birthday next week."

"I know. Have you heard back about the play park yet?" I ask.

My father sets his fork on the table and dabs efficiently at his mouth with a napkin before leaning back in his chair. We're not in an office at Quartey Workshop, we are not even in a company car on the way to an important meeting.

No, we are at a *restaurant*.

During *business hours.*

And not just any restaurant—not someplace fast, convenient, inexpensive. We are at a French restaurant in Spitalfields with several courses, with an elegant (if rather fussy) menu, and a wine list longer than many bestselling novels.

The building used to be a chapel, and so light pours through the stained glass windows and floods the space, illuminating the wooden trusses of the Victorian ceiling above us. Auden would like it. He's reliably pleased by buildings that emphasize capaciousness or history or both. Even I like it, as it's unpretentiously designed and filled with glimpses of sky, which I always crave in the city.

The surprise is that *Samson Quartey* seems to like it. The man who spent the last fifteen years eating apples and reheated rice in his office because he refused to take time away from work in order to get a proper meal for himself. The man who once scolded me for eating my lunch in the nearby park instead of at my desk.

This same man came into my office this morning and suggested we get lunch somewhere today. And this same man is now smiling at me over the table as he reaches for his wine glass. "Not yet, but I have every confidence it will be approved."

We'd decided, after a citizen's meeting about the Severn Riverfront project, to incorporate a play park into our plans. An idea that is very popular with the borough council members and significantly less popular with the borough's solicitors, since it opens up a fresh host of safety concerns. It is the sort of development that normally calls for several meetings, twice-a-day emails, and a daily visit to my office to make sure I'm on top of the situation.

But instead he's sitting here, sampling Continental cuisine in a stylish restaurant and telling me he has every confidence.

I stare at him. "You're not worried? You don't want me to call our contact at the council or pressure the solicitors into moving faster?"

He swallows his wine with a faint smile still tipping the corners of his mouth. "It's only been a few days, Rebecca. Give them time."

I continue to stare. He's been like this since he reconnected with David Markham. Warmer, smilier. *Happier.* Like the man I vaguely remember from my childhood, the man who used to carry me on his shoulders and ask me to point out the horizon.

You missed that man, I remind myself. *You should be glad he's back again.*

"Enough about work," he says, setting down his glass.

A sentence I've literally never heard him utter before. It's like waking up one day to a green sky or a slightly tilted floor—something that could be normal, but is so very *not*.

"I want to know how you're doing."

"How I'm doing?" I echo. "Not…how my projects are coming along?"

"Of course not," he says, smiling at me like I'm being the silly one. "How are *you*?"

I'm so unused to talking about anything other than work with my father that question almost feels invasive. Even though I don't want it to be invasive, I don't want it to feel like an inveiglement or an intrusion. Because this is what I wanted from him, for so many years, since we moved to London, since I took that first cursed IQ test.

I wanted him to see me as more than the vessel of the Quartey name. To see me as more than a Cartesian brain in a jar whose sole purpose is to win awards and make money.

So why do I feel resentful now that he's giving it to me?

When I don't answer, he prompts, "How are you and Delphine Dansey?"

And that's it, that's the spade driving right through the soil of my heart and hitting the rock underneath. I feel the strike of her name in my bones, and for a second I can't remember how lungs are supposed to work, how they expand out and down to draw breath, how they push that breath back out.

I'm still yours. If you want me to be.

I would like to never see you again.

"Rebecca?" my father asks, suddenly looking concerned, and it must be all over my face, how I feel and what she's done to me, and the humiliation of my feelings being known is almost as great a sting as the feelings themselves.

"I'm fine," I mutter, ducking my head and flicking away the wetness spilling from my eyes as fast as I can. My father reaches across the table and I pull back even more. "I'm *fine,* Daddy."

"You don't seem it," my father says. Kindly. "Do you want to talk about it?"

No. I definitely do not want that. I want to seal the memory of Delphine Dansey in a box and then drop that box into an Icelandic lava fissure. "There's nothing to talk about. We stopped seeing each other a couple weeks ago."

He turns the stem of the wineglass between his fingers. Grayish London light catches the glint of the glass and the gentle swirl of the burgundy inside.

"You seemed happier with her," he offers. "You smiled more. When you were at David's house, I could see how you looked at her. How she looked at you."

"She cheated on me," I blurt, and then I want to smash my face onto my plate. Why did I say that? Why did I say that to *him*? When just a few seconds ago, I wanted this conversation to be over?

Delphine broke me. That's the only answer I can come up with. I used to be molded, glazed, and fired exactly as I wanted to be, and then she came along and smashed me into a million pieces, and now nothing fits together right. Anger, pride, embarrassment, sadness, *neediness*—all of those things used to be contained inside a watertight shell. And now they leak out of me like I'm a cracked teacup or a badly repaired vase.

"Never mind," I mumble, "I shouldn't have said that, just pretend I didn't—"

A warm hand finds my wrist over the table. "Sweetheart," my father says, his eyes softer than I've ever seen them. "It's okay. It's okay to be upset."

"I loved her," I hear myself saying. Why am I still talking about this? When it hurts me so much? And in the middle of a public space where anyone can see or hear me? I don't know, I don't know, I don't know, and yet I'm still talking, words are still dripping out. "I told her I loved her and she told me she'd cheated on me. And I deserve better than that, I deserve so much better, and at the same time, I can't let go of this idea that if only I'd told her sooner that I loved her, if I'd been warmer or easier or *something*—"

I don't stop because I've come to my senses and realized that I'm spilling my deepest fears in a trendy French restaurant to *my father* of all people, and during *business hours* of all times.

No, I stop because I am crying. (In a trendy French restaurant in front of my father and during business hours.)

(Like a prize fucking idiot.)

What has happened to me?!

"Oh Rebecca," Daddy says. "I'm so sorry, sweetheart. That was awful of her. Awful and selfish."

Perversely, I almost want to defend her. To say *well, it was just some spanks and a kiss.* To say, *she's so incredibly sweet and soft and funny and she was so gutted when she told me, she was so sorry and so sad.*

"I've never had anyone like how I had her—like how I wanted to have her. I could see an entire life with us together in it, and I wanted that life so badly, and then before I had a chance to tell her all about it, it was gone. She'd taken it away from us both."

"I don't know her as you do, but I do know her parents, and they are good and kind people. I'm sure whatever she's done, she deeply regrets hurting you."

I see her face crumpling as I told her I never wanted to see her again.

I'm sorry. I know—I know that's not enough, that it could never be enough, but you should know all the same.

I'm so sorry it hurts.

"I know you will survive this, my daughter," Daddy says, squeezing my wrist. "Of that, I have no doubt. But whatever parts of yourself you found when you were with Delphine...I hope those parts of you survive too."

Daddy has a meeting across town after lunch, and so I decide to take some time to search for a birthday gift for my mother. I take the Tube to Green Park Station, and then walk to Old Bond Street to peruse the jewelry shops, not so much enjoying the solitude and fresh air as numbly accepting it.

My face is still tight from crying, and my throat feels as if someone's lodged a stone right in the middle of it, and the memory of Delphine is an acacia tree growing right through my chest, right between my lungs. Each time I try to inhale, I'm punctured and stabbed with thorns. When I exhale, those same thorns snag on my bronchioles and tear at my tattered inferior lobes.

All these years of resisting every kind of feeling, and for what? I'm still walking around the city like a raw nerve in a Cushnie trouser suit. I'm still drifting down the street with swollen eyes and dried tears on my face. I'm still leaking and bleeding and hurting, even though I knew better, *I knew better.*

I knew better.

Somehow I still manage to browse my mother's favorite jeweler's, I manage to walk and look and examine, like an automaton built for the sole purpose of shopping. Even the dilatory response from the employee behind the counter—and the way she helps an older white woman first even though she came into the shop after me—doesn't animate the numbness any. It only adds to it, like *of course, of course,* this is what my life is, this is what it means to be Rebecca Quartey. It didn't matter how many times I was photographed for the *RIBA Journal* or name-checked in *Architectural Digest,* it doesn't matter that I've played by every single rule for as long as I can remember. I can still walk into a shop on Bond Street and be ignored, I can still have my heart broken by a girl who grew up riding horses and wearing Holland & Holland tweed.

Eventually, I am approached by the employee. Eventually I find something I like: a slender gold bangle studded with rubies—bold but also traditionally feminine—something for a woman embarking on the next stage of her life. I arrange for the shop to have the bracelet sent to Accra, along with a note I scribble right there at the counter.

And then, feeling a little lighter, a little more like myself, I finish the transaction and leave the store.

See, *this* is who I am.

I set tasks and I accomplish them. I identify problems—mother, divorce, birthday, micro-aggressive shop employees—and I find tangible solutions—pretty bracelet, international shipping, taking the shop manager's business card to email them later.

That is Rebecca Quartey. Not the woman who has been sleeping curled around a fuzzy blanket because it was her ex-sub's favorite, not the woman who just cried in front of her father over a plate of clafoutis. I am the person who pushes past all obstacles—I am the person who builds things, who fixes things, who never gets hurt.

I can be that person again. Right?

I'm walking back to the station when a storefront catches my eye. It's another jeweler's, but there's something very modern about it, very arty. There's no classic blue boxes or gleaming cases of glass, no piano notes lilting through the air. Instead, all the jewelry is arranged on mannequins and sculptures and slender logs.

Yes. *Logs.*

It's very ridiculous and self-aware and trying too hard, but the pieces themselves are fascinating. Unusual. Bright where I'd expect them to be colorless, and geometric where I'd expect no geometry at all.

I find myself slipping inside the shop, drifting from display to display. Despite the alt-pop music currently droning through the speakers and the clerk with a septum piercing, all of the jewelry is just as exquisitely made—and just as expensive—as the shop with the little blue boxes where I just came from.

But this is not the kind of jewelry I would give my mother, no—not at all.

There's Art Deco-inspired brooches and playful Victorian-esque rings. Things of beaten gold and silver and tungsten; pieces wrought into animal forms, botanical forms; earrings that look like talons and necklaces that look like finely tatted lace. This is the type of jewelry you give to someone who knows what your mouth tastes like.

At the back of the shop, just when I think I'm done looking, I see it.

I see the necklace.

I've never seen it before in my life, and yet the moment I notice it, I know it's *the necklace.* For what or for whom, I don't know, but I'm meant to see it and to have it. To own it and to give it.

It hangs from the neck of a marble bust and catches the light, and when I drift closer, I see that it's more than an array of gold and precious stones. The thin collar of it drips into a sparkling fringe that would hang down the wearer's chest—but rather than dangling from the collar in a series of straight lines, the fringe fits and interlocks together to create a tableau, a narrative of metal and precious stones.

And the narrative is this: from a delicate branch, a small, exquisitely crafted wren is trying to rise into the air. One slender wing is raised in flight, while the other is snared by the branches, by their dark, glittering thorns. The bird's eye is rendered with onyx, but its wings are done in tiny pearls and pink diamonds, and there is something unearthly about it, both in its beauty and in its obvious distress. It's like a bird from fairyland caught in a mortal tree—or maybe the other way around.

The struggle is wrought in every curve of its body, in the strain of its wings and in the tiny, barely-perceptible parting of its beak. But that flashing eye is filled with defiance, and its form is still so graceful. Beauty caught in the teeth of heartbreak.

I reach out, not really to touch it, but out of a touching instinct. Even though I know it's only gems and metal, even though I know it's only a rendering and not a real bird.

Not a real beauty caught in its own painful cage.

It's trying so, so hard to fly, and if only it would stop struggling, if only it would stop thrashing—

I don't know how I end up asking the attentive shopgirl for the price. I don't know how I end up paying what is even for me an exorbitant sum. I don't know why I write down the address I do when I arrange to have it delivered.

But I do know, when I write the card accompanying the necklace, that I see not a bird in my mind's eye, but a beautiful girl washed in shades of silvery-pearl and pale pink, standing alone in the Long Gallery at Thornchapel. I know that I see that same girl crying, pleading, pretending she's okay.

I sign my name to the short card—*For you — from Rebecca Quartey*—and then I leave the shop, heading for the Tube at last and thinking of birds and blond-haired girls that hide their wounds and hurt alone.

You're supposed to be a genius. So what in God's name are you thinking right now?

Buying a gift that expensive is something one does for subs and partners and spouses, *not* for cheating exes. Because Delphine is nothing like a girlfriend or a sub to me anymore, she is nothing to me at all. Nothing but the ache in my chest and the reason I cry cuddling a stupid blanket at night. The reason I haven't been to my own club in weeks.

What are you doing?

I go back to work; I finish the day without crying again. I think of trapped birds the entire time, and when I get home, I am confronted not only with the vast emptiness of my Delphine-less loft, but with the lonely ache in my body.

I want sex.

I want a lot of it, and I want the kind that leaves you hollowed out and exhausted after. I want to zip on my favorite vinyl bodysuit, and I want to find a willing sub with a nice, plush body, and a mouth like a doll's, and big, honey-brown eyes—

Fuck.

No. See, this is the problem: I don't just want sex.

I want sex with Delphine.

It's why I haven't gone to Justine's, it's why I haven't found some other pliant sub to spend time with, even though I easily could, and even though several months ago, I would have.

And I don't know why. I'm not going to forgive her, I'm not going to take her back. She knew no one was allowed to leave marks on her body but me, and then she let some American spank her in front of everyone anyway. She was the only person I've ever trusted with myself—*really* myself, not the prodigy in the pages of *Architectural Digest*, not the dutiful daughter who sacrificed her frontal lobe on the altar of the family business.

I let her in, I let myself care about her and love her, and most damningly, I let myself be vulnerable, and she gave that gift as much thought as she would a box of unsolicited skincare products sent to her to promote on her Instagram feed. I was opened up, peered at for half a second, and then tossed aside like a bottle of artisanal lip serum.

How can I forgive that? How could I ever trust her again? Even with something as contained as an orgasm?

She was vulnerable first, my thoughts whisper. *She told you she loved you, and you acted like it didn't matter.*

But that was different. It was so different. Even if I can't explain exactly why.

Here's what I should do. I should get dressed in something

dramatic, go straight to Justine's, and then enthusiastically fuck my way out of a broken heart. Fuck my way into falling out of love with Delphine Dansey.

Yes. Yes, I'm going to do that. I even walk over to the rack of cotton garment bags where I keep my fetish clothes. I even unzip one, like I'm really going to pull on a leather miniskirt and its matching corset and go right to the club.

But when I try to imagine it, when I try to imagine someone else kneeling in front of me, or underneath me, or on all fours and waiting for whatever sweet hell I'm about to unleash on them, my brain goes all fuzzy and my stomach twists beneath my rib cage. The need between my legs collapses and cools into something that's less like lust and more like indifference.

Precisely like indifference, in fact, because try as I might, I don't want anybody else.

I don't want anyone kneeling in front of me if they're not her, I don't want anyone underneath me if they don't smell like berries and violets and money. I don't want anyone saying *yes, Mistress* or *yes, Rebecca* to me unless it's in that ridiculously upper-class voice, that voice of sharp consonants and high-falling vowels. I don't want to come unless it's against her mouth, her fingers, and I don't want to look at anyone else coming unless it's her.

Perhaps that's the piece of it I've forgotten to mourn. I've been hurt and angry about the betrayal, about my wounded pride and my ravaged heart, but I haven't yet fully grieved what I've lost. Not just a girlfriend, but a kitten, a sub. The brat I was eagerly anticipating disciplining for weeks and months—and years—into the future.

She had been mine. Her body, her cunt, her giant, bright eyes. Her giggles and her gasps. Her welts, her bruises, her everything.

There had been a person in this world whom I could pour all of the care and attention and affection I had to give, a person who filled me up instead of draining me dry.

All of that is gone now…all of it except the lust.

I drop my hand from the garment bag and go to my kitchen instead. If Auden were here, we'd do gin or whisky, or rum if I could talk him into it, and if Delphine were here, which she never will be again, we'd have champagne or prosecco or something else sweet and bubbly. But it's just me, so I pour myself a glass of red wine and sit at my desk, opening my laptop as I do.

I don't know why I bought Delphine a necklace more expensive than a holiday home in Scotland when what I really want is her lipstick smeared on my cunt. When what I really want is for her to feel this need at the same magnitude as I do.

I want her to feel this same need more than I want her to feel guilty and miserable—and not only because when I find myself wishing guilt and misery on her, I start to feel sick and clammy, like the thought of her unhappy still has the power to afflict me, like my ill wishes are rebounding back on myself. But if she were to be miserable with *lust*, with wanting what only I can give…

The thought stirs me. Imagining her alone on her girlhood bed in the Cotswolds, tossing and turning on bespoke bed linens, needing more than just an orgasm, needing the rush and catharsis that only a mistress can provide. Imagining her panting, flushed, desperate to come…

I navigate to a certain website and start scrolling. It's not pornography that I'm looking at, but a gift, and one that would be a lot more useful to us both than a necklace with a sad bird on it.

Wanting her is not forgiveness.

Lusting for her is not absolution.

She can make me wet *and* I can hate her. She can consume my thoughts and still earn my scorn. And if I'm unhappy, if I'm lonely…if there's a voice that whispers to me of all the times she opened herself to me and I walled myself off in response—well.

At least I'll be able to get off this way.

I send the gift with the same note I sent with the necklace.

For you—from Rebecca Quartey.

And then imagining her receiving it, using it while she wears nothing but a bird made of pearls and diamonds, I slide my hand down my trousers and into my knickers.

And for the first time in two weeks, I come.

6

Auden

" ollen analysis, but it could be next week, *or* it could be next
... year, depending on the twats at the lab."

I slide my iPad and some folders into my satchel, my
phone tucked between my ear and my shoulder as I step away from
my desk. It's a strikingly lovely late August evening, with rosy sunlight
still pouring through the skylight and illuminating the empty desks
and vacant glassed-in meeting rooms.

I'm the last one here, as usual, and I'm on the phone with Tobias
Talbot-Ullswater, the archaeologist in charge of the excavation at
Thornchapel, who also happens to be completely ridiculous and
completely wonderful, and also a very good friend. I take one last look
around my desk as he talks, deciding as I do that I'm going to return
to Thornchapel early this week. It's been more than two weeks since

Proserpina came back, but I still have this slow, simmering panic when we're far apart, like maybe my heart will stop beating if I'm away from her for too long. Like it's how I told her, that there's two halves of my heart, one in her chest and one in St. Sebastian's, and now with St. Sebastian gone, I'm barely clinging to life.

The only thing that makes his leaving bearable is knowing that he was right. Knowing that if he stayed, I'd destroy him, just like our father destroyed everyone he ever desired.

Tobias says something else about soil samples and palynology—pollen analysis—and I try to focus on the conversation at hand.

"Tally," I say, turning off the lights as I take the stairs to the ground floor. "I hate to be an obnoxious, landed-gentry prick, but I rather don't care about pollen at the moment."

"I find it very charming when you are an obnoxious, landed-gentry prick," Tally purrs. "It's much more charming than when you're skipping around London with your floppy hair and your Smythson bag, pretending that you're some anonymous, architect-y boy who works extra architect-y hours to impress people who patently don't care."

I think for a moment.

"It's not a Smythson bag," I finally say.

Tally laughs. Everything's a joke to him: friendships, money, sex…even his job. When he graduated with his MPhil in archaeology, there were several respectable paths open to him: a position at an aunt's vaguely-connected-to-art-literacy-but-also-maybe-a-tax-shelter foundation, a job with an antiquities firm, or the tried and true path to professorship. But no, Tally discarded all of those options and became a rescue archaeologist instead, getting very muddy with very little acclaim…and making very little money while doing it.

I asked him *why* once, and he'd just grinned and said he'd needed the cover of commercial archaeology to disguise his domestic sexual tourism. And with Tally, that's either entirely true or entirely a lie. But since I—as he rightly pointed out—am playing the part of anonymous, architect-y boy, I can hardly cast stones and demand a better answer. The fact that we've both devoted our working lives to bourgeois obscurity is probably its own answer anyway.

"Now that you've done the preliminary examination, do you know when you'll be finished with the full excavation?" I ask, locking up the Harcourt + Trask doors and then leaving the building. It's an easy distance from the office to my townhouse, and it's a nice evening, so I decide to walk. "I'm just trying to gauge what this means for the labyrinth project, and when we'll be free to resume construction again."

"Another two weeks," Tally says with complete and utter confidence.

Then:

"Actually, I don't know. Maybe four weeks. Maybe ten. We're accustomed to working fast, but you've got eight kistvaens here, you poor, prehistorically cursed sod. Even I can't blitz through eight Bronze Age graves in a week, at least not sober, and you know I can't find the gin I like out here in the hinterlands."

"So they are Bronze Age?" I ask. "For sure?"

"Undoubtedly. Younger than most of the monuments up on the moors, *possibly* younger than the stone reaves on the lip of your valley. But pre-Halstatt, naturally."

"Naturally."

"They are certainly graves as well, except for the carved chamber near the subterranean staircase. We found no burial goods or human remains of any kind in there. It seems designed to have been empty. Which is curious, because the cist facing it almost certainly belonged to some sort of chieftain or king."

I pass by the Egyptian consulate, weaving past a food delivery person with an insulated carrying box on his back. "A king? How can you know?"

"We found a torc. A torc is—"

"I know what a torc is, Tally."

"Oh. Well. I suppose you should just come and take control of this dig then, since you're such an expert."

Shoppers mill under the green Harrods awnings, and I can already hear the noise from Brompton Road. "Or you could demonstrate your proficiency in your field by telling me more about this grave you think belonged to a king."

A heavy, put-upon sigh. "You are a very needy client."

"That cannot be true."

"It is. You're lucky you're so pretty, you know, or I'd be packing up my things right now. *Poof*—there goes gentle, forbearing, noble Tobias, and now you're at the cold and disorganized mercy of the labs for all future answers."

"Tally."

"Christ. Fine. So we found a torc in the tomb closest to the chamber, along with significantly better burial goods than in the other tombs. We found amber beads, tin beads, jet beads. Axe heads, textiles, what we think might be furs, and also beakers of what might have been a fermented drink. You know, like Mardi Gras, but with more axes and tin. Typically in a cluster like this, I might expect to see other high-profile graves nearby, but there is only the empty chamber, and the other seven graves are more standard in their burial fare. Very poor in the bead department, with wooden earrings instead of gold ones, that kind of thing. Also, the torc chap was buried, not cremated like everyone else."

That does surprise me, and I find myself asking Tally to clarify as I cross Brompton Road. "Buried? You know that for certain?"

"Bones are usually a dead giveaway for that. Get it, Auden? A *dead* giveaway?"

I groan.

Tobias heaves a sad sigh. "I am very deeply undervalued by you, you know."

"So you say. But Rebecca had mentioned something to me about soil acidity and bones—"

"Yes, yes, up on the moors, the acidity is quite vicious, but we've gotten lucky with your little valley. Much more well-behaved in terms of pH. So not only do we have a skeleton instead of burned remains, but the skeleton is complete enough that we can see our king probably didn't die of natural causes. There is a preserved cord of horsehair rope around his neck and damage to the skull—which appears deliberate and not caused by any subsequent weathering or soil instability in the grave. If I were to be dramatic, then I would say you've got a victim of human sacrifice in that tomb. Killed and tucked into his eternal sleep facing the rose-carved chamber."

I stop walking for a moment as the crowds of people surge past, cars rolling next to me like a honking, metal river.

Human sacrifice.

King.

I push my free hand through my hair. "And if you weren't being dramatic? What would you say then?"

For the first time on the call, Tally's voice is more pensive than playful, and when he speaks, he speaks slowly. "I suppose I would say that it's still damned odd. The whole site. Dartmoor residents of the Neolithic and the Bronze Age preferred the moors and the outcrops for most of their monuments and burials…so why this *valley*? And if so, why not nearer to the monuments already erected close by? Why are there no other monuments marking the area, like a cairn or a stone circle? Or were there other monuments, and your terrible ancestors pulled them down in order to build a folly or a carriage house or something? If the other graves are contemporary to the king's, were those people also killed? Did they die before him? After him? And what was the empty rose-chamber used for? It demonstrates a huge amount of invested time and expertise, and then *not* to be used as a tomb…I'm not sure there's a corollary for that in the record, at least not in Britain or Ireland. Or Brittany, that I can recall."

I tug at my hair for a second before dropping my hand. It doesn't have to mean anything. These are old bones, and old bones can't hurt anyone.

The Thorn King is an old story, Auden, I can remember Poe saying. *Too old to touch us.*

And what had I told her then? *Sometimes the oldest stories are the most dangerous ones of all.*

So I don't know what I believe. I don't want this to matter, but we're past what I want now.

"Auden, I have to disclose all of this to the county archaeologist, and after that, it's very likely a discovery like this will attract some media attention. It might be worth considering if you'd like to get ahead of the interest by publicizing the finds now."

All these years of scorning my father for treating the Thorne Valley like his own private theme park, condemning him for hiding its secrets from outsiders, and now here I am balking at the idea of photographers and documentary crews swarming my property. I chew on the inside of my cheek for a moment. "May I have a bit longer to think about it?"

"Yes, but while you're thinking, consider also that the other sites on the Thornchapel grounds would provide context. Not only for people reporting on the finds, but for your dear friend Tobias, who would very much like to see this Neolithic stone row you're hiding in the forest."

Part of me is curious about what Tobias would see if he went back to the chapel. Would he see the door too? The black roses around it? Can anyone see it, or only people connected to Thornchapel or the valley?

But the rest of me is more cautious than curious. If the door is dangerous, then I don't want anyone involved who isn't already. I don't want to risk Tobias, blithe and ridiculous though he may be, nor any of the other archaeologists or journalists or researchers who might come after him. Not until I know more about the door. Not until I can verify its safety.

I adopt my best *landed-gentry prick* voice. "I'm afraid I can't help you there. You remember what I told you about the deer management scheme we've taken on?"

"I do," Tobias says. "But surely this man you've hired isn't deerstalking at all hours around your property?"

He's definitely not—because he doesn't exist—but this was the best lie I could come up with in order to keep Tally and his team clustered close to the house. "I told him to come at any time of the day, whenever was the most convenient. The roe deer are absolutely mad on my woods, and we've set a fairly high quota to achieve a decent reduction. So he's out there quite often. It's better to stay away from the woods for now, as a safety precaution."

"In case he mistakes an archaeologist for a roe deer," Tally says, his voice flat with disbelief.

"Health and safety, Tally. Can never have too much. At least if I don't want the county coming after me."

That's all nonsense, but I say it with plenty of privileged ennui— that "isn't having a grand estate such a *bother*" tone—and Tally finally seems to buy it. "You used to hate the idea of hunting," he says after a minute. "In school, remember? You never went with anyone when you were invited. What changed your mind?"

I still don't like the idea of killing animals for sport, or for any purpose that's not strictly utilitarian. Although other kinds of hunting, like stalking a dark-eyed boy through the trees and tackling him next to the river...

For a moment, my mind is filled with trees and water, with bluebells and St. Sebastian. With antlers and drums from another world. And suddenly, a breeze moves through the square as I cross through it to get to my townhouse. A breeze that feels restless and lonely, like me, and the trees shake and nod with it, as if agreeing with me that I should be running right now, I should be hunting.

I go still.

This is not supposed to happen here.

I mean, it's not supposed to happen *at all*, but I thought that at the very least, this was contained to my home, to the valley around it.

Stop it, I think. To the trees. To myself.

They stop.

"Auden?" Tobias prompts.

I step out of the square and hop the curb to the pavement that leads to my front door. And then I see—

There's someone lounging on my front steps, wearing a threadbare T-shirt and scuffed black boots—

The remaining light catches on his lip piercing and his dark eyes—

The trees start stirring again, and the wind kicks up so fast that leaves and litter scoot down the street along with it.

"Ecological responsibility changed my mind, Tally," I answer. "Say, can I phone you later? Something's just come up."

"Of course. I'll just occupy myself with not getting shot by your hired deerstalker, shall I?"

"Fine, Tobias," I say, already dropping the phone from my ear and ending the call. I reach the foot of my steps and stare at the beautiful boy lounging on them. The wind whips at our hair and our clothes as we look at each other.

He looks a little thinner than when I saw him last, a little more made of angles—or perhaps it's only how he's sitting, with his feet planted on the stair below and his elbows propped on his knees, his hands and shoulders tense. The old T-shirt stretches over his shoulders and arms and back, thin enough in places that I can see his skin, supple enough that it clings to his frame in such a way that I can viscerally and miserably imagine every swell of muscle and curve of bone.

I want to push him back against those stairs and hold him in place while I map every inch of his body, I want to scream at him for leaving me, I want to scream at him to leave me again.

I want to chase him through this leafy square like a god, and then catch him and eat him.

I do none of these things, even though the very air and earth around us seems to demand it, seems to demand that I do something, that I take or protect or speak or move—*something.*

When I step forward again, mounting the first step and looking down at St. Sebastian, the square quiets down a little. And when I speak, the air itself seems to settle and sigh.

"Let's go inside," I say.

"As you wish," says my half-brother. And I move past him to unlock the door, and in we go.

7

Auden

I close the door behind me and then look at St. Sebastian slouching in the middle of my foyer. Slouching as if he's scowly and cross about being here, even though he was the one haunting my doorstep like a lonely cat before I got home.

But I know him well enough now to know that when he seems scowly, he's actually uncertain, and to know that when he's quiet and watchful, like he is now, he's expecting to be hurt.

It gouges something in my chest to think he's come to expect hurting from me.

I want to drop to his feet and apologize. For loving him, for making us play house even when it was a terrible idea, for pinning him against a museum wall and fucking him like I was owed it.

But I also want him to drop to *my* feet. I want to haul him close and run my nose along his neck. I want to say *I don't care about what the world says, you were made to be mine*, and then I want to kiss him until we're sixteen again and he'll let me do whatever I want to his body, anything at all.

I don't know what to do with these two instincts, these two halves of myself. The part that bends toward tenderness, caring for, tending to—and the part that craves taking. No matter how much I try to ignore the latter, it never leaves me, it never stops flexing its hands and reaching for what it wants.

But of course, I don't betray any of this. I give my half-brother a polite, *I'll lead the way* nod, and say, "Follow me," as I move through the foyer and into the kitchen.

When I bought this place, it was a mess. Purchased by a Russian businessman who never ended up living in it, it had gone slightly derelict inside, and it hadn't been modernized after the 1960s.

I'd loved it for that. Not that it was ugly, but that the ugliness was an invitation, that the whole place needed to be made new again. It felt almost like consent—like the property was saying *strip me, mark me, give me a love that sands me down and knocks through walls*—and when I was inside of it, revising plans, solving problems, thumb-printing a hitherto invisible vision into glass-and-rivets reality, I felt like I do now during a good scene. Or during a feast. I felt like a king, even if I didn't have a forest to run through or a green-eyed girl to kiss afterward.

Anyway, I'm quite proud of the house as I lead St. Sebastian through to the back. Though the front is still a traditional face of pale ashlar and brown brick, the inside has been entirely opened up with windows and loads of skylights and a huge bifold door leading out to a narrow garden with a small studio built at the back. I kept the things

I loved: the original hardwoods, the beautiful staircase, the fireplaces—and then I made the rest a hymn to light.

The silver-heather light of winter.

The rosy refulgence of summer.

Light for scrolling on an iPad and for curling up with a book, sunshine for breakfast and the glimmer-glow of the city for after-dinner cocktails.

I'd done it because I liked illumination as a guiding principle, and because I wanted to liberate things like Crittall windows and pitched skylights from the faux-industrial aesthetic. And also because I wanted to stretch my architectural legs before I tackled something bigger and older, like Thornchapel.

I didn't do it because I wanted to know what the late evening light would look like reflected in St. Sebastian's eyes. I didn't do it because I wanted to know if he would shove his hands into his pockets and squint up at the sky when he walked under the glass roof of the kitchen extension. I didn't do it because I wanted each vein in his throat and every long and sooty eyelash outlined in perfectly diffused light while I stared at him.

But I should have done it for those reasons. Because seeing him here now, no other reason could ever make sense. Why would I design a house if it wasn't for the sole purpose of seeing St. Sebastian inside it? Why would I go to all the trouble of refinishing floors and refurbishing Victorian fireplace inserts and browsing through hundreds of Farrow and Ball paint colors if it wasn't to see St. Sebastian in the middle of it all, kicking his boots against the floor and stretching out his T-shirt as he ducked his head and hunched his shoulders?

Why would I ever build anything at all if he wasn't going to be inside it?

I've stopped us in the kitchen, and I gesture for him to take a seat while I pull open the doors to the garden and put a kettle on.

He doesn't sit. Instead he drifts around the space, pretending to look at things so that he doesn't have to look at me.

"Sit down," I tell the back of his head.

He tenses a little but doesn't turn. "I don't want to."

I could make you, I want to say. *I could make you sit, and then I could tie your hands together and play with your cock until you couldn't stand even if you wanted to stand.*

"Have you eaten supper?" I ask instead.

He turns his head a little. I can now make out the high curve of his cheek and the striking slant of his jaw. "I'm supposed to have a late dinner in a couple hours."

"I'm about to make supper for myself, I could—"

"Aren't you going to ask me why I'm here?" he interrupts. "Aren't you going to berate me for leaving you again, point out how hideously inconsistent I am for showing up at your house, and then make me do something utterly debasing to prove your point?"

Yes. Let's skip straight to the debasement. I want to know if you're hard. I want you to unzip those jeans and then I want to push you to your knees. I want to see what your erection looks like in the city twilight and then I want to see if I can make you come before the tea finishes steeping.

"No," I say instead. "I'm not. We've done this too many times, the game where you leave and then I chase you and bully you into giving me what I want. I don't want to be that kind of man. At all."

That does make St. Sebastian turn to face me, his hands still shoved into his pockets and a frown curving his mouth. "You never bullied me," he says. "That wasn't what I—that's not how I meant you were like our father."

"Wasn't it?" I ask, trying to keep my voice light as the kettle clicks off and I start pouring the water into a teapot. "I assumed that's what you'd meant."

He flicks the hair out of his eyes and blinks at me as I turn to face him. "There's a difference between coercion and seduction," he says. "You never coerced me."

I could coerce you now.

You could tell me your safe word, and then I could bend you over my kitchen island and lick your hole until you spray cum everywhere.

"What difference does it make?" I ask in a tired voice. "It made you miserable in the end. You can't be happy with me, and I can't live with you unhappy. It doesn't take Bex to figure out that equation."

He hunches his shoulders again, looking away. "I guess not."

"Although maybe I did lie earlier, because I do want to know why you're here, actually. Why you've come from…wherever it is you've come from."

Why, my sweet, sulky boy, why? When I've turned myself inside out trying to give you space, when I've refused to let myself know where you are, when I've spent all these nights clinging to Proserpina and wanting to cry because my bed is still too empty and still too cold?

The tea is done steeping, and I busy myself with that while he shuffles his feet, takes a breath to speak, and then shuffles his feet some more.

And then he utters the last request in the world I expect to hear.

"I need to borrow some clothes," he mumbles. "Nice ones."

I am legitimately at a loss for what to say. "You want to borrow *clothes*," I repeat instead.

His cheeks are going pink. "Yes. For my dinner tonight."

For the first time, it occurs to me that *dinner* could mean *date*. That *dinner* could mean someone else, someone new, and I suddenly can't see, I suddenly can't breathe. The jealousy is in my teeth and my bones, a primal fury is boiling my blood.

No. NO.

MINE.

It never occurred to me that he might find someone else. That Proserpina wouldn't be enough, and he would let himself be courted by…others.

Other Dominants?

I want to tear the entire world in half just thinking about it. My hands are shaking when I set them on the counter. "No."

That does seem to surprise him. "No? I can't borrow any clothes?"

"Does Proserpina know you're meeting someone for dinner?"

He looks confused. "Yes."

"And she's okay with it?"

"Why wouldn't she be? And why can't I borrow your clothes?"

I study him, every fiber in every muscle in my body quivering to pounce. If he were still mine, I'd have him on the floor and moaning in seconds. I'd have him cuffed to my bed and gasping as I left handprints all over his faithless, temperamental backside.

But he's not yours. That's the point.

"Brothers do that," he adds. "They borrow each other's clothes."

Brothers do that.

My blood burns hotter, brighter. My entire body is an alkali metal dropped into water. I might explode. I am exploding.

"Don't you dare," I seethe. "Don't you fucking dare say that to me."

His eyes narrow. "Because I left?"

"Because I would have played brothers with you for the rest of my life if you let me. *You* were the one who said we couldn't. *You* were the one who said we had to have nothing because we'd never stop wanting everything."

"I—" His jaw is tight. "I know that."

"And now you show up on my doorstep, asking to borrow my clothes so you can meet somebody else, like we really are brothers and I'm supposed to wish you well on your date—"

I see the moment he realizes why I'm so furious, the moment he understands.

"Auden," he says, something lifting his cheeks and the corners of his mouth. Something like a smile.

It freezes me mid-explosion. The fury is still there, but it's hit a wall, and that wall is the barely-there smile of St. Sebastian Martinez.

"I'm not going on a date," he explains. "I'm having dinner with Freddie Dansey."

Not a date.

Not a date.

"Oh," I manage. I could still easily shove him against a wall and bite his heart out, but I also can't stop looking at that smile. "Oh."

And then I say:

"Wait. *Freddie Dansey?*"

He lifts a shoulder in a shrug. "I know. He called me a few weeks ago, saying he'd like to get together. He said he wanted to talk to me about my mom."

I blink at him, bafflement seeping in around the fading jealousy.

"Freddie Dansey knew your *mum*? But she wasn't there that summer."

"She was there the very first summer. And Freddie was one of the first people to start everything up with your dad, along with Becket's dad," Saint says. "He told me about it at the gala."

The gala. That's right. Freddie and Daisy had been there, and I had seen Freddie and Saint talking alone together. But I'd been so preoccupied with teasing Poe with that remote-activated toy, so ensorcelled by the sight of Saint in a tuxedo, that I hadn't paid it much mind.

"And Freddie kept calling and calling after that," Saint continues, "and then he got Delphine to call on his behalf, and honestly, it was getting kind of annoying. I had some time this week to come up and meet with him, so I said we should grab dinner and talk. And then maybe he would leave me alone. I didn't say that last part to him," Saint adds quickly. "I'm not that rude."

You're never rude. You're either brutally honest or hiding yourself from the rest of us, but never rude.

"But he sent me the name of the restaurant after I got to the city today, and it's someplace posh," Saint says. "And I didn't know anyone else here and I don't have the money to buy anything nice on such short notice. You were my only option if I didn't want to be kicked out of a restaurant for wearing a T-shirt."

I stare at him over my tea, my hands still planted on the counter. His eyes run over my taut arms and shoulders, and then he studies my face.

"You were jealous," he says, a little shyly, like he's not totally sure it's true. "You were jealous when you thought I was going on a date."

"Of course I was," I say. "That will never stop, St. Sebastian. I can keep myself from reaching for you, from kissing you, from dragging you back to me, but I can't stop how I feel. I can't pretend that there wasn't a time when you were mine. Or that I don't want you to be mine still."

His eyelashes flutter as he looks down at my hands—spread and tense—and then back up to my face. "Sometimes, I think…" His voice is as soft as his eyelashes. As soft as his mouth. A whisper of silky beauty. "Sometimes I think I don't want you to stop how you feel. I think I wouldn't be able to breathe if you stopped thinking of me as yours."

Because it's how it's supposed to be. Because it's still the truth.

No matter what eternities pass, no matter how many times the door opens and shuts, you'll always be mine.

But I've learned—at a deep and slicing cost—that the restless, grasping urge of *mine* is only worth as much as a person grasps back. Wanting is not enough. Doing is not enough. Only letting go and suffering, suffering, suffering can ever be enough.

In my own way, I'm very much a masochist, you see. Except I've chosen to love St. Sebastian in lieu of whips and canes.

I'm suddenly very, very tired. "I know, little martyr. I know." I push the untouched tea towards the center of the island and straighten up. "Come upstairs and we'll find you some clothes."

8

Auden

My room faces the back of the house, and as such, it's thoroughly skylighted and windowed. St. Sebastian stands in the fading silver-gold light as I turn on a small lamp and move over to my wardrobe. Most of my clothes are tailored, which is less of a problem in the waist than in the leg, given that Saint is shorter than me. Not by much—but enough that it might show to a discerning eye.

"Where are you going again?"

"Rostam's," Saint answers.

"Ah."

"Um. Is that a bad *ah*?"

"No," I say, opening the wardrobe door and moving through the crisply organized wool and cotton. "Rostam's is rather recherché, in my view, but its affectations tend towards the voguish rather than the stuffy."

"I'm not sure what that means for clothes."

"It means," I say, pulling out a few options and laying them on my bed, "it'll be jackets on, no question, but I think we'll be fine without the tie." I turn and face St. Sebastian, running my eyes up his frame, and then I sigh at him. "You are so pretty that I often forget what you are wearing."

He looks at me with something between suspicion and amusement. "And you just now remembered what I was wearing, is that it?"

"Unfortunately, yes."

I sigh again, walking over to him and plucking at the threadbare T-shirt, *tsk*ing at the jeans with holes in the knees and the hems at the back frayed from being trod on by his boots. "I could help you revitalize your wardrobe, you know. If you ever wanted."

A stubborn chin comes up, which means he'd never let me. And I almost don't want him to—there is something rather sexy about the boots and the jeans and the piercing. And when I remember the eyeliner he used to wear with it all…

Ah. I'm getting hard now.

I turn back to the bed and subtly adjust myself. "Let's try these," I say, setting aside a pair of dark gray trousers and a matching jacket, along with a thin cashmere jumper and a button-down shirt to wear underneath it.

It's clearly an expensive outfit, and stylish if I may say so myself, but it's not stodgy or overly formal. And I think it will pair well with the slightly-too-long hair and the lip piercing.

I hand him the clothes and then make to leave, so he can change.

I don't *want* to leave—and a mere month ago, I wouldn't have—but here we are.

Growth, I suppose. Growth, and also if I never again see the look in his eyes like he had on Lammas day, it will be too soon.

It was like looking into the face of someone scourged. And then knowing that I was the one who had done the scourging.

But as I reach the door, Saint says, quietly, "You can stay. If you'd like."

If I'd *like?*

"I didn't think you'd want me to stay." But I'm turning, I'm facing him again. I'm saying this even as I walk back to him like it had been my plan along.

I wonder if he'll fight me, as we've fought so many times before. I wonder if he'll resist and I'll cajole…if he'll sneer, and then I'll snarl. But instead he says something which I *hate* because it means too much to me, and I never gave it permission to mean this much. I never wanted four words to affect me so powerfully.

He says, like it's nothing at all, "I trust you, Auden."

I trust you.

I stop coming towards him.

Nothing else in this world could undo me quite this thoroughly, and nothing else in this world could so completely ensure his safety with me.

"Okay," I say. It comes out hoarse. A little pained. "You can trust me, St. Sebastian."

The ends of his mouth deepen a little, tilt up, and I'm looking at another shy smile. We are suddenly sixteen again, looking at each other from across the abbey.

After a minute, I look away because the more I stare at that shy smile, the less trustworthy I feel. "Let's try the shirt and trousers first. If the jumper and jacket don't work, I have others."

St. Sebastian nods and is pulling off his T-shirt before I'm even finished talking. The firm lines of his back ripple and flex as he does, and when he turns to toss his shirt on the bed, the lean muscles of his stomach and chest tense and release with the movement.

A dark furrow of hair disappears into the low-slung waist of his jeans, the belt of which he works open and then leaves hanging from the loops as he reaches for the button-down.

I should stop looking. I'm going to stop looking.

He makes a fussy, petulant noise—accompanied by a fussy, petulant flapping of his hands. "What's wrong with these?" he asks. The unfolded French cuffs dangle inelegantly over his hands, and I have to laugh.

"They just need to be folded and cuffed," I say, smiling. "They might be more prim than we need for Rostam's, strictly speaking, but I can do a barrel cuff to dress it down a little." I gesture for him to button the shirt as I roll open a drawer and scan over several pairs of cufflinks organized by size and material. None of them will do. I select two tuxedo studs instead.

When I turn, he's kicking off his boots and then his jeans, and the sight nearly gives me a heart attack.

The strong, hair-dusted thighs…the hollows behind his knees which I've kissed so many times. The uncuffed and uncollared dress shirt with nothing other than boxer briefs and a silver ring around his thumb.

He looks like a *boyfriend* right now. He looks like a boyfriend in my half-done-up shirt, in his pants, with the ring I've given him glinting from his hand. And I want to shove him onto my bed and crawl on top of him; I want to thread my fingers through his hair; I want to trace the ridge of his clavicle; I want to flicker my tongue into the crescent of his jugular notch.

I want to hold him in my arms with our legs tangled and his silky hair tickling my cheek, and I want to wake up and have an utterly mundane morning with him. No bleary, post-orgy morning after, no ritual hangover. Just us waking up and kissing and snuggling and then going about a perfectly ordinary, wonderfully boring day.

I hand him the trousers, although what I really want to do is say *no trousers for you ever again,* but I behave. He shimmies into them, fastens them around his narrow hips and then looks up to me, looking totally at a loss. "Do I tuck the shirt in? Leave it out? Do I need a belt?"

I almost make a jest about how much he needs a belt, but I stop myself just in time.

I take the two steps over to him and start tucking the shirt into the trousers…and I'm trying not to die at the sheer feel of him against my hands. The juts of his hip bones, the firm slopes of gluteus muscle attaching to his back. The shuddering tension of his abdomen as I tuck his shirt around the front.

"Shirt in, jumper out, no belt," I say once I'm finished, trying to pretend that my hands aren't burning with the first real touch of him I've had in a month. "Now for the studs."

"Studs? Not cufflinks?"

I remove the first stud from my pocket and take his wrist in my hand, having him hold it up so I can start folding the cuff the way I need. "A cufflink is made to be worn with a proper double cuff—on the outside. If you wear it with a barrel fold, as I'm making now, a cufflink will irritate the skin of your wrist. But a stud is smooth on its back side, so it won't scratch or dig."

He watches as I work the stud through the holes and finally fold the cuff into place.

"You said *backside*," he says finally, and I roll my eyes.

"Next," I order, and he dutifully holds up his other wrist for me to cuff.

After he's done that, I have him pull on the jumper—which clings at the arms and stomach and hits the line of his hips perfectly—and then I step back. With the jacket, he'll look the part. Even with the piercing. He could be a peer's disaffected son, maybe, or a celebrity on the verge of breaking out. Someone with enough money that they can afford not to care about metal in their lip or having their hair trimmed regularly.

Unfortunately, one element does not look the part, and I bid him to stand still whilst I fetch a small sewing kit from the bottom of my wardrobe.

"You can sew?" Saint asks.

"You don't have to sound so surprised," I say, breaking the thread with my teeth and then threading the needle. "It's not exactly molecular neurobiology, is it?"

"No," Saint says as I kneel down at his feet and begin folding the hem up to the right length. "But I guess I never thought of rich people needing to know how to sew. Didn't you have servants for that?"

I finish folding the hem—raising it a little more to accommodate the vamp of whatever shoe he'll borrow—and use the pins from the kit to keep it in place. "Don't move your ankle or you will be stabbed and I shan't be sorry. And I didn't grow up in Downton Abbey, St. Sebastian. It's not as if I had a valet."

He makes a scoffing noise, and if he were still mine, I'd make him pay for it. Some swats on the bottom…maybe some cock down his throat so he could turn those scoffs into sounds more pleasant to my ears.

But as much as I'd like to bite that scoff right off his tongue, it does make me smile a little. He is so determined to see me as some kind of princeling that I almost wish I were one, just to please him.

"We had help with cooking and cleaning," I explain, as I start sewing, "and there was a tailor we used often, but things needed to be sent in to him. And often my mother wasn't well enough to even send things in, you see. I can't remember when I realized this, that there were things I couldn't count on Mummy to do, but I was only seven or so when I taught myself how to sew, so it must have been before then. I taught myself to cook too if there was no one around to help with meals that day, and I taught myself how to put out fires that had been left burning, how to put plasters on my own scrapes, how to schedule my own checkups and teeth cleanings—and then manage to get her there with me so I could have them done."

Saint's hand brushes the crown of my head, and when I look up, his eyes are liquid jet in the evening light. "I'm sorry," he says softly. "That I doubted you and also that the adult you were with wasn't able to take care of you."

I shook my head, looking back down. "She took as much care of me as she could. She loved me fiercely, I think, and the great shame of my life is that I never told her how much I loved her back. How much I appreciated that she *tried* to take care of me, that she *wanted* to. How much I understood that she had been doing her best, that she never gave up on being my mum, even when her disease was eating her all the way up."

When he speaks, I hear a pain in Saint's voice which is kin to my own. "I have to hope mothers know how we feel. That they know these things even if they're unsaid."

I do more than hope. I pray. But I don't say that now. Instead I finish a series of tiny stitches and roll up the hem to properly knot the thread and seal the new seam. If this were a real alteration, it would be ironed to a crisp line, but it'll pass for the night without the ironing, I think.

"I'm surprised no one noticed. Did your dad not notice? That you were doing so much to raise yourself?"

I let out a long, weak breath—not like a sigh. Something fainter. Deader. "He wasn't around very often. He traveled for work frequently."

Ralph Guest had earned his wealth—on top of an inherited fortune—in the twilight world of land and property investment. All of it legal, but much of it morally dubious. My father had the gift of seeing a bucolic sweep of land and envisioning something insidiously manicured and symmetrical. Something just lovely enough to entice buyer after buyer, but hollow enough to be a net loss for the world. Retail parks, airport expansions, soullessly curated housing estates for the upper-middles. And it was a *deep* hypocrisy, because Ralph Guest used all of his influence, money, and power to make sure that the same kind of development he made millions doing never came to his precious Thorne Valley.

They say to leave the world a little better than you've found it, but Ralph Guest left the world a little flatter than he'd found it. A little more leveled and paved.

"And when he was home," I continue, moving on to the other leg and beginning to pin up the fabric, "I think he was rather proud of my independences and irritated at any part of me that was still childlike. Which reinforced those independences, of course."

"But there must have been other adults around. Grandparents? Teachers?"

I start sewing. "There were, and I should have asked them for help, or told them what was going on. Perhaps my mother would have been made to seek treatment that way. Perhaps she'd still be alive. But you're acting like we're all little vehicles of common sense straight from birth, and not jumbles of loyalty and fear and misplaced mammalian instincts. I went out of my way to make *sure* that no one knew my mother was sick. I built my days around the pretense that everything was perfectly fine at home, that my mother was as vibrant and attentive as any other mother. I wish I could untangle why for you—if it was embarrassment, or a fear that she would be taken away, or a deep-seated belief that no matter what, my mum and I were better off together than apart—but I can't. Most likely, it was a combination of all of those things."

"I'm sorry," Saint says again.

I stitch my way around the front again. I don't look at him because I'm worried I might cry if I do. I've never told anyone about this before. I've obviously railed against my father. I've talked matter-of-factly about my mother's addiction and death.

But never have I talked about that little boy teaching himself to sew so his teachers wouldn't know his mummy didn't notice the holes in his jumpers. Never have I talked about the child who stayed up late every night to make sure all the fires were out in his house because his mum would pass out intoxicated while they were still burning.

It makes me feel little and scared all over again to talk about it, and I hate it, I hate it.

"Auden," Saint whispers, and his hand is in my hair again, and suddenly my head is resting against his thigh. It feels so nice here—he is so warm and solid through the fine wool of the trousers—and when I press my forehead against him, the rest of the world is darkened to nothing. There is only his hand in my hair, and the faint bonfire-in-winter smell of him. Only the swish of my eyelashes against the wool, and his soft, slow breaths.

"Thank you for telling me," he says, and I nod against his leg. I think this is probably against the rules, whatever the new rules are, but I can't lift my head yet. He'll see me crying if I do.

His fingers are sifting through my hair now, scratching gently against my scalp, and it feels so good to be touched like this, like there's no expectation of me, like there's nothing I need to earn because it's already earned. It feels like safety. It feels like love.

And yes, I'm kneeling, yes, I'm mid-act of service, but it doesn't bother me at all, it feels so very, very right. Maybe I'm an emotional submissive as well as an emotional masochist, or maybe sometimes even kings need to kneel, I don't know. All I know is I could rest my head here forever, and sewing up this hem forever would be a close second-best.

"I should keep hemming," I mumble, but I don't move any. "I know your dinner is soon."

"I have ninety minutes and it's only half an hour away. Plus I could probably finish hemming them myself."

"You shan't," I sniffle, offended into action by the sheer ridiculousness of the idea. "You'd probably do a...a running stitch or something."

"Oh no, not that."

I glare up at him, even though my eyes are still wet and my cheeks are still flushed, which surely ruins the effect of the glare. "It would *pucker*."

A smile pulls at his lips. A real one, not a shy one. "Auden. Now you've said *pucker*."

That works a laugh free from my throat somehow, torn right out, and once it's out, I find everything feels slightly more bearable again. I'm still wet-eyed, I can still feel that unpleasant quiver in my chin, but St. Sebastian is here. He is here and he is him, and I'm a callow, selfish man if I can't draw comfort from that alone.

His hand is still in my hair, rhythmically pulling and tugging, and I'm still on my knees looking up at him—and it seems to occur to him a split second before it occurs to me that this is how we would be if I were about to suck him off. And once—just the once—his fingers tighten in my hair to the point of pain, as if he's imagining it, as if he's playacting what it would be like to have me like this with my mouth available for his use.

I blink up at him. I don't speak at first, and I don't move, I don't want to move, because I want all of it so much. I want to touch him, to taste him, to hollow my cheeks around him.

Suddenly it feels like the only answer, the only palliative. The only cure for sad kings left with half their cloven heart and a host of rustling trees for company.

His eyes are so dark as they look down at me, and his lower lip is so soft as he worries the top of his lip piercing between his teeth. I wonder if he's thinking of our last fight, of how he admitted he was the one who pushed us into fucking on Lammas. How he was the one who couldn't stop himself from wanting.

I thought I couldn't trust you, but the truth is that I can't trust myself.

I should stay still, I should stay still, I should *stay—still—*

I lean forward. My mouth is so close to his erection that I can practically feel the heat of his body against my lips. His hand tightens in my hair, but not upwards, not away. It's infinitesimal, but I feel it like an earthquake.

He's pulling me closer.

9

Auden

I open my lips and press my mouth to his wool-covered erection. I can still smell him, the faint smokey smell, and I can smell the clean wool, and everything is perfect, and then he slides his other hand into my hair, and everything is even *more* perfect. I relish the kicks his cock gives against me, as if I'm not moving fast enough for it, which I'm not, I know I'm not, because I'm not moving fast enough for myself either.

I look up and meet his eyes as I let go of the needle, which dangles from the almost-finished hem. And then I slide my hands up his thighs. I have never knelt like this, never looked up at someone like this, and it's beautiful, it's galvanizing. It wouldn't get me hard on its own, but it's almost like I wouldn't need it, not in the end. Like the release would be someplace deeper than my groin, the catharsis still soul-rocking, no matter what fluids I did or didn't emit at the end.

Not that it's a particularly salient issue at the moment. St. Sebastian, no matter what, stirs me, and so having his urgent cock brushing against my lips and his thighs trembling against my hands and his eyes like pools of pleading midnight is enough.

"I don't want to be us right now," I tell him in a whisper. "Please, I don't want to be us."

He nods slowly. "We're not us," he says. "We met just now."

My hands move up to the waist of the trousers. "I don't know your name or where you came from. All I know is that you have the sexiest mouth I've ever seen."

"All I know is that you have adorable hair and too much money."

I grin up at him slightly, my fingers on his trouser fastenings. "I also know you need your cock sucked before you go out tonight."

"It's a good thing I found you then, because I wanted a pretty, rich boy like you to do it."

The trousers are open, and I can pull his boxer briefs down. There is fabric everywhere—cashmere, cotton blend, wool, whatever cheap stuff his underthings are made of—but he's thick and proud at the middle of it all, surrounded by flattened curls of silky black hair and capped with a gorgeous, swollen head. Veins meander enticingly down the length of him.

"We're not us," I say, looking up at him.

"We're not us," he repeats and then frees his hand from my hair to take hold of himself. I lick the tip of him—salty, slick—and then tongue-trace the crown where it flares and then dips to form the apex of his frenular delta.

"We're not us," he says again, as he pulls me forward and I swallow him whole.

He tastes like soap and skin, and he smells much the same, although even here linger traces of his sharp, wintry scent. He's as hot as a branding iron against the inside of my lips and on the top of my tongue, and thick enough that I already feel a slight ache in my jaw. And when I suck for the first time—hard and noisily—my tongue flattening under his shaft as I drew him back to my throat—his knees buckle and my hands on the backs of his thighs are the only thing keeping him upright.

"Oh my God," he says hoarsely. "What the *fuck*. Oh my God."

Encouraged, I do it again.

And again.

Alternating the sucking with flickers of my tongue, and savoring the way his hard flesh swells and swells in my mouth. My experience with this is deeply limited—I was a virgin until three months ago— and while I went down on St. Sebastian on Beltane night, we were all in such a frenzy that I wouldn't say *technique* had been a particular preoccupation at the time.

So each ragged gasp of his, each moan…each grunt as his hips punch helplessly forward…all of it is the tastiest praise, and I revel in it. I relish it.

I'm gloating, in fact, gloating like a Roman general on a triumphal march. Drape me in purple and crown me with laurel, I'm conquering this uncertain librarian with nothing but my mouth. Take me to Jupiter's temple, because I've despoiled him of every transparent pearl of pre-cum he possessed, more precious than gold itself.

"I'm close," he whispers. "Fuck. So close."

My scalp stings from his hands in my hair, and my eyes water from trying to take him down my throat, and there is the gentle ignominy of the sounds I'm making as I swallow him, of the slickness on the outside of my lips, and this is what my lessons with Rebecca missed.

She taught me how it felt to be flogged, to be bound, gagged, clamped. She made sure I knew how it felt to be thirsty or itchy or have a cramp in my leg that couldn't be stretched out because I'd been cinched into a fuckable little parcel. She wanted me to feel what a submissive would feel so when it was my turn to hold the flogger or tie the rope, I'd have a bone-deep awareness of what I was doing to their body.

I submitted to it with mere academic interest, with an impatient eagerness to be done with it all, and every lesson she taught, I was already mentally in the future, doing what was done to me to my two librarians, my priest and my priestess.

But now, being on my knees with the floor hard against them and my throat aching as I choke on St. Sebastian over and over again, feeling him pull my hair, looking up and seeing him wild and unchaste, I understand so much more. I understand so much more the pleasure of this—of service, of submission.

And there's something inside that understanding, inside this moment, something that almost feels like an answer...

It flits away before I can grab at it. And then St. Sebastian is coming, drawing in a sharp, shuddering breath and releasing into my throat with jerking pulses, again and again and again. I wonder if this is the first time he's come since Proserpina came back to Thornchapel. I wonder if he's been using those toys he used to like so much in her stead.

The thought of it has me so stiff that I'm reaching down to rub my length with the heel of my palm out of pure, self-soothing instinct, the same way I'd wiggle a leg that had just been bruised or suck on a fresh paper cut. My balls are drawn up so tight that I'm not sure I could even move right now. Not unless I come first.

"I can't believe I came that fast," St. Sebastian says breathlessly. "*Fuck.*"

I can believe it. Not because I'm brilliant at giving head, but because we've been starved for each other. If St. Sebastian so much as curled his fingers around me, I'd be spurting onto the trousers I'd just so painstakingly hemmed.

Saint looks down at me, and then he gives me a small smile. "You've got—just here…" He reaches down and wipes something from the corner of my mouth, his thumb warm and a little rough against the edge of my lip. It's his own spend, just a tiny bit, and he licks it off his thumb like it's a stray bit of cake batter. Like it shouldn't go to waste.

I could die right now.

"I should finish the trousers," I manage to say. I don't want to spoil this by insisting on my own orgasm—if never coming again in my life is the price of having St. Sebastian near me, then I'd pay it in a heartbeat—and I also don't want Saint to think I feel owed his attention and his body. I've done enough of that, I think.

But Saint, martyr though he is, won't let me martyr myself. "Stand up," he says.

"Why?"

"Because I don't want to be done yet," he says honestly.

And I could laugh or cry, because that's been our never-ending refrain since he found the letter. We steal touches and orgasms, we wrest moments away from normal life where brothers *don't*, and then we fight like mad to stay inside the bubble of stolen time for as long as possible.

It never works. We always feel worse after. And yet.

"Okay," I reply, and I get to my feet. He's already fumbling with my clothes as I fully straighten, his dark hair tumbling over his forehead and his piercing pulled into his mouth. I can't handle it, his eager hands on me, and so I help him, I work open the fastenings and unzip myself and then he's reaching into my pants and freeing me.

My organ strains between us, hard and urgent-looking, and he takes hold of it immediately, the silver ring on his thumb glinting with our family crest as he gives me a short, rough stroke.

"Fuck," I mumble, my head dropping between us. "*Ah*. Fuck."

I wasn't lying to myself earlier—I truly am about to come merely from him holding me—and then he slides his free hand around the nape of my neck and pulls me close. His lips move over mine in a whisper of skin and metal, and his tongue slips into my mouth. It's such a different kind of kiss than we normally share because it's not especially filthy or forceful.

It's how we would kiss if we really had just met on the street.

It's how we would kiss if we weren't us.

It's this sweet, wet kiss, this *utterly normal kiss*, that does me in. The slow dance of his tongue, the warmth of his lips, the buss of his piercing on my mouth. I don't even lick it or nip at it like I want to, because we're not us. We're two men who've never met before now, never fell in love and fell in hate, never ran through the trees together as a bonfire burned nearby. We don't share a father, a history, a vow.

We share nothing but this. A kiss in the London gloaming.

It's my turn to fumble at his clothes, yanking up the jumper so that it's out of harm's way. And then the harm comes, abruptly, and I'm gasping against Saint's mouth as he continues to stroke me, as he pulls heat and tension up my thighs and down my belly and right out of my flesh. We both break the kiss to look down at where I'm spending in his hand, spurting onto his stomach as I continue to hold the jumper up to his chest.

I don't know if I can use the word *romantic* right now, given the circumstances. Given what we are to each other and what we have to pretend in order to have this moment. But it feels almost…nice. Simple.

Yes, that's it. It's *simple*. Not dull or trivial—I don't mean that—but sincere. Straightforward in a way that sometimes only the filthiest things can be.

We wanted, so we did. End of.

It's feeling so good that my own knees are threatening to buckle now. So good that all I want to do is collapse back onto my bed and stare at the mess I've made of him. I've dressed him up, tailored him to a hasty perfection, and now he's all untucked, with his thick, satisfied cock still pushing through the placket of his trousers, with his jumper shoved up to his chest, and with the cotton poplin of his button-down shirt wet and spattered with my climax.

Now he really looks like a boyfriend.

I press my forehead to his. "I've ruined the shirt, haven't I? I'll fetch a new one."

"No," he says. His voice is husky and rough—barely audible. "I want to wear this one."

"You want to wear my cum on your shirt to dinner. With Delphine's dad."

I can feel more than see the lift of his shoulder. "The jumper will hide it."

"It'll be wet a while yet," I caution him.

The breathlessness in my own voice undercuts the warning in my words, however. I want him to do it—I want him to walk around London and talk with handsome men while my seed dries next to his skin. It's exactly the kind of filthy game I've spent years wanting to play with him. It's exactly the kind of filthy game that strangers don't play with each other.

"We'll never not be us, will we?" I murmur, slotting my lips against his. I don't push in when I do. I don't push my tongue into his mouth. Instead, I speak like this so that his lips move with mine as I whisper to him. "We'll always want this."

His cool piercing kneads at my lip when he says, "It's why I had to leave."

"And it's why you leaving doesn't matter."

He doesn't argue. I don't provoke.

We both know it's true.

Eventually, we have to pull apart, we have to tuck ourselves away and straighten our clothes. I finish the hem of Saint's trouser leg, and then I find him a pair of dress socks and Oxfords—deep brown, with some brogueing along the vamp and the toe cap, the kind of shoes that say *I have money but I don't care that I have money*, which is exactly the Freddie Dansey energy St. Sebastian needs to match tonight.

I kneel down and help him into the shoes, not because he can't do them himself—he protests quite irritably that he can—but because I like this feeling so much more than I can explain. Kneeling at his feet, helping him, serving him. Making sure his socks are straight and his laces tied perfectly.

I stand up and study him, nodding finally as I hand him the

blazer. "Keep the jacket on through dinner—unbutton before you sit down—and if you cross your legs, don't prop your ankle on your opposite knee because the trousers will pull too high on the calf."

St. Sebastian slides himself into the blazer and I swallow.

I've always known he was beautiful. Even when we were children and he was tearing the heads from flowers, he was beautiful...and later, when he found his uniform of boots and old T-shirts and—if I was lucky—some eyeliner, he was even *more* beautiful. The firm mouth, the high cheekbones, the black vampire eyes. The slight cleft of his chin and the cut angles of his jaw and nose. Even the way he curves his shoulders in when he puts his hands in his pockets, the way he blinks in long, almost-sultry blinks, the way one front tooth is ever so slightly longer than the other, enough that I feel compelled to run my tongue along them both just to make sure.

The lost-boy-ness of him, the sharp loneliness of him...it's the kind of beauty that makes poets reach for their notebooks and also stick their hands down their pants.

But perhaps familiarity has filtered him in my mind—or maybe I'm a shallow, moneyed jackass after all—but seeing him in quality clothes is staggering. I'm staggered by him. And for a real moment, I'm forcefully reminded that he is as much a Guest as I am, that if things had only been a little different, he would have grown up like me, he would have grown up knowing to wear a jacket to dinner. He looks fucking incredible. Still *him*, still the pout and the piercing and the hair that I'm fairly certain was last cut four months ago by a blottoed Delphine, but a him that looks more like the son of Ralph Guest of Thornchapel than Richard Davey, Devonshire painter.

I can't deny I like it. Not more than I like his usual uniform, certainly not, but I do like it. Rather a lot.

I want very much to shag him right now.

St. Sebastian mistakes my horny appraisal for judgement, and he starts plucking nervously at his cuffs. "I probably look stupid," he mumbles.

"You look like every boy I wanted to fuck at Cambridge, but even better, because you're the boy I wanted to fuck since I knew what fucking was."

He blushes, red dusting his light bronze cheekbones, and I want to push him against the wall and put my tongue in his mouth again.

But I don't.

"Truly, you look perfect."

"Is there anything else I should know?" he asks, turning to face my mirror and still fussing with his sleeves.

I shake my head as I come behind him. "It's only the usual smart restaurant nonsense. Start with the outside fork, butter your bread on the plate, and use the lavatory before the meal starts, that kind of thing."

"Not about the restaurant," he says. "Is there anything I should know in order to have dinner with Freddie? He's so…you know. Like you and Delphine are."

"And yet you successfully eat with Delphine and me quite often."

Saint huffs out a breath, blowing long strands of inky hair off his forehead. "You know what I *mean*."

Well. I do. Freddie is the sort that wings Latin mottos about in the cheerful, vaguely ironic way of someone who was tortured with Latin for the entirety of their education and then developed Stockholm syndrome with it. He has four middle names, and a signet ring so old that it's nearly impossible to make out its seal, and his great-uncle is a marquess.

But for all that, Freddie is as good-natured as anyone can be. I've known him all my life—and before Delphine broke things off, he was to be my father-in-law—and I have never known him to be cool or contemptuous. All the manifold blessings of his life have resulted in an unshakably sanguine personality, and he is genuinely friendly to everyone, because why wouldn't he be? Why wouldn't the world be full of friends for him? He goes through life with his beautiful wife and his beautiful daughter, tipsy and charming and accidentally making money even though he doesn't need it.

"Freddie is a good man, and kind," I assure Saint. "He won't penalize you for some obscure faux pas. Only the middle-classes care about etiquette-policing, you know. The real uppers can't be bothered."

"I think you and I have different definitions of *middle-class*," St. Sebastian mutters.

I smooth the sleeves of the blazer over his shoulders and biceps and our eyes meet in the mirror. "You don't need to play a part," I say. "Freddie knows who you are. This isn't an audition. Only dinner."

He nods, but we don't break our stare in the mirror and I don't lift my hands from his arms. I'm not too proud to say that I could squeeze his biceps and shoulders for a very long time and not get bored.

After a moment, he asks my reflection, "Do we look alike?"

I've asked myself this question every day since I first read my father's letter, asked and asked and asked. Is that the same high forehead, the same long nose, the same jaw? The same sharp-edged mouth? Do we have the same throat, or is that just how throats look? And do we have the same hands, or am I only imagining that his fingers are as long as mine, that our basilic veins twist up from our wrists in exactly the same way?

"What do you want the answer to be?" I ask.

His teeth catch the top ball of his labret piercing as he thinks. "I don't know," he says finally. "If we do look alike, it's almost worse, because then I feel like we should have known, somehow. We should have seen it before. We should have seen it from the very beginning."

"There's enough difference, St. Sebastian. Enough that it would have been impossible to see it before we knew. We have plenty of our mothers in us."

"Maybe. But when I look at the bones of our faces…"

Yes. He's right.

The bones are the same.

"I think we do look alike," I say. "But then again, maybe I'm wishing for it."

"Why would you wish for *that*?"

I press my face into the back of his head, burying my nose in his hair and closing my eyes. "Because then whenever I look into a mirror, I can almost see your face looking at me. It's almost like having you close. It's almost like having you back."

I feel him draw in a deep breath.

I decide I can't bear hearing whatever it is he has to say—whether it's another explanation of why we can't be together or why he has to stay away or why he almost certainly regrets what we've just done. I'm not made of stone, no matter how much I wish I fucking were.

I pull back and open my eyes, dropping my hands from his arms. "We should probably see you off. It wouldn't do to be late to dinner."

"I—" He blinks. "Okay."

Relieved and disappointed and wanting several impossible things at once, I lead St. Sebastian back downstairs to the front door. "I'll launder your clothes and bring them back to Thornchapel, and Poe can return them to you."

"Thank you," he says automatically, as if what would happen to his clothes is the literal last thing he's thinking about. He shifts on his feet and looks at me. Looks away. Looks at me again. "I'm glad I got to see you again," he says. His voice is as soft and hesitant as his gaze. "I think—I think I needed that more than the clothes."

He says this in the hushed voice of a penitent confessing sins, like he's whispering state secrets and not something that was transparently obvious from the beginning.

I touch him. Just a small brush of my fingers over the seam of the blazer, where it lays perfectly flat and divot-free on his shoulder. If we were really boyfriends, he could borrow this blazer any time. If we were really brothers, he could.

It's only here, in this strange no-man's land we've found ourselves in, where borrowing a blazer that fits him perfectly is an excuse and maybe a sin.

"I know, St. Sebastian," I tell him. I let my fingers move over to the notched lapel and I smooth it down his chest, not lingering when I shouldn't. "You didn't need to come here for clothes, not really. You could have called Freddie and asked to meet somewhere else. You could have rescheduled. You could have asked Proserpina to send you money on your phone. You could have done any number of things that weren't coming to my house."

He ducks his head. I wonder if he knows how adorable it makes him look, how it makes me want to catch his stubborn chin with my fingers and lift his face to mine. How it makes me want to slide my fingers through all that hair and yank his head back so I can bite his lips and his jaw and his throat.

"You knew," he mumbles to his feet. "How can you have known something I only just realized?"

Because I pay attention.

Because you can lie to yourself but you can't lie to me.

"Do you have money for a cab?" I say instead.

"I'll take the Tube and walk. You're saying you knew this whole time."

"Do you want to borrow an umbrella?"

"Auden, don't."

"Don't what?"

He lifts his head; the deep brown of his irises is almost obsidian in the barely-lit foyer. They remind me of the earth at Thornchapel—near-black and wet, filled with secrets. His eyes could eat bones.

They're already eating mine.

He draws in a breath. "You knew," he says in a juddering kind of voice, "because you always know. Do you know that I don't want to leave? Do you know that I want to go back upstairs with you? Do you know that I'd let you do anything to me right now? Anything you wanted, Auden, anything at all." He steps closer, his lips parted, his hands slowly turning so his palms face me in offering.

Outside, I hear the trees lashing and fretting in a sudden, gusting wind.

"Anything," I echo.

His pulse thrums just above the collar of his borrowed shirt. "Anything."

I could have him now. If I wanted.

If I pushed, he'd break. If I pulled, he'd fall. All I have to do is say yes to this churning, crashing *need* inside me, and I could have him at my feet, I could have him on his stomach and I could be inside him with my palm against his throat and this blazer crushed between us.

And he's looking at me like we're sixteen again and about to kiss in a bed of flowers, like we're starting over at the very beginning and there's nothing between us, nothing but delirious, innocent lust—*I could have him.*

I could have him.

But having and loving are only sometimes the same thing.

I take a step back. "You'll be late if you don't go now," I say. The words come out gentler than I feel them; they feel like razor-wire leaving my mouth.

"Auden..." he says. Pleads. "But I—I miss you."

He says it like I don't miss him in return. He says it like *I'm* the bad guy here, like I'm the one who left, and maybe this is the hardest part of loving someone, maybe this was always the test. Not letting him leave, but making him go.

I take his hand, wrapping my fingers around his so that my thumb rests on the Guest family ring. My hand is shaking. My entire body is shaking.

Grab him.

Bite him.

Bruise him.

Outside the trees are thrashing and behind my eyes it feels like all I can see is forest and rain. I drag in a breath, forcing the feeling down inside me, as if I can tamp whatever it is back into my belly, as if I can pretend that I don't want to run and chase and hunt. I'm not a king, I'm not so twisted up in Thornchapel that even the trees feel my lust and my pain. I'm just a London boy with a non-Smythson bag and good hair. I'm just a friend and a brother and I'm going to do the right thing, because I'll pay any price not to have St. Sebastian look at me like he did at Lammas.

Because I've finally, finally learned that I can't choose us for him. He has to do it on his own.

"Listen," I say. "You and Proserpina will always be my air and my water—the very things that make up my blood—and that hasn't changed, because it will never change, it can't. *I* can't."

I put my free hand against his stomach, pressing the ejaculate-damp shirt into his skin. *Mine,* the gesture says. *My own thing.*

"This is me. But you are *you,* and I love you as you are, and don't you see it? Don't you feel it? You were right about me. A few minutes alone with me, and I have you dressed like a doll and wearing my cum, and if you spend the night with me, I'll have you shivering and spent and marked all over. If you come back to Thornchapel, I will never stop looking and reaching and wanting. I can't be trusted."

He's shaking his head, even though I'm only repeating his own words from Lammas back to him. "*You* can't be trusted," I remind him gently. "You had your reasons for leaving. Have they changed so much that you can abandon them all now? Truly?"

He's stopped shaking his head now, and he's staring up at me with a look so hopeless I can't stand it.

This is what no one told me about love, about being the Thorn King, about everything.

You can be broken, and still you must let people break you again and again.

You must help them break you, if necessary.

You must allow your own sorrows, your own torments and regrets, to be subsumed in the face of their own.

You must cut yourself apart piece by piece and plant those pieces far and wide in the lives of those around you, and then you must not lament when they don't take root. You must cut yourself apart and do it all over again. As many times as it takes.

As many times as it takes.

"Go, St. Sebastian," I say, letting go of his hand. I can still feel the worn crest of his ring against my thumb. The G surrounded by twining, twisting thorns. "Just go."

He swallows. Whispers, "I'm sorry."

And then finally, mercifully, he turns and opens the door. I watch him take the steps with the vague stagger of a dying man, and then I watch him slope off into the evening, shoulders hunched forward and head down.

I think he's crying.

I know I am.

IO

Rebecca

"So he just went?"

Auden doesn't look up from where he's stroking Poe's hair in his lap. It's our first night down from London, and we're in the library after supper. Poe has predictably fallen asleep, curled on the sofa like a cat, her head pillowed on Auden's thigh and one hand twisted in the fabric of his trousers. Her fingers even knead and flex in her sleep, as if she's afraid her owner will get up without her and she needs to reassure herself that he's still there.

"He just went," Auden confirms.

"Well?" I ask impatiently. "And then what?"

He finally does look up at me. "And then I masturbated with my tears as lube. Twice."

His tone is dry, droll, flippant. Peak Auden.

"I can't tell if you're smiling because it's a lie and you're joking or because it's true and you're being self-deprecating."

"Do you honestly want to know the answer?" His mouth is still on the verge of a grin, his voice still wry and teasing, but there's something in his eyes... something like pain. Like he's still bleeding internally from St. Sebastian's visit.

"I want you to be happy," I say. "Emphasis on the *you*, by the way."

"I thought he'd become your friend too."

"I can be chums with someone and still not forget the time they left my best friend for dead in a graveyard."

The corner of his mouth drops. No more smile. "It was more complicated than that," he says quietly.

"Everything about that boy is complicated."

"But that's why I—" He stops. Sighs. "It doesn't matter. The whys don't matter. I only wish that I didn't have to be the strong one and *make* him hurt me. It was hard enough when he did it all on his own."

I watch him go back to rubbing Poe's hair between his fingertips, and my own fingers tighten around the stem of my martini glass.

I'm jealous.

I'm so jealous it hurts.

If Delphine were here...

No, I'm only jealous of the *idea* of a sub tucked against me like a kitten. It's not that I want a *specific* sub here, it's not like I'm imagining sunshine hair all over my lap or the way certain doll-like lips would feel against my finger as I traced them.

"I suppose that's growth," I say. "Given that you threw a glass at him last time he left you."

"It wasn't *at* him," Auden says, exasperated.

"Tell it to the constables."

He gives me a *ha ha very funny* expression.

I sip my martini and then sigh down at it. Auden never puts in enough vermouth. "I think you did the right thing, although I'm still vexed with Saint for making it necessary. Also why don't we just drink the gin straight from the bottle if we're going to make the martinis like this?"

"Winston Churchill said the ideal martini was a glass of gin while looking at a bottle of vermouth, and who am I to question the great bulldog himself? As for Saint, I would like to think that I've gotten stronger or wiser in the last month. Or at least better at hurting myself to help him." Then Auden's shoulders drop, and his eyes close before he speaks again. "Doubt isn't permission. That's what I've learned, I suppose."

Doubt isn't permission.

I think about this as I take another drink and Auden opens his eyes and resumes stroking Poe's hair. Over by the fire, Sir James stretches and groans like he's had a long day of work, when in reality he spent most of the day barking at the archaeology team and then napping with Poe after he was banished for bad behavior.

"Doubt isn't permission," I agree, "but sometimes it's very, very enticing. Especially to people like us."

"Enticing," he says. "Yes."

"Those moments of doubt..." I'm thinking of Delphine, uncertain and delicious in the leather lingerie I made her wear. I'm thinking of her honey-gold eyes flashing up to mine as Auden watched her eat my cunt. "That moment when there's nothing but hesitation, nothing but fear. When all the reasons *why not* are hanging in the air like pollen, just waiting for you to blow them away, and then you do.

When you turn hesitation into relief, into eagerness, when you turn fear into pleasure. It's a kind of alchemy. It's addictive."

"It's more than the alchemical moment, though, isn't it?" Auden says. There's remorse in his expression when he looks at me. "It's tempting on its own. The pushing, I mean."

"We don't need safe words because we're safe lovers, Sir Guest."

"No," he says. The fire gives a lonely pop, with a single, stray spark tracing down to the foot of an andiron. "I suppose not."

I take another drink, thinking of Delphine.

"Although," Auden says after a minute, "easy surrender is very sweet too." He's looking down at his sub now, a small, fond smile on his face, and I snort.

"They haven't invented something yet that Poe would say no to. You could wake her up right now with two fingers inside her, and all she'd do is purr at you."

His smile widens into an asymmetrical grin. "I know."

"She's a good sub."

"She's a good everything," he says. "I love her."

Jealousy slices me into sheets thinner than Bible paper, and I drain the last of my martini.

"I worry about her sometimes, though," he says softly.

"That she doesn't say no enough?"

He nods, smile fading. "Not with kink—well, not with that necessarily—but with life. With everything else. I love that she's curious, but sometimes…" He trails off.

He doesn't have to finish. I know what he means. I know he's thinking of Poe plunging eagerly into the world of Thornchapel, of pushing us to do the feasts, of wrapping herself in the love of two boys who thought they hated each other. Who stayed even after she found her mother here.

She's too many *yes*es, and not enough *no*s. If she were a kitten for real, she'd be the kitten who gets stuck on top of cabinets and trapped inside the sleeves of jumpers left lying on the floor.

"You'll be there to keep her safe," I assure Auden.

"I hope so," he murmurs. He runs a palm down her arm and then settles it over her heart, as if to convince himself that she's still here and okay and hasn't gotten herself stuck atop a cabinet he can't get her down from.

I had that responsibility for Delphine too. For a few brief months.

I stand up before the thoughts can bloom into memories of welts and velvet. "Another martini? I'm making them this time, by the way, you're barred from the mixing from now on."

"Yes, fine."

I'm at the sideboard we use as a bar when Auden says, "I invited Tally to stay the weekend here, starting tomorrow, so we should take care not to mention the door. Or anything else in the woods."

I'm not bothered by this—although Tobias is exactly the type of British boy I rarely have patience for—but it does feel strange keeping so much of Thornchapel from an archaeologist who's actively studying Thornchapel. "Do you think maybe we're being too secretive?" I ask as I turn and carry the drinks back. "I'm not proficient in archaeology, but I do know context is vital for its application. Geographic context in particular."

Auden's brows are drawn together above his nose. He accepts the drink and sets it on the small table next to the sofa, and says, "Have you been out there? To the door?"

To the door, he says. Not *to the chapel*. As if the door is swallowing up the things around it, and it's all that's left.

"Not since Lammas."

He chews on the inside of his lip, looking down at his lap and then up at me again. "You should go," he says. "You should go see it."

"What, tonight?"

It's past dark already, and wet, and the gin is already cool and tickling in my veins. But Auden still nods.

"Tally and his team will be back tomorrow morning, and then he'll be staying the night, and he'll almost certainly be using supper and drinks to wheedle us into looking. I think you should see it before then."

"You could have mentioned this earlier," I grumble, but I don't sit. Now that the idea of going to see it is out and floating around inside my mind, it's hard to pack it back away.

"I could have," he says. "I'll admit that my thoughts have been...tangled...today."

Because of Saint's visit to him yesterday. I understand more than he knows. I can still vividly recall the taste of my own tears as I wandered around London and ached for Delphine. As I bought a necklace I had no business buying.

"Does Tally still think you're culling deer on the estate?" I ask.

"I don't know. It was a flimsy lie to begin with—"

"It was."

"—and I don't know how long it will hold up. Especially if he's here for much longer."

I fix my oldest friend with a look that he winces at. "Rebecca, don't. I know you don't like lying, but..."

I take a drink without my eyes leaving his face, making my response clear without words.

"…but I think you should go look at the door first. If you see it and still think we should tell Tally the truth for the sake of archaeology—"

"—and for the sake of not being our parents—"

"—then we'll talk about it." He blinks at me. "Wait, what about our parents?"

I swallow the last of my second drink and walk the empty glass over to the sideboard. "Our parents, and everyone else who's ever lived in this valley, has stayed silent about the chapel and the door. If they hadn't, if they'd simply told other people or told scientists or authorities or *someone*, then maybe Poe's mother would still be alive."

"So you agree with Poe's father, then? The door should be studied by men in plastic suits with ticking instruments?"

"I agree more with David Markham than my own father, who thinks God put the door there," I sigh, and then I walk over to the sofa, swipe my phone from the cushion, and look at Auden. "I'll go out to it tonight. But for the record, I don't think ignoring the door like my father did is any better a strategy than fucking with it like *your* father did."

"You may change your mind," Auden murmurs.

I give him another look. "We shall see."

I started my day in London, and so I'm still in clothes meant for pitching designs in glassed-in conference rooms—not for tromping around Thornchapel in the dark. I take the stairs up to my room to change into something more practical, and once I get there, I pull out a pair of jeans and a thin jumper and start stripping out of my blouse and trousers.

Which is when my phone buzzes on the bed where I tossed it. One buzz. A text.

It's probably Ma. Or Daddy.

But my hand is shaking when I reach for the phone, because I don't want it to be Ma or Daddy, I don't want it to be work, or some half-drunk message from Auden downstairs, too lazy to come up to say it and too impatient to wait for me to come back down.

No, I want it to be someone else.

I pick up the phone and swipe across the screen.

New Message From Delphine Dansey.

Heat sears up my arm from the hand that's holding the phone, as if I've just plucked a living coal from a fire. It's her. She's texted. It's her and I don't know what to do, because I shouldn't open it, I shouldn't have sent her those gifts, I was the one who ended things—

My thumb moves anyway, out of habit or excitement, I'm not sure, and then I see a picture. A beautiful necklace, glittering with all its diamonds and pearls and gems, still resting inside the jeweler's box with its lid propped to the side. The box is sitting on a white dressing table, with lipsticks and things scattered around it. In the mirror, I see a room that I know must be her bedroom at the Dansey cottage in the Cotswolds: attractively rustic beams in the ceiling, a partially open casement window, a bed made with an ivory duvet that is wrinkled and puffy in that particular way that very expensive duvets have.

She isn't anywhere in the picture.

I've had two gin martinis, which is not enough to do what I do next.

I want to see you wearing it.

I send the text message and immediately regret it. What I am doing? What am I *actually* doing? I can never forgive her for what she's done, and that's something that won't ever change, so why—

Delphine sends me a picture, again with no other message attached.

Oh, my brain thinks slowly. Stupidly.

That's why.

She sent me a picture of her wearing the necklace…and nothing else. The diamonds wrap around her throat and drip down her chest, ending right at the fullness of her bust. One hand is holding the phone aloft for the selfie, and the other is wrapped coyly around her breasts, enough to press them up, but not enough to hide glimpses of pink areolae that match the colors of the trapped bird perfectly. Her hair tumbles over her shoulders in tuggable waves, I can see enough of her hips and thighs to know she's not wearing knickers, and though I can't see her eyes from this angle, I can see her perfect doll's mouth, painted in a color that reminds me of candied violets, that reminds me of the berry-sweet, violet-y way she smells.

The curve of her upper lip means I can see the white of her teeth, teeth I used to chase my tongue along the edges of, teeth that have scraped gently across my skin when I've permitted them to. Goose bumps pebble up and down my arms.

I want to lick those teeth. I want to lick that violet mouth.

I knew what I was doing when I asked for a picture, and still, the angry, panicked lust which slams into me takes me completely by surprise. I want to mark her, taste her, hold her down and stain her with her own shame.

Desire is not forgiveness, I remind myself.

Very good, I text. **And my other gift? Did that come in as well?**

I know it has—it was delivered this morning. I also know she hasn't turned it on yet, because the gift comes paired automatically with an app on the purchaser's phone, so I can see when it's turned on, when it's used, and for how long. I can also control it from my phone, if I wish. Which I do, I do wish.

There's a long pause, and then Delphine replies:

Do you want to see me wearing that too?

I'm sending mixed signals, I know I am. I'm acting like a lad at uni all over again. I'm acting like fucking around in the present moment has no future emotional consequences, but I don't care. I could blame the gin, or I could blame the lack of sex, or I could say, *look at Saint and Auden, they do this nonsense all the time, and they're both still fine*—but the truth is more than any of those things. The truth is that I want her. I want her so much that I don't care if it's not fair to either of us.

I want her so much that I don't care if it hurts afterward.

You know that's exactly what I want to see.

Three dots appear, then disappear, and then appear again. I'm not moving, I'm not breathing. I have Delphine-apnea.

The dots disappear again, and this time they don't come back. I pull up the app for the toy on my phone, checking to see if it's been turned on or used, and it hasn't.

And she's still not replying.

The silence is its own response, I suppose.

Maybe she's being sensible enough for the both of us, or maybe her self-preservation instincts are finally kicking in. Maybe she knows that no orgasm is worth the torment that will inevitably come after—although even as I think that, I know it's a lie, because after everything that happened, I still can't regret fucking her. It felt too good, so good, the kind of good worth losing a heart over.

Maybe even worth losing a heart over a second time...

Stop. That's your clitoris talking.

Hating myself, but too horny to care, I bring up her picture again, propping the phone against a pillow as I stretch out on the bed and push my fingers into my knickers. She's so fucking sexy in this picture, all curves and skin and the diamonds I bought just for her, and that *mouth—*

Even as the climax comes, swift and sharp, I know it won't be the last I have looking at this picture. I know it won't even be the last I have tonight, which should dent my self-respect some, but apparently when it comes to Delphine, I don't have any left to dent.

In fact, I *know* this is true because the first thing that occurs to me once my cunt is finished contracting is not that I want more sex, more filth, but that I want her in my arms to hold and to snuggle, to kiss and to pet. I want her to fall asleep with her head on my shoulder, and then blink herself awake looking at me, and I want us to be so tangled together that neither of us want to leave the bed ever, ever again. I want to hear her voice, her laugh, her sleepy murmurs.

I want her here.

I roll onto my back as I pull my fingers free and lick them clean. This is the problem with Delphine Dansey, I think. The problem with loving someone beautiful and charming and perfect. Her sex slides seamlessly into her beauty which slides seamlessly again into her playfulness and her wit and her cheer, and there's no winnowing out one thing from the other. There's no *only* wanting to fuck her, because then once I'm thinking of her, I'm thinking not only of plush thighs and a pouty, rich-girl mouth, but of giggles and gossip in the dark. I'm thinking of the purring noises she makes when she's happy.

I'm thinking of how she sees me like no other person ever has.

Yes, this is the problem with Delphine Dansey.

Once I've cracked the door for lust and lust alone, all the other feelings come barging right in after anyway.

II

Rebecca

I do end up changing, and then I make my way back downstairs, creeping quietly through the hall and to the mudroom in the south wing. I doubt Auden and Poe would be able to hear me anyway, but the hall and windowed corridors have a funny way of carrying sound, and I don't feel like talking to anybody at the moment, in case my furtive wank is somehow written all over my face.

In case *This Girl Still Stupidly Loves Delphine* is somehow written on my face too.

I find a torch and wellies in the mudroom, slip into a raincoat I keep there, and concede defeat to the German shepherd currently prancing circles around me.

"Fine, all right, you can come," I mutter, and Sir James gives me an answering whine, like he can't be *sure* I've said yes until the door is actually open and his paws hit the grass.

I open the door and he tears off into the night, disappearing immediately, although I know he'll find his way back. In the meantime, I click on my torch and set off across the lawn.

It's one of those evenings that can't decide if it's warm or cool, rainy or not, and so the air is a clammy sort of in-between. Even the mud can't make up its mind—firm in one place, sloppy in another—and it takes me a long time to pick my way through the expansive dig site on my way to the path out to the chapel.

I swing the torch light over the mess as I go: grids made with thick white string, abandoned sieves, a small canopy tent with trays and trowels piled haphazardly underneath. They're still in the thick of the excavation, even though they're working with incredible speed, and strictly speaking, I haven't been needed at Thornchapel since this started.

I've come anyway.

Even though I could do more work in London, even though there's truly nothing I can do with the site right now—because the alternative is…what? Drinking wine in my flat alone and regretting impulsive jewelry purchases? Missing Delphine and arguing with myself about going to my own damn club? No, it's better to be here. In London, I'm restless, stifled, trapped; here I can stretch and breathe and see. Here even my squashed and mangled heart is easier to carry.

I used to think it was the simple recipe of air and trees and grass, I used to think it was the appealing prospect of design to be drawn, of a vision to manifest, but it's more than that, I think, it's more than work and opportunity. But what it *actually is* remains a mystery to me. It's a formula with too many variables. A riddle meant to be recursive. There's no solving for x, there's no curve to chart.

The question is Thornchapel and the answer is also Thornchapel and that's as clear as it will ever be.

Sir James rejoins me as I make my way into the trees, his ears up and his nose to the ground. He occasionally darts off into the dark, ready to pounce on some small furry thing he scented or heard, and by the time we reach the clearing, he's panting and totally wet, like he detoured through the river on his way back up to me. "I'm not drying you off when we get back," I tell him in a stern tone. He just looks up at me with his tongue hanging out of his mouth, totally unfazed by my scolding, and then gives my free hand a lick, as if to remind me that we're friends and friends don't river-shame each other.

Untidy, lovable beast. I scratch behind his ears as we approach the stone row, and he licks me again.

"Stay with me," I say, and I meant it as a command and only in the interest of him not being a muddy mess when we get back, but it comes out as a plea. I don't want to be alone. I don't believe in ghosts or magic, and I've never been afraid of the dark, but as I step between the two menhirs and my torch beam cuts through the dark, something adrenal starts happening in my body. Goose bumps, a speeding heart, a trembling stomach. Waves of heat everywhere.

Fear.

Stray raindrops streak in front of the torch, not enough to truly be rain, but enough to make me blink away water. Enough to patter and hiss on the leaves. My beam catches the broken arches of the windows, the ruin of the doorway, the rose-covered walls, but only in brief flashes. Only in quick, shaking slices.

It's stupid to be afraid. Utterly childish. I'm the only person here, and I have a giant, loyal dog, and nothing is going to hurt me. This is merely a chemical response to the sensory deprivation of darkness, this is just evolution reminding me that humans who go wandering where they can't see fall into holes or get eaten by bears.

It would be better, though, if my torch were stronger. Brighter.

As it is, it won't even reach the far end of the chapel. It illuminates the silvery-wet grass until almost the altar and then everything dims and blears to impenetrable darkness—

"Oh," I breathe. "Oh no."

It's not my torch at all. It's the chapel itself—or rather, it's the roses covering the chapel walls and spilling onto the ground beneath. Black roses, I think, or very close to black. Big and full-blown, so many of them that they cover the stone completely. The altar is covered with them, and behind the altar...

I've seen the door before now, at Lammas. I've seen its pointed arch, its weathered wooden door banded with old metal, the quiet clearing on the other side of its threshold. But there'd been no black-red roses on Lammas, none at all. Only the usual pink and white ones lingering on from June, only red hips and blue sloe and green leaves everywhere else.

I don't mean to take a step back, but it happens anyway. My neural programming is whispering that I should go, that unknown things in the night are *bad*, that I'm alone and in danger and the correct response is to run away.

Even Sir James is whining and pacing behind me right now, as if he also wants to leave but won't let himself leave without his human alongside him, and it takes all of my willpower to talk myself down.

I'm not afraid of the dark. I'm not afraid of roses.

I'm not afraid of a door.

Forcing myself to take a step forward, I swing the torch around the chapel, trying to get a sense of what I'm really seeing. The most logical conclusion is that the roses seem to have started near the door and crawled outward, and when I examine the leading edge of the growth, I see that the roses farthest from the door—and closest to me—are barely budded. Brand new.

Sir James Frazer huffs behind me, as if to say *why are we still here, why aren't we going back to where it's safe and Auden-y?*

"We're not afraid," I tell the dog. "It's just some roses."

Fast-growing roses. In a color that's not possible. Spreading from a door that should not exist.

I use the torch to trace the shape of the door, following its contours until I drop the light down into the middle, shining it at the opening. I say *at*, because the light of the torch doesn't seem to pass *through* the opening, impossible as that is. As if there's something invisible blocking the way, some transparent but still impermeable barrier.

I step forward, and forward again, until I have to step into the sprawling ground cover of the roses. I'm grateful for the wellies— which are impervious to the thorns—and grateful too that Sir James decides to hang back, although he makes a big production about it, chuffing and complaining.

"I'm not bringing you back to Auden with a thorn in your paw," I say. "That would be unpleasant for all of us. Stay."

I turn back and press on toward the door. There is a sort of path through the roses, roughly three feet wide and edged by thorns, which winds to the rose-covered altar and then forks around it, leading back to the door. It's not a perfect path, however, still strung with sprouting canes and invaded by reaching sprays of the plant, and I snag my jeans on the thorns more than once before I get around to the door.

Finally I'm there, and even from right here, the light from my torch won't pass the threshold.

No, that's not quite right. It does pass the threshold, only it's much fainter than it should be, as if I'm shining it through gauze or some other thinly woven fabric. The light filtering must only go in one direction, because I can see what's through the door with perfect clarity.

Wrong. Bad. Run.

I ignore my whimpering amygdala and click off my light.

There's no mist or drizzle on the other side. There's only a crescent moon hung in a sky filled with stars, only a clearing stretching into the velvet-dark woods beyond. Aside from the lack of cloud and mist, it looks exactly the same as our clearing, as our woods.

It could be the same world.

"Why does your light pass through and mine doesn't?" I murmur. It made no sense. If there were some sort of barrier preventing light from passing through, it should work both ways, right? And if light from my torch couldn't pass through properly, then could *any* light pass through properly? Did that mean I wouldn't be completely visible to someone standing on the other side of the door? But Proserpina had told me that Estamond had seen a shadow on the other side of the door and it had known what she was doing…so what should I make of that?

That was at Lammas—so did the time of year make a difference?

I touch the stone architrave rimming the door. I don't know what I expect to feel, but it's as cool as stone should be at night, and as damp. It's the same Dartmoor granite that makes up the chapel—and the altar and the standing stones and the manor house too. And as far as I can tell through the patchwork of rose canes and blooms, it's as worn and weathered as if it's been facing the elements for centuries.

I don't believe in magic. Whatever this door is, it's not that. But it might as well be magic, for as little as can be understood about it.

Which is frankly irritating. Very few things are beyond the limits of what I can assimilate, if I'm given enough information and enough time, but the door is not differential geometry, it's not organic chemistry. The door is not a landscape to be transformed or an engineering problem to be solved. If I had to guess, I would say answers about the door and its nature lie in some obscure field of physics. Very theoretical physics. A fold in time and space that can only be explained by particles no one has definitively proven to exist yet.

"All the more reason to bring in the men in plastic suits," I say, with some defiance, with some bravado, as if the door can hear me.

If it does, it doesn't care. My words fall flat and pointless to the earth, and nothing changes. There is still only the mist on my side of the door, and a clear night on the other. Still only Sir James whining at my back and the roses gathering raindrops at my feet.

Primal unease continues to pluck at the nape of my neck. Telling myself this is only a quirk of physics, a strange crease of energy and particles, is one thing. But standing here, looking at a weathered stone threshold that light won't cross is another.

On a hunch, I look down at my feet for a pebble or stone and settle on a small rock the size of my palm. I toss it at the door, knowing, *logically*, that the rock should land on the soft grass on the other side. The rock should pass right through the doorframe and arc downward to the ground, just as it would if I threw it on my side of the door. Just as it would anywhere else.

But it doesn't do that.

It stops right over the threshold, right between the jambs, as if it's struck something solid, and then it drops to the ground.

On my side of the door.

I pick it up again and throw it, overhand this time, with enough force to carry it right into the trees, but again to no avail. It still stops at the threshold and falls to the ground.

I throw it again. And again. Not because I think I'll have a different outcome, but because I'm trying to discern why I'm having the outcome I am. Because there's no noise when the rock stops, there's no bounce, nothing that would indicate exactly *what* the invisible barrier is made of. The rock itself seems unchanged by its contact with the door, which almost makes me tempted to reach out and touch it myself, but I remember what happened to Freddie Dansey when he tried to shut the door, and I'd rather not put that to test when I'm in the dark, alone. Touching the space inside the door seems like a…a daytime activity.

I don't try the rock again. Now I merely stand and consider the problem in front of me.

My father said the door was dangerous, and Samson Quartey does not say such things lightly. If he believes the door is dangerous, then I'd be foolish to dismiss that as a data point. I'd also be foolish to dismiss my observation—which is that the door seems fairly inert. Aside from the roses crawling everywhere—admittedly weird and unsettling—and aside from the near-constant prickle of danger that comes from standing near it, the door doesn't seem to be able to *do* much. It repels rocks thrown at it…and that's about it.

Auden's instinct to ignore it may not be a bad one after all. If it can't hurt us, then what's the harm in letting it stay out here? And given enough time, I could probably convince Auden we should give experts or the government or *someone* permission to examine it—

Sir James gives a soft bark behind me, followed by a whine. It's the same bark-whine combo he uses on Auden when Auden won't let him run after rabbits or jump into uncovered Bronze Age graves. Like he sees something he would like to chase and then spend the rest of the night chewing on.

I don't have to turn back around to discover what it is, however, because it's right in front of me, through the door and on the other side. A small bird has hopped into view, flitting up into the door-world's trees and then moving from branch to branch in flashes of pearl and gray.

A wren, I think, with its plumply curved breast and its flouncy little tail, although it's not quite the right color for a wren. It's too silvery, too pale—nearly pink in some places.

In fact, it looks rather like the bird from Delphine's necklace. Rather a lot.

Down to its bright, black eyes.

I step as close to the door as I can without going over the threshold, holding my breath. I must be wrong, I'm certain I'm wrong, because there's simply no way this bird looks like it does, but there it is anyway, hopping onto another branch and tilting its head back and forth. It lets out a little chirrup, watching me, hopping a little, and then watching me again.

I can hear it. Interesting. So sound *can* move through the door too. At least in my direction.

Satisfied now that I'm not moving toward it, the bird moves to a branch lower down and gives another trill, eying me again. Its upright tail waggles every time it sings or moves, and whenever it stops to glare or sing at me, it stamps its little feet on the branch, adorably defiant.

Even though I'm looking into a world that's decidedly not this one, even though I'm looking at a bird eerily like the one made of jewels I gave Delphine, my uneasiness abates a little. The bird is *cute*. And something about it reminds me of Delphine, with its tiny glares and little tantrums.

"It's okay," I murmur to it. It tilts its head again, like it can hear me. I wonder if it can, if it's like the light from my torch, where it comes through, but only very faintly. "I won't hurt you."

It stares at me a second and then hops to the next branch down, glaring at me again, as if daring me to stop it. It reminds me so much of Delphine again that I almost laugh.

Which then makes me want to cry.

The bird finally stops on a branch midway to the ground and hops towards the trunk, which I see now is twined with a flowering vine of some kind. I don't recognize it, or its flowers even, because some are small and possibly purple and others are pale with dark centers, but in the faint moonlight, it's hard to tell the colors exactly. But what can be discerned is that the vine has thorns as long as nails, like teeth biting right into the air, and the bird is hopping closer and closer to them.

"Careful," I whisper to it. "Careful."

It turns and trills at me, as if to tell me to mind my own business, and then it lifts off the branch and flies right into a snarl of thorns.

"Wait—" I breathe, but it's too late. The little wren is now caught in the thorns, one wing pierced and snared, the other wing flapping frantically. Its chirps are now desperate, high-pitched, and its feet push and strain at the branch below it, as if it's trying to take flight, and it can't, it can't.

All around it, flowers shiver and tremble from its struggle, and drops of dark blood start running down its pearly wing.

"Oh God," I say, "Oh God, oh God."

I want to help it; I need to help it. But I can't, I can't get to the other side, and I'm forced to watch as it twists and struggles against the thorns.

And then the crows come.

One by one, they start flapping into view, cawing at each other, cawing up at the trapped and bleeding wren. It freezes for a long moment, like it hopes the crows won't notice it, but when the first crow lands just outside the thorns, the wren struggles harder than ever. Blood stains its wing and drops on the flowers below, and the crows seem to jeer at this. More flap up to the wren's branch, a few find perches just above or just below, and soon the wren is surrounded not only by thorns but corvids too.

"Go away," I say. "Shoo! Shoo!"

The crows glance back at me, looking amused, and then they throw a few dismissive caws my way. The crow closest to the wren takes a step closer, leans in, and tears a chunk of flesh right from the wren's breast.

The wren screams. I scream.

The crows jeer and flap some more, and then the lead crow tears off another bite, and another, until its friends fly up and start tearing too. I get a single glimpse of the wren's desperate eye, glinting in the moonlight, before the crows completely obscure my view, flapping and ripping in their frenzy.

It only lasts a minute. Maybe less.

And as quickly as they started, they stop. They hop back from the wren, they clean their feathers. Until finally—tidied up and sated on wren flesh—they fly off.

The wren is unrecognizable now. Nothing but flesh and feathers, the wing that was caught in the thorns now torn to shreds.

Blood drips onto the flowers below it. Dark, so dark in the moonlight.

And in something almost like slow motion, the corpse of the wren tips forward and pitches onto the grass, landing with a light but final-sounding thud. I only realize I'm moaning *no no no* once I stop. Once I suck in a breath and hear my own silence.

Stop it, I tell myself, a little wildly. *Stop it now.*

Everything gets eaten, everything dies. That is nature, that is the way nature has always worked.

Everything dies. Even sweet, tantrum-y little birds that remind me of Delphine.

And the bird *wasn't* Delphine, that is what I need to remember. It was just a bird, and the crows were just crows, and the world beyond the door can't touch me here anyway.

It's nothing personal or contingent or specific to me. It's the world going about its sometimes-deadly, sometimes-mysterious business.

It's not magic. It's not an omen.

I've almost convinced myself of this when a wind picks up on the other side of the door. I can hear it murmuring through the trees, blowing over the grass in the lea, plucking at the leaves and the flowers on the strange, thorny vine that snared the bird.

Two of those flowers tear free and tumble across the clearing until they roll almost all the way to the threshold of the door. Mere feet away from me. I can see the blood on their petals, I can see where they were tattered and torn from the bird's thrashing panic.

And then the flowers blow right through to door to rest at my feet.

For a moment, I don't move at all, I don't think. I can't think. Something from over *there* has now come over *here*, and I didn't know that could happen—in fact, I'd empathetically convinced myself that it couldn't happen.

Fear prickles at my skin as I fully apprehend what's just occurred, as I bend down and pick up the flowers. And then I see what the flowers are, and the fear is more than prickles now, it's knives and broken glass all over my body.

A roselle—a hibiscus varietal native to West Africa—and a violet.

A violet.

I stagger back, I stumble. My hand is wet with the bird's now-cooled blood, and I'm carrying two flowers that should not be in season, that should not grow on vines, and I can't ignore, I can't pretend any longer, that these flowers are not somehow meant for me. That the tableau with the dying bird was not somehow meant for me.

That all of this was not somehow meant for me.

I push back through the thorns, past the roses, half jogging now, half scrambling, one fist clenched around the bloody petals and the other around my torch. Sir James prances and spins when I reach him, giving me a bark of canine relief, and together we bolt out of the chapel like we're being chased. Like the door has opened wide and let out something even more terrible than flowers and blood.

All this time, this entire year, we've been worried about the danger of going *in*, about what would happen if we touched the door or came near it.

But we've been wrong. So wrong.

We should have been afraid of what could come out.

I2

Within Thy Wounds Hide Me
St. Sebastian

The dinner with Freddie went like this:

Saint got there on time, he wore his jacket to the table but unbuttoned it when he sat, he buttered his bread on the plate and didn't clank his silverware around. They made polite conversation until the food came, conversation that made Saint feel a little poor and unworldly—but in a way that felt familiar and also in a way that was clearly unintentional on Freddie's part.

And then Freddie started speaking of Jennifer Martinez.

It was painful and wonderful to hear new stories of her. To hear about a time when she'd been young and carefree, a young journalist who'd chased her curiosity all over the world and then fell in love with a hidden little corner of it. Every word Freddie spoke—every past tense verb, every fond, sad syllable—reminded Saint that his mother was dead, that it had been almost two years since he'd seen her eyes twinkle at him over a mug of tea or had heard her infectious giggle. But also it reminded Saint that she *had* lived. That she had mattered, that she had left a Jennifer-shaped hole in the world when she left.

He didn't know if he could bear any more.

He also wanted Freddie to talk about her forever.

After dinner—and two bottles of wine shared between the two of them (in vino veritas, Freddie had rumbled cheerfully)—he and Freddie walked to the door of the restaurant, and Freddie asked him if he'd like to take a walk along the Thames. Saint almost said no—he had a late train back to Bristol and also it had only just stopped drizzling in that damp, hushed way that suggested it would start up again at any moment—but there was something about the way Freddie asked, something about his face as he did. Hesitant and bashful, almost nervous.

Saint found he couldn't say no.

So they walked to the river, moving in silence until they reached the stretch of paved walkway above the bank, and then Freddie finally said, "I didn't ask you here solely to tell you about your mother."

Saint knew what was coming next.

Freddie was about to ask about the chapel and the door. He was going to do what David Markham and Samson Quartey had done, and warn Saint away from it, warn him of its many dangers. And Saint wasn't sure what he would say in response—*I'm not living there anymore*, perhaps, or *we haven't gone near it since Lammas*—but as he braced himself to speak, Freddie said, in a very quick rush, something that Saint could never have expected.

"There's a chance Ralph isn't your father."

For a single second, the words weren't words but noise. Noise like the cabs and buses on the road above them, noise like the river sloshing against its walls. They meant nothing because how could they mean anything, because they were sounds and nothing else.

And then they became words, and Saint stopped walking.

"Pardon?"

Freddie stopped too, shoving his hands into the pockets of his trousers. Aside from the fine lines around his mouth and eyes, he could have been a man in his thirties, not his early fifties, and Saint could see what his mother would have liked about him, all those years ago. He was handsome, easy, warm. Even right now, with his posture tensed in what seemed to be discomfort, he radiated an earnest and boozy cordiality that was hard to resist.

"I mean," Freddie answered, "that it was never certain whether Ralph was the one who fathered you."

"How—" Saint stopped himself. *How* was not the right question, although he also didn't know what the right question should be in its place.

Freddie seemed to understand his problem. "You know about the feasts," he said quietly. "You know what they were."

"Yes."

Freddie moved over to the railing overlooking the river and leaned against it. After a moment, Saint joined him, looking not at the river but at the man next to him. The flaxen hair and the honey-gold eyes, so much lighter and warmer than Saint's own.

"Did you know that the Guests used to have many, many children?" Freddie asked, eyes on the water below. "Ralph found that out, when he was trying to revive the old ways. That any child born in the village to an unmarried mother was paid for and cared for by the lord of the manor."

"Because he was the father?"

Freddie shook his head. "Not always. Sometimes he might have been the father—given what happened in the chapel, I'd be surprised if that wasn't often the case—but his protection extended to all children conceived in the village during a feast, any child at all that was born to an unmarried mother. Ralph was very taken with that idea, I think. It appealed to how he thought of Thornchapel and his family: benevolent guardians of the valley and such. And so that first year, we all agreed that was how it would be. The lord of the manor would claim responsibility for any children made if birth control methods failed." Freddie snorted then. An inelegant noise for such an elegant man, but on Freddie it worked, because everything worked on Freddie. "As if it would be that easy, what Ralph wanted, that simple. As if children are bottles of wine to be swapped around or handed out like gifts."

"Freddie," Saint asked, feeling like a giant fist was clenched around his throat, "what are you saying?"

"I'm saying," Freddie said carefully, "that Ralph promised to take responsibility for any child conceived in the chapel, but even though your mother was his May Queen, the feasts were not only—"

Even in the faint light of the streetlights, even with the wine already glowing in his cheeks, Saint could see that Freddie was blushing.

"The feasts weren't hemmed in by those kinds of boundaries," Freddie continued haltingly. "That any one person belonged to any other. In the chapel, all of us belonged to one another, you see."

"You're saying you slept with my mother too," Saint said, although it was more of a statement than a question.

"Yes. Every feast. And on Samhain, in particular, we were very much…together. You were born on Midsummer's Day, correct?"

"Yes, but I was born five—"

"Five weeks early," Freddie said first. "I know."

Freddie looked at Saint then, his honey eyes full of regret. "A Samhain conception date is very likely. And Ralph and I were the only ones who were with her that night—you see the problem now, don't you? Jennifer withdrew after that first year, and I didn't know she'd had a child until years and years later—and by the time Ralph told me about you, you were already in the States. I was told that Jennifer wanted you to think you were her late husband's child, that you'd been raised believing it, and that Ralph was already helping financially. It bothered me, not knowing the truth, not knowing *you*, but I didn't feel I had a right to intrude on Jennifer's wishes. I didn't think I had any right to say anything at all until we spoke at the gala and you mentioned being Ralph's son." He took a long breath. "I thought if you'd learned the truth about that much, then I could tell you the truth about the rest."

Saint tried to think about what should be said next, about what should happen next, but his thoughts weren't here in London with this man who might be his father. They were at Thornchapel, they were with Auden.

It might not be true. Maybe it's not true.

Oh God, what if it wasn't true? What if these last four months could be forgotten like a bad dream?

We could be together again.

"So you don't know who my father is," Saint clarified. "It could be Ralph still."

Freddie nodded slowly. "It could. But it could just as easily be me, St. Sebastian, and if it's okay with you, I would like to know. I don't know how many wrongs I can make right at this stage, but I want the number to be more than nought."

Saint didn't have to think long. He didn't know Freddie well, and he didn't know how much he needed a father at age twenty-five anyway. But he did need answers. He did want the truth.

Especially if the truth would bring him home to Auden.

"Yes," Saint told Freddie. "That's okay with me."

And so a week later, as Saint sits in his cramped, sub-let flat in Bristol swabbing his cheek, he wonders if the possibility is enough. The mere possibility that he might not be Ralph's son, that he is *Delphine's* brother and not Auden's. Does he really have to wait for proof to see Auden's face again? He should—he should wait—but he can't. He can't. He finishes the swab, he packages it and drops it in the post where it will be mailed off to the paternity testing company, and then even though it's already evening, he gets in his car and braves the fading light in order to find his way home.

Rebecca

On the night she saw the wren, it didn't take Auden and Poe long to understand that something was wrong, deeply wrong with the door. She told them about the spread of the roses, she told them about the bird, she showed them the roselle and the violet crusty with dried blood.

She'd changed her mind about it, she explained as Poe bent over her leg in the kitchen and dabbed antiseptic on her thorn-bitten legs, as Auden stared at her with serious eyes and a grimly set mouth. It wasn't safe, she told them.

It took him a moment to speak after she finished, but finally he nodded.

"We should close it," he said.

"Thank you," she replied, the relief of being believed almost as heady as the relief of knowing she'd have help.

Poe smoothed a bandage over Rebecca's leg and looked at Auden. "I thought you wanted to leave the door alone?"

Auden ran his hand over his face. "I've already tried closing it before now."

Poe stared at him in shock. "What do you mean?"

"Before you came back. I tried lighting fires. Singing. Dancing. The first time I saw it was Beltane, so I thought maybe…I don't know, that there was a connection. But none of that worked, so I thought the next best thing was merely leaving it alone."

Auden met his submissive's eyes with a gaze both imperial and apologetic. "What Rebecca saw was specific to her and Delphine. I can't risk—I won't risk the people I love being hurt by this. We find a way to close it and stop whatever it's doing. I'm sorry, but that's my final decision."

Rebecca sensed Poe had something to say about this, but the librarian merely pressed her lips together and resumed bandaging Rebecca's legs instead. If Poe had been her submissive, Rebecca would have made her speak, but Poe wasn't her submissive, and anyway, Rebecca had other things on her mind.

"I wish…" Auden started, but then he paused, looking down at his fist where it was clenched on his thigh. "I wish the others were here. I wish I could call them back to me. Move them like how the trees move for me."

"If you could bring people to you with the sheer force of your will, then you could also make them not be tits, and then we wouldn't be in the position of having to call them back anyway."

"Right you are, Quartey."

"When? I don't want to wait long."

"As soon as Tally's done," Auden said. "The day he wraps up the dig, we go out there and close it."

And so here they are, a week later. The last of the archaeological excavation is packed up, Tally has been feted with celebratory cocktails, and now there's no one left but Poe, Auden, and Rebecca. Now there's nothing left to do but go to the door, armed with fading sunlight and determination. Poe has a bulky bag slung over her shoulder which clanks as she walks. They all have torches.

The weather today seems to remember it's still technically summer, and so it's warm and dry as the three of them make their way out to the chapel. The breeze ruffles through the still-green leaves, and Sir James has plenty of furry things to chase along the forest path. Eventually he disappears, on the trail of something interesting, and Rebecca suspects he'll be wet and muddy by the time he returns. Auden was extremely prescient in installing a dog shower in the mudroom when he renovated it.

"What's our plan?" Poe asks as they enter the clearing. "If we try to close it and it doesn't work?"

They've been talking in circles about this all week. The simplest way to close it would be to reach through the door's opening, grasp the handle, and pull it shut. That's what Freddie Dansey tried, and that was what rendered him unconscious. However, Rebecca doubts that they'll be able to reach through the threshold at all, which she reminds them of.

"It makes no sense," Poe says. "If flowers can come one way, why couldn't you throw a stone the other way?"

They're inside the chapel walls now, picking their way through the roses and the thorns. They all click their torches on, even though the sun has only just disappeared into the sheep-flecked hills on the rim of the valley. And while it doesn't make much material difference to how much they can see, Rebecca senses that they all feel better with the torches on.

"I'm not sure," Rebecca finally answers Poe. "I can only imagine it's something happening at the quantum level."

"Not magic?" Auden asks. Rebecca notices a machete and a sledgehammer resting against the altar. The machete has been used: the path to the altar is wider, and the altar itself is currently free of roses. The sledgehammer looks shiny and unnicked, as if it's just been purchased and hasn't seen any work yet.

"Not magic," Rebecca says.

"You're only saying that because you don't believe in magic," Auden says.

"Everything looks like magic until you understand how it works," Rebecca answers impatiently. "The stars, the weather, crops, diseases, earthquakes—for thousands and thousands of years, humans thought those things were just as magic as you think the door is now."

"I didn't say I thought the door was magic," Auden says mildly.

"I'm only pointing out that you're dismissing the possibility out of hand."

"And what evidence points to the door being magic and not a natural phenomenon that we don't understand yet?"

"Its irregularity in appearing. Its interaction with people like Estamond. Its response to sacrifice. The way it knew you were watching when it showed you the wren's death and gave you the flowers."

Rebecca is about to counter this when she decides she can't entirely. The memory of the wren's screams are still too loud in her head.

She's also decided she doesn't care about why or how the door works. A first for her, maybe, a first in a life built around understanding the essential principles of the natural world. What she cares about is the door knowing Delphine. What she cares about is keeping Delphine far away from it.

She changes the subject. "Did you come out here earlier and clear away the roses?"

Auden shrugs. "It seemed like it would make it easier."

"They're farther out now," Rebecca observes. "They're almost to the front wall of the chapel. They're growing faster than roses should."

Auden only nods at this comment, as if he's already noticed and come to the same conclusion.

"And the sledgehammer?"

"For in case nothing else works," Auden says cryptically. Then: "All right. Are we ready?"

Rebecca steps up to the door with him. She's past ready. Delphine may no longer be hers, she may never forget the ways Delphine has hurt her, but she'll be good and goddamned before she lets a threat like this go unanswered.

The door can kill all the wrens and bloody all the violets it likes. Rebecca will never let it hurt the girl she loves.

Proserpina

After settling her bag on the ground, Proserpina runs her hands along the altar as Rebecca and Auden talk. It's quite clear that roses covered it until just recently, since a few canes still cling to the sides, and dark petals drift along the top. She takes a minute to skate her hand over the *convivificat* carved into the altar—the very word that brought her here to Thornchapel—and then she takes another minute to remember that she's standing on her mother's grave. Or what was once her mother's grave.

A grave made because someone thought her death necessary to close the door.

When Proserpina turns to the door, she doesn't see the horrific scene that Rebecca saw. There are no carnivorous birds, no unnatural flowers. Just a clearing and the forest surrounding it. Just a twilit world of late summer beauty.

She reaches for the opening without thinking much about it. In fact, she thinks as much about reaching for the opening as she does about cracking open a book she's found in the library. Like it's the most natural thing in the world to ask her questions with her body as well as her mind.

Auden says her name and steps forward in a panic, but it's too late. Proserpina's hand is already there, already touching the unseen barrier between their world and the world of the door. She presses her hand flat against the barrier as Auden sags in relief.

"You're okay," he breathes. "Jesus Christ, you're okay."

"When Rebecca threw the rock at the opening, she said nothing happened to it," Poe points out.

"A stone is rather less biologically complex than a librarian," Rebecca says dryly. "I don't believe our standard for safety should be: 'but it didn't hurt a rock.'"

Poe smiles, activating a dimple which she knows will disarm the two Dominants she's with. "Even if our standard was Freddie Dansey, we'd still know I'd be okay. The worst that happened to him was sleeping for a day, and I do that all the time anyway."

Auden comes up and pulls her tight to him with one arm around her waist, sliding his free hand into her hair and tugging her head to the side. "Just remember," he murmurs into her neck, his lips moving over her skin, "that any risk you take is not a risk you take with yourself alone."

He is cool and elegant as always, but clearly pissed, and his anger has her abruptly wet and shivering. She would love to kneel for him right now; she would love to feel the sting of his displeasure all over her bottom and breasts.

But instead he lets her go with a bite and a swift, thudding swat over her jeans.

"What does the barrier feel like?" Rebecca asks.

"I think you can feel it for yourself," Proserpina says, moving aside to make room. "It didn't hurt me to touch it, after all."

Both Auden and Rebecca step forward, reaching out as she had a moment earlier. "It felt like cloth to me," Proserpina supplies as she watches them. "Like a cloth strung tightly between the jambs."

"A thin one," Rebecca says. "Like butter muslin. There's give to it almost. A flexibility."

"It's smoother than that," Auden observes, running his fingertips along it one last time before stepping back. "Butter muslin would be rough, but this is more like…silk."

"A veil," Proserpina says after a minute. "That's what the *Record* mentions. A veil between worlds."

"A veil," Auden repeats. It's impossible to tell from his tone what he's thinking.

It's quickly apparent that they can't close the door the easiest way—by reaching through the doorway and pulling it closed.

Auden then tries his next idea. Setting his torch on the altar, he pulls a small knife from his pocket and uses the tip to prick his thumb. He lets the blood drip onto the threshold of the door.

"What's this?" Rebecca asks.

He shrugs, his attention on where the blood is dripping onto the stones that make up the bottom of the doorframe. "All that talk this summer about Estamond's sacrifice and John Barleycorn—I don't know, I thought maybe a little blood would do the trick? It seems to respond to that sort of thing."

Proserpina would have assumed the same—she *does* assume the same—but she and Auden are both wrong, it seems. Auden's blood is now spattered all over the threshold and nothing has changed. The door is still open.

He puts the knife away and then gestures for Proserpina to part her lips. He slides his thumb past them and rests the injured pad atop her tongue.

"Suck," he orders, and she does, relishing the copper-salt taste of him, relishing the look of faint relief that flits over his face as the throbbing in his thumb abates. After a minute, he pulls his thumb free, but he gives Poe a look she interprets to mean she'll be cuffed to his bed the minute they get back to the house.

"Well," Rebecca says. "What next?" She's pacing around the door, probing at the wall surrounding it as if searching for weaknesses.

"I pulled some of Thornchapel's books about superstitions," Proserpina says, taking her bag and setting it on the altar. "There are some old folk customs meant to protect people from gates to fairyland—or later on in the tradition, doors to hell. I gathered some of the supplies this week, although I'm not sure exactly what to do with all of them. Or if they're even worth our time to try."

Auden scrubs at his hair in that Auden way of his and offers the two of them a *what-the-hell* kind of smile. "Seems reasonable enough to try anything we can. If we opened the door using old rituals, surely they might also help us close it?"

So they go through everything in Proserpina's bag.

They drench the jambs in holy water. They hang the architrave with an old iron chain Poe found in a potting shed. They string the doorway with red yarn. They cast salt on the doorway and all around the altar too.

They bury a small figure made of ash wood in front of the door; they hang the yarn with rowan berries; they smear the juice of the rowan berries on the lintel, jambs, and threshold. They even turn their clothes inside out and walk backwards from the altar to the door, an old trick for becoming invisible to fairies.

None of this works.

The door remains as it is. The clearing just past it remains silent and empty too. It's almost fully dark now, and all they've accomplished is festooning the door with random crap and turning their clothes inside out.

Poe expects Rebecca to look displeased about this, to look grumpy that they've done a bunch of silly things for nothing, but when she catches sight of Rebecca's face, it is not irritated or peeved, but panicked.

"Auden," Rebecca says. "We have to shut it. I don't care what we have to do, but I can't stand the thought of it just *here* and *open* and *waiting*. If things can pass through it, if it knows Delphine..."

"It knows you too," Auden answers, looking over at his friend. "Are you so little concerned with your own safety?"

Rebecca's face and voice are completely earnest, completely serious. "She comes first for me. Always."

Auden's eyes flick over to Poe, but she doesn't think his thoughts are mirroring Rebecca's words, not entirely. Because while he'd do anything to keep her and St. Sebastian safe, she also knows he'd do anything to keep the others safe too. So that Delphine is in danger is enough for him.

It's enough for Proserpina too, it's only that...well, okay, she doesn't know exactly why she has reservations about closing it. She shouldn't have any reservations at all. In fact, she should hate the door for all it's taken from her and her family. But she doesn't. And she feels like she's missing something obvious about it. Some answer that she read in a pamphlet or came across in a book, but she can't remember exactly what it is.

Auden takes a few minutes to readjust his clothing, offering Poe pleasant glimpses of lean muscles and a firm ass, and then with his clothes righted, he takes the sledgehammer from the side of the altar and approaches the door.

Unease curls in Poe's stomach as she watches him, and a stiff wind seems to pick up in the chapel, blowing past the roses and ruffling their hair. Poe can't tell if the wind is some kind of admonition or encouragement, or if it's merely mirroring the intensity in Auden's face as he lifts the hammer and swings it at the side of the door.

There's a crack of steel on stone, and Proserpina feels it in her teeth when it collides. The noises reverberate through the chapel and throughout the trees, and they all stand still as Auden drops the hammer to look at the place on the frame he struck.

There's no change. Even though he swung with enough force to scar the face of the hammer, the stone is unchipped, undented, uncracked. Auden could have tied a red yarn bow around the stone for how much effect the strike had.

He looks back at Poe and Rebecca. Poe wants to say something, she wants to stop him, but she's not even sure why she wants that, she's not sure what reason she has, except that she thinks there's an answer somewhere and it's not this.

But what about Mom? she thinks. What about the laughing archaeologist who used to hunt for fireflies with her in the backyard? Who read her Greek myths and Bible stories and let her sleep in the big bed when she had bad dreams?

If someone had closed the door with a sledgehammer before she came to it, Adelina Markham would still be alive. So why does thinking of her mother—imagining her standing in front of this open door and looking through it—make her more confused and not less?

"Again, Auden," says Rebecca, and shoulders bunching and feet bracing, Auden heaves the hammer and swings it at the door.

The crack resounds throughout the chapel and the clearing, and once again when he drops the hammer, the stone is unchanged. He shifts enough to take aim at the old wooden jambs, which should splinter easily on contact, but they don't. He hits them over and over, at the bottom, at the middle, at the top, and they remain whole and secure to the doorframe, not budging an inch.

Rebecca takes a turn with the sledgehammer, with the same results.

The hammer is scratched and nicked, both Rebecca and Auden are panting and sweaty, and dangling yarn and smashed berries are everywhere, and the door is unchanged.

They haven't shut it.

They haven't even come close.

"Fuck," Auden says, still panting. He wipes his brow with his forearm and leaves behind a smear of berry juice as he does.

"Fuck," Rebecca agrees. Poe doesn't think she's imagining the glassy shine to Rebecca's eyes or the working of her throat.

Which is when they see the beam of a fourth flashlight swaying over the roses. They turn to see Delphine in one of her *I go shooting in the Cairngorms* outfits, a thin summer jumper and gray knickerbockers. She tromps up to them in her knee-high boots, her cheeks flushed and her eyes bright. She looks quite proud of herself.

"Are you doing something at the altar? May I help?" And then: "Golly! What happened to your clothes?"

Delphine

She'd put on the necklace every night.

Some nights, she put it on for only a few minutes, turning this way and that on her dressing table stool and watching the jewels glitter in the light. Other nights, she put it on and wore it to bed, savoring the weight of it on her chest and throat.

It felt like a collar would feel, she imagined.

Cool, heavy.

Final.

When she closed her eyes, she could almost pretend Rebecca was in the room with her, watching her from a chair while she commanded Delphine to do all sorts of depraved things wearing the necklace and the necklace alone.

And then the past two nights, when she felt so low that she might as well be buried, she put on the necklace and then knelt. She knelt to no one, she knelt for no reason, really. The world was not changed by her kneeling, and Rebecca certainly wouldn't be, because how would she ever know?

But still Delphine felt soothed by doing it. Like if she could wear this gift of Rebecca's—this unexpected, expensive, lovely, lonely, sad, sexy gift—*and* she could kneel thinking of Rebecca, then she was somehow closer to the version of her life that she should have been living. The version where she hadn't fucked everything up by being needy and lonely—and then lying about being needy and lonely.

Then there was the *other* gift Rebecca sent. The gift that was also meant to be worn, but in a very particular way.

Delphine was still new to wanting penetrative play—had been new to it before Rebecca had broken things off—but when she took it in her hands and studied it, when she found all the buttons and inspected all its curves, she felt not trepidation, but a forbidden kind of excitement.

But still she wondered what it meant. Surely the aim was for

Delphine to use it—to fuck herself with it—but did Rebecca want to know when she did? Did Delphine want Rebecca to know when she did? If they were broken up, then what was the point of sending a vibrating toy that looked to be the absolute latest in vibrating toy technology? Of sending a necklace that cost more than a purebred Lusitano?

She didn't know. And so she couldn't quite let go of the fear that Rebecca was playing with her somehow. That if Delphine did as she wanted and used the toy—if Delphine sent Rebecca videos of her masturbating while wearing only the necklace every single night—disapproval would wait at the other end. Or rejection. Or—worst of all—disgust at Delphine's clinginess, at her trying-too-hard-ness. And Delphine'd had enough of being the needy one, she really had. It made her feel crazy and lonely and alone, and being dumped and still in love was already lonely enough.

Maybe she wouldn't have her orgasms but she would have her dignity.

There really ought to be a Latin phrase for that.

And now, today, she's tormented by the necklace and the toy both, tormented with what she no longer has.

She misses Thornchapel, she misses it so much. She misses Poe, who would let her sit in the library and flop around and sigh while Poe scanned in book after book. She misses Auden and his crooked smile, and the hugs he never stopped giving her when she needed them, even after she abruptly ended their engagement last winter. She misses Becket's warm reassurance. She even misses St. Sebastian and the way he scuffed around the corners of each room, scowling at Auden and Proserpina like he personally blamed them for every beat of his heart.

It's more than that. She misses the house, the huge Jacobean library and the rustling trees, the walled garden and the forest. She misses seeing the hills glowering above them, and she misses the chatter of the river below. She misses drinks by the fire, sparklers with Poe while barefoot on the lawn, she misses the cute little village and Sir James snuffling her hand and Abby's delicious suppers and fucking in the chapel and watching bonfires spit sparks into the night.

She misses Rebecca too, of course, but that goes without saying. That's like saying she misses water when she's thirsty or air when she can't breathe—it's implied.

She looks around her bedroom and realizes that at some point, this ceased being *home*. She's not sure how it happened or when, and she's not even sure why, because she still loves this house with Daddy and Mummy and Rumswizzle and Gimlet, their naughty springer spaniels. She grew up here, her stables are just over the hill, all her favorite stuffed animals are still perched on her bed, all her favorite books are still here on the shelves.

But it's no longer home.

She wants to go home.

Once she makes up her mind about this, all other considerations fall away. She doesn't bother herself with whether anyone's down from London—Poe will be there, certainly, or Abby can drive up from the village to let her in—and she doesn't bother herself with whether Rebecca will be there or not.

Not because it doesn't matter, but because it doesn't change anything.

She packs her things—clothes, makeup, random cords and lights and equipment for content production. She packs the necklace and the toy too. And then with a kiss on her mummy's head, and a quick explanation that she's going to stay with Auden and Poe for a bit, she walks out the door.

Her mummy follows her out to her baby blue Aston and gives her a big hug before she gets in. Delphine's spent the last several weeks toggling between therapy and tears, and she can tell her mother is a little reluctant to let her go. But when they pull back from the hug, Daisy seems relieved too. Relieved to see Delphine excited and animated and sunny about *something*.

"Call me every day," Daisy makes Delphine promise. "And please come home whenever you need."

"I will, Mummy."

Daisy makes a specific kind of maternal expression—the *it's my job to worry about you* expression. "I want you to do the things you want and keep living your life."

"But...?" Delphine prompts, expecting Daisy to cite Delphine's mental health and the breakup with Rebecca as reasons why she shouldn't go.

Her mum shakes her head. "No *but*. Full stop. I want you to go where you feel called to go. Just know that Daddy and I are yours. First and foremost, we belong to you. If you need us, we'll be there."

"Mummy, I know," Delphine says, giving her mother a final kiss on the cheek. Her parents are *good*. Good parents. They were not at all like Auden's father, grasping and cruel and cold. "I know."

And then she gets into the Aston and drives south.

When she gets to Thornchapel a few hours later, night is already settling in, and the house is empty. Auden's car is there, the car Poe uses is there, but when Delphine pushes her way past the unlocked front doors, she finds an empty hall, an empty dining room and library.

She climbs up through the stairs in the south wing, all the way up to the tower, calling their names and making kissing noises to summon Sir James Frazer. Still nothing—although when she looks out of the tower's windows to the sloping lawn and the gathering forest, she thinks she sees torch beams bobbing in the distance. Very faint, very deep into the woods. In the direction of the chapel.

They're out at the chapel. *Without her.*

Smiling and also fussy about all the fun she's missed while off licking her wounds—and also smiling some more because she's so excited to *see* Auden and Poe, she's so excited to be in the chapel again—she retrieves one of her bags from the Aston and trots up to the story with all the bedrooms. For a moment, she considers using the one she and Rebecca briefly shared, but then she decides she's not ready to see it, she's not ready to be in there, and so she picks an empty guest suite instead. She puts her bag on the crisply made bed, which is dressed in a bespoke linen set she'd had commissioned when she and Auden were engaged and she thought she was helping renovate her future home.

She has her yoga clothes, but as the nights are cool and damp, she settles on her more autumnal outdoor things, and dresses quickly. The great tragedy of her fashion life is that she loves tweed and cashmere and suede as much as the next horse-mad girl, but finding these things in her measurements is beyond difficult. Most of the companies specializing in those clothes don't carry anything close to her size, and the ones that do only have extremely limited options. But if there's one thing Delphine is ever truly stubborn about, it's dressing the way she wants, and so she spends her time searching for dupes or having bespoke versions made. She pieces together outfits store by store, tailor by tailor, because she doesn't always have the energy to fight fatphobic doctors or too-small Tube seats or the unceasing waves of trolls online, but she can do this. She can wear the things that make her feel like who she is.

After she's dressed, she finds a torch in the mudroom and then goes out to the woods, practically skipping as she goes. She missed this, she missed all of this. The dark, the magic, the mystery. The sex and the parties and the fun. She wonders what they're doing now—a ritual? Something less than a ritual but still more than a party?

But then as she approaches, she hears something unfamiliar, something jarring. Totally inharmonious with the sounds of the forest around them. And then she sees that there's not two torches—but *three*.

Rebecca.

Rebecca is here.

Rebecca is here like Delphine both hoped and feared she would be.

Brazen your way through. Brazen brazen brazen.

"Are you doing something at the altar? May I help?" she chirps. "Golly! What happened to your clothes?"

Rebecca turns to her in her oddly inside-out clothes, and there's horror on her face, pure horror, and seeing it hits Delphine in the chest like a cannonball.

She stops.

Rebecca takes a step forward, and in the torch light, Delphine can see that both Rebecca and Auden are breathless and sweaty. And then she sees Poe—also in inside-out clothes—and then she sees the door.

"Oh," Delphine breathes. She's not sure which is making her the most twisted-up and nervous—Rebecca's obvious displeasure at her being here or the presence of this silly door that they'd all tried so hard not to open. She has to admit right now that there's nothing silly about the door. There's nothing silly about it at all.

"Is that another flashlight?" Poe asks, clicking hers off and squinting past Delphine to the entrance of the chapel. "I think that's another flashlight."

"I didn't see anyone at the house," Delphine says, turning to see someone tall moving through the roses. "Oh, hullo, Father Hess."

Becket

If his counseling in Plymouth was a chore, then his retreat in Argyll was a revelation. The cottage designated for clergy retreats was at the edge of an ancient churchyard, set on a knoll overlooking a cemetery and a crumbling church—and the steel-gray water beyond it all. Across the loch, stern hills rose, green at the bases where the sheep grazed, rusting with heather at the top. Though these hills were bald and mostly bare, they reminded Becket of the mountains back home. Warm Virginia mountains with trees upon trees upon trees.

The retreat was meant to clarify Becket's commitment to the Church. He was meant to spent the day in ordered contemplation and prayer, and indeed, that was his aim when he'd arrived there. He *did* feel shame for what he'd done—not the act itself, but the flagrancy of it, the carelessness, the way its situation cheapened what sex and Poe meant to him. And he did feel a deep confusion about what his purpose was and where his path was supposed to lead.

He did need clarity. Above all, he needed it.

But once he arrived at the cottage, already stocked with plain but hearty fare and plenty of tea, he found that his plan to account for every moment with disciplined, scrutinizing prayer simply…melted away. He stepped out of the cottage after setting down his bags and looked out over the graveyard, over the loch, and for the first time in a long time—for the first time since Beltane, maybe, or the last time he'd been joined with Poe—he felt like he could breathe.

Living with zeal was never easy. It felt like living with another version of himself, but one that was nestled just inside his skin, a version that cried out for deserts and blood. But there were times when it was easier, when the zeal felt more like a river flowing than a vast and hungry ocean.

It was easier here. With the air on his throat, because he wasn't wearing a collar, with his hours open and open and open. He let the zeal off its leash and did what it asked.

Instead of reciting a set number of prayers, he bent over his Bible and murmured until his voice went hoarse. Instead of forcing himself to eat regularly, he ate when he remembered to, and spent the rest of the time talking to God. Instead of going to Mass on Sundays, he sat on the knoll and watched fog swirl through the gravestones and had Masses inside his own heart. He spoke the words to the lift of the wind and to the distant wash of the loch.

Pray, my brothers and sisters, that our sacrifice may be acceptable to God.

Let us proclaim the mystery of faith.

There was a time, Becket knew, when holy people were not safe. When they were not tame. When they were not the gentle shepherds, but the keepers of mysteries and the guardians of fire. As a priest, he turned wine into blood and bread into flesh—why had that ever become a tame thing, a safe thing? God was not safe. The numinous was not safe.

So why then had he hemmed in his faith with safety? His hunger with rules? His zeal with bloodless, methodical praxis?

He loved rituals, rites, and liturgies, that was unchanged. He loved the motions of them, the ancient words, the less-than-ancient words made to sound older than they were. But he'd been reduced by them, he saw now. Or perhaps not him personally, but his understanding, his relationship with God and belief. He'd hoped to wrestle it into submission, that relationship, and make it something that matched the way other people believed. He'd hoped to hide his zeal, stuff it into the corners of himself, bind it and lash it to his heart so it could never make it to his mouth or to his hands and deeds. So that it could never make itself known.

All he'd wanted, all he'd ever wanted, was to believe like other people did. Communally and pleasantly, and with glad hearts that could easily bear the distance between themselves and God.

Not wild and alone. Chasing after God like an abandoned bridegroom.

But it was the wildness that terrified you that summer, he reminded himself. *It was the zeal that led you to ruin that day.*

Indeed, he had hurt someone in his zeal before. And for that sin, he atoned daily, hourly, with prayers and self-denials and tears. But he also couldn't live like he had been, not for a single day more, not for a single moment more, and it was there above the loch that he found the clarity he was looking for.

Yes, the zeal was dangerous. Yes, it could consume him if he wasn't strong enough.

But he was tired of fighting it. Tired of pushing away love and sex and feral fun, tired of keeping his hunger for God locked in a box because he felt like he had to.

He would leave the Church, and he would return home. To Thornchapel.

But there's no warm welcome waiting for him when he gets there a week later. The front door is cracked open as if someone forgot to close it on their way in, but there's no sign of Proserpina or anybody else—including the dog. Becket sets his bag in the hall—he's never needed a permanent place to stay before, but he's been asked to vacate his belongings from the rectory within the week, and so he'll ask Auden if he can live here until he has a plan for his new, post-collar life.

A worry for another day. Right now his plans begin and end with Thornchapel.

He walks through the house to the terrace overlooking the lawn, thinking perhaps the others are having an evening party in the walled garden or maybe they're in the small glass-and-wood outbuilding that houses the pool. But there is only the breeze and the darkness, and Becket stands in the doorway a moment, debating what to do.

Footsteps echo behind him, and he turns with a smile on his face, already knowing the only person that scuffing, heavy tread could belong to. St. Sebastian emerges through the doorway in his usual boots and jeans, blinking at Becket as he transitions from the cozy light of the mudroom to the velvet dark of Dartmoor.

"I was just looking for everyone," Becket says. "You wouldn't happen to know where Auden is, would you? Or Proserpina?"

Saint kicks his toe against the pale stone of the terrace. "I don't know, sorry," he says. "I've been gone for a while."

"I see," Becket says kindly.

"You've missed quite a bit while you've been away. Are you done being punished or whatever?"

"Completely done."

Done with all of it.

Saint squints out into the woods. "I wonder if they're at the chapel. That's the only place I can think of where Sir James wouldn't hear us." He walks back into the mudroom, and then returns with a flashlight. "Here, take this. I'm going to bring in my bag and then I'll be right behind you."

"I don't mind waiting," Becket volunteers, although for a man who tries not to lie, it's very close to lying. He doesn't want to wait. He wants to be with the others. He wants to have his face in Proserpina's hair as he holds her close.

The austere weeks in Plymouth and the retreat in Argyll had been bearable because of course there would be distance, there was supposed to be distance. He was supposed to be alone and atoning for the right to be alone for the rest of his life. But now that he's chosen another way, now that he's back, even the distance between the house and the chapel is agonizing. Even the twenty or so minutes it will take to reach Proserpina is a torment.

Saint's already going back inside, giving a sort of dismissive flap with his hand as he goes. "I'm not scared of the dark, Becket," he answers. "I'll be fine."

Becket decides to take him at his word and strikes for the woods. But when he gets there, he finds no fire, no fun, no cozy gathering of blankets and wine. Instead he sees something he never thought he'd see again: the door, open.

For an instant, he's fourteen again, shivering under a Samhain sky, thoughts tangled with zeal and tears running down his face. For an instant, he's fourteen again, seeing Adelina Markham being buried behind the altar.

The door had been gone then. Closed with her death.

And the time between those two moments—well, there is his reason for hating lies now. Because he's been lying about what happened that day for years.

Becket forces himself into the present, into the chapel filled with roses, and into the strange little scene in front of him. There's Auden, looking haggard and grim, and Rebecca, looking equally grim…and also wearing her clothes inside out. Delphine stands in front of them, her head tilted slightly to the side like a bird's.

And then there's Proserpina.

Becket's feet move before he gives them permission to, and then he's next to her, sweeping her into his arms and forgetting how to breathe when she hugs him back.

"I missed you," he murmurs into her hair. His hands run over the seams of her cardigan where they line her shoulders and arms—she too is in inside-out clothes—and she nods into his neck, giving him a little kiss there.

"I missed you too," she whispers.

He pulls back before he says or does anything else. His body is aching with weeks of pent-up need, and despite the eerie roses and the cold power of the door nearby, he is very close to begging to fuck Proserpina.

There will be time, he promises himself. He has nothing but time now.

"What have you been doing?" Becket asks, keeping Proserpina's fingers laced with his. He catches Auden's eye and Auden gives a subtle dip of his chin, a *yes, you may.* "And is that a *sledgehammer?*"

Auden

St. Sebastian arrives not long after Becket, his piercing glinting in the dark along with his insufferably pretty eyes. Rebecca is explaining to Becket and Delphine that they were trying to close the door and how—which is a lucky thing, because Auden wouldn't be able to speak even if he had to right now. The sight of St. Sebastian here, at Thornchapel, is a knife plunged right into a lung. Brutal and breathless.

What is he *doing here*?

But then again, what is Becket doing here? And Delphine?

Auden looks from his half-brother to the door. It can't be a coincidence that tonight is the night he chose to destroy it, and it's also the night everyone is coming back. But to what end? And *what* is drawing them back? The door? Thornchapel? Can the two even be separated?

A memory comes, unbidden, of him wishing for his friends, for his priest and his ex-fiancée and his St. Sebastian. Wishing so fiercely his bones ached. Wanting them here, here, *here.*

But no. That's not how things work. That can't be. Not even when Thornchapel is involved.

Even though it's only been a few weeks since Poe has seen Saint, she pulls her hand free of Becket's and runs to him, giving him a swift, eager kiss. Becket doesn't seem upset by Poe's defection—his expression is generous and gentle as he watches the woman he loves run to the man *she* loves—but Auden hurts for the priest anyway. At least for Auden, the jealousy is part of the fun, woven tightly into his kinks and his possessiveness. At least he chose this. Auden isn't sure where Becket draws his comfort from.

From God, he supposes.

"I thought you wouldn't be done in Argyll for another two weeks," Auden says as he and Becket watch Saint kiss Poe back and then pull away to goggle at her inside-out clothes.

"I'll explain everything tomorrow," says Becket.

"That sounds dire."

Becket gives him a beatific smile—a saint's smile—and even in the dark, his eyes are a vivid blue. "It's entirely the opposite, Auden. It's wonderful. Now, what were you all doing to the door?"

Delphine, who's been running her torch over the door to inventory the yarn and chains and rowan berry corpses, seconds Becket's question. "What indeed? It's a dreadful mess out here, Audey. Just ghastly."

"We were trying to close it," Rebecca answers, stepping forward as Delphine moves closer to the door, as if to intercept her. "Nothing worked."

"Nothing worked," Auden echoes, turning back to look at the door, and then turning to look at his friends. Standing there in the dark, surrounded by roses and encroaching fog, with only their torches and their equally worried expressions, they are the most beautiful and terrifying thing Auden has ever seen.

Beautiful because he loves them.

Terrifying because he could lose them.

The door yawns at his back like a cold, unsatisfied mouth, and the only thing natural about the door right now is that Auden is standing between his people and it.

"Inside," he says finally. "I think we've done enough for one night."

"We need to do more," Rebecca says in a low voice. Her eyes are on Delphine. "We shouldn't rest until it's closed."

"We need to rest in order to close it," Auden counters tiredly. "Come on, Bex. No one's getting hurt by the door tonight. We'll deal with it tomorrow."

"Then everyone needs to promise," Rebecca says in a firm voice, "that no one comes out here alone. Not until it's closed."

"Why?" Delphine asks, tilting her head.

"It's not safe, Delly," Auden answers her. "We'll explain once we're inside and warm again."

"Oh, all right," Delphine concedes, dropping her torch and stepping back. She gives a big, adorable yawn, a yawn so sweet and so cute that Auden's heart gives an extra beat. It wasn't for nothing that they were engaged once.

"Perhaps," Becket observes, "we should discuss all this tomorrow, when we've had a chance to rest. I for one have traveled a long way today, and I suspect Delphine and Saint have as well."

"I guess"—Delphine yawns again—"that would be fine."

"Any objections to having a meeting tomorrow about this?" Auden asks.

There are none. With a nod, he indicates they should start filing down the rose-lined aisle to the chapel's entrance and the stone row beyond, but once they spill out into the clearing, Auden catches up to St. Sebastian.

"I want you in my room tonight," he says.

St. Sebastian swallows. "For what?"

Auden's never been good at dismissing his fantasies of muffled groans and sweat-slick skin—he's rarely tried, if he's honest—but he dismisses them now, fixing Saint with a serious look. "To talk, St. Sebastian. About why you're back."

"Proserpina," Auden says, snagging her hand as she's about to split towards the kitchen. "I want you upstairs with Saint and me."

She looks up at him, brows pulled together. "I thought you two might want space to talk." He'd told her everything that had happened in his townhouse that day, and so she knows the most recent pain between them.

Auden shakes his head. "I'm tired of space. And it doesn't help anyway, remember? All I did was blow him, and all he did was make me cry."

Proserpina rolls her cat eyes. "You two are a mess."

"I know." He pulls their joined hands up to his mouth and kisses her knuckles. "It's because we're supposed to be a three. Please." He squeezes her hand once, twice. The slow beat of a joined heart.

She softens a little and nods. "I'll bring up some tea?"

"Or something stronger," Auden suggests and then releases her hand with a final squeeze. "Don't tarry."

"Yes, Sir," Proserpina salutes, which earns her a couple quick swats before she manages to escape to the kitchen.

Upstairs, Auden finds St. Sebastian sitting on his bed, rubbing his hands on his thighs and looking uncomfortable. Auden takes a moment to remember that for one wonderful night, this was St. Sebastian's bed too. For one night, the three of them were well and truly together, well and truly whole.

But never mind. He's learned since then. He's learned that whole isn't whole just because he wills it so.

He takes a seat opposite St. Sebastian in his desk chair, bracing one elbow on his desk and leaning his head against his hand.

Saint says nothing. Only stares at him with that tragic, onyx stare that's captured both Auden's heart and his cock since they were teenagers.

"You'll be staying?" Auden inquires after the silence begins to gnaw at them. "In the area, I mean?"

Saint gives a jerky nod. "I—um. Yeah. I think for a bit. I decided I really needed to list the semi, but I can't until I deal with Mamá's things and fix a few things up."

"Wherever you were…you can leave there that easily?"

Saint lets out a breath. "I was in Bristol. Doing work for Augie still, but remotely, you know, the accounting and ordering and things. I was—well, it's so dumb at this point, I feel like an idiot even saying this—but I had decided to go back to school. I've been accepted at the University of Bristol. They've worked out a thing for me to transfer my other credits, and if I go full-time, I'd have my degree by next summer."

Auden only stares at him. His brave, bashful Saint. He wants to hold him so much right now that his body is shivering from the strain of staying still.

"I don't think that's dumb at all," Auden says. "I think it's wonderful." And then Saint's words fully catch up with him. "What do you mean, you *had* decided? Are you saying you're no longer going to do it?"

Saints rubs at his thighs again, the ring on his thumb catching the light as he does. "I'm saying I'm not sure," he responds after a moment. "The semester doesn't start until October, so I still have a few weeks to consider it, but I just...well, the library still hasn't filled my position and said they'd take me back in a heartbeat. And mostly— it felt wrong being there, in Bristol. Being far away from Thornchapel. And you."

Their eyes meet across the room, and Auden draws in a deep breath.

"St. Sebastian—" he starts, and then Proserpina enters the room with a tea tray. There're also three lowballs and a bottle of Macallan on it too.

Auden falls silent. He's not sure what he was going to say anyway. *Stop talking like that*, maybe. Or maybe, *please talk like that some more, please tell me how much you need me, because I need you so much I'm forever bled dry with it.*

Proserpina serves them, and then sinks into a graceful lounging position against his leg, her head against his knee while she traces her finger around the edge of her teacup. And with her there, her silky hair just at the perfect height for him to caress, her bottom tucked lush and warm against the side of his foot, everything feels so deeply and legibly good. Like they are a garment that's finally been stitched together or a chain that's finally been linked or a keystone set into an arch made of wounds and purposes instead of stones.

This is how it should be. And so he can be as he should be.

"Why are you here, St. Sebastian?" he asks. "It cannot be only that you're doubting school, can it? There is another reason."

St. Sebastian fiddles with his thumb ring. "I have something to tell you. Both of you, both of you should know. I hadn't said anything yet, because I'm still not sure—I mean, I still don't know for sure."

"Know what?" Poe prompts gently.

Saint takes a breath like he's about to step off a cliff. "Freddie Dansey thinks he may be my father."

"What?" she whispers.

Auden says nothing. He doesn't think he can.

"This means Ralph wouldn't be my father," Saint adds, as if to clarify. As if he thinks Auden isn't grasping the implications of it. "Freddie would be my father, which would make Delphine my half-sister, but you wouldn't be my brother. We wouldn't be related at all."

"Why does Freddie think this?" Auden asks, as calmly as he can. His mind is racing. His pulse is racing. He doesn't need to look outside to know the forest is stirring for him too.

Saint explains about the Guests and the children of the manor, and how Ralph wanted to carry on the tradition. Of how Freddie had learned of him, and how their conversation at the gala had prompted him to tell Saint the truth. "So you see," he finishes all in a rush, his hands fluttering above his knees. "Maybe Ralph isn't my father at all. Maybe everything can be—we can be—Auden, will you look at me?"

Auden's been looking not at St. Sebastian's face, but at his hands. At the silver ring around his thumb, the one with the worn crest of Auden's family stamped into the middle. A strange loneliness folds itself into Auden's chest, and he tries to ignore it, because he's not sure what it means.

Auden hasn't met Saint's gaze quickly enough, it appears, because Saint moves from the bed and lowers himself to his knees in front of Auden. He puts his hands on Auden's thighs.

"Don't you see?" Saint asks urgently. "This means—this changes everything, Auden, absolutely everything. All the reasons we couldn't—*the* reason—it's gone now!"

"And that's why you came," Auden says. He shouldn't touch St. Sebastian right now; it's not safe. It's not safe because for the first time in so long, Saint is kneeling at his feet. Saint is kneeling at his feet and offering…offering everything. And it's not just relief or joy that Auden feels coursing through his veins now, but possession and power, and if he touches Saint, he might never stop.

He touches him anyway. He presses his thumb to Saint's lip piercing. He remembers how that piercing felt on his cock all those months ago, when Saint caught him in the tower. When Saint crawled to him and licked him clean.

He's hard. His cock has lengthened down the leg of his trousers, pushing against the fabric, aching for him to notice that his two subs are right here at his feet. It's mirrored by the ache in his chest—the ache from having both halves of his heart here again.

God is cruel to give him this. God is cruel to wave this miracle before him, to offer him cool water to finally, finally quench his thirst.

Auden drags in a breath and forces himself to remember. He must remember what he's learned. He must not forget now when it matters the most.

"This changes nothing, sweet martyr," he tells St. Sebastian. He manages to lift his thumb from Saint's lip, and the lifting hurts, like he's plunged his hand into a bed of coals. But still he holds strong. "This changes nothing."

Saint's mouth opens. His pupils are blown so big now, and Auden realizes he's having the same physical reaction to kneeling in front of Auden as Auden has to him doing it.

"Why?" Saint whispers. "Why does it change nothing?"

Anger arcs through Auden so fast that he nearly catches fire with it. He is so *tired* of being the strong one, the wise one. He is so tired of being this new version of himself, when the old version would already have Saint and Poe on his bed in a sprawl of skin and sex.

He is angry enough that he does what he's wanted to do since the moment he saw St. Sebastian in the chapel, and he threads his fingers through Saint's dark hair and drags his mouth to where Auden's erection pushes against his trousers.

"If you put me in your mouth right now," Auden says in a low, furious voice, "if I told you to bend over this desk and allow me to use you—if we spend the next few days doing every depraved thing that we think we're owed—and then it turns out not to be true, then what? Then what, St. Sebastian? If you get those results back from the lab and Freddie isn't your father after all, how do you think you will feel?"

Poe's hand curls around Auden's ankle. A subtle reprimand.

With an unhappy hiss, Auden releases Saint, who has shock and hurt written all over his face.

Ignoring the stiff throb of his erection, Auden leans forward. "Even if you get the answer you want from the test, what happens if the lab comes back in two years and says there's been a processing error? That they've gotten your results mixed up and you really are Ralph's son? What if that happens in five years? Ten years? What if we're married by then? What then, St. Sebastian? Will you leave me then? Will I always be afraid that you'll be yanked away from me?"

Saint's lips are trembling. "That's not—that's not going to happen."

"That the lab could make a mistake or that you would leave me if it turned out they did? Tell me what you *want*, St. Sebastian. You know what I want. You know everything I'd be willing to do to have it. But all you seem to know is what you *don't* want."

"I want *us*," Saint bursts out. "The three of us. I want to be yours, but God, Auden, you can't expect me to choose us without some fucking certainty that we're not brothers!"

Auden is roiling with the need to *make*, to hurt, to fuck. He rubs his hands over his face, the roar of his instincts louder than anything else—louder than wisdom, than compassion, than logic.

Take him to your bed.

Show him all the certainty he needs.

Fuck. No. He won't do that.

He loves St. Sebastian too much to have this discussion in a language he knows he can win in. Because Saint would go to bed with him. Saint would let himself be fucked and spanked and handled, and Auden will have won, but only for a time. Only for a night, maybe for a few nights, if he were lucky.

He won't have won his little martyr back. Not for good.

"You have to decide," Auden says. His voice is shaking, and his body too. There's something caught in his throat and prickling the backs of his eyelids. "You have to choose. If you come back to my bed, it won't be temporary, and it won't be contingent on a phone call that could come at any point down the line. If you come back to me, it will be because you're ready to accept whatever may come, without fear and without shame. Because you're ready to choose me, even if we are both Ralph's sons."

Saint is looking up at him like Auden is the cruelest man he's ever met. "So it doesn't matter to you that I could be yours right now," Saint says dully. "Tonight."

The obstruction in Auden's throat is downright painful now. "Of course it matters, Saint. *You* matter. Which is why I'm not going to fuck you on the chance Freddie's claim is true, and then have you hate yourself when the tests come back and you are still Ralph's son. You have to be the one to decide it doesn't matter. You have to learn to forgive yourself for this, independent of whatever alleles you and Freddie may or may not share."

Saint looks over to Proserpina, and whatever he sees seems to fill him with defeat. "You really mean this," he says. "You're really pushing me away right now."

Auden's eyes burn when he says, around the knot in his throat, "I'm only a man, St. Sebastian. I can only lose you so many times before I lose myself too."

He and St. Sebastian look at each other for a long time, Auden's breathing labored and Saint's eyes wet. And then finally Saint gets to his feet. "Fine," he says raggedly. "Have it your way."

"My way is having you—don't forget that. It's only that I'm asking you to choose me. For better or for worse, as the vows go."

"Just like in the chapel when we were young," Saint says. He's pushing tears off his cheeks, but there is a small curve to his mouth.

"Just like in the chapel," Auden agrees.

And then St. Sebastian leaves.

Auden's barely even opened his mouth to speak before Proserpina is tucked in his lap, her fingers curled into his jumper.

"Do you have a lecture for me?" Auden asks as he shoves his fingers into her inside-out jeans. She's only a little wet, so he lifts his fingers to his mouth and licks them, so he can work them inside her hole. She squirms for him, squirms so prettily. The inside of her cunt is like the softest, silkiest thing against his fingertips.

He would like to fuck it.

"No," she says as he stands her up on her feet and starts tugging at her jeans. "You did the right thing."

"Did I?"

"You know you did."

"I don't even know what's right and wrong anymore." Her jeans are off now, and so are her knickers, and soon she's wearing nothing but a soft, slouchy jumper that keeps sliding off one ivory shoulder. "All I know is that I've chased him and chased him and chased him. And it never works. It never sticks."

His throat still aches something bloody awful and his eyes hurt even worse, but when she frees his erection and positions it against her opening, he forgets about all that. There's only her, only her green eyes and her wet cunt.

"Kings were chosen by the people they would lead. Not the other way around," she says, sinking into his lap. They take a moment to shiver like that, just like that, her bottom on his thighs, her thighs around his hips. She's too short for her feet to properly brace against the floor, and so she is suspended almost helplessly in this position.

Auden loves it. He wraps his hands around her plush hips and savors it, her needing him for balance, her sweet powerlessness. "What are you saying?"

She slides her hands behind his neck and kisses him as he fucks her. Her breath is hitched when she speaks, and even through her bra and jumper, Auden can feel that her nipples are bunched into needy points. "You can't choose *for* him," she says. "You can't chase him into choosing. But you can remind him of why you'd be a good choice."

"Oh, can I?" The inside of her caresses him, kisses him. Strokes wetly up and down his cock. He is close. He wedges a thumb against the ripe berry of her clit. "And how should I remind him?"

She nips at his lip, which earns her a low growl. He spanks her to settle her down, and then—deciding that's not enough—he rises to his feet with her thighs wrapped around him and her backside firmly in his hands, and carries her over to the bed, where he flips her on her stomach and ruts into her without mercy.

The roughness, the prerogative, has her coming in an instant, and it's that same prerogative that sends him over the edge. He loses himself in the utter sensation of her, and with a series of vicious grunts, he pumps his release free of his body and into hers. Enough that it trickles out around them and onto the duvet. Enough that he thinks maybe he'll never stop coming, and this is his new heaven, his new eternity.

He wouldn't complain if it were.

He stays on top of her for a long time after he's done, because they both like it, and when he finally rolls off and pulls her against his chest, she answers his question. "By being yourself, Auden. You remind him by being yourself."

"And if being myself is being a kinky pervert?"

She laughs against his chest. "Isn't that why he fell in love with you in the first place?"

Later that night, when Proserpina and Sir James are both snoring on the bed, when Delphine and Rebecca and Becket are asleep in different rooms, when Saint has disappeared back to the village, Auden walks up to the south tower and looks out over the lawn and the dark, muddy stain of the excavation.

He can't sleep: his eyes hurt, his chest hurts, he's hard all over again. Saint should be in his bed. Delphine and Rebecca should be in bed together too. And Becket shouldn't be orbiting Proserpina like a lonely moon, but Auden doesn't know how to fix that any more than he knows how to fix anything else.

All of them are miserable. Sick with love for each other.

He can't seem to blink and see properly, like there's something caught behind his eyelids. Something more than his feelings, anyway, and there in the tower, with the moonlight streaming in and making rosy, thorny patterns on the floor, he starts to cry.

The tears feel like hot knives, big, slicing, burning, and he is blinded by them and felled by the pain. He's never had tears *hurt* before, not like this, not like something is inside his head and trying to climb out through his eyes, and there's a flash of real fear that he might need serious help—A&E help—when he finally succeeds in crying something free from his right eyelid. It tumbles down his cheek to the floor.

The pain abating, his vision clearing, Auden looks down at it.

In a way, he's almost not surprised.

A single rose petal rests between his bare feet, wet but untorn. A red so dark that it's nearly black.

13

Proserpina

"Are we all quite settled then?" Rebecca asks.

We're all gathered in the library, some of us—me, Delphine and Becket—are sitting in pools of September sun, while others—Rebecca and Auden—are on their feet, pacing. St. Sebastian has returned from the village and, as usual, is slouched in the shadows, his eyes on his boots and his lip piercing glinting out from the dim cove of bookshelves where he's currently hiding.

We are all together, all about to talk Thornchapel business, and so everything should be as it was. It should be like old times, all of us crowded on chairs and sofas, Delphine wondering if it's too early to drink, Becket giving an impromptu history lecture, Sir James begging for ear scratches.

But it's not like old times.

Delphine and Rebecca are situated a painful distance apart, as if repelled by some kind of force field, and they're doing their best not to even look at each other. Saint also seems to be doing his level best not to look at Auden…but of course, Auden only has eyes for Saint, like he can rich-boy-smolder his way past Saint's moral defenses.

And Becket? Well, he is here from his retreat early, and he's not wearing his collar, and he's not mentioned going to St. Petroc's once— so none of that can possibly bode well, but Becket doesn't look like a man bereft of his calling. In fact, he seems as content and charming as ever. Maybe even more than usual. And the looks he keeps fixing me with…

But. I also can't stop the guilt that twists my stomach or the worry that cinches in my chest. *I* was the reason Becket was caught. *I* was the reason he was sent away. And the worst part of it is that I don't know if there's any silver lining to that. I don't know if I can offer him anything that was worth losing everything.

I don't know if I'll ever be able to love him like he loves me, not in this life at least. Not when my heart is already sewn to Saint's and Auden's and has been since I was twelve years old.

"We have to close the door," Rebecca is saying, walking up and down the length of the first library table. She has her braids down today, and they sway with each and every step she takes, with each and every click her ankle boots make against the old wooden floor.

Delphine is watching Rebecca's feet like how people in deserts watch rain fall.

"That much is certain," Rebecca continues. "And the sooner we close it, the better."

Delphine looks very much like she wants to ask why but can't seem to make herself speak to her ex-Domme. She turns to Auden instead. "But why? I know you didn't want the door to appear at all, but it is *just* a door after all, not a landmine. We won't walk through it, or whatever it is you're so terribly worried about."

Auden sighs, giving Delphine a smile that seems reserved only for her. Gentle and indulgent, utterly fond. "It's more complicated than that. You've seen the roses."

She waves a hand. "So the chapel will smell like the Chelsea Flower Show? Who cares?"

Rebecca stops pacing. For the first time today, she stares down at her ex. "This isn't a joke, Delph." She corrects herself with a small shake of her head. "Delphine."

"I never said it was, *Bex*," Delphine says, sitting up straight in her chair and glaring at Rebecca. Even from here, I can feel the thing between them—sharp and charged with anger and longing. Even from here, I can see the way Rebecca's eyes drop to Delphine's lipsticked mouth. Even from here, I can see the pulse in Delphine's throat.

Rebecca steps back with a soft oath and turns away.

"Quartey, tell her what you saw," Auden says. "She deserves to know."

"I *know* she deserves to know," Rebecca says brusquely. And then her shoulders slump and she raises a shaking hand to her forehead. "I just don't like talking about it," she says. "That's all."

Delphine sits quietly, a furrow between her dark blond brows.

"I'll tell you what I saw, and then you'll understand," Rebecca says, and then she explains to Delphine—and Becket and Saint—about the night she went to the chapel alone, and what she saw through the door. She explains about the bird and the blood and the flowers that blew over the threshold.

Delphine's hand flutters to her chest as Rebecca describes the wren—its snared wing and its pearly-pink feathers and its bright, black eye—and when Rebecca describes its death, Delphine shivers and shivers, like she's just caught a draft.

And then the violet and the roselle, both bloody from the bird's miserable death, and Delphine looks up at Rebecca again. The stubbornness has left her face now, and what's left is something that looks to me like trust. Like even now after they've broken each other's hearts, Rebecca is still the person Delphine trusts most in this world.

"My scent," Delphine says to Rebecca. "It's violets."

"I know," Rebecca says tiredly. "I know, Delph."

There's no correcting the nickname now, there's no stepping back. They look at each other and a shared understanding arcs between them.

After a few seconds of this, Delphine nods. "Well. I suppose this changes things."

"If I may," Becket cuts in. "Have we considered that the door wasn't showing Rebecca the wren's death out of some sort of ill will?"

Auden half sits on the edge of the library table, crossing his ankles and curling his fingers around the edge of the table, drumming them in apparent thought. He's in a cream turtleneck and velvet slippers and trousers the color of Japanese maple leaves in fall, and he should look ridiculous, but he doesn't at all. With the hair tumbling over his forehead and the muscles moving under the thin cashmere of his sweater, he looks like money and sex and I wonder if it would be too distracting if I went over and sat at his feet right now. If I bent over them and started kissing the bare skin above his slippers.

"Are you saying that you don't think there was intention behind what Rebecca saw?" Auden is replying as I move over to him and settle on the floor. He drops a hand to cup the back of my head while he continues to talk, and despite everything—despite the unhappiness everywhere else in the room—I'm so content I could purr. I press my face against Auden's thigh as Becket responds.

"I'm saying intention doesn't signify malevolence."

"What other purpose could there be?" Rebecca asks. "It wasn't exactly a fucking Disney scene, Becket. It was slaughter. Gruesome, *pointed* slaughter."

"But is there no other alternative?" Becket asks. "Is there no way that it could have been something more…neutral?"

"More neutral than death?" Auden interjects, a tad incredulously.

"It's a vision," Becket explains. "They aren't always meant as literal signs. In the Bible, Daniel sees a lionlike beast with its wings getting torn off, and he later sees a beast with iron teeth which gnash everything in its path, but the beasts weren't meant to be seen literally. They were symbols of—"

"Of the Babylonian empire and the Roman Empire respectively, yes, I did my catechism too, Becket," Auden interrupts impatiently. "But we're not talking allegory here, we're talking about a threat. To one or more of us."

"This is the danger with symbols and omens," Becket says. "They can be read more than one way, and yet we often pick one interpretation and stand by it. All I'm asking is if it's possible that— like Daniel with his kingdom-beasts—the omen might be more explicative than existential?"

"Hasn't Daniel's book been used to predict the end times?" a voice says from the edge of the room. I crane my head to see Saint, but all I can see are his boots under the table as he leans against the shelves next to him. "I remember that much from Sunday school. And the end times seem pretty existential to me."

"Also Daniel was a captive in the same foreign empire that destroyed his city and exiled his court," Auden points out. Still impatiently. "What seems merely political to us may have been very existential to him."

"I'm not arguing that," Becket says calmly. "I'm only pointing out that what Rebecca saw might have a meaning beyond terror. That's all."

"What else can it be if not a threat, Becket?" Delphine asks him.

"I don't know," Becket says, leaning back in his chair. "I really don't. I only know that we can't be certain the door means us harm."

"It could be a warning," I hear myself say. Auden's fingers slide into the base of my braid; my face is tilted up to his.

"What do you mean?" he asks.

"If it's not a threat. It could be a warning instead."

"A warning of what?"

"I don't know either," I say. "I'm just guessing. But warnings and threats *are* cousins to each other. Read wrong and one might look like the other, you know?"

There is a silence among us all a moment.

"If it is a warning," Rebecca says, "could it not still be a warning of itself? Of some force that lays beyond the door?"

"More saliently," Auden adds, releasing my hair and then standing up straight, "the price of ignoring a warning seems lower than ignoring the price of a threat. That is, if we close the door thinking it means us harm and we are mistaken, then we lose very little. But if we leave it open and then we are mistaken about doing that, we could lose quite a lot more. It's a risk I'm not willing to take. Not with Delly or Rebecca or anyone else here."

"I'm not opposed to keeping our friends safe," Becket says. "All I want is to be sure it's necessary. That we're choosing this knowing we might be wrong. Knowing that we might not be able to qualify the door in terms of good *or* bad *or* neutral, and that there might be some blessing or transformation to come from it that we can't yet fathom or perceive. That's all."

"That's all, huh?" Saint says dryly.

I can feel the tension in Auden's body, and after giving his knee one last nuzzle, I stand up and take his hand. He seizes my grip with palpable relief as he speaks. "If I'm being asked to weigh the possibility of the door hurting one of us versus a conceptual gift, then you must know what I'll say, Becket. Don't you? You are a shepherd yourself, and you know that shepherds can't lead their flocks near to a cliff because the shepherd thinks the view might be worthwhile. The danger is too great. The flock comes first."

It is a testament to what we've been through and how we've all come to see each other that no one objects to Auden being the final voice, the deciding vote.

Which is good, because if I was asked to vote, I'm not sure what I would say. Rebecca and Delphine *do* come first, but yet—there is something about the door…something I am certain I'm missing…

Everything is possible.

Convivificat.

"The flock comes first," Becket finally concedes. "Although you are wrong about one thing, Auden. I am no longer a shepherd."

A stunned silence fills the room.

"I'll move my things out of the rectory this week," he says.

Delphine is the first to digest this. "Oh, Becky," she cries, flying to the sofa and giving him a massive hug. "Have they fired you? What bores they are in the Church, I've always said this!"

Becket returns her hug, smiling at the rest of the room over her shoulder. "No, I wasn't fired. I quit."

"You quit?" I ask. Guilt is moving through my blood, dark and grainy. *I did this.*

Auden gives my hand another squeeze, sensing the shift in my mood, and Becket pulls away from Delphine so he can look me in the eye. "It was my choice, Proserpina," he says gently. "My own. I didn't feel forced or pushed into it."

"But I…" I trail off. "You love being a priest, Becket. I saw you there, week after week, thriving and happy…"

"I'll still be a priest," Becket says. "Did you know that? I was forever marked as one at my ordination, my very soul was transfigured. Ontologically, I will always be a person of God. It is only in practical matters—saying Mass, hearing confessions, *working* as a pastor—that I will no longer be of service. My clerical state is revoked, although my soul is unchanged."

"What does that even mean?" asks Saint. "How can you be a priest without being a priest?"

"I honestly don't know. Which doesn't change the fact that such a thing is possible," replies Becket. "Clearly, since I am here before you now as both a priest and not a priest."

Auden pulls me over to Becket, and Becket stands to greet us. And then Auden pulls him into a hard, long hug.

"You have been dear to me as my confessor," Auden says softly. "As my Father Hess of St. Petroc's. But you will be even dearer to me as my Becket of Thornchapel."

I see the wet in Becket's eyes as he nods, and then I hug him too, and then Delphine is there, and then Saint has emerged from his corner, and then even Rebecca, who hates churches and hugs equally.

And we are all hugging him, and we are all in our own whirlpools of shame or anger or fear or longing or all of those things mixed together, but we are together in this moment, we are together in this. When one of us hurts, we all hurt. And when one of us needs, we all need.

We are all of us bound together by thorns. We are all of us a family like the world has never seen.

Eventually, the moment ends. Eventually Delphine calls for drinks and Saint mumbles something about needing to go but he never does go and Rebecca tries to get us all back on task. Eventually, we circle back to the business of the door, and I decide to help Rebecca by indexing all the things we've tried on a blackboard Auden and Becket have carried down from the attic.

"We've done iron, salt, holy water, rowan, rowan berries, ash, red yarn, talismans, prayers, inside-out clothes, and blood on the threshold. Auden said he did fires and dancing on his own. We've also of course tried just pulling it closed." I tap the blackboard with my chalk. "There are two things we haven't tried yet that we know might make a difference."

"A sacred day," Becket suggests.

"Exactly," I say, writing on the blackboard. "The door seems to respond to holy days. So perhaps these things would have a greater effect on equinox or Samhain than say, a random Thursday."

"A rite," Delphine adds. "That's the second thing you're going to say, isn't it? That we could do a full rite."

"Yes," I say, adding *rite* under *holy days* on the board. "Auden saw the door after Beltane, although it didn't stay. But there's the possibility that rituals may affect it."

"But we didn't do a ritual on Lammas," Delphine muses, her forehead wrinkling. "Nobody went into the chapel at all. So maybe I'm wrong."

Auden clears his throat, and when I look up, both he and Saint look uncomfortable.

"That's not...*entirely* true," Auden says. "St. Sebastian and I were out there that day. And we...well, it wasn't a rite, necessarily, but..."

"We acted out a sacrifice," Saint admits. "The two of us."

"Let me guess," Rebecca says, eyebrow arched, "instead of killing your king, you, what? Gave him a blowjob?"

"Give me some credit," Saint says. "I got to home base."

Auden makes a choked noise—either a laugh or a groan, I can't tell.

"At any rate," he continues, "we should take all that into consideration."

"Yes," Becket adds. "Perhaps for the purposes of the door, what you two did was ritualistic enough in nature and execution to influence it."

I asterisk the word *rite* and scrawl *king-killing kink* underneath it. "Okay. So that's what we've got left. Holy days and holy rites."

"There's one more thing," Becket says.

We turn to look at our not-a-priest.

"Sacrifice," Becket says.

"No."

That was from Auden.

Becket holds up his hands. "I'm not personally advocating for it, but it must be mentioned. Poe told us what Dr. Davidson said, and we all heard Poe and Rebecca's father talk about their summer here. We know what Ralph and Estamond believed."

"John Barleycorn is a memory," I say, echoing the words of my dream.

Auden gives me a sharp look.

"Exactly," Becket says. "Remember Paris Dartham? Here—" He digs for his phone and scrolls through his camera roll until he finds what he needs. He reads the image he took of Reverend Dartham's journal aloud.

"*They*—that's the people in the valley—*can all explicate in meticulous detail how the Thorn King was killed in the woods and whereby his blood fed the land.* And then some local history, and then—*if the door should appear, then the Guests have done their duty by the land and gone to the altar in the woods.*"

Becket finishes and then sets his phone on the library table. "It may be off the table, but it should still be in our minds. People have believed for centuries that a death can close the door. And we know for a fact that Estamond's death *did* close it."

"And my mother's," I say, a little tremblingly, although it hurts less and less to talk about it these days. "At least, I assume it was her death that closed the door that time."

"A sacrifice doesn't have to be a person," Rebecca points out. "It could be an animal."

"I don't like that," Auden says.

"Or grain, like Cain offered," Rebecca suggests.

"Which worked out so well for Cain," mutters Saint.

I write *sacrifice* on the board. "We can try blood again on a holy day," I say as I write, and then I step back and think. "But I wonder if it has to be bigger. Blood isn't truly a sacrifice, is it? Not when it's only a few drops. Not when we have bandages and antiseptic to make sure a wound can't hurt us."

"No sacrifices," Auden grits out. His eyes flash hazel around the room. "Not animals. Not people. No. Sacrifices. Whatsoever."

"Of course not," Delphine says soothingly.

"Obviously," Saint says.

"Not even a goat?" asks Rebecca, but I think she's joking. Mostly.

But when I meet Becket's eyes across the room, I know he's thinking something similar to me. That it's easy to dismiss centuries and millennia of sacrifice as misguided superstition…but what if there's some truth hidden there? What if we're not the first people to try to find another way, any other way, and can't?

I don't erase sacrifice from the board, but before Auden can object, his phone rings.

"It's Tally," he sighs. "One moment."

As he walks away to his friend, I turn back to the others. "We need to learn more," I say. "I think—I keep thinking there's something we're missing here."

"A clue?" Delphine asks, a little excitedly. "I like the sound of that. It makes it all rather like a mystery, doesn't it?"

"Yes," I agree. "A mystery I'll need help solving."

"And what is this mystery exactly?" Rebecca asks. "What kind of clue do we need?"

"My dad told us that Ralph was searching local folklore and fairy tales for information about the door," I say. "And we know he was searching for those things here in the library too. I think there's a possibility that we might find more explicit texts about the door here, in the books around us. But I'll need help."

"I don't know how much help I can be," Rebecca says, a little doubtfully. "I know nothing about fairies."

"There's not that much to know," Saint pipes up. "They don't age like we do, they don't like iron or salt, and you can't eat fairy food, or else you have to stay in fairyland forever."

"The fairies aren't the point," I cut in. "The fairy *tales* are, because they might have some abstracted mentions of the door. That's what we're after. No one needs to have their PhD in fairy lore after this."

"Fine," Rebecca says. "But I'm not a librarian. You'll have to tell me what you want me to do."

I think a moment, spinning slowly to take in the rows and rows of shelves. Even though I've been here nine months, I've still barely scratched the surface of this collection. I've catalogued only ten percent of it, and I've scanned even less. There're entire sections I haven't even looked at, much less searched.

"We'll need to do an organized hunt. Divide the library into sections, assign those sections to each of us. Becket and Saint, seeing as how you're currently unemployed—sorry—you'll take bigger sections, as will I. Auden, Delphine, and Rebecca still have their own work to do, and so they'll take smaller ones. We'll pull books one by one and assess them for potential. Maybe we can find an answer that's better than dead birds or human sacrifice."

"There's that optimism I love so much," Auden says cheerfully as he walks back to us. "We can do better than human sacrifice! Say it with me now!"

"You're in a better mood," I observe as he kisses my cheek and then pinches my bottom.

"Tally's just told me that the lab has started on his samples, which means we are getting close to the excavation being formally over."

"Good," Rebecca says. "And while you were on the phone, Poe has devised some homework for all of us."

"If it means we can stop all this mad sacrifice talk, I'll happily do any manner of library drudgery."

"Wonderful," I say. "We'll start tonight then."

14

St. Sebastian

A week or so later, I'm standing in the middle of the lane when a sporty little Ford comes up behind me and rolls to a stop.

A handsome blond head pokes out the window. "This isn't how hitchhiking works, St. Sebastian."

"Har har," I rejoin, looking back down to my phone, where I'd been dialing the Livestock Society. Becket parks his car and hops out to join me.

"Hi, yes," I say for the Society's voicemail. "There's a dead sheep on the road between the village and Thornchapel. Doesn't look like it's been dead very long. Hasn't been hit by a car or anything, seems to be alone." I rattle off a few other details that I notice—no sign of injury, a smear of green paint on its back, and then I hang up as Becket squats down to look at the sheep.

"Do you reckon we should move it?" I ask. "It's in the middle of the road."

"I wouldn't," Becket says, eyes still on the dead animal. "In case it died of some communicable illness."

"Are you sure? I don't think your car can get through to the house otherwise."

I'm being polite. The lane here, while somehow *legally* a road, is practically only as wide as Becket is tall. In Texas, this would be a footpath. There's hardly enough room for a motorcycle to pass by the side of the sheep, much less a hatchback.

Becket sighs and stands. "Right you are. Can I park at yours? I'll walk the rest of the way."

"Of course. And I'll wait, if you'd like."

And so about ten minutes later, we are walking to Thornchapel together, a brisk wind kicking up and rustling the leaves above us as we go. I'm not cold, despite being only in a T-shirt, but Becket has a chunky cardigan pulled over his shirt and keeps fussing with the shawled neck of it, trying to raise it higher around his throat. Even though equinox is still a few days away, Dartmoor autumn is already announcing itself.

"Were you clearing out the house?" Becket asks as we walk.

I nod. I've been splitting my time between helping Poe in the library and getting my mother's house ready to sell, which is less emotionally exhausting than it was the last time I tried to clear out her things, but also more time-consuming than I anticipated, due to her habit of saving anything and everything she thought might be useful, like gas station receipts and half-used skeins of yarn and plastic tubs that once held spreadable butter and were now used to hold everything from earrings to batteries to—yes—gas station receipts.

But I don't have a choice about combing through it all, because I have to sell the place. I need the money, seeing as I won't have a job when I'm in school.

If I'm in school.

Becket seems to know which way my thoughts are bending. "Term starts soon," he observes. "Have you decided whether you're going to go?"

I shove my hands into my pockets. "No."

"May I ask what's influencing your decision?"

No, you may not, I want to say, but I make myself remember that collar or no collar, Becket is my priest and also my friend.

I make myself remember that I don't want to be the person who hides from friends anymore.

"I want to be here at Thornchapel," I admit.

"Bristol is hardly on the moon. You'd be able to come back as frequently as you like."

"I know," I say, "I know. It's just…"

I can't put it into words, I really can't, because when I try to, it sounds so stupid I can't stand it. It sounds pathetic.

But I've underestimated Becket. He brushes his shoulder against mine as we walk, and tells me, "I quit the only work that's ever given me meaning because of this place, St. Sebastian. Nothing you say will sound melodramatic to me. Nothing will sound like it's not a good enough reason."

His shoulder feels nice against mine. I suddenly think of the nights I used to spend in St. Petroc's, kneeling in not-prayer with him sitting a few rows behind me in silent companionship.

I decide to try to explain. For him. And for me.

"I've spent four years like this," I say. "Being here, being the town's librarian, being a good son. But also being a person of half-starts, of broken attempts, of unfinished ideas. It eventually became part of me, the attempting, it became who I *am*, and I know—I know that who I am, or who I let myself be, was more about Auden in the end than about me. I was making myself into his opposite. He was in London and I was here. He went to uni and I didn't. He had a big fancy job and I shelved picture books. He was building cool shit all over the world and I was giving up on the guitar after three weeks. It was like...I don't know. If I couldn't be with him, couldn't be near him, then I had to be as different from him as possible. I had to put so much distance between our lives that even if he did walk into the library one day looking for me, even if he did suddenly decide he didn't hate me anymore, a future between us would still be impossible."

"And then," Becket notes, "it would be your choice. The distance between you two. It would no longer be this animus out of your control, but a wall that *you* erected—not him, not the past. You."

Becket is uncomfortably perceptive. But then again, that's what had made him such a good pastor before. "Yeah," I say. "That."

"And if you leave for school, what happens then? That distance erodes? Your control fades?"

I sulk a little at being read so easily . "I guess."

"And what happens after *that*?" Becket presses. "If you no longer have the illusion of control? If you're no longer pushing him away before he can push you away?"

I know the answer to this. I know what will happen.

I think of his words in his bedroom, of his line in the sand.

You have to decide.

If you come back to me, it will be because you're ready to accept whatever may come, without fear and without shame.

"I'll have to choose for real," I say softly. "All these years, I've been in a kind of stasis. A cocoon that was mostly lonely and mostly boring and also mostly safe. But if I tear that cocoon open...there's no more safety. I will have to choose my life and then accept the consequences that come after." *I'll have to either choose him...or not. For good.*

"It's terrifying," Becket agrees.

It's beyond terrifying. It's existential. "I still love him," I blurt out. "It seems so simple to walk away from it all, to keep Poe close but leave everything else behind. But then I see his eyes in the sunlight...or he smiles at me with that lopsided smile...or he says something in that ridiculous accent, and it's like I'm sixteen again, staring at him from across a church and wishing I was his."

Becket makes a humming noise as we turn onto the drive and are greeted by crenelations and windows peeking through the trees. "As someone who has chosen the uncertain path," he says, "I can honestly say that my only regret is not choosing it sooner. I can't define your morality for you, St. Sebastian, and I would never try, but consider what will be lost and what will be gained. Is the illusion of safety worth the starving of possibility? Is there a world where you can allow yourself a choice more nuanced than *stay* or *go*?"

"You make it sound so easy," I complain as we approach the front door. Augie's crew is gone for the day, the tarp-covered piles of supplies and splatters of paint on the gravel the only trace that they were here earlier. "It's not that easy."

"*Easy* is a misleading word," Becket says. "And in your case, I think the wrong one."

"So what's the right one then?" I ask Becket as we round the corner from the hall and walk into the freshly renovated dining room to see Poe and Auden already seated at the table.

Auden looks at me, hunger all over his mouth and blazing from his hazel eyes, and then he says, "Sit next to me, St. Sebastian. I've missed you."

I go. I go like I'm compelled, and I hear Becket answer behind me as I do:

"Inevitable."

Delphine is keynoting some influencer conference in Edinburgh, and Rebecca's been called away for an emergency meeting with the Severn Riverfront people, so it's only Auden, Poe, Becket, and me for dinner. Abby's made a sumptuous feast of local venison served with caramelized white asparagus, mushrooms, and hazelnuts, and then for dessert, we have an apple soufflé with a butterscotch sauce. We mostly talk about what we've found while digging through the library for information on the door, but the conversation wanders to Becket's ongoing house hunt after we help Abby clear away the plates.

"You know you can stay here as long as you need," Auden says as we prepare to decamp to the library. "I have more than enough room."

"Or you could stay with me," I offer. "At least for a bit." I've been sleeping in my house in the village since I came back, too chickenshit to sleep here at Thornchapel. I've been using the preparations for selling the house as an excuse, but we all know the truth.

I can't trust myself to sleep here.

I can't trust myself not to crawl to Auden's door and beg for him to let me in.

"I appreciate the offers," Becket says, "and I love staying here obviously. But I should find a place of my own too. I can't tax your hospitality that much."

"Why not?" Poe asks. "The rest of us do."

"I genuinely don't mind," Auden says seriously. "The new wing has six suites. The old wing will have three more. There is room to spare."

Becket's gaze slides over to Poe briefly as he folds his napkin and sets it on the table. The longing there is naked, palpable—even as he shutters it as quickly as he can—and suddenly I understand. Becket can't live here any more than *I* can live here.

Because Thornchapel is home to someone he loves. Who is also someone he can never have.

"I'll eventually need my own place anyway," Becket says, trying to force cheer into his tone. "I may as well look sooner rather than later."

Auden says nothing, but a line appears between his brows.

"Have you given any more thought to what you will do?" Poe asks him. She doesn't ask about money or how he will afford to buy property, because he's being robustly supported by his parents—which, to his credit, is something he's been very candid about.

It makes me very, very aware that I'm scraping every last pence from my bank account to pay for the shitty flat in Bristol. It makes me very aware that every class I will take isn't truly paid for yet, not by me, and that there's now a student loan account with my name on it.

So much for Ralph's high-minded *children of the manor* talk. He didn't leave me anything when he died—not money, not family jewelry, not even an old car. Meanwhile Freddie has already offered me—in that coded but somehow still awkward way of wealthy people who like to pretend money doesn't exist—help with housing and schooling.

I refused. Because I'm a stubborn arsehole and I'd rather eat Pot Noodle on a used mattress than take charity from a stranger, even if he did furnish me with half my DNA.

"I'm not sure what I'll do next," Becket is saying to Poe. "I've considered teaching at the university level—although for that, I'll need more than an MDiv, so I'll need to go back to school myself first. I suppose that's the most likely course of action."

He doesn't sound enthused as he talks about it, but he doesn't sound unhappy either. He doesn't sound *anything* really, nothing more than polite. Small-talky. Like he's talking about an acquaintance's nephew and not about what he's going to do after he left the Church in a cloud of exhibitionist-sex-related disgrace.

"You'd be a good teacher," Poe says warmly as we all get up.

She's wearing a tight, long-sleeved top with a deeply scooped neck and a short plaid skirt which hits mid-thigh, and when she smooths it down over her legs, I can practically hear the shared mental groan between Auden, Becket, and me. She is all curves tonight, with that low neckline and short skirt, and my cock gives a lazy stir behind my zipper. I fucked her in the library earlier when it was just the two of us, her hand twisted in my hair and me stabbing into her as hard as I could, but I'm ready for more again, I'm ready for more right the hell now. Especially knowing that there's nothing underneath that little skirt of hers but soft skin and pink places.

Auden and Becket are clearly aware of the same thing, because Becket clears his throat and says he's going ahead to stoke the fire in the library, and Auden extends a hand toward Poe, who nestles obediently into his side. He murmurs something in her ear while his hand roams under her hem and kneads what he finds, and she nods at what he's saying and then murmurs something back, which has him laughing a little. They have this quiet meeting even as she's spreading her feet apart so he can inspect her bottom and cunt more easily.

I can tell the moment his fingers push inside her, because she gives a happy sigh and her eyes flutter to mine, as if to say *why are you so far away? Why are you over there and not over here?* And when Auden looks at me, his eyes say much the same thing.

Except they also say *my fingers could be inside you too. All you have to do is come to me.*

I shiver and quickly excuse myself to join Becket before I do something stupid. Like go over there and slide my own fingers inside Poe.

Like drop to my knees and crawl to them both.

I've been avoiding being alone with Auden for just this reason, and he hasn't pushed me, he hasn't chased me, but he's watched me. God, how he's watched me. And the look in his eyes isn't resigned or forbearing, it's not patient and watchful. His stare is avid, raw.

Maybe even…mischievous?

Yes, that's what it is. *Mischief.* Devilishness. His eyes glint with the same spark they had when he tackled me in the lavender and bit my lip hard enough to make it bleed. When he straddled me in a graveyard and Sharpie-d an entire mural over my chest and back.

Playful. Arrogant. Bossy.

It makes me think *oh God what is he up to,* and it makes me want to weep with a gratitude I don't understand, and it should terrify me too, because I've never stood a chance against Auden like this. I can face his anger, I can face his indifference and even his tears—but his wickedness? His haughty, naughty misbehavior?

It took me no time at all to crumple before it when I was sixteen, and it will take even less time now, because now I know. Now I know the tender, hungry king behind it all, and there's no resisting that king, there's no fighting him.

There's only hiding and hoping that you can outrun your own thoughts. That you can become invisible to your own heart.

"Are Poe and Auden still coming?" Becket asks from beside the fire. He's coaxing it into a merry little blaze, one hand curled around the poker and a tulip glass of fizzing prosecco dangling from the other. With the chunky cardigan and perfectly fitted wool trousers, he looks like he's just stepped off the pages of a magazine shoot about English country houses. For a long moment, I'm totally captivated by the strong throat above the collar of his shirt and the muscles of his thighs straining against his trousers. The taut curve of his arse.

Fuck, I'm messed up today. I'm so horny that I'm leering at Becket while he's doing nothing but stirring the fire.

"Yeah, they're coming," I say. I throw myself onto a sofa and scrub at my hair, trying to get my simmering blood under control. "They were right behind me."

I hear whispers and giggles in the hallway, and then they're strolling in, Poe's cheeks stained with lust or excitement or both. Auden gives me a smile that could be called flippant except for how smug it is, and then sits on the velvet-upholstered sofa across from mine, propping his ankle up on his knee and leaning back with his arm along the edge. The picture of indolence, with that rumpled hair and those glittering eyes.

"That should do for now," Becket says, straightening up and putting the poker away before he sits next to me on the sofa. "It was downright chilly today, I hope that isn't it for the warm weather this year. Oh Saint, I forgot to ask you if you wanted something to drink?"

"Poe will get it," says Auden, and Poe nibbles on her lower lip to stop a smug smile of her own.

"I'll get it," she repeats in a purr, walking past the table to the sideboard, her bottom swaying hypnotically under her skirt as she goes. We watch as she pours the drinks—scotch for Auden and me, something clear and lime-wedged for her—and then she walks back over. She's barefoot now, and as she walks toward us and the fire, I can see she's no longer wearing a bra. Her nipples are dark shadows under her top, and her breasts move as she steps, and oh my God, Auden is responsible for this, I know he is.

My suspicions are confirmed after she sets her drink on the mantel. She hands me the scotch and then rather than walk around the table to hand Auden his, she leans over it instead. Her skirt lifts as she does, pulling up over her bottom, showing Becket and me the plush heart-shape of her backside. And then the soft cleft between her legs, revealing the tiniest, narrowest hint of glistening pink.

Becket lets out a ragged breath, leaning forward and shoving his head into his hands, like he can't bear to look.

"It's rude," Auden says coolly, "to show off something you don't plan on sharing. Especially with guests. Where are your manners, Proserpina?"

She looks over her shoulder, giving us a faux-contrite look. "I'm so very sorry," she says, not sounding sorry at all. "How unforgivable of me."

"Over my lap," Auden says, patting his knee. "Come on."

She practically skips there, and she's summarily arranged over his thighs with her skirt flipped up and her backside ready for punishment—which Auden delivers with swift, unforgiving measure.

Each slap against her skin has her whimpering and begging, and each lift of his hand has me shifting on the sofa. I can see the muscles tensing in his shoulder and his arm, I can see the flex of his hand before he strikes, I can see how his other hand holds Poe securely over him.

I can see the thumb rubbing soothing circles over her hip even as he punishes her, as if to say *thank you.*

Thank you for hurting for me.

Fuck.

I wish it were me I wish it were me *I wish it were me—*

Becket is in abject misery now, watching through his fingers, breathing like he's running a half-marathon uphill. Auden gives Poe a final swat and then looks over at us, one hand smoothing idly over her reddened skin as he does.

"You have to forgive my girlfriend's bad manners," he says calmly. "But she's going to make it up to you, isn't she?"

"Yes," Poe murmurs, her voice sweet and tipsy-sounding, like she's taken several shots of vodka instead of several swats to the arse. "I am."

"Good girl. Since you liked bending over like a slut so much, how about we do that now? How about you crawl onto that table on your hands and knees, and apologize to our guests?"

"Yes, Sir," Poe says dreamily, and Auden lifts her easily onto her feet, nudging her toward the coffee table. Our eyes meet before she crawls onto it, and I see nothing but happy, horny joy reflected there, like she's in heaven right now, like this is her land of milk and honey. A dark library with an arrogant Dom and plenty of watching eyes.

I'm a swirl of needing to fuck her like this and also needing to be fucked like this. If only it were my skin burning with his marks, my pride he was roguishly stomping on…

Poe is in front of us now, facing Auden on all fours. Already we can see her spank-flushed bottom and the shadow of her pussy, but then she lowers her head to the table, resting her head on her arms, and her cunt is on full display. Pink and wet, swollen and waiting.

"I know what you're doing," Becket says hoarsely to Auden.

"And what am I doing?"

"You know."

Auden leans back in his chair, crossing his leg over the other again, and smiling at his friend. "I'm afraid I don't know."

The wicked gleam in his eyes testify otherwise however, and we all know it. He knows we know it. His smile hooks even higher.

"You're teasing me with this. Because I haven't asked for it yet."

While they speak, I lean forward and stroke Poe's ankle. She peeps at me from underneath her arm, giving me a saucy wink. This must have been the plan all along, this must have been what they were whispering and laughing about. This whole moment was engineered so that she'd be arse up on the coffee table, her warm cunt spread wet and inviting. And at such a tempting height…

Becket breaks before I do. He gets to his knees and leans forward to kiss the wetness between Poe's legs, a slow kiss that's more romantic than carnal, despite what he's kissing. I hear Poe sigh as he does, a slow hum of contentment.

"I have wondered why you haven't asked to borrow her," Auden says. He's leaning forward now too, stroking the dark silk of her hair, but his smile is still aimed at Becket, who's just pulled back from licking Poe's slit. "And I wondered if perhaps you were punishing yourself. Abstaining. Starving yourself like sometimes you do."

Becket's pupils are dilated, the iris around them a vivid blue.

"Maybe I was," he says. "It seemed right that I should…punish myself for my appetites. But not for the reasons you're thinking."

"Oh?" Auden asks. "And what other reasons can there be?"

Becket runs reverent fingers along the dark, pink petals, his eyes on Poe's body. "I wanted to be sure," he murmurs. The fire is reflected in his eyes. "I needed to be sure."

Auden doesn't speak, doesn't urge Becket to. Instead he watches as Becket caresses Proserpina, as Becket thinks over his answer.

"I needed to be sure," he says again, "because for years, I walked a path so well-worn that I didn't have to think about where to step next. It was a path with its own gravity, its own momentum, and being a priest meant everything was decided, every choice already made. There were different ways to be a priest, of course, different versions of sanctioned holiness, but nonetheless, my steps were bounded, and now they are not. I feel like I'm in the middle of the woods or up on the moor, far, far away from any road. And it is wonderful and liberating, but terrifying too because each step is my own. Made with my own gravity and my own momentum. I want to make sure each step is the right one. That it takes me closer to where I want to be."

"And where do you want to be?" I ask.

"Where I've always wanted to be," is his quiet reply. "Near to God."

Auden meets Becket's gaze over the curved offering of Poe's body and nods. "You are a new kind of priest then. Or a very old kind."

Proserpina shifts the tiniest bit, and when she looks at me from under her arm again, I can tell she's bursting with a thousand things she wants to say. Auden knows it too.

"Later," he says down to her. "You're still apologizing." But he gives her an affectionate, almost conspiratorial tug of her hair, as if to let her know he's only saying that for the benefit of the scene.

"So," Auden says. "Are you sure now?"

"I'm sure," answers the priest, getting to his feet. He smooths a hand over Poe's upturned bottom. "I'm very sure."

"Well, then," Auden says. "You should show me."

15

St. Sebastian

ecket pulls in a long breath, and then he unbuttons his cardigan and shrugs it off. He doesn't pull off his shirt, but he doesn't need to for us to see the shuddering seize of his stomach and ribs as he sucks in breath after breath or for us to see the way his nipples have bunched into little points or the trembling in his arms. He unfastens his pants, his cock falling free from the placket the minute he does, and then he stands there behind Poe, his eyes closed and his chin to his chest. He is half country house, half obscenity, and it heats my blood back to full boil. Yes, apparently I have a type, or one of them at least. Generational wealth mixed with vulgarity...

I am shamefully susceptible to obscenity framed by expensive wool.

"Go on," Auden tempts, his fingers still tangling in Poe's hair. "Take. You may have to find your own way to God, but I know the way to heaven, and it's right in front of you."

Becket exhales slowly, opening his eyes. And then he reaches down to take Poe's hand. "Thank you," he tells her. His voice is shaking, and I can already see the pre-cum beading at his tip.

"Don't thank me yet," Poe rejoins, voice muffled by her arms.

"Hush," Auden says. "Or I'll hush you myself with a cock in that pretty mouth."

"Promises, promises. Ow!"

Auden has pinched her arm. His eyes dance wickedly in the firelight. "I'm not averse to taking you over my knee again, little bride. Maybe I should give Becket a turn spanking you this time, hmm? You think he'd like that?"

She moans a *yes* at the same time Becket does, and he lets go of her hand to guide himself to her opening. "Thank you," he says again, and then he breaches her body with his.

It is painfully erotic, agonizingly so, to watch his thick erection slowly spread her open. The room is hushed as he sinks in, and even the fire seems to hold its breath, flames unnaturally still until he's all the way in. He stays flush against her a moment, as if savoring the clasp of her around him, and then finally he draws himself back and gives her a true and full stroke.

The spell breaks across the room. I let go of the breath I've been holding, and Auden sits back on his sofa. The fire dances once more.

Poe is the picture of obedience as she receives Becket, but I can see her little toes curling, the flash of teeth as she bites her lower lip. She wants to writhe and squirm and move—but more than that, she wants Auden to take her ability to do those things away. For people like her and me, pleasure is best when it's razor-sharp with humiliation or pain.

Or denial.

"St. Sebastian," Auden says lazily, his head resting against the back of the sofa. "Come here." He pats the seat next to him without moving the rest of his body. "I want you here."

"I can see better here," I say, although it's a weak protest and we both know it. We both know I want to say yes.

"Yes, but I can talk to you better over here," Auden says.

"What do you want to talk to me about?"

"Come and find out."

Of course, I cave. I cave because I want to cave, because I want to be close to him, I want to be ordered around by him. I want his knee to bump mine while we watch a sexy ex-priest fuck our girlfriend.

I take my drink with me, as if it's some kind of talisman that will keep me safe from my own temptations, and sit on the far edge of the sofa, far enough away that Auden would have to reach with his entire arm to touch me.

He gives me an amused look as I adjust my legs and try to take a casual drink of my scotch. "Afraid I'll bite?" he asks.

"Yes," I say honestly, and he laughs. A full-throated laugh that I feel on the soles of my feet and on the inside of my veins.

"Well. Rightly so, I'm afraid. What if I promise not to bite hard?"

"Auden."

"What if," he lowers his voice and rolls his head along the back of the sofa to look at me with fire-glazed eyes, "I promise not to touch you tonight at all. Would you sit closer then?"

I notice how carefully worded his promise is. *Tonight. At all.*

That means his restraint is temporary, but complete. Even if I beg and plead, he won't touch me. Because he knows that what I need is not assurance from him, but insurance against *myself*.

As an answer, I slide closer—close enough that we can whisper together, far enough apart that our knees don't quite touch.

I take a long swallow of scotch, feeling my control fracturing already. I can smell him now, lavender and lemon and pepper, and even staring at his knees is painfully arousing, because right above his knees are his thighs, and his trousers pull so eye-catchingly over the sculpted muscles of his legs…

I turn my attention back to where Becket works himself in and out of Poe's body with a fervor I've only seen from him in the thorn chapel, and that's a mistake, because the sight of her arranged so pliantly, so accessibly, for use…the sight of her full breasts moving with each thrust and her long lashes resting on her cheeks as she pants…

"It's very stirring, isn't it?" Auden asks, in a voice like he's talking about the weather. "Watching our bride get fucked."

"Stirring is one word for it," I mumble. My cheeks are hot; my cock is a throbbing bar stretching diagonally to my hip and chafing in its prison. And then I look over at Auden and see that despite his cool, dispassionate voice, he's in the same state. A flush dusts his cheekbones, and his erection is beyond conspicuous, and when he rolls his head to look at me again, his eyes are black with desire. He presses the heel of his hand over the shaft straining against the wool fabric of his trousers.

"You want to see it?" he asks in a low voice. "I'll show it to you."

Flames are licking at the base of my spine. "Yeah," I say, voice coming out dry, cracked, and needy. I swallow. "Yeah, I want to see it."

He doesn't make a performance of unfastening his trousers and pulling his cock out to show me, but because it's Auden, it's still almost like art to watch. Those clever architect's fingers on the buttons, the play of the tendons on the backs of his hands as he parts the fabric of his trousers. The care he takes in hooking his boxer briefs down past his testicles, and the deliberate way he braces his thumb at the base of his cock so that his organ points straight at the ceiling.

I suck in a breath. And another. There's not enough air in the entire library for this. For Auden's cock gleaming in the firelight and Proserpina's soft whimpers and Becket like a Greek god in rut behind her.

"Now you," Auden says. He still hasn't taken himself in hand, he's not fisting or stroking himself, and it feels like he's displaying his need, like he's proving a point. What that point is I don't know, but I don't care either.

I fumble at the button and zipper of my jeans, at my boxers underneath, and then I have mine out too, throbbing in the cool air.

"You're already wet," murmurs Auden, and he's right. Slickness coats the taut, velvet skin at the head of my penis. I'm surprised there's not more. I'm surprised I haven't come yet.

"Proserpina, look at what you are doing to us," Auden says, and Poe looks up, her expression drunk. Her full lips part as she takes in the sight of Auden and me, our cocks out and hard. She reaches out a hand and sets it on Auden's knee, like a plea.

"I want you," she says to him, to me, to Becket too it feels like, because she rocks her hips back into him as she says it. "I want more."

"You get to watch," Auden says. "You're still apologizing, remember?"

"Yes," she whispers, her eyes fluttering as Becket gives her a series of short, fast strokes. "Yes."

Becket lifts his eyes from where he is riding my girlfriend, and looks up to me and Auden. "I'm going to come," he confesses. "Fuck, I'm going to come, I—"

He goes still—as still as someone in prayer—and then lets out a long, low sigh as his cock begins pumping her full, and he stays there until his release is complete. And before anything else can happen, he is on his knees behind Poe, his mouth on her cleft, his hands digging into her bottom to hold her against his eager mouth.

"Fuck," Auden groans from next to me, and I'm already gripping myself, already jerking off, because there's something so unutterably filthy about Becket doing that, about someone licking through their own release to service someone else, and it's almost too much to watch, too much to endure because I know I'm only seconds away from coming myself.

Poe beats me to it, however, her feet kicking against the coffee table as Becket expertly brings her off, rocking back against his mouth and gasping as her muscles go tense and she shivers her way through an orgasm that lasts a very long time.

Lasts until finally Becket releases her, and she slumps halfway to her side with her feet still tucked behind her bottom and her skirt around her waist, like a slutty human comma.

Becket stands up, his mouth wet, and Auden looks up at him.

"Come here," he tells Becket, and Becket listens, his maleness still wet and half hard, his eyes as dark as Auden's. When he gets close, Auden tilts his face back even farther. "Kiss me with that mouth," he says, and Becket wastes no time. He bends down and presses his swollen lips to Auden's, and Auden groans up into the kiss, probably tasting both Becket and Proserpina.

My cock leaps in my hand, and Auden tears his mouth away from the priest's. "Kiss Saint too," he rasps. "Make him taste," and then Becket does, he does make me taste. He presses his firm lips to mine, and I taste the bitter salt of his release and the honey of Proserpina's, and I'm so close to coming now, I'm so close—

"Again," Becket says as he pulls away from my mouth. He looks at me and then Auden. "If this is to be the night where I inaugurate my new path, then I want to come again. Help me."

He pulls off his soft cotton T-shirt and shucks his trousers, and then he kneels in front of our sofa, his knees spread wide and his cock already hard again. The meaning couldn't be more clear. He wants to be fucked.

"St. Sebastian?" Auden asks, like he's passing around a plate of appetizers before he takes one for himself.

"I'm sorry, I—" I'm blushing. I've been jerking off in front of everyone for the last fifteen minutes, and *now* I'm blushing. I look at Becket. "I've never done it. That. I don't think I'm ready?"

That's not entirely true. I could be ready.

There's just only one person I want to be ready with.

Becket looks to Auden. "Please," he murmurs. "It's been since Beltane since you—"

"I'll have to be me about it," Auden says, meeting Becket's eyes. "Is that okay?"

Becket shivers. "Yes."

"Tell me if it's too much," Auden says, and then he stands and starts undressing, revealing lithe, flat muscles which gleam in the firelight.

"Are you doing okay, sweetheart?" he asks his slutty human comma as he disrobes.

Poe gives him a limp thumbs-up, and the lust clears from his face long enough for him to give her a huge smile. His affection and love for her is so fucking palpable and it makes my chest tight to see. Tight with happiness because I love her as much as he does, and I love seeing her be loved. Tight with jealousy because I want him to look at me that way too. Tight with misery because he *would* look at me that way, if only I'd let him. If only I'd choose him.

"St. Sebastian," Auden says, draping his clothes over a high-back armchair and walking back into the circle of firelight. He's completely naked now, and so beautiful my bones hurt. "Spread your legs."

"I thought you promised not to touch me," I say, and if there's a note of illicit hope in my voice, he ignores it.

"I did, and I'm not. But you look as if you'd like to have your cock sucked, don't you? Wouldn't that feel so good? To have Becket lick you and kiss you? And then pull you into his mouth and let you empty yourself there?"

"Shit," I mumble, my entire body clenching in response. "Yeah, that sounds good."

Auden gives me a smug look. "I thought so." He bends down and scoops the loose and dozy Poe off the coffee table, depositing her on the sofa and tucking a blanket around her drowsy form. "Do you need anything?"

"Just to watch you fuck," she says, both sleepily and naughtily, and that earns her a long, pleased kiss. My chest goes tight again.

"On the table," Auden tells Becket after breaking away from his doll. "Hands and knees, so your mouth and your hole are available."

His eyes hood. "Whatever you want."

Lube is produced from somewhere, and I have a dire, Pavlovian response to watching Auden slick himself up with it. I have to pull down on my testicles to stop myself from coming then and there.

"Stand up, St. Sebastian," Auden says, the muscles in his right arm bunching and releasing as he strokes himself. "Becket's mouth is waiting."

I obey and stand because, yes, I want Becket's mouth on me, but also I want Auden's words to be my will, I want to do as he says. I want to be his, just like Poe is his. Just like Becket is his right now too.

I step in front of our friend and savor the coarse picture he makes like this, his tall body and long limbs arranged for fucking, his full lips already parting to take me. I squeeze my eyes shut the moment I feel his lips touch my tip—and then I open them again because I want to see. I want to see my thick erection disappear into his holy mouth. I want to see the way his cheeks hollow and move around me as I savor the silky flat of his tongue and the grip of his throat around my crown.

"Feel good?" Auden asks, watching me. His cock is so hard that it's a dark, dark red, and it points up toward the ceiling, all slick and ready to fuck.

"So good," I mutter, sliding my fingers through Becket's golden waves. "His mouth is so good."

Auden steps behind him, widening his stance and gripping one of Becket's narrow hips. "Keep sucking," he tells Becket as he pushes the fat tip of his cock against Becket's entrance. "Keep sucking while I use you."

Becket makes a helpless noise. I make a helpless noise too, because, Christ. I keep forgetting. I keep forgetting how Auden does it, how he twists himself up inside me, makes me a thrall to my darkest needs. And this is what he meant by *I'll have to be me*. He's no more made for vanilla sex than Becket is for celibacy.

Auden wedges himself into Becket's channel with a steady, inexorable force. Becket is trying to catch his breath around my cock, his inhales cool around the sides of my shaft, his exhales warm and damp. The muscles in his back tense and quiver as Auden pushes in, and then with a rough gasp from the former priest, we're all joined, all three of us. I meet Auden's eyes over the damp topography of Becket's back, and he stares back with unrelenting greed. He wants it to be me he's fucking right now. I want it to be me.

It can't be me.

I've seen Auden fuck before, of course, but there's something about this, right now, that seems to be etching itself onto my brain. Maybe it's the quiet of the room, maybe it's that he's wearing nothing, which he so rarely is. Maybe it's that there's not the drunken panoply of a ritual around us.

Whatever it is, I'm enthralled. By the working of his throat as he drags his cock in and out of the man in front of him. By the tousle of his messy hair, by the grip of his fingers around Becket's hips, by the corrugated lines of his stomach and the firm expanse of his chest. He is magnificent, stunning in his crudeness, and he uses every muscle in his body to fuck his priest, his every tendon and sinew braced and tensed towards one goal.

Becket for his part is one long shiver—six feet and some inches of shuddering male arranged for sex—and even Poe on her sofa is with us, her hand moving under her blanket as she watches.

I look down at Becket's face, at the fluttering eyelashes and the hectic blush on his cheeks, and then back up at Auden, gleaming faintly with sweat, the hazel in his eyes swallowed up by black, his restless hands all over Becket now, gripping and stroking and bruising. He is all Thorn King now, and beautiful, and although it's Becket's face I cradle as I come, although it's Becket's tongue sliding against me, my orgasm is all for Auden. Every last drop of it.

I grunt as my cock gives a series of sharp, urgent jerks, spilling into Becket's mouth, and then I see that Becket's body is mirroring my own, that he's come to his peak along with me. He's ejaculating in long, full pulses, his seed spattering between his knees, and he's moaning around my cock as he does, sending sensation racing back up my length and nearly buckling my legs.

"Jesus," I swear, staggering back a step and pulling my cock free of his mouth. It's wet in the firelight, and I'm not quite finished coming, and so the final two pulses drip from my crown and then run back down my shaft. Becket leans forward to lick them before they drop onto Auden's antique rug.

A desperate noise leaves Auden then, desperate and possessive, like he's just watched Becket drink the last glass of water in hell, and then his entire body tenses. With a shudder and a series of deep, hard strokes that have Becket whimpering, Auden tumbles over the edge, throat bobbing, jaw tight. Eyes like obsidian mirrors.

He doesn't need a forest to be a wild god, and we don't need a ritual to indulge our wildness. He can be a god right here in the library; we can be his playthings atop a coffee table. It's wonderful and terrible, because how can I live any other life than this? How can I go to Bristol, how can I live without this if Freddie isn't my father after all?

Auden finishes, having filled Becket full of his spend, and then slowly withdraws.

"Thank you," he tells his friend and bends down to kiss where he's just been.

And then he turns to see Poe grinning up at him. She's still snuggled onto her side, but she holds up her wet fingers for him to see. "Did you enjoy watching, little bride?" he asks, leaning down to suck her fingers into his mouth.

"Obviously," she says, laughing as he nips her fingers. He gives them a kiss and then finds his trousers, pulling them on and surveying the room. I'm now slumped back on the couch, my pants still undone and my limbs everywhere, and Becket is still trembling on the table, like he came so hard that he doesn't trust himself to move without fainting.

"I'm going to get towels and some water," Auden says, buttoning his trousers. He's shirtless, his feet are bare, and his hair is all rich, sensual drama. If I could move, I'd drop to his feet and beg him to fuck me.

As it is, he gives us all a fond look, so soft and warm I could curl up in it forever. "I'll be right back," he promises, and leaves.

Poe sits up and goes to Becket, who now has his head on his arms, much like Poe herself did earlier. She kneels down in front of the table and strokes his thick hair.

"Hey buddy," she says. "You want to get off the coffee table now?"

"I need a minute," he mumbles.

"I know that feeling."

"Stay?"

"Of course." She presses her dark head to his golden one, and they're both quiet a moment. I find the energy to tuck myself away, but not to move, and so I hear when they start murmuring to each other.

"I feel responsible for this," she's saying, and somehow I know she doesn't mean him arse up on the table, seed splattered between his knees—but *this*. Him being here at Thornchapel and not at St. Petroc's, his throat bare of a collar and his future void of direction. "I feel so responsible."

"You're not, Proserpina."

"And I feel guilty."

"You shouldn't."

"But you gave up so much and I—"

"I gave it up for me, Poe, and no one else. I know—I've always known—what you can and can't give me."

She pulls back enough to kiss his temple, and he lifts his head, catching her lips in a sweet kiss. My chest aches to see it, because his longing for her is so clear. And though she obviously cares for him, loves him back in her own way, I also know what she looks like when she kisses Auden and when she kisses me, and it's not like this.

It is an unequal love between them, and I wish I could fix it. But I can't.

Auden returns with towels and damp washcloths, and he tends to Becket while the rest of us clean ourselves. And then Becket finally—and shakily—comes off the table with Auden's help and is reunited with his wineglass, which Poe has helpfully refreshed with more prosecco. I gather up the towels with Auden and carry them to the laundry room at the end of the old wing.

"You kept your promise," I say as we walk. "You didn't touch me."

A small smile curves his lips. "I know."

"But I still came for you in the end."

The smile gets bigger, more crooked. He seems very pleased with himself. "I know that too."

"You're trying to tempt me," I say as we go into the laundry room and drop the towels on the floor near the washing machine. "You're not just waiting for me to make my choice, you're trying to tempt me into it."

He's still shirtless, and the air is cool. Goose bumps pepper his skin, and all I can think about is how they would taste against my tongue. Like salt and soap.

"I'm not trying to tempt you," he says silkily. He steps forward, crowding me against the washing machine, and caging me in place with hands braced on either side of the machine behind me. He doesn't touch me, though. He's still keeping his promise. "I'm only reminding you of what you get if you choose."

He smells like Thornchapel, like the forest, and it's hard to think. It's hard to think with him so close, with his eyes so bright, and his mouth so pretty, and his chest and arms and stomach so *naked*. "What do I get?" I ask faintly, my entire body trembling with the urge to nuzzle against him and beg forgiveness.

Another crooked smile and then he straightens up, letting air and space and logic pour between us once more. "You get me, St. Sebastian." And then he leaves without waiting to see if I'll follow, his bare feet padding softly on the flagstone floor.

I'm in so much fucking trouble.

I'm in trouble, I'm in trouble, because I don't know how much longer I can resist this.

I don't know how much longer I *want* to.

16

Rebecca

"I wish you could see the dress I'm wearing, Rebecca, it sets off the bracelet perfectly," my mother is saying through the phone.

I smile, even though she can't see it. I'm glad she likes her birthday present, but I'm even gladder that she sounds, well, *happy*. "The signal isn't strong enough out here for me to do video," I tell Ma. I'm out wandering around the excavation site now that the weather's warmed up a bit, and while the house's Wi-Fi is decent, I'm too far away for it to help. "But I'm glad the bracelet suits."

"It suits indeed!" Ma chirps. "How have you been this week? How is your...girlfriend?" Ma's voice is still friendly and bright, but I can tell from the awkward cadence of the question that this is still new for her. That maybe it's going to be new for a long time.

I hesitate before answering. After the episode in the French restaurant, it became clear to me that I'm not capable of discussing my personal life without having emotions, and accordingly, I'm no longer allowing myself to discuss anything more intimate than work and what audiobook I'm listening to. I used to solve this particular problem by not having a personal life to speak of, but alas. Yet another villainy to lay at Delphine's pedicured feet among the many others she's inflicted on me. Other villainies like unceasing loneliness...and unrelenting horniness...and a punishing, aching need to have her tied to my bed and whimpering my name.

"Delphine's fine," I lie to Ma. I don't like lying, but it's better than the alternative, which would involve the *truth*, and right now the truth involves tears. And even though it's ultimately pointless since I *don't* actually have a girlfriend, I don't want to spoil this new progress between us. After all this time, to have Ma ask about a girlfriend—even if she's stilted and ambivalent as she does—is...affecting.

It's better than affecting. It's good. It's progress where I never even thought to hope for it.

"I'm glad," Ma says. I can practically hear her search for the right words. "Do you think she'll ever come home with you? To Accra?"

My throat goes tight, imagining this thing that will never happen. If I brought a husband home, he would be fussed over and fed, there would be not-so-subtle interrogations about grandchildren. We'd be able to go everywhere and expect fondness and welcome wherever we went.

But if I brought Delphine home, that would not be the case. Even if Ma is ready, our family might not be. Her friends and her church certainly wouldn't be. And our safety in public—at the very least, our *peace* in public—wouldn't be assured. Not that it's assured anywhere else, but at home, we would have to take real care.

I blow out a breath and remember that this is all fake anyway. I don't have a girlfriend for my mother's church friends to make faces about anymore. I don't have a Delphine to protect from side-eyes or insults or snubs.

"You may have to meet her the next time you come to London," I say, and that lie is strangely the one that hurts most of all.

We talk for a while longer, and it ends up being pleasant, actually pleasant, and then we end the call, and I'm smiling. *Smiling.* After a call with my mother.

What a world.

I slip my phone into my pocket and continue wandering around the site. Tally and his team have left and taken everything with them, and so where there used to be a maze and then a swarm of archaeologists and their associated detritus, there is now only dark, bare soil and the sporadic stone boxes of the graves.

Auden told me he wouldn't be bothered if I wanted to implement my original plan—a labyrinth of gravel and turf—but it would necessitate covering over the kistvaens and the thought bothers me. I'm not sure why, since they've been buried for millennia, but it feels wrong somehow. Like Thornchapel has offered us something and I'm contemplating kicking clods of dirt back over it and consigning it to obscurity.

After a while, I find a grassy patch to sit on near the terrace, and I simply look out over the space. I have my notebook with me and a pencil, but the notebook is empty, the pencil unused. Landscape architecture is really about two things when it comes down to it: need and response.

What is the need of the project?

And what is the project responding to in its environment?

The answer to those two questions—and the interplay between those two answers—is usually the seed of the idea. The core of any inspiration.

But now I'm stumped. Empty.

What is the need here? Of Thornchapel?

And what am I responding to?

The house? The woods?

The graves?

I'm deep in thought when someone comes and sits next to me. Knee-high boots and leggings. A jumper and a scarf. Blond waves everywhere and lipstick the color of kousa leaves in autumn.

My belly clenches as I turn to look at her. I've been trying to avoid her for a week and a half, doing my damnedest to keep an eye on her to make sure she doesn't go out to the door while also keeping a large enough distance that I won't be tempted to do more.

Like ask about the toy I got her.

Like ask if I can see her wearing the necklace.

Like ask if she'll pull down her knickers and show me her pussy.

And I was doing damn good at all of that—even if I did have to slip up to my room for a wank now and then—but now here she is. Looking like a fuckable pumpkin spice latte and close enough that I can smell her, smell her berry and violet scent.

I pick up my notebook just so I can have something to do with my hands that's not grabbing her.

"Yes?" I ask, trying to sound brisk and indifferent, but I forget that my brisk voice is an awful lot like my mistress voice. And she likes my mistress voice too much.

She gives me a little pout, a bratty little pout, and I nearly die with the effort it takes not to pull her over my lap. "I just wanted to see what you were doing."

"I'm working," I say.

She leans over to peer at the blank notebook page, her hair and her big scarf and her jumper all brushing against my shoulder. I have an abrupt and vivid fantasy of tying her wrists together with that scarf and then shoving her jumper up to her chest so I could look at her tits.

"Doesn't look like you've gotten very much work done to me," she says doubtfully.

"I'm thinking, that's all. Thinking is work too."

"Especially for a genius," she teases, and I have to close my eyes.

Why does she have to be so sweet? Why did she have to hurt me and then go and still be so perfect?

I'm suddenly tired, so, so tired. Of her being so bewitchingly her and of my heart being so stupidly besotted.

"Why are you really here, Delphine?" I ask, looking over at her. She bites her orangey-red lip as she looks back at me, blinking those big, honey-brown eyes. With her gold hair and pink cheeks, she is every color of autumn at once, a full harvest of loveliness.

She's also brave. So brave to come to me when I've thrown up every wall between us that I possibly can.

"I want to know why you care about the door," she finally says. "I want to know why you care if the door can hurt me when you so obviously hate me."

"I don't hate you." It's automatic, pulled right out of me. "You know I don't hate you, Delph."

"But you haven't forgiven me."

"Did you expect me to?"

The hurt that flashes in her eyes is gone as soon as I see it, and she draws herself up a little, as if this was a wound she'd already known she'd receive. "No, Rebecca. I didn't. But you still haven't answered my question, not really. Why do you care about the door if you no longer care about me?"

I should tell her that just because I can't trust her with my heart doesn't mean I want her harmed or dead. I should tell her that she's still a friend of my friend, that she's part of this little clan of ours for better or for worse, that she's a fellow human and therefore I have the duty to see to her safety when I can.

I should tell her all those things, and yet what comes out is, "You're still mine."

I want to fling myself backwards and scream the minute the words leave my mouth, because they are so idiotic and reckless, because I didn't know they were true until I spoke them—but here we are. In my deepest parts, in my guts and in my marrow, I want Delphine Dansey to belong to me. I want her heart. I want her body.

I want her.

I've struck her speechless, I can tell. Her pretty, fall-colored lips part and then press together and then part again. I let go of my notebook and nearly reach for her, but I dig my hands into the cool grass instead, refusing to make a confession of my body along with a confession of my words.

But the words are still there, chasing circles in my mind, demanding to be spoken again and again…ideally while my hands are tangled in her hair and her tongue is between my legs…

You're still mine.

You're still mine.

I grip the grass harder. It's lush and thick, tickling my palms.

"Rebecca…" she finally breathes.

"Yes," I say. I don't know whether I'm acknowledging my name or confirming what I said earlier.

She doesn't seem to know either. And then she's getting up, all grace and supple movements, even in boots and a giant scarf.

I don't want her to go—*don't go*—

"Delph, wait—"

"I'll see you at supper," she says quickly, already walking away. "Tomorrow's the equinox and we need to plan, and I…I'll see you at supper."

She's up the steps and disappeared into the house before I can do a single thing about it. Fuck.

"You're still mine," I murmur to the spot where she was sitting. I murmur it to hear the words aloud, to hear if they sound as true as they feel. "You're still mine."

The grass beneath my left palm is tickling even more now, and I finally let go. I make to get my notebook and go inside and work—as if I'll be able to concentrate until I can see her again—but when I look down to pick it up, what I see nearly stops my heart.

There's a violet. Right where my hand had been. Right where there had only been grass before.

A violet in September. A lone violet with no others around.

A violet grown under my palm, as if I willed it into sprouting and blooming just for me.

I pluck it and then stare at it for a very long time.

17

Delphine

I'm wearing A-Go-Go by KVD when I sit down in my room and stare at myself in the mirror. My cheeks are flushed, my eyes are bright. I look like I've just stepped off a sailboat or climbed out of a speedy little convertible.

I look like a girl exhilarated.

You're still mine.

I get up again and pace. I press my hands to my cheeks. My heart is like a church bell inside my ribs, tolling great big tolls with each and every beat. I want it to be true; I feel like it's true. I have to still be hers—of course I'm still hers. The necklace. The toy. The fact that she's here while I'm here, even if she does avoid me most of the time.

But I can't mistake this for love. Or even for forgiveness. I threw all those things away when I kissed Emily Genovese.

I stare down at the dressing table, which is covered in makeup and things, even though I've only been here a week. I pick up a tube—*the* tube—and uncap it, staring down at the bright red lipstick inside. It's been smoothed over from use even though it's only a few weeks old, and there's a ring of red around the rim from where my shaking hands had made a mess of capping the tube the first few times.

But now—now I can look at it without shaking. I can touch it, think about it, even wear it, and still be a human girl and not whatever mess of tears and panic I used to be.

Cherry Tree.

I don't put it on my lips now, but I do rotate the tube so that the red little ingot of lipstick is exposed, and then I draw a line of it along the inside of my forearm.

This is how we started, Dr. Joy and me—this is how we worked our way up to me being able to wear the lipstick again. Or more accurately, this is how we started after three weeks of foundational exposure therapy. I would sit in her office and she would have a bowl of cherries on her desk. I would stand by the window and say the words *cherry tree* over and over again. I would drape my legs in an old ratty afghan she had with a cherry pattern appliquéd on; I would color a cherry in a children's coloring book with colored pencils; I would watch videos with Dr. Joy where cherries were picked, processed, and jarred.

It was bad, at first. So bad. When Dr. Joy and I first began working on this, and she mentioned having a bowl of cherries on her desk as a possible exposure, I remember thinking, *that's not so difficult, I can do that at home, on my own.* All of the exposures sounded so innocuous, so *easy*, not at all like something that would require someone's help to endure.

And yet.

I burst into tears when she set the bowl of cherries on the table.

I threw up during the first five minutes of saying *cherry tree.*

When I colored the cherry in the coloring book, I begged between sobs to be allowed to go wash my hands because they'd touched the picture and I could *feel* the cherry on my skin.

If anyone had been watching, they might have thought they were watching an unethical psychological experiment from the 1970s, they might have thought they were watching some perverse, creative form of torture. But the torture was the cure. Dr. Joy said loads of things about neural connectivity and emotional down-regulation and reconsolidating memory, but what it boiled down to was this: for trauma reasons, my brain had forged a link that didn't need to exist, a link between Cherry Tree lipstick and existential violence. And every time I balked at cherries, avoided them, panicked at the thought of Cherry Tree anywhere near me, I was tacitly informing my brain that the link was necessary and helpful. That my amygdala was correct to flood my body with cortisol and adrenaline whenever I encountered— or even thought of—a particular lipstick and its namesake fruit.

It was like grooves on a record or paths worn into an old rug. A feedback loop. An association grown stronger and more potent with time, like a whisky or a wine.

So we made new loops. We emptied the casks.

From the ashes of that visceral, terrible panic, we began untangling my brain. I would remember that awful night and talk through it, I would describe what was happening in my body as I did. That my fingers were numb or my skin clammy or my neck hot with the urge to run or that I could smell wet grass and spilled beer.

Processing is what Dr. Joy called it.

Misery is what I called it.

But it worked. With time—so many sessions a week, every week since mid-July—and grit and a healthy dose of mindfulness and breathing, Cherry Tree's hold on me began to wane. And so did the hold of that awful night.

It is still there, of course, and it will always be there, but it is more scar than wound now. More seam than tear. And I can smear Cherry Tree on my forearm and still breathe, still think, I can still be me.

But right now, I'm staring down at it and regretting that I hadn't been honest with Dr. Joy and my parents and Auden and Rebecca from the start. It lost me years.

It lost me her.

I put the lipstick away and clean off my arm. Supper will be soon, and I'll need a few minutes to prepare for the sight of Rebecca. Every time I see her, it's like—I don't even know—like the only response I can possibly have is dropping to my knees. Because she's so perfect, so sharply beautiful, so deserving of worship, and any moment not worshipping her is a moment wasted.

Seeing her sitting in the grass with her braids gathered in a messy knot and her brows furrowed had me trembling to kiss her feet, so watching her eat and lick and swallow during supper might kill me— although I'd die happy at least. I'd die with a smile on my face.

I stand up, thinking maybe I'll change for supper, and it's when I'm restlessly grazing through the closet that I see it. The toy. Tucked in a discreet velvet bag and resting on a shelf next to the necklace Rebecca sent.

I think of her slender fingers in the grass, how the lithe, narrow muscles of her forearm lifted and flexed as she dug her fingertips into the earth. I think of her lips—naked except for a clear gloss, parted in thought—and I think of her dark brown eyes as she stared at me.

You're still mine.

Could I still be hers even if she resents me for it? Refuses to love or forgive me in spite of it? Can you belong to someone if they're not sure they still want you?

Do I even care?

I take the toy off the shelf, and before I can talk myself out of it, I'm shimmying out of my boots and jeans and scarf, wearing nothing but my jumper and my knickers (and of course, the A-Go-Go on my lips). I climb onto the bed and lean back on the pillows, rooting around a little until I'm comfortable, and then I turn the toy on. It vibrates in my hand, a buzz so gentle it's more tickle than anything else, and then I drag my phone over, pulling up the app that controls the toy. I can make it vibrate harder, I can make it pulse, I can toggle between where it vibrates internally and the slender branch that's meant to lay flat against my clitoris, or I can have both vibrating at once.

Rebecca would have lube, or I would have been made to work my clit until I was dripping, or I would have been tied down and licked, but I find that I'm nearly wet enough to use it merely knowing it's from Rebecca. Merely from the memory of her fingers in the grass and the gloss on her lips.

I turn the toy to its lowest setting and then slowly, carefully, ease it inside my pussy. A thick curve of it rests against a certain spot on my front wall, and the clitoral part is nestled between my lips, and the whole toy is designed to hold itself in place. I slide my hands free from it and close my eyes, savoring it, imagining that Rebecca is here with me. That she's teasing me with it, laughing in that low mistress laugh she has when I whine about wanting to come. That she's kneeling between my legs right now, her eyes on my cunt, a smile curving her lush mouth as she watches my breathing hitch and my thighs quiver.

That she's waiting for the perfect moment to turn the vibration higher…

A deep surge of pleasure radiates out from between my legs, catching me by surprise and making me moan. I grope for the phone—I must have accidentally hit it with my elbow or something and adjusted the controls—and then another surge comes, as the toy kicks up in intensity. It's almost too intense, but in the best way, and when I open my eyes to look at the app, I'm not sure yet if I'll actually turn it down or leave it where it's at.

Which is when I see that the app has changed colors, from a lavender to a deep, scarlet red.

Mistress R. is in control, the app tells me, and indeed, when I try to adjust the controls myself, they don't work. *She* is the one setting the intensity, *she* is the one guiding the pace. I could pull the toy out, I could turn it off. I could text her and say, *not to be a bore, but I don't want you making me come whilst you still detest me.*

But I don't want to.

If this is all I get of my mistress—this and a necklace that glitters more than the Dartmoor sky at night—then this is what I'll take.

And as if she knows I've consented, she sends me a text.

Press your knees together, the text says, and eager submissive that I am, I immediately obey, sucking in a breath as I discover why she told me to. The sensation like this is different—deeper—harder to move with or squirm away from. My thighs lock everything in place, and without being able to arch my back as easily, there's no relief from the buzzing pleasure of the toy.

It's inside me. It's on my clit. Everything between my legs is one jangling knot of tension, all of it cinched so tight it nearly hurts.

Everything is her. This is her.

Her tension, her buzzing. Her will.

For the first time in months, Rebecca Quartey is making me come.

The orgasm slices through me like a hull through water, like a saber through a bottle of champagne, and I cry out as it shakes me and takes me, making every intimate muscle clench, turning my cunt into a starburst of bright, sharp bliss. I curl into the feeling, the immense feeling of it, because it's not just a climax, it's a climax given by *her*, and after the waves pass and my vision returns, I feel the tears sliding effortlessly out of my eyes.

I don't know what I'm crying for exactly—joy or satisfaction or renewed longing or the knifelike loneliness of being the only one in the room—but the tears come faster than I can wipe them away.

If Rebecca were here, she'd kiss them away. Not to comfort me, but because she reverenced my tears the same way I reverenced her control. Because they got her wet when she knew she was the one to put them there.

The toy is still buzzing, too much now against my sensitive flesh, and I text her **thank you** before I drop my hand to pull it out.

The toy stops vibrating before I actually do it though, and then I see her reply.

Leave it in for supper.

I don't pull it out. I think for a moment.

And then I leave it in for supper.

"I know this isn't strictly door-related, but did you know there are records of plague in the Thorne Valley?" Poe is saying to Auden.

"*Not* the Black Death plague," Becket cuts in. "Some sickness that overworked clerks nonspecifically called the plague."

"It could have been the bubonic plague," Poe counters. We're sitting around the dining room table, having finished a scrummy meal of chèvre tart tatin and Cornish crab, and I am very, very aware of the toy inside me as a fresh bottle of white is opened and passed around.

The toy is not buzzing. It hasn't buzzed once since I came down to find Rebecca already at the table, eyes glittering and phone in her hand, but I know it *could* buzz at any moment. I know with a swipe of her thumb, I could be trembling in my chair and panting through another insane orgasm, and the possibility of it, the denial and threat of it, is almost as delicious as the buzzing would be itself.

Even more delicious? The way Rebecca smiles every time she sees me twitch or stir in my chair. Which is usually when I see her look at her phone. I swear she's handling it more than she ever does at the dinner table simply to tease me, to keep me wondering if she's going to put me out of my misery and turn the bloody thing on.

"The first record you found mentioned it was the same sickness that came to the valley during the reign of King Stephen," Becket says. "That's too early for it to have been the bubonic plague, because *that* plague didn't reach Europe until the 1300s."

"Fine," Poe says impatiently, "but lots of people did die. In plague-like numbers, one might say."

"Any idea what illness it might have been?" Rebecca asks. She doesn't look at me as she does—she keeps her eyes on Poe—but she traces the screen of her phone with one long finger.

I shiver.

"There are lots of sicknesses that have since disappeared," Poe says, "so it's hard to say if it's something we'd even recognize or just some lost disease."

"Lost disease?" echoes Auden.

"You know. Like the sweating sickness, and...okay, the sweating sickness is the only one I can think of, but diseases in the historical record whose symptoms don't match anything we know of today."

"Ah," Auden says. He runs his fingertips along an eyelid and then takes a drink of wine.

A quick, soft buzz, like a kiss, reverberates through my body and I gasp.

"Are you okay, Delly?" Auden asks, looking concerned.

"Yes," I say quickly. The buzz is gone. Rebecca's face is totally impassive—save for her eyes, which seem to dance. "Just realized I forgot to charge my ring light upstairs."

This has the effect of immediately boring everyone at the table, and the conversation moves back to plagues. And as Poe and Becket start debating again, talking about the difference between the records in the early medieval period and the Restoration, the toy jolts inside me, a powerful pulse that has me squeezing my legs together and forcing myself to breathe.

Another pulse.

Another.

I can barely sit still now, the vibrations are coming so quickly and with so much strength. But she's making them sporadic, clustered and then spaced in such a way that I can't brace for them, I can't find a rhythm and ride my way through them.

I dare to look up and meet Rebecca's eyes—they are more than dancing now, they are positively saturnalian, and her mouth is curled in pure delight. As I watch, she catches her lower lip between her teeth and slides her finger across her screen.

Sensation explodes inside me, and I want to whimper, I want to moan. I want to grab the edge of the table and hold on for dear life, but I can't, I won't, I will see this game through if it kills me.

Acutely aware of my nipples poking through the silk blouse I'd changed into for supper, and very aware that I must be flushed and breathing abnormally hard, I keep my eyes on my lap and my hands on my thighs. I resist the urge to fuck myself on the toy—although it's very hard not to fuck, because I'm basically sitting on it and every little move has it rubbing deliciously inside me—and I try to keep my trembling to a minimum.

And when the orgasm comes, as of course it must, I manage not to cry or laugh or otherwise give myself away. I close my eyes and breathe quivering, uneven breaths as my clit surges and my womb contracts and wetness slicks me down below.

It takes forever it feels like, eons and eons, but when the shudders finally leave me and my pussy relaxes around the toy, Poe and Becket are still talking about plagues and Auden is still idly rubbing his eye.

Rebecca is watching me over the table like I'm her next meal.

"Let's do dessert in the library," Auden finally says. "We can talk plagues in there and we need to make some decisions about tomorrow."

Everyone accedes to this and rises to their feet, Auden going ahead to find Abby and let her know. Rebecca lingers and so do I, until we're the last two in the dining room.

She takes measured, deliberate steps over to my side of the table. "I'm glad you're in a skirt," she purrs. It's the first time she's spoken to me directly the entire meal. "Bend over."

I bend.

My skirt is shoved up and my knickers moved aside. My ballet-flatted feet are kicked apart and then her fingers are all over my slit, stroking where her toy meets my wet skin.

"I should fuck your mouth right here," she says breathlessly. "I should push you to your knees and use those pretty lips and that pretty pink tongue. Would you like that? For me to use you?"

God, yes, of course I'd like that. I've thought of nothing else for nearly two months. "I'd like it better if I was wearing the necklace while you did it," I say, and I feel her rest her forehead on my back, as if the mere idea has undone her and now she can no longer stand.

"Tomorrow," she says against my silk blouse. "Equinox. If we all fuck, then I fuck you. You can safe out if that's not okay, you can tell me no. But otherwise, you're mine. Understood?"

My sore internal muscles clench around the toy, quickened back to life by her words.

Even if this is all I get of you, it will be enough.

It will be enough.

"Understood?" she asks again, and this time I answer.

"Yes, Rebecca. Understood."

18

Auden

"I feel like you're not listening to me."

I adjust the phone closer to my ear as I walk down the wooded path to the chapel. I've got a roll of blankets under one arm and a jug of water dangling from my hand, and trying to balance everything while listening to Tally talk about pollen analysis is almost too much.

"I'm listening," I say, awkwardly readjusting the blankets. "You said something about a pollen sample from one of the cists?"

"Yes, we took a sample from each grave—it helps us see what additional plant matter might have been put inside the graves along with the cremated remains. And we also took a sample from outside the graves too, for a sense of what flora was native to the valley at the time."

"Ah," I say. "So what pollen did you find in the graves, then?"

"That's just the thing, my little country lord. We found the same thing both inside and out of them."

Shafts of early afternoon sunlight dapple the path in front of me, and the trees are still full green, still heavy with summer. The oaks are holding on to their acorns, the rowans their berries, there's no catkins dangling from the hazel or elder yet. The wild apple trees at the fringes of the path are still dangling with small, rosy globes.

But there is still an inhale in the air, a subtle shift—something saying *summer is over*. Something saying *it's coming*.

I can feel it even when I can't see it, and even as I think the thought to myself, an oak above drops a single half-green acorn onto the ground, as if to agree.

It's coming.

Like the altar says—convivificat.

It stirs.

"So you're saying the people in the cists weren't buried with any plants around them," I say to Tobias. The birch and beech and hawthorn begin to thin and the stone row comes into view. "So the pollen analysis was pointless."

"First of all, you are breathing *very* heavily. Are you fucking right now? Do you have that pretty librarian in your lap while I'm trying to talk to you about important paleoecological things?"

"I'm walking, Tally. And if I remember correctly, you are the only one of us who's spoken on the phone in flagrante delicto."

"I was calling you for a *good reason* that night," Tobias answers, sounding miffed. "I needed someone to take me back to St. John's after my date ended."

"Yes, but as I recall, your date hadn't *finished*, and you were bent over the arm of a chaise longue while you were calling me like a cab service."

I can practically hear the shrug I know Tobias is giving right now. "What can I say? I knew I'd be ready to leave once he was done. Those rowing boys never give as good as you think they will."

"*I* was a rowing boy," I point out, weaving through the stone row to get to the chapel. The roses have climbed all over the walls now.

"And you were tragically a virgin, as I recall. And if you are still a virgin after holing up in a gothic manor with all those very delectable friends of yours...*and* after being affianced to a genuine socialite-celebrity for two years, I will be greatly disappointed in you. Why am I talking about this again?"

"Because I'm walking," I reply, going to the platform and depositing the water and the blankets. The others won't be out for a couple more hours yet, but I spent the day getting everything ready for our impromptu ritual: water, blankets, wood for the fire. A coolbox full of beer and bubbles and the little cakes Abby makes for us. I imagine she thinks we eat them during breezy, Edwardian-style picnics on the lawn.

The problem is that nothing in the *Record* or any of our other texts mentions an equinox ritual. So we're making it up as we go along. Some fire, some sex, throw in the proverbial cakes and ale...maybe it will be enough.

Maybe we can close the door.

"Oh, yes, that's right—you called my pollen analysis pointless. Pointless! As if I would deal with the boffins at the lab for no reason, Auden, really. There is a point. And the point is that on at least six or seven separate occasions, your property has been covered in roses. Enough polleniferous rose material to leave a significant deposit on the record. Which is an unimaginable amount of roses, I would think. The lab people were certain they were wrong, and kept re-analyzing, but here we are."

I stare at the door for a moment, and then I turn and look back at the entrance to the chapel. The roses haven't left the ruins yet, but with as fast as they've grown inside the chapel, surely it's only a matter of time...

"Roses," I say. "Are you quite sure, Tally?"

"Positive. And here's the intriguing thing—the roses aren't a varietal the palynologists can identify. They're definitely roses, that much is certain, but they don't match any known rose on record."

"Interesting," I say. My voice rasps a little when I speak, and my eyes prickle. I wonder if I'll cry another petal like I did the night St. Sebastian came back.

"Yes, Auden. It is interesting. Interesting as in there is literally nothing like this that I've ever seen or studied—or even *heard* of in a hotel bar at an archaeological conference, and you hear all sorts there."

"It can't be that unusual," I say, although I don't believe it. I'm staring at an ancient church covered in bruise-colored roses; behind me is a door that shouldn't exist. I can make the trees move when I'm sad, and apparently I can weep rose petals like a miraculous statue.

Unusual doesn't even begin to describe my ancestral home this year.

"Let me explicate to you, once again, dear friend, what I've found in your back garden. I've got eight graves in a valley when they should be on a hilltop. I have a mysterious chamber covered in carvings that is totally empty of remains, objects, or anything else that could indicate its purpose. I have a person buried with incredible wealth who appears to have been ritualistically murdered, and I have rose pollen everywhere from roses that *apparently* don't exist anywhere other than in the Thorne Valley. And even then, it appears only a handful of times from the Restoration back to the Neolithic. You see the problem here, Auden."

I emerge out of the chapel, heaving a deep breath. The trees heave it with me. "Yes," I agree. "I see the problem."

"We talked some time ago about how I'll have to make a report to the county archeologist—have you given any more thought to how you would like to handle the inevitable public interest?"

I wince. I'm not proud of the solution I've come up with, but I can't have people out here, not until the door's shut, and even then, I can't be certain how safe anything is. But even though it's a matter of safety rather than secrecy, I still feel like my bloody father when I say, "I'm going to ask the county archaeologist to keep it quiet. For now."

Silence greets me on the other end.

I go on. "We'll of course abide by any determinations about future construction and so forth, and allow them whatever latitude they need to do their own surveys. But I don't want television crews out here, Tally. I don't want to end up on an Ordnance Survey map. I don't want pricks from Oxford or wherever crawling all over my woods and demanding more digging."

"Obviously I would never let someone from *Oxford* come near my site," Tobias says. "But Auden—"

"My mind is quite made up," I say firmly. "Do whatever you need to do legally, but please understand, I'm not ready for Thornchapel to become a thoroughfare for documentarians, rambling tourists, or swotty history types in cargo shorts."

"Are you implying," Tobias asks in a dangerous tone, "that I wear *cargo shorts*?"

"I would never."

"Good, because I refuse to be so maligned by someone who insisted on wearing his rowing shorts everywhere, even when not rowing." A pause. "Not that I minded seeing you in them."

I walk up to the menhirs that guard the entrance to the stone row, and then look back. Above the forest, the hills rear up in a hazy spread of purple heather and yellow gorse, and above that is a sky so clear and blue that it's hard to believe summer will ever, ever end. I wonder if the people who dug the graves are the same ones who erected these stones. I wonder if they stared up at these same hills.

I wonder if the door opened for them too.

"Why do you think they did it?" I ask. My voice is soft, uncertain, so unlike the bossy little lordling I just pretended to be. "Why do you think they made those graves where they did? How they did?"

"That is a *very* stupid question," Tobias says bluntly, and I have to laugh.

"And why is it a stupid question?" I ask, still smiling as I press my palm to a sun-warmed menhir.

"Because you've got all sorts of modern assumptions bound up in your *why*. You're trying to think about this logically—you're imagining these Bronze Age people decided to build their kistvaens like how a multi-national supermarket chain decides on a new store location—and that's not right at all. This is symbolic thinking we're dealing with, and unfamiliar symbolic thinking at that, and symbolic thinking is entirely different from reasoning, it's entirely different from the kind of rationale that we would use to build a supermarket. *Mythos* and *logos*, Auden. Aren't you friends with a priest? Shouldn't he be telling you these things?"

"He's no longer a—actually, never mind. It's a long story."

Tobias continues as if I hadn't spoken. "If I were in your shoes—which I'm not, I'm in mine, which means I already know the correct questions to ask—I would ask myself what the makers of these graves were trying to achieve. I would ask myself what symbolic language they were speaking with these burials. Were these graves a reflection of the world—or how they saw the world? Or some kind of transactional process, like a payment or a bargain with nature or their gods? Or was it an atonement? An attempt to right some wrong? Or an act of worship or reverence?"

"I fail to see why the word *why* is an unhelpful synecdoche for all the things you just said," I respond, and he scoffs.

"That's why I do the digging and the question-asking, and you walk around London with a scarf and a pout."

"Don't forget the bag."

"All scarfy boys need a way to carry around their Midori notebooks and magnetic Apple Pencils. The bag was implied."

"Ouch."

"You deserved it. I have to dash—Mummy is calling—but I'll give you a shot over the bow when I contact the county archaeologist, so you can begin your classist and corrupt machinations. I'll also send you a copy of the preliminary report I'm giving her, if you'd like it."

"I would." I give the menhir a pat and push myself away from it. "If it's not too much trouble."

"Of course it is, but you're worth it. Especially if you still own rowing shorts," he adds. "Tatty-byes, darling."

And then Tobias is gone, and I'm alone in the clearing with my thoughts…and the roses.

And the door.

19

Auden

It's not part of the ritual. It's not called for or remotely necessary. But since I have another hour or more before the others come down here, I decide to do it. Not for any rite or reason, not for the door. But for me.

I shrug off my shirt, I toe off my trainers, and I run.

My feet dig into the grass—long, ticklish, and cool—and soon I'm moving between the trees, the white trunks of the birches flashing past, leaves whipping, the grass giving way to loamy soil and the occasional fern and the sometimes soft, sometimes scratchy carpet of old leaves and moss.

More acorns have tumbled here, and as I run, I see flashes of movement through the trees, sepia and russet. The deer I've been pretending to cull. They're in season, and they're bounding all over the woods with me, darting in and out of view.

I don't have antlers tied to my head today. I'm not playacting the part of a wild god. It's barely even a special day.

And yet.

Yet they are here. There are more of them, and more, until the herd is tearing through the trees with me, kicking up leaves and leaping over logs and moving like one entity, one creature broken into many bodies. It's me and them, not me hunting, not me chasing, simply me with, and together the deer and I push into the deepest part of the forest, to where the equinox sun only barely reaches the forest floor, to where mushrooms and moss grow plentiful and thick.

Birds flit from tree to tree here, and the huge oaks have spread their branches, and it's so old here, older than Thornchapel, older than the Guests. Older maybe than the Kernstows and the stone rows and the graves. This is a ghost of the forest that once covered all of Devon—all of Britain. This is the forest that the first mesolithic hunter-gatherers filtered into from Europe, following the herds of red deer and horses, this is the forest that the first post-glacial Britons would have seen.

Trees and mushrooms and deer. Abundance growing and decaying. Light and shade, wet and dry, life and death. And I can feel it all as I run, I can feel all of it threading through me like the mycelium threads through the forest under my feet. I can feel the world blooming and wilting and sprouting and falling, and I can feel the hinge of the season in the very air I breathe, and I can feel the woven circle it all makes, the budding, the dying, the turning, the turning, the turning—

And it's almost there again, that answer I needed when I was on my knees for St. Sebastian. An answer that grows through every part of me like roots through soil, like a river through a moor, like a bright vein of metal through rock. Or is it the question that runs through me, and not the answer at all? Is it this excruciating contradiction, this incessant entropy, this chaos that more and more seems to define Auden Isaac Guest than anything else ever has?

Because I don't know how to hold all the parts of me—the conquering and the cherishing, the taking and the serving, these angers and these aches and these loves and hurts—inside myself any longer.

I don't know how to carry all this seething, restless, tender, keen *existence* inside only one heart, and inside only one body.

I don't know how I am supposed to *be* all of it, just like the forest is all of it, life and death and light and dark, and I don't know what that means for the people I love. That I want to hurt them as much as I want to love them has been the awful shadow stitched to my heels since I was twelve, and that I savor the ways they hurt me back has been a secret even to myself until just this year.

Surely it is hard enough to be one person, one whole person, who loves like normal people love, but to be *this*—to be the teeth in the dark and the hands that soothe—and to not even be *that* properly? Because I want to hold everyone I love inside me and hollow myself out so they can nestle right against my bloody ribs, but how can I trust myself to do that? Why should anyone trust me to do that when I know exactly what kind of man I am, what bruises I long to leave?

Why should anyone see the teeth in the dark and willingly, happily bare their throats?

I don't know, and that this is all happening when the forest is doing this, when Thornchapel mirrors my own moods back to me, and I can run through the trees with the deer as if it's the most natural thing in the world...

I have no idea what to do with that either.

Have all Guests been able to do this? Or the Kernstows before them?

Was my father able to do this?

And why, why, *why?* Is it the valley or the door that gives Guests this power? Or does the valley have power *because* of the door?

Does it matter? When I'm crying rose petals and running with deer, isn't the question of *why* a little academic at this point?

I don't know, just like I don't know anything, and as I canter in the direction of the river, I feel the answer sliding away before I can grab hold of it. Flitting away just as the deer do when the river comes into view.

And the moment is over, it's done. The herd is gone, the world is no longer a heavy, bursting, rotting, and growing thing inside me, it's just the world, just the place I occupy while I sketch plans for tourism centers and shop online for floggers and spreader bars.

It's just the ground I stand on while I miss St. Sebastian.

I stagger to a stop near the water, air sawing in and out of my lungs, and drop to my knees. Sweat trickles down my back and my stomach, and the bank is damp enough that I can already feel the wet seeping in through my jeans. My head hangs between my shoulders as I struggle to get the oxygen I need.

I can be the Thorn King when it's this—and only this, I think. The king who thunders through the forest with the deer beside him, the bare feet and the stabbing sides and the blur of branches as I race past. Who couldn't be? Anyone could be a king if that's all being a king was, whispering through the world alone.

But that's not all it's supposed to be. That's not what Estamond meant on that cold day when she informed me that kings walk to the door.

Kings are kings of people, and I don't know if I can be that. I don't know *how*, not when I still don't understand my very self. Not when the answer to my question keeps slipping away, like raindrops on a window.

"Just like old times," a voice says, and I turn to see my biggest question of all coming toward me.

My river boy, my St. Sebastian, my maybe-brother.

"I think you were wearing less during those old times," I say, my voice still ragged from my run, and St. Sebastian smiles down at me. He's in his usual boots, jeans, and T-shirt—this one another summer reading program shirt from the library—and he has an extra shirt slung over his arm.

It's mine.

"We've found more creative ways to sneak glimpses of each other's underwear since then," he says, handing me my shirt. "I found this in the clearing. And your shoes—although I suppose you'll want to wait until after you wash your feet in the river to put them on."

"Thanks," I say, taking both the shirt and trainers and setting them next to me. Even though I can breathe now, I still don't stand. It feels safer for me to be down here.

And by safer for me, I mean safer for *him*.

"I remember the first time you found me here," Saint says, looking over to the deep, clear pool that used to be our haunt. "I still don't know how I survived you pulling my shirt off me. Or you seeing my cheap boxers."

"I wasn't assessing the cost of your underthings, St. Sebastian," I clarify. Eight years too late it seems. "I was trying to see your cock."

Even now, even after all the things we've done, I can still make this man flush. Red darkens along the high curves of his cheeks, and he blinks down at his boots. "Ah."

"I would have thought it obvious, given that I was hard by the end."

Our eyes meet. "You were, weren't you?" he says softly.

"Then and every other time I was with you. Do you know how hard it is to hike through gorse while stiff, St. Sebastian? And yet I persevered. For you."

The corner of his mouth sharpens and tips up. Nearly a smile. "It still surprises me that you wanted me."

"What?"

"Well, I—" He chews his lip a moment. "You were you and I was me, and it just didn't make sense to me how you could—you know—*want* me." And then he gestures to himself, a sort of head-to-toes gesture, which only baffles me more.

"How could I want the sulky boy in eyeliner and ripped jeans? How could I want the boy with the mouth I hadn't stopped thinking about since I was twelve? How could I want the boy who'd gone from mischief to pretty misery?" I lift up on my knees a little, enough that I can ease the strain behind my zipper.

Nothing has changed really—not the river and not us—and my body still responds to his like the only thing that will stop death is fucking him.

He notices, his eyes tracking down to the front of my jeans, and then slowly back up my damp abdomen and chest to my face.

"You're on your knees," he says after a minute, as if he's only now noticing.

"Remind you of anything?"

His breath shivers in and out, and I know he's hardening too. That flush is still high on his cheeks. "Don't tease me," he whispers.

"I'm not teasing."

"You are. You've been teasing me since I came back."

"No," I say, "I've been honest with you since you came back. There's a difference."

He narrows his eyes at me. "Don't be coy. You know that your honesty isn't—it's—well, it's *flirting*, Auden, and you know it."

Maybe I do know it a little. After Lammas, I did what I thought I was supposed to do, I did what I thought was right: I stayed away, I didn't chase, I gave him all the room in the world to build a life apart from me.

I gave him that, even though it felt like dying to do it.

But he came back. He came back and there is a chance now, a real chance.

And if I'm honest, abnegation felt as wrong as arrogance. Restraint felt as wrong as reckless taking, and so now here I am trying to find a middle path between the two, ne quid nimis and all that. And anyway, Proserpina said I should remind him of why he should choose me, even if that means reminding him that I am a kinky pervert.

"Are you accusing me of being a coquette?" I ask, raising up on my knees a little more. I'm vain enough to know I'm setting off my body to its best advantage and that the sunlight is filtering down through my eyelashes right now to leave fan-shaped shadows on my cheeks. I know when I lick my lips, I'm drawing attention to the wideness of my mouth, to the small hitch on one side of my upper lip. I know that when I lean forward, my hair tumbles over my forehead and light moves over my sweat-sheened muscles.

"Of course," I purr, "a coquette doesn't perform what he promises, does he? He'd be all talk."

His Adam's apple bobs up and down. "Are you saying you wouldn't be all talk?"

"That's precisely what I'm saying. If you allowed it, of course. If you so chose."

I crawl forward on my knees. One movement and I'm so close that I have to tilt my head all the way back to see him. All he'd have to do is unzip himself and he could be in my mouth.

He seems to realize this too, and he lifts his hand as if to do it. And then drops it again.

"I noticed," he said hoarsely, "that you didn't promise not to touch me during the ritual."

"Do you want me to promise?"

Another swallow. "No."

"Would you like me to move away from you right now?"

"N-no. You can stay."

I peer up at him. In this moment, he is very nearly the same St. Sebastian Martinez I fell in love with that summer. Despite the way his slender frame has filled out with muscle, despite the shadow of stubble on his jaw, despite the piercing set in the middle of that perfect, undrawable mouth, I still see the same soul I saw by the river that hot day. Eyes glittering, mouth sullen and delicious. Torment etched into every line of him.

It was how I noticed he was beautiful at first, that torment. Not only because I like the taste of torment in certain circumstances, but because there was something so singular about it—both that it was unique and also that it was unified. His entire person was complete, choate; he knew himself, and even through the smudged eyeliner and loud music, that self-knowledge burned bright. He wasn't broken into two halves—a half that longed to hurt and a half that longed to be hurt in turn—he wasn't marred by contradictions and contrasts and multiplicities. He wasn't forever his own foil.

He was, simply, him. And that he radiated with a fever of grudge and melancholy, that he came with a pre-lacerated heart—well, then.

All the sweeter.

"Would you like me to be honest with you? Would you like to hear all my coquettish promises?"

He breathes out a *yes*, and I'm already talking, already confessing and pronouncing and lobbying. Already building realities out of words like I build structures out of pen strokes.

"I want to suck on you," I'm saying, low and urgently. "I want to put my mouth on the place where your cock grows from your body. I want to run my nose along the curve of your groin. I want to kiss the crown of you until it's wet for me, and I want to push the tip of my tongue into your slit. I want you to make noises for me, and I want your knees buckling for me. I want you so undone for me that when you finish, you hate yourself for it. You hate yourself for spilling your seed and ending what you wished would last forever."

His eyes are wild and his jaw flexes as he tries to breathe and seems to fail. "Christ, Auden—Jesus Christ. I can't even imagine what you would say if I were the one on my knees."

"You don't want to know," I say—and I say it as honestly as I say it grimly. He doesn't want to know. Not because it would scare him—although it would—but because he'd want it too much. Because he'd shudder and beg me for it, and then we'd find ourselves how we always found ourselves: spent and bruised in our different ways.

"I think I do," he whispers. "I think I do want to know."

"Do you know what I was doing? Before you found me here?"

"You were running." He touches his tongue to his piercing. "Like on Beltane."

"Do you remember what happened when I caught you? Right here? What I did after I pushed you into the bluebells?"

I can see the hitched contractions of his ribs under his T-shirt; when he speaks, his words are stilted with lust. "Of course I remember."

"I caught you and then you were mine. I fucked you like it. And that's only the beginning of what would happen this time, because this time I wouldn't be catching you, I'd be taking you back."

"Fuck—Auden—" Saint drops abruptly to his knees, his face in front of mine. He stares at me with desperation, with a surrender which is beautiful and yet all too wrong, and I know what he's going to say before he says it, and I know that I'm going to hate it.

"I don't know how I thought I could fight this," he mumbles, letting his forehead press against mine. "I don't know how I thought I could resist. I can't. I can't anymore. I give up. You win."

It should be perfect. It should be what I want.

It's not.

"I win," I say, hearing my own voice and knowing it sounds flat.

"Yes, Auden," he says, nudging his nose against mine. "You win."

I can smell him over the damp of the riverbank and the leaf-churned woods. I can smell his fire-in-winter scent, and I breathe it in deeply, as deeply as I can. I breathe it in like I'll never be able to draw another lungful of air ever again.

I pull back so I can see his eyes. Rings of coffee around a jet center. Defeat is all over him.

Defeat I haven't earned.

"I feel like a starving man," I murmur, studying his face, "looking in on a feast, seeing a banqueting table stacked with pies and meat and wine. All I crave is right there, all that would sate my hunger and slake my thirst. If only I'd be let inside."

"What—"

"And then someone comes out with a crust of bread to give me instead," I finish over him, my throat aching, pain thudding behind my eyes. "And how can I refuse it, Saint? How can I say no when I'm starving? But yet how am I supposed to feel? Knowing I'm being given a scrap when just beyond the wall there is a carnival of plenty?"

St. Sebastian draws back now too, hurt pulling on the edges of his mouth. "This isn't a scrap, Auden. This is what you *wanted*."

"No," I say, my throat and eyes hurting even more. "No, I wanted you to choose, and you haven't chosen. You've only given in, you've folded, you've crumpled. That's not choosing a life with me, St. Sebastian. It doesn't even meet the legal definition of consent."

"You're asking too much of me," he says. His mouth is trembling and he's blinking fast. He's trying not to cry. "You always ask too much."

I press the heel of my palm to one burning eye. "I know this, St. Sebastian," I say, my voice raspy and choked. "Which is why you have to ask of it of yourself first. *You* have to choose. You'd let me rut into you right here, right now, and then in a few weeks' time, you could get those test results and curse yourself for every stroke I gave you, every pinch, every kiss. We both deserve better than that inevitable regret."

I can barely see as his chin drops to his chest. A familiar panic crawls through my ribs and up my spine as my vision fades, as I struggle to breathe around the agony stabbing at my eyelids, and then suddenly I'm hunched over and leaning on my hands, weeping petal after petal onto the ground. Dark red, near black. Wet but whole.

When I'm done, there is a scatter of petals between my hands.

I finally suck in a real breath, actual tears running down my face from the effort and the pain of it. My head hurts.

"Auden..." Saint whispers. His eyes are wide as he looks from me to the rose remnants on the soft dirt of the riverbank. I make myself stand up and then I wipe at my eyes with the back of my hand.

"The others will be waiting," I say, stepping over the petals and picking up my shirt and trainers to carry with me. "We should go back to the chapel."

"Auden, what *are* those?"

I shake my head, not in the mood to share anything with him, much less something I don't understand. Much less something that terrifies me.

"Nothing," I say. "They're nothing. Let's go."

20

Suffer Me Not To Be Separated From Thee
St. Sebastian

The others are standing in an awkward semicircle outside the chapel when he and Auden arrive. Becket, Delphine, and Poe are silently passing around a big growler of beer while Rebecca paces in front of the rose-lined entrance. They all look up at him and Auden as they come into the clearing—Poe and Delphine with relief, Rebecca with impatience, and Becket with something deeply inscrutable.

"Auden's crying rose petals," Saint says. He doesn't know why he says it, except there's this reflexive instinct to assure everyone they hadn't been fucking by the river. And it's an instinct he doesn't really understand, because hadn't he begged Auden to do just that not twenty minutes ago? Wasn't he the one to kneel at Auden's feet on the night he returned and say *everything's changed now*?

But he's feeling differently now anyway. Embarrassed, ashamed, angry. All the messy feelings that come with rejection.

At any rate, Auden reacts like a younger brother who's been tattled on, scowling and glaring. He still hasn't put his shirt on.

"Auden?" Poe asks, sounding concerned.

"It's nothing," Auden says shortly. "It's just—it's like the trees moving or the river rushing. It's peculiar, but it doesn't seem to do any harm."

"Yet," Saint points out. "It doesn't do any harm *yet*."

Poe and Becket exchange a glance, and then Poe says, "I think Saint has a point."

"What are my options?" asks Auden. "Go to a doctor? Find an ophthalmologist whose expertise is in ocular plant matter?"

They're all silent. The options are limited and they all know it.

But that doesn't mean Saint has to like it.

"I just don't want you to be sick is all," he tells Auden, although he sounds more stubborn than doting right now and he knows it. "I don't want you to hurt."

Auden's eyes soften the tiniest bit, but his mouth is still etched into a line of displeasure. Displeasure that Saint put there.

But what is Saint supposed to do? He thought Auden *liked* surrender, but all of a sudden, surrender on its own isn't good enough? Saint has to make promises along with it? He has to swear oaths and pledge vows to a future that is only one test result away anyway?

This is more of Auden's incomparable arrogance. More of that rich-boy hubris. This is the same Auden who withheld money from Saint's mother just because he could.

All of the reasons why Saint used to hate Auden Guest are so very clear right now. So very loud. Maybe he hates him still—at least it feels a lot like hate, knowing Auden has rejected his open submission twice now.

"I think I can grow flowers," Rebecca says suddenly, and everyone turns to where she stands in the chapel entrance. "No, I know I can. Watch."

Rebecca

It's only been roselles and violets so far, which makes a frightening kind of sense when she thinks about it. And she has been thinking about it, all day. All day while she's been pacing the perimeters of Thornchapel, testing, testing, like this is an experiment that must be refined for variables, and not what it so obviously is, which is *insanity*.

And so far she's learned this:

She can grow flowers—under her palms, not inside her eyes or whatever fucked-up thing Auden has going on—on the Thornchapel grounds, but nowhere else. The minute she passes the equinox stones to the east or Reavy Hill to the west—or the river to the south or the stream crossing Thornchapel's drive to the north—she is like every other gardener who must buy seeds and water them and wait.

She can only grow one flower at a time, but if she uses both hands, she can grow two at once.

She cannot grow them with the soles of her feet or her knees or her elbows or her lips.

Yet.

And there is a price, which she only learned an hour ago when she was conducting her experiment here in the clearing.

Or maybe it's not a price, as such, but a consequence. A reaction.

She kneels now and presses her hands to the grass. It takes a moment, but soon she feels the now-familiar tickle of plant tendrils against her palms.

"Watch the rose canes around the chapel entrance," she tells the others. "Watch what happens."

They watch. And soon they see that as Rebecca grows two flowers—two violets this time, delicate, innocuous—two dark roses bloom along one side of the ruined chapel door.

She lifts her hands all the way, and the violets bob among the soft grass in the cool September breeze.

"Fuck," she hears St. Sebastian say, at the same time Poe and Delphine explode with awe and excitement.

"That is *so cool*—"

"That is marvelous, Bex, really so marvelous!"

Becket says nothing, but his gaze is far away, like he's considering the implications of this. Only Auden meets her look with something like what she's feeling. Something like worry.

"The roses," Auden says after a moment. "If you grow something—"

"Then the roses grow too. Which means...I don't think Thornchapel and the door's roses are the same thing, Auden, which means Thornchapel and the *door* aren't the same thing. They are different, even though they are tied together. Or maybe not tied, but..." She searches for the right word. "Correlated? Responsive?"

Auden runs a hand through his hair, his eyes on the roses beside her. "Sympathetic," he says after a minute. "They resonate together. Like strings on a hurdy-gurdy or something. And so a change in one provokes resonance—or change—in the other. You think?"

"Makes sense to me."

"Not to me," sniffs Delphine.

Rebecca abruptly regrets spending all day wandering the valley and the moors when she could have been playing with Delphine's toy again. *Tonight,* she promises herself. It may be a terrible idea, but it's too late, she's flung herself right into this terrible idea's teeth and she has no plans to free herself from it. She will take what she wants, come what may, and face her feelings tomorrow.

"If they are sympathetic to each other," Delphine goes on, tossing her thick blond waves over one shoulder, "Thornchapel and the door, then we should have been able to close the door ages ago."

"Why?" asks Auden curiously.

"Because *you* seem to be Thornchapel's hurdy-gurdy too. Or maybe Thornchapel is yours—but either way, if you and Rebecca have resonance with Thornchapel, and Thornchapel has resonance with the door, then shouldn't you be able to affect it somehow? By the transitive property of flower magic or whatever?"

It's a fair point, and Rebecca can see that Auden has no more answer to it than she has.

"Well," he says, drawing a deep breath. "On that note, perhaps it's time to light the fire. Maybe we can conjure up that transitive magic tonight."

Proserpina

The mood in the chapel is different tonight, and she's not sure whether she hates it or whether this thing that feels like hate is actually sadness instead. Sadness for what they've lost, nostalgia for what they had. Regret...but for what, she doesn't know.

She does know that she doesn't share the wariness Auden and Rebecca both have for the door. She does know that when she dreams, more and more often she dreams of it. She dreams of Estamond here in the chapel, she dreams of the Guests who came before Estamond too. She dreams of the Kernstows—she thinks—although those dreams are different. Blurrier. Merrier even.

She dreams of fires.

She dreams of blood.

She dreams of a golden torc flashing in the dark.

And once, just once, she dreams of the cists, of their builders. They dig graves in a forest covered in roses and they weep.

"We'll start with singing," Becket says, "if that's acceptable to everyone. I also suggest we drink."

If the response to singing is rather tepid, then the response to drinking is beyond enthusiastic. They scramble for the cooler while Auden and Rebecca work on the fire, all of them needing the escape, the excuse, the energy. They've brought no energy of their own for revelry tonight, they've brought no excitement or hope. Only fear, and in Proserpina's case, curiosity.

The fire catches and they drink and Becket begins to sing—and they drink. The last of the equinox sun sets directly to the west, sinking into the moors and dying a slow red death. They drink some more.

Gradually, habit takes over. They sing with Becket, they move around the fire. They smell the sex hanging in the air like smoke, they breathe it in.

But they do not forget why they're doing this.

They do not forget the door.

Delphine

The fire is high when Rebecca finds Delphine. A brush of fingers against hers, and when Delphine looks, the fingers snap. Delphine drops to her knees like the earth has rocked underneath her, and Rebecca gives her an approving nod.

"Platform," she orders, walking away from Delphine without looking back. With utter confidence that Delphine will follow.

It's that confidence she missed, that authority…and the clarity that came with submitting to it.

Mostly she just missed Rebecca. The sway of those slender hips, the cascade of braids over that shoulder, the architectural way she holds the fingers of her right hand as she walks.

The tips pressed together, the knuckles arched. Poised for a sharp, Domme-y snap.

Rebecca didn't specify that Delphine should crawl, but the platform is very close, and Delphine would like to crawl. It would make her happy. She knows that she's only getting a sliver of Rebecca—a sliver that's still undoubtedly poisoned by what Delphine did—but she is determined to make the most of it. If all she gets from Rebecca is the impetus to submit, then Delphine will submit the bloody hell out of herself. She'll wring herself dry with it.

Rebecca reaches the platform and sits, watching Delphine crawl toward her with a stillness that belies danger. The fun kind.

When Delphine reaches Rebecca's feet and dares to look up, she sees the fire reflected in Rebecca's eyes. Rebecca pulls up on the long, scarlet dress she's wearing today, exposing her bare feet and smooth calves, and then the firm lines of her thighs, which she parts. Even though dusk has faded and the shadows are everywhere that the firelight is not, Delphine can still make out a subtle wetness there.

There is nothing between Rebecca's flesh and Delphine's mouth but air, and Delphine can't stand it, she can't stand being so close.

"Please," she breathes. "Please."

Rebecca studies her. "It should be earned."

"Then I'll earn it. However you like. Please, Mistress."

The honorific seems to affect Rebecca, because she closes her eyes and swallows. Her hand clenches tight around the hem of her dress. "I've missed hearing that word on your lips."

"I'm sorry," Delphine blurts, even though she knows she shouldn't, she shouldn't disturb this unspoken game of pretend. "I'm sorry. You must know how sorry I am, how sorry I'll always be. I love you and I hurt you, and I wish every day I'd done differently. And I will never, ever do it again."

Rebecca opens her eyes. They are impossible to read like this, with the jumping flames mirrored in them, with the shadows everywhere else. For a moment, Delphine thinks that she might respond. That she might accept or refuse the apology.

But she does neither. She merely slides her free hand into Delphine's hair and pulls Delphine's mouth to her waiting cunt.

Becket

He cannot be here now and not think of *then*, that other autumn, that fateful Samhain. He cannot see the door and not think of Adelina Markham.

He cannot be here without thinking of the logic that underpins the Eucharist and rituals like it.

Sacrifice and love. Offered flesh. Blood and blood and blood.

Death to secure life.

The door will demand more than a stilted, fearful rite. He knows this. Its price is too steep to pay with fire and sex alone, and he worries that the price will be paid by the wrong person. He looks at Auden, his exposed skin gleaming in the light of the fire as he makes love to Proserpina. He looks at Rebecca perched on the edge of the platform, her head thrown back and her hips bucking mercilessly against Delphine's servicing mouth. And then he looks at Saint and Proserpina, currently kissing as Auden ruts between her thighs.

He knows what Ralph believed. Ralph believed it had to be a king or a Kernstow, since the Kernstows used to be kings. But Becket believes differently. After all, his own god wasn't a king alone, but also a priest in the order of Melchizedek, and the king of the grove at Lake Nemi wasn't a king in truth, but a priest of the goddess Diana.

It has been priests as often as it has been kings. Perhaps more often than not.

This is to be part of his untaming then. Or his atonement.

But not tonight. Tonight he will kiss his friends and take his pleasure with them. He will watch with a familiar, fond jealousy as Proserpina sighs in the arms of their king, he will watch Auden and Saint dance around each other, not taking or touching save for with Proserpina between them. He will indulge, because summer has already sighed into autumn, and Samhain will be here soon enough.

And perhaps…perhaps there is another way. He would like there to be another way.

Take this cup from me. That's how the verse goes.

He will search for another path, but since he was fourteen, he'd suspected this was a cup he would have to drink from someday.

And he would rather be the one to drink than anyone else.

Auden

The door is still there when they finish.

"Perhaps it will be closed when we come back in the morning?" Delphine suggests, and they all make noises of agreement, although Auden is certain that no one actually thinks this will happen. They all seem to know, judging by their faces and their lowered eyes, that it didn't work. Whatever they were trying to do failed.

Unlike Beltane, they do not sleep on the platform afterwards. With the fire and blankets, it might have been warm enough, especially if they'd all piled in together, but no one wants to sleep surrounded by the roses or watched over by the door. Least of all him.

He wouldn't be able to sleep for a single moment at all, not with those he loves most in this world so near to it.

So they troop back to the manor with blankets and things carried between them. Auden goes last, burying the last of the fire and taking a look around to make sure everything is safe and secure for the night. And when he flashes his torch over the doorway, he thinks he sees something on the other side. Someone.

But it's gone the moment he perceives it. He would like to believe he imagined it; he tells himself he imagined it. He tells himself that nothing can come through the door, even though that's a lie.

Back at the house, they meet a fussy Sir James, who'd been left alone on the pretext of convenience, but everyone knew it had been because Auden was worried about Sir James being in the chapel while they were trying to close the door, and they all shower and go to bed. Delphine and Rebecca to separate rooms, Becket and Saint to guest rooms they'd claimed earlier. Auden slips into bed with a shower-damp—but already asleep—Poe, and pulls her into his chest, where she nestles so pleasingly that Auden finds himself praying that the rest of this night will last forever, that the rest of his life will be holding her and feeling her fingertips twitch against his chest as she dreams.

God is not in the prayer-answering mood, it seems.

Auden dozes and wakes, and dawn has come, and with dawn, a persistent kind of dread.

He climbs out of the bed, carefully tucking the covers back around his submissive and smiling as his dog takes his place.

Sir James lays his head on Poe's shoulder, heaving a giant sigh like it's unconscionable that a dog should have to lay on pillows and beautiful women with such little notice, and then closes his eyes.

Promising himself that he'll be back soon to reclaim his Poe-cuddling rights, Auden dresses quickly in jeans and a jumper and then slips on his trainers before heading out across the lawn.

The sounds of sheep bleating from the hills carries all the way down to the valley, and the forest is flush with the whispers of morning—voles going to bed and rabbits waking up—bats finishing their last feeds, birds bitching at each other—and Auden is almost lulled into a hazy, sleep-deprived kind of hope.

This is how Dartmoor is supposed to sound. This is how

Thornchapel used to sound before this year. Maybe…maybe the ritual worked. Maybe he'll get to the chapel and the door will be gone and he won't cry rose petals anymore and everything will go back to how it should be.

But it's a fool's hope, an iron pyrite hope, and he knows it before the clearing even comes into view. Which is fortunate, because what he finds is enough to steal his breath and weaken his knees.

He stops just at the edge, still in the shade of the forest, still in the place where everything sounds like it should on a country morning in late September. But in front of him…in front of him, nothing is as it should be. Nothing is good or right.

The roses are everywhere now.

In the space of a few hours, they've crawled from the entrance of the chapel to the stone rows to the clearing beyond, carpeting the floor of the glade and starting to climb up the trunks of the birches and the oaks. They cover everything, dark and fully bloomed, and they bob in the early morning breeze like heavy heads of grain.

But this is no harvest.

Resonance. That was what he and Rebecca had settled on. Like the strings plucked on a Hardanger fiddle or a viola d'amore, one string vibrating the other.

They did this. Somehow. They plucked, and they plucked wrong, and now the resonance is here in the form of silky petals and curved thorns.

And if they pluck wrong again?

No. No, he can't think like that. He won't.

Or at least that's what he tells himself as he trudges back toward his house, rubbing a petal free from an eye as he goes.

21

Proserpina

"This is all of it, I think." Becket sets a stack of books next to me and then leans against the library table I'm currently staring down at. "Poe? Proserpina? You here?"

I manage to break my attention away from the small piece of paper I was staring at and offer him a grateful smile. "Yes, hiiii. Thank you for bringing these over here! Is that everything from the cart?"

"It is," Becket says, folding his arms and smiling down at me. He's so tall, and even though I know he's not necessarily a dominant person, it trips all my submissive wires, and I want to twine around his legs like a cat. "What were you looking at?"

"Oh," I say, moving my attention back to the table. "I read Dr. Davidson's book about ancient British religion. She mentions the Thorne Valley quite a lot—and evidence for human sacrifice at sites near here—but it's the introduction my mother wrote that I've been mulling over. Here." I flip the book to the pertinent page and read, "*The Romans were curious; it is said that when they first encountered the Dumnonii living in the Thorne Valley, they asked the Britons why the altar in the woods was so deeply sacred to them. We don't know what words the Dumnonii used to explain it, but we do know how the Romans translated what they said.* Convivificat."

I look up at him. He's staring down at the book. Or rather, just past the book at the well-creased piece of paper beside it.

"That's the note your mother wrote," Becket states, nodding down at it. "The one you were sent late last year."

"Yes. I thought—I don't know what I thought really. That looking at it for the millionth time would help me understand something about it, I suppose. Understand something about the altar. About the door."

"And it hasn't?"

I run my thumb along the bottom of the note. "No. And it's probably stupid to hope it could help me understand a riddle like the door when I don't even understand a riddle as tiny as who stamped the envelope this came in. Who sent it to me in the first place."

The paper is soft along the bottom, the fibers getting worn and fuzzy from handling. It's thick paper with a significant cotton content—stationery paper, something for indoor work. It couldn't have come from a field notebook—my mother swore by Rite in the Rain, never used anything else—and it wasn't from an airplane or a hotel. It had almost certainly come from her desk, which meant she'd written it before she came back to England.

As if he can sense the way my thoughts are tending, Becket asks, "Why do you think she wrote the word down? The altar was covered with grass by the time she came here. By Estamond's time."

I trace the pad of my finger over the sharp c of the word, thinking. "This is the real question, isn't it? The chapel was still in use as a church through the medieval period, and then as a hidden meeting place for recusants in the Valley during the Reformation, so I have no doubt that the carving on the altar is attested in the historical record somewhere. But why write it down herself? Why think of it at all? Why bring it with her here?"

"It quickens," Becket says to himself. "It comes awake."

"Does it refer to the door?" I ask. "It must. That's what awakens in the chapel. That's what stirs. And that's what's so remarkable about what the Dumnonii told the Romans, not that there *is* a door at all, no, but that the door comes *back*. That was the most important thing to know about the door. Which is a troubling thought."

Becket tilts his head. "It is?"

"Yes. Because if the door comes back and has done since before the Romans came, then that means there's no closing it for good, is there? It will always open again, even if you pay the highest price." I lift my finger from the c, thinking not of the note, but of the c carved into the altar. Thinking of my mother's skull with dark soil clinging to the arch of her orbital bone.

She had paid the price. And then my father and I paid a price of our own. So it hadn't only been the sacrifice of a single life when she died, but the destruction of many.

"Maybe there was no other way," Becket says, and his voice is deep and a little strange, but when I look up at him, his eyes are a bright and normal blue, and he's giving me a warm smile. He is just Becket and not the sapphire-eyed being I once found in the shadows of the Kernstow farmhouse.

"Or the people there believed there was no other way," I say, frowning at a nearby glass case of artifacts. The torc is in the middle— the torc my mother holds in that picture with the other parents. The torc Estamond wore before she died. "Or they were taught there was no other way."

"Ralph wasn't taught," Becket points out. "He seems to have come to this belief through research. And intuition maybe."

My frown deepens. It's painful enough that my mother was murdered, and by someone she used to care for. But I can't decide if it's worse thinking Ralph killed her because he believed he had no other choice or because he had a mere *intuition* it was what should be done. "If he came to it through research, then he should have known it's the Thorn King who's supposed to walk to the door," I say. "The king alone."

"Unless someone chooses to be the king in their stead. Remember Estamond?"

I sit back in my chair. I had never considered—it had never even occurred to me—that my mother might have been complicit in her own murder. That she might have chosen it, to be the king, to be killed.

"You're saying that she might have consented to her own death?" I'm not saying it defensively or rhetorically, but as a genuine question. "Like Estamond did?"

"Is it not a possibility? Could it not explain why she was there that day?"

I think for a moment, trying to remember her as she was and not as I've added on to her memory and deleted from it during these last twelve years without her. Could she have been the kind of woman who'd willingly die? Was she someone who would have believed there was no other way to shut the door?

"I don't know. I do know that she wrote often about human sacrifice—mostly in the ancient Mediterranean—and she told me once that in ancient Greece, even the sacrificed animals had to consent to being killed." I can recall her telling me this in the kitchen, fresh coffee beside her well-traveled laptop and pictures of patinated human bones all over the table. "If there was no consent—if they couldn't make the animal nod its head or if the bones burned incorrectly after—then the sacrifice was considered tainted or impure. For the sacrifice to work, there *had* to be consent. At least for the Classical Greeks. The Bronze Age Greeks seemed to believe differently."

"There's a logic to this that's very compelling," says Becket. "Even Jesus consented to his death."

"But it doesn't matter," I say suddenly. "Whether she was willing to die or not, she still died for nothing. Everyone who's died at the door has died for nothing because it will always come back. Always."

"Maybe there is a way other than death," Becket says, but when I look over at him, his face is all doubt.

"We can't be the first people to try to find another way." I rub at my forehead again, staring down at the note. "Convivificat. Convivificat. There has to be a reason for why it mattered to her."

"Perhaps she wrote it as a warning," he says.

"Do you think the Dumnonii meant it as a warning to the Romans?" I ask, looking down at the book. "But then why did those who followed carve a warning onto an altar? Why worship there, in a place of danger?"

"A warning is a powerful thing, spiritually speaking. The Ten Commandments are warnings. The implications of damnation are a warning. Maybe the people who worshipped there saw the warning as a gift. Or as a kind of protection."

That could be true. "They've found witches' marks on churches," I say. "Not to hurt the churches, but to protect them. A mark against the evil eye, a talisman. Sigils meant as a threat to outside forces but a comfort to those within."

"It seems like our choices are limited then, in how we interpret the word and its meaning," Becket says, straightening up. "Which makes it difficult to know what your mother meant by writing it."

I offer him a self-deprecating smile. "And now you see why I was staring at nothing. My thoughts go in all these circles, the same circles, again and again. The door is scary. The word is a warning. But I'm missing something, because I know—*I know*—that the thorn chapel can't be all blood and invasive flora. There has to be something more to it."

"You think so?"

"I know so," I say, closing Dr. Davidson's book and standing up. "Because we've pulled hundreds of books, pamphlets, tracts, and surveys over the last two weeks, and I can't find any kind of unifying imperative when it comes to the door."

Becket seems surprised by this. "You can't? The sacrificial imperative seems very strong to me."

"It is—in certain texts. And then in others...." I reach for one of the books I was paging through this morning, a dusty, cloth-covered book called *The Riddling Rose and Other Devonshire Legends*. "Here, okay, listen to this. In the story 'The Riddling Rose,' a peddler learns there's a fairy market once every seven years, where he can buy up all sorts of fairy wares. When he finds the way to the market, he discovers the gate to fairyland is blocked by a rose bush—which makes him a bargain. If he can answer three riddles, it will allow him to go to the market and come home again unchanged. There's a bunch of back and forth about the riddles, blah blah blah, but the upshot is that he answers them right and wins the rose's bargain—he can go into fairyland and leave again safely. He does a good business there, and then returns to the path the next day to come home. But once he steps through the gate, he realizes everything has changed. The path he walked on—well marked and well trod—is now covered in brambles and weeds. The village he passed through just before coming to the gate has new, tall houses and a new stone market in the middle—seemingly sprung up overnight. And he recognizes no one there—not the innkeeper though he stayed at the inn nor the blacksmith though the peddler had shod his horse on his way through."

"Ahh," says Becket. "So the rose lied."

"The rose didn't technically lie but had tricked him nonetheless. Time passes differently in the other world, and so while he indeed left the market unchanged, his world changed without him. A hundred years had passed over here, and the peddler no longer knew his own land. Everyone he'd ever known or loved was dead."

"Quite a price to pay for one night at a market."

"Depends on the market, I guess. Okay, and this one"—I set *The Riddling Rose* down and take *Amusing Tales of the South-West*—"Here a young maid catches the eye of the fairy king during his May Day dance. He returns for her on Halloween, and abducts her through the door into his fairy hill. She learns that the door to the fairy hill will open out to her world again, and after waiting a long time, she manages to escape—after several misadventures obviously, because it's that kind of story. She returns through the gate mostly unscathed, but pregnant with the fairy king's child. She builds a home from rowan and elder, studded with iron nails, but because she ate the food on the other side, she soon sickens and dies without it, and the child follows her to the grave. The fairy king is said to search for her and their child still, riding over the moors whenever the seasons turn, refusing to accept their deaths."

Becket considers. "So there were no true sacrifices in either story."

"There was *return* in both stories. And these aren't the only ones. All this local folklore about people accidentally getting caught up in the Wild Hunt or being swept off in a fairy dance to fairyland—almost all of the people return. But in this one..." I rest my fingers on a third book.

It's a small leatherbound volume which has no title embossed on the front—nor a true title page. Where there should be a title page is only a chromolithograph of a knight encountering a door in the middle of a forest.

The door is ornate, covered in gilded carvings and things, and there's no hint of a chapel or any other structure nearby, so it's not our door, not our forest. Not Thornchapel.

But the illustration still raises goose bumps along my arms.

"In this one, a knight finds a beautiful woman riding in the woods on Halloween. He pledges his fealty to her, and she accepts only on the condition that he give her his entire life, and never do so begrudgingly. The minute his heart falters, he is to inform her and leave her side, because she only wants a true and willing defender. When they ride into fairyland, she tells him that he can only return to his former life if he leaves her right then, because the way to the human world will close at dawn. She tells him this thinking he will leave her, abandon her out of longing for his old life or maybe fear. But she underestimates her knight, and he stays loyal, not only staying by her side, but eating the first fruit he finds in the fairy realm to ensure he is bound to her forever. Rose hips, by the way. That's the fruit he eats."

Becket makes a face. "Not the fairy food I would choose."

I stack this volume, *The Riddling Rose,* and *Amusing Tales* on one side of me, and then Dr. Davidson's book on the other. "I know there's only so much we can glean from stylized sources like these, but I think there's something here, some common kernel of truth we can uncover. If the door has been used *like* a door, for moving back and forth, for taking lovers or for doing business or even just for wandering around, then that has to mean there's some other way to live with it other than what the Guests and Kernstows insisted on."

"Do you think the door used to appear more often? Do you think it could appear and disappear on its own, without human—or mortal, as it were—intervention?"

I'm already shaking my head because I don't know, I don't know yet. "Let's start by dividing what we've found across the sacrifice watershed. Books mentioning death and sacrifice go here, and anything else goes *here.* And then we can begin indexing anything useful from the non-sacrifice pile."

"Auden is going to be so pleased," observes Becket as he picks up a book to page through.

"Well, maybe less pleased when we make him help us later tonight."

22

Proserpina

Three nights later, the only sounds in the library are the popping of the fire, the melancholy drone of Becket's indie playlist, and the sound of pages turning. The first long library table has become a mess of stacks and piles that only makes sense to me and the spreadsheet I've made to tabulate everything. The second table is the shared workspace of everyone else as they flip through each text and scan for mentions of what we're looking for. Only Rebecca is spared going through the books tonight, as Tobias has forwarded over his official archaeological report, and she seems to have an irritated interest in familiarizing herself with the tombs that so rudely interrupted her labyrinth project.

"If I read another Victorian version of Tam Lin, I will crawl into the fire," Auden says calmly, shutting his book.

"What happened to being open to all manner of library drudgery?" I ask, batting my eyelashes.

"I said that before I truly understood how many books were in this room. I feel like we must have looked through every single one of them by now."

"Not even close, lord of the manor."

"What I want to know," Delphine says, giving a big stretch and then a very pretty pout, "is when we can be done for the night."

"Tired?" asks St. Sebastian from where he's reading, his boots propped up on the table.

"No," Delphine answers pertly. "Bored. We used to have *fun* here, remember? What happened to having fun?"

Becket left the priesthood, Saint and Auden learned they were brothers, and Rebecca learned that you let my ex-Domme spank you in public.

"Poe," Rebecca says before I can translate any of that diplomatically, "didn't you say there were plagues here during the medieval times and during the Restoration?"

"Yes, although as Becket pointed out a couple weeks ago, we don't know what kind of illness precisely—"

Rebecca waves a hand, her eyes still on her iPad screen and Tobias's report. "That's all right. I was actually more curious about the dates, if you have them handy."

"I have the records catalogued. One moment."

"Take your time," Rebecca murmurs, eyes scanning her screen.

It takes more than a moment, but soon I have a healthy stack of church registers, Elizabethan travelogues, and bound editions of medieval coroners' rolls. Since Becket and I have recently combed through them, it's easy to find what I'm looking for inside each one.

"Okay, the first recorded in real time, as it were, was during the reign of King Stephen, so the mid-1100s. But later, during a sickness that came in the 1400s, a clerk calls it the *Saxonn Morbus*, and mentions briefly that it came with Wessex in the sixth century and has repeatedly cropped up in the valley ever since. But then travelogues from the late 1500s describe a claim by locals that Merlin the wizard cursed the valley with the sickness before the Saxons ever made it here. There's one more episode of illness in the 1600s, recorded by a traveling clergyman, who claims the sickness was inflicted on the villages of the valley—Thorncombe and the denizens of Thornchapel in particular—by God for refusing to abandon their papist ways."

Rebecca has looked up from her iPad and is looking over at the tables with a line carved between her brows. "Auden," she says in a tight voice. "Every one of those dates lines up with Tobias's pollen anomalies."

Auden squints. "The roses, you mean?"

"Yes. Whenever a plague has come to the Thorne Valley, the roses have come too. Or I suppose we could say that whenever the roses come, so does the sickness. Except Poe's texts only refer back to the Saxon era, while Tobias's pollen record shows two more incidences in the Neolithic. One of which is contemporary with the cists and the rose-carved chamber. The only significant gap seems to be between the time of the cists and the time of the Saxons. A period of almost fifteen hundred years without the roses showing up once."

A minute passes as the six of us think about this. As the six of us digest the fact that the roses are currently crawling through the woods toward the rest of the valley now.

"Proserpina, do these sources describe the illness at all?" asks Auden. His voice is cool, but I can tell this news about the roses and the sickness bothers him. A lot.

"Um, it's a fever primarily," I say, looking back down at the books in front of me. "Marked by delusions, visions, waking dreams, that sort of thing. Once the delirium sets in, the victims are said to bleed from small wounds and…well, this is a thing—smell distinctly of roses. After several days of this, they succumb to a deep sleep, and from that sleep they never wake. Oh, and the sheep get sick too," I add, flipping through one of the travelogues. "Some of the later writers speculated the disease actually came from the sheep, since the sheep started dying earlier than the people. One visiting doctor in the 1500s even called it *ovium languorem*—the sheep sickness."

"The sheep sickness," Auden says strangely. "Are you sure?"

"It's right here."

Saint shifts. "There was a dead sheep in the road the other day."

"And one near the equinox stones," adds Auden. "Is there anything else epidemiological in there? Any other indication of how it spreads?"

"Only that it seems to spread along the line of the river—of the valley. And only once, during the 1100s, does it sound like it spilled out of the valley and across the moors. Until it simply stopped."

"Was there any kind of cure?" Delphine asks. "Or were they able to halt its spread somehow?"

I shake my head. "It sounds like once it started, it would spread through the valley unimpeded, but then it would abruptly end. And when it ended, those who were sick at the time were wholly recovered."

"So the door brings the roses," Saint says. "And the roses bring the illness?"

"The roses are growing now though," Delphine says, sitting

forward and looking at us all now. "Does that mean we're going to get sick? Has anyone been feeling sick? Other than Auden with his flower-cataracts?"

Becket's music ends, and he stands to go start another playlist. "To be fair," he says as he goes, "I think Auden's flower-cataracts are different from what's being described in the historical record."

"Because he's the Thorn King," Saint says. "Like the Fisher King. His body and the land are tied together, so what happens to the land happens to him."

"I'm not sure about the Fisher King angle, but we can safely assume they're not the same for the simple reason that he doesn't have the same symptoms," Rebecca says. "If the records mentioned smelling of roses, surely they would mention human tears made of rose petals too."

Auden seems not to be listening to this, as if his own illness isn't something that concerns him in the slightest. "Do you think the sick people recovered *because* the door was closed?" he wonders aloud. "And if so, does that mean the cure is closing the door?"

"It seems plausible," Rebecca says.

He lets out a deep breath. "That would explain a lot. It explains why someone would be willing to give their life to close the door. Because it's not about closing the door at all, it's about stopping what the door brings with it. Protecting people from it."

Silence settles over the room. Becket's still by his phone and the speaker, but he hasn't turned on anything else. Instead, he folds his arms and looks down at his feet.

"What are we thinking then? If the illness comes again—"

"It hasn't yet," Saint cuts in. "I'm in the village every day, and nothing bad has happened."

"But if it comes again," Becket says in a solemn tone, "then what does that mean? If people *do* get sick and start dying, then what are we willing to do about it?"

This is when Auden will tell us in no uncertain terms that sacrifice is off the table, that he'll hear no talk of it. This is when he'll tell us that no matter what, he draws the line at death, and that we will find another way.

He doesn't.

Instead he stabs a hand through his hair and stands.

"I need a drink."

A few hours later, and Delphine and Rebecca have gone off to bed—together, I've noticed, just as I've noticed Delphine sporting marks on her ass when we were using the indoor pool yesterday—and Becket's gone up to bed too, claiming he's still struggling not to keep priestly hours. Saint hasn't gone home yet, and Auden and I haven't gone to bed yet, and the three of us are sitting out on the terrace looking up at the stars. It's a chilly night, and Auden's in a peacoat and I'm wrapped in a blanket. Saint is in a T-shirt.

We're passing around a bottle of scotch.

The two of them have struck an uneasy truce for me, tolerating each other's company so long as mine is the company being sought, even though I know they're both deep in their feelings about what happened in the woods on the equinox.

He rejected me, Saint said about it, face twisting with angry shame. *I offered him everything and he said it wasn't good enough.*

He's not ready, was all Auden would tell me.

As per the usual with them, I'm guessing the truth is somewhere in the middle. I think Auden is right to wait until St. Sebastian is able to choose him no matter what—but at the same time, I miss being a three. For one night, one wonderful Beltane night, we were together as we should be. And then Ralph's sins tore us apart.

Well, Ralph's sins, and the stubbornness of two certain boys I know.

I suppose these months since May have given us practice in being a split triad, a three-pointed line with me in the middle, and so we've been limping along somehow. But it's not the same, it's not the same, and I'm so tired of being the hinge between them, of being the fulcrum on which they teeter and totter.

But something's shifted tonight. Tonight, under the stars, it's not only them who are distant from each other, but it's me who is distant from them. My thoughts are still in the library. My heart is still at the door.

"I've decided to go to school," St. Sebastian says. We've turned off the lights in the back of the house, so that there's nothing but starlight above us, and his voice seems to come out of the night itself. "I think…I think it is the right choice."

"It is," Auden says. "If you feel that it is, then it is."

"I'll be listing the house soon too, so I need to decide whether I'll stay in Bristol full-time or not."

"You're welcome here," Auden says firmly. "I hope you know that will never change."

"No, I—I know. I know."

"Good."

The silence spills in again, like water sluicing from a gate. A fast, cold rush.

Even in the darkness, I can see stacks of books. I can see black roses around a door.

Missing something. You're missing something.

"Proserpina," Auden says softly. "Is everything all right?"

No, I want to say. *We're missing something. My mother died because our parents missed it too.*

But what can I say that hasn't been said already?

"Yes," I say to the two men I love. "Everything is totally fine."

23

St. Sebastian

After a long five days in Bristol learning how to be a student again, coming back to my childhood home is a relief, although I'm not sure why. It hardly even feels like home now, with most of the furniture donated or sold, with most of my mother's things either packed away or gotten rid of, with my sprawling collection of books given to charity shops and the YOI in Exeter.

It's a house of bare shelves and naked walls. There's no more half-read magazines or pictures of Jesus watching me from the hallway. There's no more old cookie tins filled with sewing things, there's no more well-worn blankets folded over the back of the couch, there's no more anything that says *Jennifer and St. Sebastian Martinez lived here and were mostly happy.*

Nothing, that is, except for my mother's office, which is still a monument to disorder and imagination. More than anything else—her clothes, her books, her half-empty bottles of shampoo I left untouched for two years in her bathroom—her office was her. Not just her space, not only a retreat and a nest of paper and research, but her mind. Her thoughts and her energy extrapolated and manifested in secondhand books, photocopies, journals, organizational systems that were halfway utilized and then quickly abandoned. Pens and highlighters and little colored flags that she loved to stick everywhere—not only on her work things, but on her leisure reading and on where my homework needed correcting and on her bills too, until our entire house was filled with little stickies of yellow and blue and red.

Walking from a mostly empty house into this time capsule is shocking. Not only from the sight of all her things mostly as she left them, but the smell too, paper and ink and dust and a lingering hint of coffee and vanilla. It's been almost two years, and it still smells like it did when she was alive. It smells like she just got up from her chair to go to Mass.

For a moment, I can barely move. It's one thing to consciously remember her, but to have these sensory memories flooding in…

It's awful and powerful and evocative. It's unpleasant in such a way that I want to do it over and over again, like licking a battery. Like for that brief moment as I'm confronted with her scent, her things, the remnants of her thoughts, she's *so close* to being alive again. So fucking close.

I go back to the kitchen, to the cabinet that's just cereal and booze—all I need to live, really—and make myself a gin gimlet in a coffee mug and enter the office again. It still stuns me, it still nearly lays me flat, but I can push through it. I can keep going.

There are reasons beyond the emotional that I've avoided this room. It's a mess, and I don't mean that in a cutesy, "aren't writers so charming" kind of way. I mean it in a "I could probably invite a reality show in here to clean it and it would make for good television" kind of way. Luckily, I'd already made a start of it this spring, and the desk is mostly tackled at least. That only leaves the two other tables, the bookshelves, and the floor—which is cluttered with enough paper to cover another two or three tables.

With a sigh, I get to work.

With my mug-gin and some music going, it's not as bad as I feared. The two-year-old bills and bank things can be trashed, most of her notes and research can be tossed too. There's a fair number of things I suspect need to be returned to various local societies, so I set those aside. And then there's the things I keep for purely sentimental reasons: a clipping of her first article published in the local paper; a love letter from Richard Davey; a St. Michael the Archangel holy card with bent edges; a picture of mermaids that Richard and I drew (well, he drew and I "helped").

Soon the tables are done, and then I move to the floor, which is mostly photocopies and printed journal articles, and I sit cross-legged on the old carpet, tossing folder after folder into the recycling pile until I can see one whole side of the room.

I drag over a metal box—not big, but not small either—and flip it open, expecting old checks or cut-up credit cards or something. I'm already reaching for my mug-gin, deciding I'll slip into the library to use the branch manager's shredder for the checks—when I pause, my brain finally metabolizing what I'm seeing, what's sitting in my lap, which is not old checks at all.

It's money.

Lots and lots of money.

Pinky-orange colors. £50 pound notes. Hundreds and hundreds of them, some in rolls, some in stacks, some just loose. Some stuffed in crumpled envelopes and smashed into corners. So many that they spill out of the box like dry sand over the top of a beach bucket, sliding into my lap and onto the carpet, utterly incongruous with the faded and worn fibers there.

I stare at them like they're fairy money that will turn into leaves the moment I touch them. I stare at them like they can't be real.

How can they be real?

We weren't ever going to end up on a television program about contemporary poverty in Britain or anything, but there was no missing that money was tight in our household and had been since Richard Davey died. And while my grandfather's business in Texas makes good money—very good money—my mother was prideful to the point of stubbornness about asking for help. If we could get by on our own, then we would. Even if it meant stretching every pound like it was made of rubber.

And when Mamá died, there'd been so little to her name that I was able to buy a few rounds for everyone at the Thorn and Crown after I closed her accounts and that was it—and never, not once, not when we were in the shops getting food and searching for bargains, not when there were late notices on the utilities, not when our car refused to start or died in the worst places on the B roads of Dartmoor—not fucking once did she say, *oh well screw this, I've got a metal box with thousands of pounds in it.*

Not. Once.

I count the money with shaking hands. There's nearly fifty thousand pounds here. *Fifty thousand pounds.* Money that would have changed her life—our life—and yet she'd just stuffed it into a box? She hadn't let a single whisper slip about it?

There's more than just money in here though. There's brochures—one for UCL, one for the University of Exeter, one for the University of Sheffield. Two for American universities. And there's an envelope pressed between them, its sides creased as if it had once held money, but now it only holds a letter. A short one written in a tidy, assured hand.

I was wrong.

Forgive me.

—Auden Guest

I stare at that for I don't know how long, and then by the time my reasoning has caught up with me, I'm already halfway to Thornchapel, my blood simmering and the box in my trembling hands.

"St. Sebastian," Auden says, coming out of his chair. He's wearing a soft waistcoat buttoned over a thin jumper with trousers and bare feet, and he should look ridiculous, but he looks perfect, damn him. I'm too angry with him for him to look so handsome right now, and it only makes me angrier. How dare he look like a porny Evelyn Waugh character, how dare he give my mother money, how dare he never say anything about it?

How dare he?

"To what do I owe the pleasure—"

I drop the box as loudly as I can on a table nearby. It makes a thudding *clunk* they can probably hear in Wales, but I don't care.

Auden stops walking toward me, his forehead wrinkled in—

damn him again—adorable bemusement. "St. Sebastian?" he asks.

I flip open the box, which had barely closed again around all the notes, and they spill over the edge and onto his expensive wide-planked floor, a pink and white scatter of guilt.

His mouth opens. Then closes. "What is—" His voice is a little wavery at the edges, a little choked. He clears his throat with a small cough. "Where did you find that?"

"In my mother's office. This letter was in the box too." I extend my hand—the note clutched there is now damp and wrinkled—but Auden only shakes his head.

"No need," he says quietly. "I know what it says."

"How long, Auden?" I demand. "How long did you give her money?"

He looks like he's considering lying, but I see the moment he gives up, his shoulders slumping a little and his hand going to his hair to pull at it. "I started two weeks after you came back, and I kept going until she died."

"But." My words stop there. They stop at the *but*.

Because the timeline wasn't that, the timeline couldn't be that.

"I went to Cambridge to confront you about it," I finally manage. "Three weeks after I got back."

"Yes."

"But." My words are gone again. All the way gone.

Auden sighs and sags against a low bookshelf. "Go ahead and ask. I know you want to."

"I *hit* you, Auden. Don't you remember? I found you at that indoor rowing tank thing and I bloodied your nose in front of all your teammates."

"You did."

SIERRA SIMONE

I nearly explode in his direction; I want to explode, I want to destroy him for lying, for hiding, for depriving my mother in the first place and making me come home from Texas. "*Why?*" I rage. "*Why? Why* did you allow me to hit you—spit at your feet—call you every name I could think of—why when you'd already started sending her money again?"

There's a solemnity in his face when he answers. "Because I deserved it, St. Sebastian. I deserved the bloody nose, the spitting, the names. I deserved to be punished. I did the wrong thing for wronger reasons, and I knew it even then. I knew it deeply."

"But you—" I'm still trying to wrap my head around this. "I just don't understand why you wouldn't have fought back—tried to defend yourself—*explained*. I wasn't some tornado of anger that couldn't be reasoned with, Auden. If you'd told me the truth, I would have listened."

"I know you would have, but you're not listening now," Auden says impatiently. "I deserved all of that and more that day at the rowing tank, and I craved it even. Just because I'd started doing the right thing didn't erase the hurt I'd caused doing the wrong thing, and I—well. It felt craven to try to bargain down to a lower sentence, as it were. Your anger was justified no matter that I'd already laid a verdict on my own guilt and tried to make amends."

"How Catholic of you. But you never thought to tell me the truth since then? All these times we've fought about the money, you didn't think to volunteer the fact that you'd given her fifty thousand pounds?"

"No," Auden says, straightening up and padding toward me in his bare feet, "and for all the same reasons. It felt childish and stupid of me to pretend that giving away money I could easily spare changed what I did. I imperiled your mother's survival—or at the very least her independence—and I interrupted your studies and your life, and made you come back here. I earned your fury, and I don't take things I've earned lightly. Not at all, St. Sebastian."

He stops right in front of me, and I want to hit him again, just like I did in Cambridge. I want to hit him and I want to drop to my knees, and I'm so fucking *furious* at him for being better than I'd thought, for being a better man than I believed he was, and all I want is to tear the world down around us so that I'm not so full of loving him and hating him and hating how much I love him.

"Do you want to hit me again?" he asks curiously.

"Maybe," I say, although I don't really, I think. I want to hit the money, I want to hit the wasted years and anger. I want to hit every wall that the last twelve years has erected between us.

"I'd let you, if you wanted," he says.

"Whatever," I mumble, glaring down at my boots.

"Or you could let me do something to you," he suggests.

I snap my head up to look at him, and while he's keeping a respectful distance between us, there's nothing respectful about his carnivorous gaze or his flexing hands. There's nothing respectful at all about that mouth, about the way his tongue wets his lower lip, as if already tasting me.

"Like what?" I ask, despite myself.

He lifts one shoulder in an elegant, cashmere shrug. "I could spank you. Bite you. Pin you to the floor and run my fingernails everywhere."

Heat gathers low in my stomach, stirring my blood and stiffening my flesh. "Oh?" I say, my voice more strangled than casual. "I thought you needed me to promise you forever first."

"I'll make an exception today. You seem like you need it."

"Oh my God, fuck *you*," I hiss, shoving his shoulder. "You'll make an exception for me? Will you? How fucking benevolent, you fucking dickwad—"

My words are cut short as his mouth comes down hard on mine—hard enough that I can taste blood from where our teeth cut into our lips. My organ is fully erect within seconds. My entire body aches for invasion and violence. It aches for possession.

It aches for Auden.

He slams me against the wall, something metallic rattling somewhere, my breath leaving my body in a sharp grunt, which he steals with his kiss, pushing his tongue into my mouth and stroking and stroking, seeking and seeking, until I'm so starved for air that sparks fizz at the edges of my vision and my knees go soft. Only then does he let me breathe, tearing his mouth away from mine with a vicious oath.

"Please," I whisper once I've found air again, once I can stand. My hands are on his jumper, searching underneath for firm, warm skin. "Please, Auden."

"I'm tired of being the thing you regret," he says, his voice as hollow as it is rough with lust. "But I'm even more tired of not having you. I don't think I can hold out any longer, St. Sebastian."

"Then don't."

I don't know who starts it—I never know who starts it—and does it even matter? But somehow we're both moving, shoving and pulling at each other's clothes, somehow the kissing has turned to fighting and the fighting has turned into what it always is at its core: Auden winning because I want him to win.

We stagger over to his desk, still shoving and kissing and grabbing and biting, and then I'm shoved down, bent over his desk like a schoolboy about to be punished. My jeans are yanked down to my hips and a drawer is opened, and then I hear the click of a lube bottle.

"Hurry," I say. "Hurry."

"Because you're worried you're going to change your mind?"

"No. Yes. I don't know—does it matter?"

"It should," answers Auden darkly. But he doesn't clarify, and the only other clarification I get is a slick fingertip rubbing against my opening.

I bury my head in my arms on the desk and groan, because this is something that never feels as good alone, this is something my own touch, my own collection of toys can never replicate. It's not just the slipperiness or the touching itself—it's the impatient way he does it, it's the authority he does it with, the utter prerogative, like of course my arsehole is his, of course he has every right to fuck it in the middle of his own goddamn house. Of course I should be bent over for him, available for his use, whimpering at his irritable need as much as any sane person would whimper at a sensual kindness.

No, a toy can't give that to me. I can't even give that to me.

There is no preamble to him pushing in, there is no warning. There is only the absence of his fingers and then something broad and hot—and then the intrusion. Thick, too thick maybe, and unrelenting enough that I'm making all sorts of noises into the mess of plans and L-squares and liner pens on his desk.

I hear a grunted *fuck* from behind me as Auden buries himself deep, and I'll never tire of hearing him so completely undone, so unraveled and rough for me. All that studied elegance tumbles right away, and what remains is ferocious, hungry male. And if I'd known when I was a teenager and fumbling around on the internet to find out what I liked that one day I'd have the lord of the manor himself grunting behind me, then I'm pretty sure I would have been at Auden's feet the very next time I saw him. I'm pretty sure I would have found him after Mass one Sunday and said *I will do anything for you, please just let me.*

"So stubborn," he's murmuring now, but it's not a soothing murmur, it's an angry one, it's a murmur like he could fuck me until the sun sets and still not be done punishing me for punishing him. "So pretty and so stubborn. You feel like heaven around me, did you know that? Pure hot joy. All this time you've denied us this, all this time…"

"You have," I breathe. My fingertips are scratching at the plans on his desk, pens are rolling everywhere. "I wanted this, remember?"

"That's right, isn't it?" Auden says, giving me a full stroke that nearly kills me. "You wanted exactly this. A rough fuck to scratch your itch. Something fast and mean to remind you of how it feels to be mine."

I'm given several more ruts, and even though it's trapped beyond the edge of the desk and out of reach, my erection gives a sharp, sudden surge in response. I'll come soon, just from his words and the fucking, and I can't even care that it'll be all over my boots and all over his floor. It feels right, necessary, like of course it should be as filthy as possible. Of course this shouldn't be clean or sweet or romantic. Not when it started like this.

"You could be mine," continues Auden, his hand cracking along the curve of my arse. "You could, St. Sebastian. It'd be so easy. All you have to say is *I don't care what happens next, I'll love you anyway.* And then it's done. You, Poe, and I will be together again, and I'll fuck you any time you like, I'll keep you in my office like a pet and use you whenever the fancy strikes, I'll find a way to marry you and Poe and leave lovely little marks on your skin until we die. It could be us, St. Sebastian. It could be the three of us."

I open my mouth—but the words don't leave it. I'm not sure why, if it's because I'm scared or because there's a sexy, posh boy fucking me like I'm the last lay in the world, or because I'm simply not ready until I have those test results in my hand, I don't know.

But I don't speak.

And Auden snaps.

"Fine," he seethes, his hips merciless and his hands cruel. I can barely breathe for how fast he's jamming into me now, for how brutally he's fucking. I can barely breathe for how that brutality stirs my body like nothing else. "That's fine. I'll use you anyway. And when you're feeling me tonight and tomorrow, think about us. Think about the three of us. Think about what we could be if you would only promise to stay. Stay no matter what comes next."

"I just—need—to know—first—" I manage.

"Then know," he says in something like a snarl. "But you'll still need to promise after that. No matter what changes, no matter if there's a mistake. Because I am fucking tired of watching you leave."

His hand moves under the desk to find my trapped cock, and he doesn't stroke it or play with it, he merely inspects it, testing to see if it's wet at the tip. And then he's back to fucking me with harsh, unrestrained thrusts. I have the feeling that if someone walked up here right now, he wouldn't stop, he'd keep going, he'd make them watch as he extracted his due from me—

"Auden," I groan, "I'm going to—"

"I know," he says, and for the first time since he bent me over his desk, I hear something deeper and warmer than anger or lust. "I know, Saint."

He loves me.

It's not a secret. He's never kept it a secret. Even when we were teenagers, it was there, radiating from his bites and his sketches on my skin, if not his words. But sometimes I'm still struck sideways by it, by the fact that *Auden Guest* loves me, by the fact that he loves me still. After everything.

My balls seize up, tight, tight, and then something shears inside me, something critical and structural, and a lewd heat rushes up my cock as I cry out into the desk. Cum sprays from the tip, thick spurts of seed that land somewhere I can't see, and it's so *dirty* to come like this, so impossibly *rude*, to just ejaculate onto the ground like an animal, and I love it, I love that he's made me do it, that he's reduced me to this.

Even as I hate that I can't surrender to what he's asked of me. Not yet.

Auden crams me full one last time and lets out a low grunt that curls my toes. Then he's filling me up, his cock swelling and pumping and swelling and pumping, until his grip loosens on my hips and I hear him draw in a tattered breath. One final pulse and he's drained. He gives me a quick thrust before he pulls out—not for me, I know, but so he can feel his seed inside me, and then it's done.

We're done.

I don't move for a moment, not until Auden pulls away completely, and then I stand up to see him holding out some tissues. We both clean up, and then after I'm put back together and zipped, I notice the floor under Auden's desk.

"I came under your desk," I say.

"It's fine."

"No, I should—" I crouch down and clean up my semen with a tissue and then stand. "Sorry about that."

"I said it's fine."

"Auden—"

He looks at me, and we're so close right now that I can see every crypt and furrow in his irises—slender rings and radial threads of emerald, jade, coffee, and amber. Eyes like the forest outside. Except at the very edges, around the very outer ring, the irises have darkened to a color I've never seen in his eyes before.

A reddish-black. The color of a deep, hours-old bruise.

"Auden," I say again, but this time it's a question. This time it's because worry has begun to crawl up the backs of my legs and up my spine.

But he waves me away before I can say any of that. "Go," he says hoarsely. "We're done here."

"But—"

He pushes the heels of his palms into his eyes. "No buts, little martyr, please. Not today. I asked, you said no, now we keep up this awful thing where the three of us are unlinked and apart." He drops his hands, his eyes with their strange new color at the edges burning into mine. "And you know it's wrong. I know it's wrong. Every time we're with Poe together or separately, every time you and I are together or apart, we can feel the wrongness like...like—" He gestures at a window, in the direction of the chapel. "We can feel the wrongness growing, and I'm terrified that at some point, it's going to be too late."

"I'm not asking for much," I maintain. "I just want to know if Freddie is my father. I feel so sure that he is."

SIERRA SIMONE

"Wait, then, if that's what you want to do. But I will have a promise from you then."

"Of course," I say, "of course I'll promise then."

"Even if there's a possibility the test could be wrong?"

"Yes, obviously."

"If you say so," Auden says, and I wish I could fix all the doubt I hear in his voice then, I wish I could smooth all the sadness away. I wish I could promise him forever *right now*; I wish I didn't care so much what my mother would have thought.

I wish, so much, that we were a three again.

I nod my goodbye, and with heavy bootsteps and an even heavier heart, I take the box of money and go back home.

24

Rebecca

The trees are turning.

Outside the library windows, I can make out wet smears of gold and orange and red among the green. Alder like a blaze of sunshine, ash like dried blood. Yellow hornbeam and birch, deep orange beech, red rowan. And the yews with their scarlet berries and deathless needles and trunks like skinny fingers, knuckle bones and all.

If the last week of rain and fog hadn't made it clear, autumn is here at Thornchapel. The land is bleeding with it. Burning with it.

I close my folio where I've been answering a few last minute emails before my car arrives to take me to London, and I stand and stretch. I rarely work in the library if Poe is working in there too—I prefer complete silence, and Poe is a symphony of sighs, tuts, and small talk—but today is a short day anyway since it's a travel day, and I wanted to be near the fire while I worked. I'm glad I did—the rain pattering against the glass and the occasional snuffles from Sir James Frazer were a welcome infusion of Thornchapel before I head back to the city and the sterile offices of Quartey Workshop.

And anyway, Poe was a very pleasant work companion today, totally silent other than the soft thump of books on the table and the sporadic clack of keys as she took notes and entered in metadata.

I bend down to give the dog a final scratch behind the ears before I go to fetch Delphine—she's riding with me back to London—and then I see Poe sitting on a table, her knee pulled up to her chest and her head resting on it. She's in a short red dress with mustard yellow tights, and she's all color and curves as she stares out into the rain-haunted forest just beyond the library's windows. Books older than the country she's from are piled all around her, and a forgotten notebook with a pencil sits on the keyboard of her laptop, the screen of which is dark. She's been sitting like this for some time then.

"I'm about to go," I say, coming toward her. She nods against her knee but doesn't lift her head to look at me. "You all right, love?"

"I'm fine," she murmurs.

I'm close enough now that I see what I didn't notice this morning, when I was deep in my emails and she came shuffling in with coffee to start her day. There are bluish smudges under her eyes—which are glassy and unfocused—and there's color high in her cheeks. She still doesn't look at me, keeping her eyes on the trees outside as if they're speaking to her in some tree language made only of fluttering leaves and swaying branches.

"You don't look fine," I say, which I know isn't strictly polite, but all my mistress instincts are flaring, and I suspect a direct approach is best. "You look lost."

"Lost," she echoes. She lifts her head just enough to tuck dark hair behind her ear. "That's the word."

Her nails aren't bitten; her lips are plump, rosy, and soft; her hair is clean and brushed; and she's wearing an outfit with components—not just a dress but opaque tights and cute little Mary Janes and a coordinating bracelet on her wrist. There's a crumb-dusted plate and a reusable water bottle nearby. I can see that she has made some headway on her work today, before succumbing to whatever reverie this is.

I relax a little after taking my inventory. She is lost, but the kind of lost that I can trust her to unlose herself in.

At least I hope so.

"You're not sick, are you?" I ask, and she shakes her head.

"No. I don't think so."

"You don't think so?" I press my hand to her forehead. It feels a little warm to me, but that could be because the room is so cool.

"What were the symptoms again? Visions? Sleeping constantly?" She gives a wan smile. "That's already the daily life of a narcoleptic, so perhaps I wouldn't know if I was sick if it came down to it."

"Don't forget the smelling like roses." I study the blue-dark skin under her eyes. "Has your sleep been restful?"

"No," she says, the already-faint smile fading into nothing. "It hasn't."

"Dreams?"

"Scenes. Visions. Memories that aren't mine." She closes her eyes. "Every time I sleep, I see the chapel and the door. I see the roses. I see people dying. But it's like"—she opens her eyes and makes a gesture like she's using her hand as a knife to slice something apart—"slivers.

Little cross-sections of memory, and then they're gone, and there's no context, there's no way to glean anything from them, other than that people put on the torc and walked to the door. The Kernstows seemed less sad about it than everyone else, but I don't know why that's the case. I can never see more than a few moments at a time."

I touch her shoulder. "Does Auden know?"

"About the dreams? Yes."

That seems like an unnecessarily specific answer, but when I start to ask what he *doesn't* know, my smartwatch chimes. My car is here, and I need to get Delphine and go. But my inner Domme recoils at the idea of leaving Poe uncared for.

"Come on, then," I say, pulling her off the table. "You're done for the day."

"I am?"

"Yes." I pull her to the sofa and urge her to lay down. Her skirt pulls up and exposes a pleasing bottom that I have fond memories of spanking, and I give it a quick squeeze before I pull a blanket over her. "You sleep. I'll let Auden know to wake you for supper."

"That's a good idea," she says tiredly, already closing her eyes. "You always have the best ideas."

"Of course I do."

Sir James, spotting an opportunity, comes and curls into a ball directly underneath where her hand dangles over the edge of the cushion, earning himself a few sleepy strokes. I kiss her cheek—soft and maybe a little warmer than it should be—and leave to go find Delphine.

"I love your office," Delphine says later that night, wandering around the room and peering at site plans and elevations laid out across various surfaces. She has a photoshoot tomorrow morning in Shoreditch, so I should take her to her place, I should remind her that the hour is late and she'll want some sleep.

But she doesn't bring it up and I don't mention it, and I know why I don't. I want her to stay at my place tonight. I want to fuck her until this twisting, grasping need in me is sated for a few hours at least.

But if I say it aloud, then it's real.

It's not like Thornchapel, where things can happen in a forested cloister set apart from the real world. No, if we fuck here in London, if we accidentally-on-purpose fall asleep together while post-sex here in London…

Then I'll have to face the truth. That I want her, that I want to forgive her, that I want every day to be filled with her, and that I want the filling to start now.

Delphine leans over another table to examine the infinity-th iteration of the Severn Riverfront project, and my mouth goes dry. She's wearing these incredible pants—not quite leggings, no, they're something more expensive and more horse-related than that—and knee-high boots with a tight shirt and a cropped moto jacket over it. She looks like she left on a purebred horse and came back on a deviant's motorcycle, and when she bends over, there is nothing hiding the lush curves of her bottom, the bite-worthy temptation of it. I could go right over there and run my palms up the contours of her thighs up into the flare of her hips; I could stroke my fingertips over the rise of her cheeks just under the waistband of her pants. I could mold my hands to the luscious form of her backside and then rub my thumbs along the crease where her cheeks meet her thighs.

I could.

And so I do.

I come up behind her and fill my hands with her, leaning back so I can watch, so I can take in the sight of my fingertips pressing into her bottom, so I can see how her body moves as I squeeze and plump and play.

Ever an eager sub, Delphine allows me this with a contented sigh—even arching her back so the parts of her I want are more accessible. Fuck, she's perfect, so perfect—just firm enough to squeeze, just plush enough to sink my fingers and teeth into.

I hear people say sometimes, usually as some kind of euphemism, that fat bodies are *generous*. *She has generous hips, generous curves, generous thighs*—a way to say *fat* that feels safe, I suppose. But as a Domme, I've only ever seen the word *generous* as the literal truth of a fat partner, because this...this is a gift. A body reminding me that I can't grope fast enough or grip hard enough to take in everything at once. It makes me so horny I could growl with it.

And suddenly, fondling and palming her is not enough. Pulling her tight to me and sliding my hands under her jacket is not enough; crushing her tits until she moans isn't enough. None of it is enough, and none of it ever is, because the only thing that's ever enough with her is uninterrupted days and days, and even when I had them, my imagination still never ran dry, plans for her pleasure and pain never stopped coming. I never stopped being hungry, hungry, hungry for this upper-class girl who needs it so very much, so very hard and so very often.

"To your knees," I say hoarsely, unzipping the trousers I'm wearing and shoving them past my hips. "Right now."

Even though I've given her no other warning—even though when she kneels, she's kneeling in front of the floor-to-ceiling window behind my desk, visible to anyone who happens to look up—she does it without hesitation, without even a blink. Like she's been waiting for it since the moment we walked in here.

She drops gracefully, so gracefully, years of ballet and dressage coded in her every movement, and I wish I had time to savor this, I wish I had the patience to just sit and observe her following my orders.

I don't even have the patience to undress her.

Instead, the moment her knees touch the floor, I'm stepping close, sliding one hand into her hair and bracing the other against the glass behind her. Without preamble, I pull her mouth to me, guiding her to kiss and nuzzle my cunt through the thin silk of my knickers.

Her mouth is soft and her breath is warm, and when I look down at where I hold her to me, I see delicate smears of lipstick all over the silk. I want to hiss in triumph, I want this to be my national flag, my coat of arms, the sigil of my house. Rich-girl lipstick all over my knickers, a painting in pink and ivory. A masterpiece.

But even this can't scratch the itch, even this can't blunt the desperation I have for more of her. I drop my hand from the window and draw my knickers to the side, exposing my nakedness to her mouth. She flicks a look up at me that is pure slutty, submissive gratitude, and I want to cry. I couldn't have dreamed her up even if I tried, and now here she is, fitting every puzzle-piece tab and slot of me, and I don't know if I can keep her. I don't know if I can let her inside the tenderest, rawest parts of my heart ever again.

The first buss of her mouth over my cunt is heaven. The parting of her lips and the lingering trace of her tongue down to where my clitoris pushes itself between my lips is the hottest fires of hell. I press my hand back against the window because I don't know if I can stand otherwise, I don't know if I can keep myself upright. She uses the tip of her tongue to find my clit, and then she licks again with her tongue flat—pressure, then velvet, pressure, then velvet—and I shove her face harder to me.

"That's it," I tell her. "Just like that."

She hums in response, and I pull her hair a little, wishing briefly that I were at home or at Justine's, someplace where I could have her naked and clamped, or at the very least, someplace I could be stinging her heart-shaped bottom with a riding crop while I used her mouth. But the wish is gone nearly immediately, because I know I wouldn't have the patience for it anyway. I used to love elaborate scenes—I used to thrive on the drama, the pacing, the props. I would spend hours tormenting subs with all sorts of choreography and gadgets, and it had become such an integral part of my identity as a Domme that I would never have thought I could be a mistress without it. Without a stage, without a script, without an entire room of implements.

I would never have thought I could be just as much of a Domme with only this—only my trousers around my thighs and my fist full of hair—and yet here I am, here we are. Here she is being used and loving it, on her knees where she so loves to be.

"Suck," I tell her, and she does, sealing her lips around my bud and drawing it against her tongue. "Good girl. Very good girl. Keep going."

She makes a happy noise against me, like she wished on her birthday candles to be granted permission to do exactly this, and there's another flare of heat behind my eyelids. Why does she have to be so otherwise perfect for me? Why does she have to fit me so well when she's the same one who cut me apart with a careless ten minutes and a kiss?

But she sucks on me again, nursing on me until I can barely breathe, and soon the only feeling thrumming through me is jagged, unfiltered lust. I angle my hips so that she can push her tongue into me. With my trousers around my thighs, there's only so much she can do, but she tries valiantly, stroking my seam with her tongue and searching out my hole, letting me ride her mouth until her kiss is so wet and slippery that her lips slide against me. Only then do I haul her mouth back up to my clit to finish what she started, widening my legs as much as I can, leaning on the hand against the glass and fucking her mouth with selfish thrusts.

Though the hour is late enough there's no foot traffic at all, I imagine what we look like from the street were someone to look up and see us in the window. Delphine, like a slutty secretary on her knees, and me with my pants down past my hips, fucking her mouth with crude abandon.

The image is suddenly too much, the idea of it, that Delphine is my secretary who I can call into my office to use whenever I need—

Holding her face tight to me, her hair bunched in my fist, I come against her mouth in several hard, shuddering spasms, each one lasting longer and longer and longer until they eventually recede into a warmth settling in my stomach and my thighs. My breathing is harsh and ragged as I guide her mouth away from me, my clit giving one last kick as I see how her lipstick is smeared across her mouth, as I take in how it all looks with my trousers shoved down and her lips all swollen.

"My God, Delph," I breathe. "My God."

She smiles up at me, and I know I can't be done for the night, there's no way I'm done for the night. I haven't even tasted her, I haven't felt inside of her yet. I want to push her toy inside her cunt, and I want to tease her with it the entire trip back to my flat, and then

I want to tie her to my bed and make her come while I flog her breasts into hues of pink and red.

I help her up, and then while she uses makeup wipes in her bag to fix her lipstick, I pull up my trousers and button them shut again. "Come back to my place," I blurt. "I know we haven't talked about it, but I want you there. Tonight."

She drops the makeup wipe in the small bin by my desk and turns to look at me. There is something in her face...not hesitant, maybe, but wary.

"Just for tonight?" she asks. "Or until we go back to Thornchapel in three days?"

It's a fair question, and the answer's obvious:

Yes, of course.

Of course I want her there all week.

I want her to fuck and to play with and to leave beauty rubbish all over my bathroom counter; I want to wake up with her using me like a long teddy bear. But as soon as I part my lips to tell her yes, I want her to stay, panic chokes me like cold seawater. I nearly sputter around it, and suddenly breathing is hard and thinking is hard, and all I can feel is that awful feeling on that storm-tossed Lammas, when it felt like she'd plucked my heart right out of my chest, twisted it from my aorta like a grape from a stem.

All I can feel is what it felt like to love her and have her hurt me.

She sees. Of course she sees, and she ducks her head, so that I can't see her in turn.

I've hurt her.

And despite what I said to her in the Long Gallery the day I found out about Emily, despite what I thought for weeks after, I don't want to hurt her. I don't want her to have to shield her heart from me.

It's only that...well, I don't want to have to shield my heart either, and yet here I am, here I'll always be, because it's the only thing that keeps me safe. She taught me that lesson more than any other person in my life, and maybe it's only fair that she should know how it feels too.

"On second thought," she says, and I can't see her face, only the flutter of her eyelashes against the fading sex-flush on her cheeks, "I do have an early morning tomorrow. I should probably get a cab and go home for sleep."

"Delph, I—" My hands drop to my sides. "I don't want that. Come over tonight."

When she looks up at me, her eyes are wet and her chin is dimpled and quivering. But her voice is strong. "I've changed my mind," she says. "I really should get home."

"I want you to come over," I say, and it's so stupid and hypocritical, but now I'm filled with panic that she doesn't want to come over, that she doesn't want to stay. "And yes, you should stay until we go back to Thornchapel. Because we should keep doing this, shouldn't we? Logically, it makes sense: I need a sub and you need a Domme, and we both like sex, and this serves us both." I know I'm saying the wrong things, I can hear the wrong things pouring out of my mouth like rainwater from a gutter spout, but I can't stop myself because if I stop myself then I might say the right things, and if I say the right things, the honest things, the other panic will come back, and I'm not ready for that either. "This can be fun, you and me, it could be easy, Delph, so easy between us."

The word *easy* makes her blink once, hard, as if I've just hit her. And then she swallows and says, "No, thank you."

"No, thank you?"

"I mean, no thanks. I don't think it's a good idea for me. I did—I really did think I could do this, that if all I got from you was Mistress Rebecca, that would be enough. But I think I'm realizing it's not enough now, and I'm sorry, but no, thank you."

I stare at her like I've never seen her before. And maybe I have never seen her before like this, all vulnerability and surety tangled together. I have the abrupt, acute sense of something very important slipping through my fingers. Something so important that I might die without it.

"Why?" I ask in a numb voice. "Why can't we go on like we have been? Because it has been easy, you know it has."

She shakes her head slowly, her honey-brown eyes pinned to mine. "Easy for you, perhaps. But I don't even think it's been that, has it, Bex?"

I want to tell her she's wrong. I want to tell her that casual sex with her is the easiest thing I've ever done as a kinky adult.

But I can't.

She gives me a long appraising look, as if my silence is answer enough. "I wanted to be easy for you, you know," she says. "My whole life, that's all I've ever wanted, actually. How funny is that? Some people grow up wanting to be smart or ambitious or brave, and all I wanted was to be easy. Because that was something I could change about myself, even if I couldn't change my body. I could be easy, pretty, graceful, fun. Not anxious or messy or difficult or afraid. Frictionless, you see, because I'd used up all my points on having this body, so I had to make sure that I was otherwise marvelous to be around, because if I wasn't, then who would like me? Who would love me? And then somehow, at some point, and I don't know when, wanting to be easy turned into hiding. And the hiding turned into lying, and you know what the lying turned into, Bex, you know what it led to. I don't want to do that anymore. I don't want to hide, and I don't want to contort myself into knots pretending that I don't still love you and that I don't want you to love me back, so that I'll be easy enough for you to keep around. I've apologized for what I've done and vowed to do better, but this is something I deserve. I deserve the right not to be easy."

I don't know what to say, and I find that I'm pacing, pacing in front of my desk in the flats she gave me this summer because she hated my other traveling shoes so much.

"Delph, do you honestly think I have no idea what that's like? You think I don't understand having a body that the world judges on sight…what it's like to have only a certain number of points that are already spent merely by being who I am? You think I don't understand what it's like to have to be *easy*? I'm a Black woman—an immigrant— and I'm queer—you don't think that I've ever had to negotiate exactly how ambitious I'm allowed to be, how messy, how *difficult?* I can do those equations in a split second, on a moment's notice. I can do the math—the differentials, the multivariable integrations—of being easy in my head while I'm giving a presentation or talking to a cab driver or trying to order at a restaurant. The necessity of easiness was spliced into me at birth, Delphine, you don't have to explain it to me. Fuck."

I'm shaking a little after I say all this, things I've never said aloud to anybody—not all at once at least—and I step back until I find the edge of my desk and can prop myself against it. But when I lift my eyes to Delphine, the shaking eases a little. She is not defensive. She's not crying because she felt that was hard for her to hear. She is nodding, listening, her eyes warm and clear all at once.

"You're right," she says softly. "Of course you're right. I'm sorry

I didn't understand that before."

"No, I—" I lift a hand and then drop it. "I appreciate that. But I didn't say it to win a fight, Delph. I'm saying it because I *get it*. I get it. But do you? Because if we're going to talk about *easy* and who's allowed it, then you have to know that you'll always be allowed more. So much more than me."

She lets out a long breath as she nods again. It's a slow, thinking breath.

"Yes," she says after a minute. "There is a value to my skin, isn't there, that will always shield me, lift me—and that value goes beyond size, it reaches past it. I should have seen that. My reality is shaped by that value, and so everything else—being fat, being easy or difficult—it will always be layered with it."

She gives me a rueful kind of smile. "I don't want to perform the *mea culpa* at you, because I know the performance means nothing without really understanding—without action—but I am sorry for not seeing, and reflecting on it, Bex, I'm so sorry. Of course you get it. You get it so much more than I ever will have to."

She's right that I don't want performance. What I do want is much simpler.

Not *easier*—definitely not that—but simpler.

"I know you know this, Delph, deep down. I wouldn't have been with you if I thought you didn't. And I'm not invalidating what you felt or what's happened to you to have made you feel that way—I just need you to accept my reality too. To make room inside yours for what I experience as a Black woman, because you will always have more latitude than me, more social and functional legal capital. More safety."

"Yes, Rebecca," she says, and she says it not like a submissive, but like a friend. Like someone who is ready to earn trust. "I will."

I have to look down, suddenly, because there're too many feelings—radiating from her, boiling in me. Boiling, boiling, because even though she says she understands—even though maybe she *does* understand—she's still ending this. Ending us.

"I'm not saying this to win a fight," I say, looking up again. "I'm only saying I don't let it excuse my mistakes."

Her voice is still soft when she answers, but it's firm now too. "I'm not either," she says. "I know what I did to you; I'm responsible, and I'll apologize as many times as you want to hear it. All I'm telling you is why I can't do this anymore."

"This. Us."

"*Not* us. This isn't us—this is a shadow of us, a ghost of us, and we both know it. And I can't make myself into nothing hoping that one day you'll give me a crumb of something. And I hope you know in return that you never have to be easy with me. I can't promise you much else, but I can promise that. Even if we're not having sex, even if we're only friends, I will always hold room for you to be all of yourself. Without the multivariable integrations, without the points. All of you, as you are, and as you want to be."

My throat hurts; my eyes sting. It's all I've ever wanted a lover to say to me. All I've ever wanted anyone to say to me, maybe.

With me, you can rest.

And then my muscles are tightening with panic, with imminent loss. She's really leaving right now. She's really saying no.

And the worst part?

It's for a good reason.

Even I, wanting to keep her as I do, see that it's a good reason.

She slings her bag over her shoulder. "I'll see you back at

Thornchapel, Rebecca. And I—" She hesitates and then says it anyway. "I love you. You don't have to say it back or feel it back or anything. You don't even have to forgive me. I just want you to know."

And then she leaves me alone with damp knickers and tears already beginning to fall before she's stepped onto the lift down to the lobby.

It's a long week. A terrible fucking week.

I hate it. I hate every single day of it. I'm out of sorts and I can't sleep and even my bones ache with missing her, and I hate it.

Finally, though, it's nearly at an end, and I'm in my flat packing for Thornchapel—and trying to decide what I want to say to Delphine when I see her again—when I hear the buzz of someone at the door. My chest seizes like it's just been caught up in a giant's fist, and I run down the stairs like a teenager expecting someone they fancy, smoothing my clothes and licking my teeth for stray lipstick as I go.

But it's not her.

It's my father, standing there with Auntie Yaa's groundnut soup and banku. "Supper?" he asks, as if I'm going to say no to hot groundnut soup. I step back and let him in, and he trots easily up the stairs.

I notice again how much warmer he is now, how much happier. But instead of stirring resentment inside me, it only stirs sadness for my own lonely state, and a melancholy kind of joy for him. *I'm glad he's happy*, I realize, feeling for the first time that it's really, honestly the truth. *I'm glad he's happy now.*

"I won't be long," Daddy assures me as he starts laying out the food on the table. "But I'm going to America tomorrow, and I wanted to see you before I left."

I'm stunned. "You're going to America? But you haven't said anything about it at all—and we haven't planned for it at the Workshop—"

"It's only for a week, and if anything comes up, my capable daughter will be able to handle it most superbly," Daddy says. "What's the point of being the boss if I can't give myself time off now and again?"

It's still startling to hear my father talk about work like this, like it's only part of life and not all of it like I've been raised to believe. And yet—yet, I do smile a little this time around. Maybe I'm getting used to this version of my father. Or maybe I'm starting to untangle all the ways perfection and hard work were knotted up with love for me, and so I can finally understand why he's been able to let go of perfection too.

I pour us each a glass of Beaujolais, and we sit down to eat, talking a little bit about work and the latest gaffe in the mayoral race, and then out of nowhere, he asks, gently, "How is Delphine Dansey?"

Her name burns through me hotter than any scotch bonnet pepper, and I take a drink of water, stalling for time. "Fine," I manage to say after a moment. The word sticks in my throat, but I somehow dislodge it. "She's doing fine."

My father leans back and gives me the famous Quartey Stare, his dark eyes scraping over my face. "And how are *you* doing?"

I start to say *fine*, and then I can't manage it, I can't force out the lie. I take a drink of wine instead, swallowing it and looking out the window instead of at him. I don't want our new family tradition to be me crying about Delphine Dansey over food.

I can feel the heat of his stare a moment longer, and then I hear him reach for his own wineglass. I see him swirl the Beaujolais out of the corner of my eye as he says, "Your mother and I failed you in a lot of ways, Rebecca."

I swivel back to him, ready to protest this. Whatever their faults, Daddy and Ma gave me the best of everything—and they pushed me to be the best in turn. And as exhausting as the latter was and is, I can't say that I wish they'd done any differently.

But my father holds up a hand, forestalling my objections. "No, no, not like how you're thinking. But in other ways, we have failed you, and I know this because we failed ourselves too. We didn't show you there are ways through hurt and pride. We didn't show you a way to navigate conflict that wasn't avoidance or shielding or separation. I wish that I had been braver and more direct with Lydia before this year. Not only for us, but for you too."

I'm shaking my head as he speaks. "It's different," I say. "Delphine and I are different."

"Because she cheated on you? I cheated on your mother."

"Is it so wrong of me not to forgive her for it?" I demand. "I gave her something I've never given anyone and she spit on it. What kind of a woman would I be if I allowed people to do that to me? Without any kind of consequence?"

"But you love her?" Daddy asks, his eyebrow crooked ever so slightly. "You miss her and want to be with her?"

"Yes, of course I do," I say in exasperation. "That has nothing to do with forgiveness."

"I think it does, Rebecca. If she's apologized and pledged to be better, then she's made the amends she can. And if she's made her amends, then why not admit your own feelings as evidence in her case? Why not allow yourself something you want for the simple reason that you want it? No one can tell you what choices to make in a circumstance like this because no one is you, and no one else will reap the rewards of loving her."

"Or suffer the consequences," I mutter.

The eyebrow quirks up the tiniest bit more. "Is your pride really more important than your happiness?"

Indignation flares through me, followed by a sharp kind of sadness. "Daddy, if I don't protect my pride, no one else will, don't you understand that? I'm the one who has to fight for it, to guard it, to know what I'm worth, because I live in a world where it's not a given. And it's not a matter of my pride versus my happiness, it's a matter of what I deserve. And I deserve more than being cheated on."

He gives me a long, uncomfortably gentle look. "Of course," he murmurs. "Only I worry that you're using the wrong math here. Arithmetic instead of algebra, fractions instead of irrational numbers. You've flattened your thinking into something two-dimensional: this or that, safety or hurt. Me or her. Loving someone isn't about rigid, oppositional certainties, loving someone is…it's quantum. It's subjective and alchemistic. It's difficult to measure and impossible to see with the naked eye, and even more impossible to explain."

"Quantum."

"Both things can be true at once, Rebecca," Daddy says. "Just like light can be both a particle and a wave, it can be true that she hurt you and also that loving her could be the smartest and most wonderful thing you ever do. Now, let's finish this good soup and talk of easier things, hm?"

He reaches across the table to take my hand, like it's the most natural thing in the world for him to show me this kind of affection, and it breaks something in me, something as old as my Red Dress Barbie.

I start to cry, and when I start, it's not just for Delphine and me, but for him and me, for Ma and me. For the simple fact that we as the Quartey family have our own complicated, quantum love, and I think I finally, finally understand exactly how beautiful it is.

And will be.

Later that night, I'm opening windows to let in the wet October air. I can't decide if I'm hot or cold, and so it seems better to err on the side of a cold room and then huddle under blankets if I need to.

I have the second window swung open when it happens. I see something in the glass behind me, a fluttering, and I turn to see a wren perched on the top of my headboard.

"How did you get in here?" I murmur, stepping toward it as it tilts its head and studies me with one eye. It chirps and sidles a little toward the side of the headboard, then flies up to perch on a bar I have mounted to the wall for perverted sex reasons. "Come on then, let's get outside with you—"

The bird chirps once more and then disappears. Not flying away, not hopping down, not moving at all. It's simply there one moment and gone the next, and I am frozen with a confusion I've never felt before. Because even with the things we've seen at Thornchapel, I've never, never doubted that I saw them. I knew I had, I knew they were real in their own fashion.

I've always been able to trust my senses.

But that wren was never really there.

It takes me a very long time to fall asleep that night, long enough that the sleep doesn't even feel like sleep before the morning comes, it feels like a fitful, foggy haze instead. And when I wake up, chilled and sweaty and aching, I know something is wrong.

I wrap myself in the warmest, softest clothes I can find and go to Thornchapel.

25

Auden

The girl at my feet is exquisite. She is artful obscenity.

She is living surrender.

Marks already decorate her tits and thighs, her hands are bound, her full lips are parted for my cock, which she takes and takes and takes, until I withdraw, leaving it jutting between us like a sword.

I reach down and untie her hands. "On the bed. On your stomach."

She is naked, with a thick braid draped over one pale shoulder, and when she nods, the end of it brushes against a stiffened, lovingly abused nipple. "Yes, Sir," she says, and moves to obey. I can see the pale flash of her soles as she walks through the shadows to our bed, and I think after we're through tonight, I'll play with them. Massage them and pet them until she purrs.

But she doesn't need to purr right now, my little bride, she needs to cry. For the past two weeks, she's been growing more and more withdrawn, and sleeping worse and worse, and she says she's fine, but it's apparent to all of us that she isn't. I've tried ordering her to rest, to take time off, I've tried pampering her, watching over her, until Rebecca, wrapped in her blankets by the fire and shivering with fever finally told me I was doing it wrong.

"She needs spanking, not spa days," Rebecca said. Though her lips were dry and her eyes glassy, her voice was steady still. She'd come to Thornchapel more than a week before that with a fever and intermittent hallucinations—a wren, she said, always hopping away from her. She's visited a doctor twice—was admitted once overnight in Exeter for observation and then released—and there's nothing the doctors can find as the source of her fever. They've sent her on to a rheumatological specialist for a consult in a handful of weeks.

I'm terrified, if I'm honest with myself.

I'm terrified that she is ill with something that cannot be cured—or that can be cured by one thing only, which is closing the door.

But that is a worry for later, a problem for later. I have another problem draped across my bed at the moment, and it's a problem I'm determined to solve. Rebecca is correct, and there is no getting to the treasure inside Proserpina without first breaking the lock. Much like her namesake's mythical fruit, she is meant to be peeled open, and so peel I shall.

Checking to ensure that she's comfortably positioned and can breathe easily—my mattress is firm and the blankets stripped back, but I still feel better knowing—I climb onto the bed with a few choice supplies, straddling her thighs on my knees and giving her backside a nice swat, loving the way it moves when I do, loving the way she moans in response.

"Reach back," I tell her, "hands on your arse. Pull yourself apart for me so I can see you."

She does, her fingers pressing into her cheeks as she spreads herself, and I'm grateful that I turned on a few lamps around the room, so that even with the October twilight seeping in through the windows, I can still see her. I can see her soft pink hole and the wet seam beneath it, and I can see the place where her seam opens into another pink hole for me.

Lust clenches every muscle I have, and for a moment, I stay there, straddling her with my cock bobbing painfully in the air. She is beautiful. Always in her brilliance and curiosity and warmth, but my deepest sin is that she is just as beautiful to me in debasement and surrender, holding herself open so I can use her any way I please. In fact, I could come from this, maybe not even touching myself. I could come just from watching her do this for me.

I can barely stand it, how much I love her; I can stand even less how much I love her like *this*. I've starved this part of myself for so many years that finally indulging it is not only thrilling but terrifying. Because is this really who I am? Not the architect—or the young ex-fiancé of Delphine Dansey—or the former boat club boy who likes dogs and graphic novels and gave up art to make money like his father said he should. But the man currently straddling a woman's crop-marked thighs as he clicks open a bottle and slicks her back entrance with lube until it's ready. The man who will fuck this woman until she begins to cry, and then fuck her some more. The man who can't unsnarl love from pain no matter how much he spent his adolescence and early adulthood trying.

That is me. And even though it terrifies me that anyone trusts me with their bodies and their affections, some things just won't be denied.

Once her rim is slippery, I push a finger inside, going slowly so that she can relax around the invasion, so that she can let me in. And then I add a second, giving her more time, time to breathe and adjust.

"Tell me how it feels," I say, giving my erection a quick pump as my other hand continues opening her, stretching her.

"It feels okay," she breathes. "There's pressure, but it's a familiar one. It's not any more than the plugs you've had me wear before."

"Ah, yes. The plugs. Do you know how much I enjoy it when you're wearing them? How hard it is to focus on work knowing that you're in the library, feeling my toy inside you every time you move? Do you know how good it feels to fuck you while you're wearing one?" I slide my fingers free and then reach for the bottle, painting my organ with lubricant until it's shiny and nearly dripping with it. "It feels so wonderful, Proserpina. Nearly as good as this is going to feel."

She whimpers in an aroused kind of anxiety as I wedge the fat head of my erection against her. "You're so good," I soothe her. "Such a good submissive, aren't you? Such a good little bride, making sure I get to fuck you. Hold very still now. Hold still."

The sight of my tip pushing against her shiny entrance as she holds herself open to receive me is almost more than I can bear, and my testicles are already drawn up tight, my entire groin filled with a hot, sharp, shivery tension that threatens to shear me apart. I've never fucked her here, and the knowledge is like a carnal drumbeat, thumping in time with my pulse. I'm about to fuck her tightest, most secret place—*I'm about to fuck—I'm about to—*

The first half-inch is a grip so hot and slick that I have to remember how to breathe…the second nudge forces my crown all the way in. I stop for a minute just like this, drawing in lungful after lungful of air, desperate not to come yet, but it's so tight and hot, it's like a fucking fist, and seeing the sweat mist on her back, seeing her hands shake as she valiantly attempts to hold herself open—it's too much to see and to feel all at once, *fuck*. I have to wait until I'm in control, I have to wait until my own hands aren't shaking, and then finally I push deeper, all the way, loving the resistance and the friction of her entrance around me as I slide into the silky heat. I bury myself until there's nothing left of me to give, until her hot opening is around the hilt of me, and then I lean forward, shifting inside her enough to make her gasp.

"How does it feel?" I ask in a hoarse voice. I need to make sure she's okay, that it's not too much—except only in the precise way that I want it to be too much.

"Full," she says, her voice trembling. "I feel so full, Sir."

"Uncomfortably full?"

"Yes."

"Good uncomfortable or bad uncomfortable?"

One must always ask with Poe.

"Good uncomfortable," she murmurs. "Very, very good."

She already has plenty of endorphins dripping from her pituitary gland, making her floaty and agreeable, and now that I know she's ready, I plan to give her more. I straighten up—my cock still deep in her backside—and I begin to ride her this way, fucking in and out with long punches of my hips as she gasps and sighs underneath me. The sensation of it, of her, of her delicious gift to me, is streaking up my shaft and going right to my spine, arcing lightning through my belly and thighs, until everything below my chest is crackling with dark, primal urgency.

That's when the door opens, revealing the silhouette of St. Sebastian. "You texted to say when I got in from Bristol I should—" He stops short as he takes in the scene, me kneeling over a prone Proserpina, fucking her arse with rough, punishing strokes as she holds herself open for it. He closes the door behind him and comes closer, rubbing a hand on his jaw, already breathing harder. "You said I should come by?"

"I did," I tell him, not stopping or slowing down. "I'm going to finish and then you're going to mount her and fuck her while I watch. Is that acceptable to you, or would you like to say *May I* to me?"

The words might sound pointed, but I mean them honestly. I want him here, I want to toss off while he fucks our girlfriend, but no one is less sure than I am if I have the right to command him like this.

I yearn to. It's better than the fucking itself, seeing their chests flush and their pupils dilate. And more than anything other than having St. Sebastian close to me forever, I want him to be that shuddery, blissed-out version of himself he is when he's made to submit.

But despite what happened with Becket in the library, despite the lapse in my office where I took him over my desk, I can't be certain that he wants this. Actually, that is a lie, because I am very certain he wants this. But I can't be certain he *wants* to want this, and that matters too.

But perhaps it's Poe, perhaps it's the pull of the three of us just as it has been since we were children in the chapel, perhaps it's the lashing rain against the glass…whatever it is, St. Sebastian succumbs almost immediately.

"No," he says, swallowing hard. Already an erection pushes against the front of his jeans. "No, I don't need to say *May I*. I want to stay. I want to fuck."

"Of course you do," I grunt, slicking back into Poe with a forceful rock. "You want to watch me come?"

"God," he breathes, "yes."

"What do you think, Proserpina?" I ask her, smoothing a hand up the contour of her damp back. "Should we show Saint how hard you make me come? Hmm?"

"Yes," she murmurs, and I can hear the smile in her voice. The endorphins are really trickling through her now. "Yes, Sir."

Saint comes to stand near the bed, his piercing caught between his teeth as he stares at us. As Poe turns her head so she can stare at her other boyfriend with glassy, happy eyes. Saint is rapt looking at her now, like a pilgrim who's just stepped into his temple for the very first time. And his thick length is now pressing so hard against the denim of his jeans that I can trace the shape of it with my eyes.

"You want to take it out?" I ask him in a rasp. "You want to touch yourself while I take my turn?"

"Yes," he says quickly, his hands already at work on his jeans to free his erection. He's already got his cock fisted and is punching his hips into his own hand before his other hand has finished dragging down his jeans. His breathing has joined mine and Poe's—hard, harsh, quick—and having them both here, together, is everything, fucking everything.

My two loves, my one heart. If I can't have them both in my arms, at least I can have them both in my bed.

I turn back to Poe, who is quivering underneath me with the effort of keeping herself held open and also from the hard railing I'm giving her arse. She won't come like this, she needs more stimulation against her clit, but I'm hunting more than her orgasm tonight, I'm hunting her catharsis, the breaking open, the crashing through. I have a plan for that.

"You can let go now," I tell her. "And you no longer have to hold still."

Confused, but obeying, she brings her hands up by her head, which means all of a sudden, my root is buried not only in her channel, but in the plush give of her bottom. Her cheeks now press against me each time I thrust, and it's heaven to feel, it's so wildly scrumptious to feel how much my thrusts push against her body, how much of her curves I displace in my quest for invasion. I bring my palm cracking against the side of her bottom as I fuck her, relishing her sharp cry as I do.

Saint's hand moves faster, shuttling quick and urgent on his penis. He never can take his time, which is one of the reasons I think he responds so well to being dominated. He loves to be forced to go slowly, because it's the only way he can manage it.

"Use your left hand," I tell him as I deliver another hard strike to Proserpina's backside. "Put your right hand on the bed and use your left."

He gives a furious curse, but does as I ask, because he knows it will be better this way. He knows his clumsy grip will keep him miserable and frustrated, and that is exactly what my little martyr boy wants in bed, and he looks like he both hates and loves me for knowing that.

For my part, I only smile wickedly at him before giving Proserpina a flurry of spanks that have her moaning. I start matching my strikes to my thrusts, both as hard as I please, a dark abandon filling me. I give in to it, even as I watch and listen to her, tracking the moment her moans turn wet and hiccupy with tears, measuring the way she bucks and rolls underneath me to get away from the pain. We are practiced enough at this that I trust her to safe out if the time comes—truly, the miracle of Poe is that she's far more experienced at kink than I am and has no qualms about asking for what she needs—but my one eternal fear is that she will be so lost in the high that she won't feel when too much becomes *too much*, and so my abandon must always be laced with vigilance, as it is now.

My vigilance tells me she's not there yet, not yet where I want her to be, and so I let myself off the leash even more, riding her so hard the bed shakes, fighting to stay mounted even as she bucks and twists, and when she instinctively tries to crawl away from a particularly vicious slap to the bottom, I lean forward and cover her entire body with mine, giving her the heavy, rough pounding we both crave. Every muscle in my arms and stomach and thighs is corded and tight; even my calves are working, even my toes are working, every cord and sinew bent toward the singular task of pumping her pretty arse full.

"I love my beautiful slut," I croon in her ear, and she sobs underneath me as I fuck and fuck and fuck. "I love my wonderful whore. My bride."

And she says in response, choked with juddering, racking tears, "I love you so much, oh God, Auden, I love you so much—" She seizes up around me, her core convulsing around my cock and massaging me, milking me, and all while she screams into the mattress with a scream I could wank to every night for the rest of my life, and then it's over for me too. A noise tears free from my chest, a low roar of satisfaction. My organ gives a heavy jolt and then starts rhythmically pulsing her sheath full of seed.

"Ohhhh fuck," Saint moans, his left hand moving jerkily. "Fuck."

I growl and finish fucking my way through my pleasure, loving as always the feel of my orgasm inside my lover, loving how Poe is still coming too, still sobbing as her body trembles out its release, and then with a few final spurts, I'm finished ejaculating and I straighten up.

I pull free of her body—slowly enough that I can enjoy the way her entrance is still open after I leave it—and then wipe myself with a flannel I set nearby earlier. I gently roll her over to take stock of my Proserpina, my future wife, and find it's as I expected. She's close to that breaking point, but she's not all the way there yet. She's sobbing, she's all marked up and flushed, she's got her thighs clenched together from the last waves of her climax—but she's not broken yet.

I move to the side, sitting against the headboard, my semi-erect penis draped over my thigh. "Take her," I say simply, and then Saint is scrambling onto the bed, boots and all, eager as a teenager to fuck. She parts her legs willingly, easily, so limp and open, and Saint slides in with no resistance, his back moving with shuddering breaths through the thin cotton of his shirt as he sinks inside.

"Poe," he says, like a prayer. "Oh Poe."

She lifts a weak hand to thread through his hair, pulling him down for a kiss, which he groaningly gives her as he starts to rut. My cock is stiffening again now, and I don't even bother to fight it. I get the bottle and lube up my fist to fuck as I watch.

"Press your hips in, rock upward with each stroke," I order him, hissing a little at the cold lube on my skin as I start to masturbate. "Make her come again."

"Yes," Saint says in a rough voice, and then what follows has us all freezing. "Sir."

Sir.

I can't remember the last time he's called me that. My throat hurts, like my heart has slithered up there to choke me.

Sir.

Saint unfreezes first, his dark eyes meeting mine. "Yes, Sir," he repeats, perhaps so there can be no doubt. For right now at least, I am his Sir. His king.

Oh, how that fires my blood.

I start handling myself rougher and rougher as Saint gives Proserpina long, rolling pumps of his hips, which gives her the friction she needs as he moves. Her toes curl and her nipples are tight, turgid points, and her head starts thrashing on the mattress, her throat working as she tries to breathe, tears still sliding from the sides of her eyes. Her hand searches out my free one and grips it hard, and in this moment, there is no barrier, no chasm, nothing between the three of us. We are feeling, moving, respiring, existing as one, as one thorny heart.

With another sob, the muscles in Proserpina's stomach jerk and she starts coming again, and Saint follows, pulling out to spend on her belly, his pearly cum pooling in her navel as he holds himself above her and spills onto her skin. I am the last, grunting both their names as warm semen spurts up my shaft and then runs over my fingers, dripping everywhere.

For a moment, there is nothing but this. All of us wet with our pleasure, all of us exhausted with it. The only sound in the room is the rain against the window mingled with Proserpina's quiet sobs.

"Help me?" I ask Saint, and he nods, and I get off the bed and scoop her into my arms, handing her off to him once he's on his feet and then going to change the sheets.

Within a few minutes, the sheets are changed, and we are mostly cleaned up, although I know Proserpina will need a shower before she sleeps. I make a gesture of invitation toward the bed, and Saint nods, joining me as I lift our little bride onto the mattress and tuck her into the blankets I've bought just for her—the softest I could find, soft enough they won't chafe against a well-abused bottom.

She's still crying after we settle in on either side of her. I pull her against my chest, and Saint curves his body around hers, his chest to her back, and lays his arm over her waist, making a cage for her out of lovers.

Because she is on her side and I am on my back, his hand comes to rest on my undressed abdomen, and I feel him jolt the moment his fingers touch my skin. But he keeps his hand there, and I in turn lift up my free hand to toy with his too-long hair, which he allows with a bite of his lip.

We are all three together, pressed shoulder to ankle, twined and touching, and even if it's only for right now, we are as we should be. As we are fated to be and have been since our wedding in the chapel all that time ago.

It makes me want to join Proserpina in her tears, but I don't.

Instead I ask, in a tone as gentle and firm as I can make it, "Will you tell us what's bothering you now? And if you use the word *fine* at any point in your explanation, I shall take you over my knee again."

She huffs out a wet little laugh against my chest and then gives a sniffling kind of nod. "Yes, Auden."

I kiss the top of her head. "Good."

"You can tell us anything," Saint murmurs. "Anything at all."

She angles herself so that she's facing the ceiling, her head pillowed on my shoulder, and then she speaks. "It's not like I've been hiding it on purpose, or that I've been too embarrassed to speak about it, nothing like that. It's like there's this new—I don't know—*shape*, maybe, in my mind. Or it's like a presence, but not an alive one, not something separate from me. More like an idea. But I feel like I've come to it in the fog, like it's mostly obscured from me somehow, and I can't even make out the boundaries of it, I can't even survey its foundations. All I know is that it has something to do with the door. And my mother."

"Poe," Saint says, "what happened to your mother…it's understandable that you would be thinking of her—"

"I'm not grieving," she clarifies. "Or I am, but that's not all this is. Instead, I keep thinking about why she came back, about what Ralph could have said to her on their last phone call to make her get on a plane straightaway. And I keep wondering if…I'm wondering if she chose to die that day. On Samhain."

Neither Saint nor I expect this, I think, because our eyes meet over her head, and I register the same shock in his expression that I'm feeling now.

"You think she might have chosen to have my father murder her?" I ask.

"We don't know that he murdered her," Poe says.

"Becket saw—"

"Becket saw Ralph with her body," Poe says slowly. "Burying her. We don't know what happened before that. We assumed…but what if we assumed wrong?"

"But why…?" Saint asks and then trails off, like he doesn't want to finish asking so he won't have to hear the answer.

She doesn't respond for a moment, and then she says, softly, "I think she would have chosen it. If she felt there was no other way."

"We can't know that," I tell her firmly. "We can't know if she consented, and we can't know what her reasons for coming here were."

"Convivificat," Poe says to the ceiling. "She brought that word with her. I keep thinking, why would you fly across an ocean with a warning in your pocket?"

"Because my father asked her to come, Poe," I say. "She called and he did whatever it was that he did so well—bending people to his will. He made her come here and then he killed her."

"Like you said," she agrees after a beat, "we can't know for sure. But it's this possibility that she consented to it, and I can't stop *thinking* about it. About what happened, about what she felt and thought as she walked through the stone row that day. About why she might have chosen it."

A chill, deep and relentless, is settling into my marrow.

A true king would never let anyone go in a king's place.

A Kernstow told me that once.

"And I can't stop thinking about the fairy stories down in the library," adds Poe, dragging me free from my thoughts.

Saint releases his piercing from where he's been tugging on it with his teeth. "Because the door is safer in those stories? More benign?"

She shakes her head against my chest, silky, tangled hair sliding over my skin. "Not benign, not at all. If anything, I think the door might be more powerful in those stories, because they go further in describing the world beyond the door. It's more than an omen, it's a path."

"No," I hear myself say. "It's not. Freddie Dansey tried to reach through and couldn't, remember? It can't be a path."

Poe's voice turns thoughtful. "I think there must be certain times when it's open in both directions, but that can't be all of it. There must be something else as well."

She sighs, a sad, frustrated exhale. "And I keep thinking that if I can find the answer to that, then I might have answers for all the other questions too."

26

Auden

When I wake, I have a moment where I've forgotten everything since Beltane, and there's only a warm curl of satisfaction in my chest as I open my eyes to see two submissives asleep in my bed. We'd showered after talking, and then Saint—without any prompting from me—had climbed naked into bed, and we'd cuddled Poe between us, letting the rain lull us into a cozy, snuggly sleep.

It's only as I roll over and register wet leaves stuck to the window—buttery gold and startling crimson—that I remember it's October and that maybe St. Sebastian is my brother and that my best friend is sick with something that might kill her.

I remember that the door is open.

I push myself to a sitting position and look over at my lovers. Poe is a lush sprawl of sleep—deeper sleep than she's been getting lately, which is probably related to the man curled behind her, his legs tangled with hers and his arm thrown over her stomach. For his part, his lips are pressed together and his eyes are moving under their lids—he's dreaming.

My two dreamers.

Though it's still early, it's not so early that I'll be able to go back to sleep, so I dress myself quietly and go into the en suite. I don't have the energy to shave away the stubbled shadow that's cropped up overnight, and all that's left to do is brush my teeth and tame my hair.

I stare at my reflection when I'm done, studying my irises.

All my life, I've looked in the mirror and seen brown and green; ever since I can remember, I've had my father's eyes. But since the equinox, my eyes have been changing. It started with a ring of deep crimson around the edges, and then the ring began to bleed inward. Threads and tendrils of its fresh-bruise color, staining my irises all the way up to the starbursts of coffee and amber around my pupils. Perhaps by Samhain, they will be completely changed.

I'm not sure what happens then.

I finish, check on Poe and Saint one last time, and then go downstairs for tea. I find Rebecca sitting at the kitchen table near the range, a puffy blanket over her shoulders and a mug of steaming tea between her hands. There are plasters on her fingers and on the inside of her forearms.

"Doing all right today, Bex?" I ask with forced cheer as I fill the kettle with water and then flick it on.

"The same," she says tiredly. "This fever, and now these little wounds. And I keep thinking if I could just rest…but then when I try, I dream of the wren…"

I come to sit next to her and carefully put my hands over hers, looking down at her wrists and arms, where a few small wounds are beaded with tiny scabs. They look like pinpricks.

Thorn pricks.

"Bex," I say, "I think you need to tell your father that you're sick."

She gives an emphatic shake of her head. "No."

"He's going to deduce something's wrong eventually if you continue making excuses not to return to London," I tell her. "And if you're really sick with—well, with whatever this is—then he deserves to know."

Another shake. "I've already been to the doctor, Auden. They're already sending me to a specialist. I have no answers yet, no solution, and I refuse to worry my parents with this until I do. And besides, he thinks I'm staying here because I'm making nice with Delphine. Which is nearly true."

It is. I can tell from the tension strung between them that they still haven't resolved whatever it is that's made them both so miserable, but despite that, there is no more devoted nursemaid than Delphine. She's been fussing over Rebecca since the day Rebecca showed up, clammy and peaked, and hasn't stopped making her broth and wrapping her in blankets ever since. At first, it was a little surprising, since Rebecca usually hates anyone doing anything for her that she can do herself, but once I saw the way she looked at Delphine, with confused, complicated longing, I understood that it wasn't about the nursing and the fussing for Rebecca. It was the intimacy of it, the proximity. The having Delphine curled on a nearby sofa editing photos while Rebecca slept, the familiarity and affection in Delphine's touch as she tucked blankets around Rebecca's lap or wound a scarf around Rebecca's braids before bed. It was submission laced with indelible love, and in Rebecca's shoes, I wouldn't have been able to resist it either.

"Speaking of, where is your little nurse?"

Rebecca flicks her eyes up to the ceiling. "I made her sleep last night. She needs it. And I thought I could sneak down here and work, but I haven't even made it through one email yet."

The kettle clicks off, and I stand up. "You shouldn't be working," I say, trying to keep the impatience out of my tone. "Tell your father you have a cold or something, but then stop expecting so bloody much of yourself when you can't even lift a tea mug without your hands shaking."

I turn to see a hot glare bent my way. "I can still work," she says stubbornly.

"You're practically ready for A&E." I sit down with my mug and level a look at her. "Which reminds me, have you thought any more about—"

"I'm not going back to the doctor until my specialist appointment," she says firmly. "And I'm not going to A&E. Christ, Auden, what do you think they're going to do with me? They'll either send me home or treat me for something I don't have, because what I *do* have is an ancient rose disease they've never seen before."

"We don't know that they can't help," I maintain. "We have antibiotics now, antivirals, steroids, scans—we don't know that they can't help. And we still don't know it's the same illness—"

"Stop, Auden. Just stop," she says, closing her eyes for a moment before opening them again. "We can be reasonably certain it is, and I'm not saying I won't go to the hospital if I'm very, very ill, but I am saying that they won't know the cure for this, and we do."

"The door," I say, fear pushing on my chest like the gravity of a hostile planet. "Closing the door."

"We can decipher this without anyone having to die," she says, gentler now. "And I want to be here to help when the time comes."

I put my hand back over hers. Her fingers are clammy and cool. "Promise me that you will take care of yourself. That you will make the choice to go to the hospital before it's too late."

"Of course," she says.

"Because I will do it for you if I have to," I tell her.

She doesn't argue with me, although I can tell by the hard twist of her mouth that she would fight me every step of the way.

"And you know Delphine would help," I say, which is perhaps cheap of me, but I don't care. Keeping my friend alive is more important than fair play.

As I predict, she softens a little at Delphine's name. I drop my hand from hers and take a drink of my tea. This is the closest to a truce we'll get today, and I decide to take my victory and not push for more. She also sips her tea, and we sit in a companionable silence, watching the wet trees wave outside the window.

"Your eyes, Auden," she says after a moment.

"I know."

She looks down at where the steam curls from her mug in twisting, ephemeral blooms. "What have we gotten ourselves into?"

A question I've asked myself often.

"And what," she asks, lifting her face to the glass, where the trees burn with autumn against a dark gray sky, "happens on Samhain?"

The other question I've been asking myself.

The answer I refuse to name.

After I finish my tea, Sir James finds me and starts his morning circles in front of the door until I let him out. I pull on a navy peacoat and some boots and go out to the south lawn, where my dog is currently finding every puddle left by the rain last night.

Though thunderclouds frown above us, there is still plenty of fog clinging to the grounds, and it gets thicker closer to the river and the trees. I walk the borders of the forest like a farmer checking his fences, noting that the roses have breached the cover of the woods and are climbing toward the house again. I've directed the team that comes in twice a week to tend to the grounds to cut them back, I've told them that it's an invasive species that must not be allowed to spread to the lawn or the other Thornchapel gardens, but every time the gardeners trim them, the roses return, thicker and even farther onto the lawn than before. As if desperate to make it to the house.

The rose bushes hulk ominously in the fog today, and last night's rain drips from the blossoms like tears. I think of Tobias's report, of the pollen analysis showing layers and layers of an unknown rose pollen, and I wonder if my battle against this stupid plant is pointless. I wonder if it's all pointless.

Scrubbing at my face with my hands, I walk back out of the fog and up the slope to the house, which is when a figure resolves itself out of the misty air. For a moment, I think it must be Becket—the trench coat and upright posture means it can't be Saint—but no, this person is too short, and their hair a bit too long—

"This looks a right mess, Auden, I hope you know that," Tobias says as I approach him, gesturing toward the muddy scar where the maze used to be. The cists—empty and with their lids replaced—cup rainwater in little pools along their tops, reflecting dark sky back at us.

"You only just finished tearing into everything, you twat," I say fondly, giving him a handshake. "Why on earth are you here?"

"They've found a potential earthwork from the Battle of Bovey Heath, which is where they would like to build a Lidl or something, and obviously the earthen bank might contain evidence of revetting and palisade construction—I'm sorry, *am I boring you?*"

I make a face at Tobias. "Yes."

He gives me a sulk, all sapphire eyes and pretty mouth. "I listen to you when you talk about—I don't know—building permits and things."

"When have I ever talked to you about building permits?"

"That's rather beside the point at the moment. Because as I was saying, I had to come to Bovey Tracey to do an initial survey, and while I was mourning what a waste of my immense mental acumen it was for me to be there, I had a thought about your graves."

"They're not my graves," I say automatically. But I'm deeply curious to hear what he thinks, especially with the keen interest in his face as he looks at them now. I'm also deeply grateful that the fog is currently hiding the roses from view. If Tobias sees them, I have no doubt at all he'll be able to extrapolate all the correct assumptions about pollen layers and mysterious rose varietals, and then there'll be no keeping him away from the chapel. Or the door.

"Well, this might sound strange at first, but it's a very clever theory, so if you're astute enough, you may be able to keep up. Also have you done something to your eyes? They look...odd."

Tobias peers at my face, and I use the same lie I used last time I was in the Harcourt + Trask office. "Contacts," I say lightly. "They act as sunglasses."

"Sunglasses," Tobias says, lifting his eyes meaningfully to the storm clouds above us. "Yes, I can see why you'd need those today."

"I've been struggling with proper pupillary dilation lately," I explain. "Anyway, back to your very clever theory."

Tobias narrows his eyes at me a final time, as if to say *I'm watching you*, but then with a theatrical sigh, he gestures back at the cists.

"A microcosm," he says.

"The graves?"

"Yes, the graves. Druids built their temples in these irregular shapes, you know, the Romans used to make horrible fun of them for it, but it turned out those lopsided squares created triangles which lined up precisely with the elliptic motion of the sun, and then they would walk the path of the sun on crucial days. The later Celtic saints did it centuries later too, when they consecrated churches and wells and things. Walking a microcosmic path that mimicked the macrocosmic path of the heavens above."

I look out over the cists, which are dispersed across the grounds in the most random possible order. "These are like the irregular temples then. There's a logic to the pattern."

"Precisely," Tobias says, pulling something from the pocket of his Burberry trench coat. A paper. "I had to have a friend dig into some archives for me yesterday, since you hate the search for knowledge and stymy all attempts at scientific inquiry, and I managed to find the surveys from the excavation done on the chapel in your woods. Coupled with the Ordnance Survey of the valley at large, I was able to make this." He unfolds the paper to show me a rough rendering of the monuments around Thornchapel. "Look familiar?"

I see it instantly. The way Tobias has drawn the landmarks—to miniature scale and with none of the interference of trees or sheep or medieval manor houses—I can see it.

I pivot slowly to look at the graves furthest to the east. "Those would be the equinox stones then."

"And here"—Tobias says, tapping the paper—"I think this succession of three is meant to be the river."

"So then these two would be the menhirs," I say, stepping around a puddle to reach the two closest to the king's tomb. "Which means this one, where you found the murdered figure with the torc—"

"Would be the grass-covered altar, yes," Tobias says, getting excited now, rocking a little on his feet. "If I had to guess based on the organic materials we've pulled from them, I'd say these cists are a fair handful a centuries younger than the monuments around them. Which means there's no doubt in my mind these tombs are referencing an existing sacred landscape. They're not scattered or disordered at all, but placed *by design* to connect with the environment."

"You told me last time I needed to ask what symbolic language they were speaking—this is it, isn't it?"

"And now it's my turn to ask *why*," Tobias says, giving me a dimpled grin. "What would have prompted them to do this? An enduring worldview? An acute crisis?"

I think of the roses, of the illness, of the graves filled with the cremated dead, and I wonder if I already know the answer.

"The only flaw in my genius—yes, even I have flaws, let that come as a comfort to you—is that the carved chamber doesn't correspond to anything on any map I can find, not the archaeological survey undertaken by Dr. Davidson, not even the Ordnance Survey outside your property lines, nothing at all." He walks over to the king's cist and the empty chamber directly across from it, the two structures set so closely together that it would be possible to hop from one stone lid to another.

"This *must* be the altar, of course it must be," Tobias murmurs, mostly to himself. He looks between the grave and the hand-drawn map with furrows carved into his forehead. "But there's nothing else for the chamber to be then. The edge of the forest, perhaps? Or maybe there's a buried monument in the clearing? Or a monument that was quarried for stone for the chapel—which has happened before, you wouldn't believe what people have done to standing stones in days past. Broken them up for barns and drystone walls."

I let him talk. I let him talk because I already know what the rose chamber must represent. I know what the grave builders had meant it to be.

It is the door.

It is the door, and there is a murdered king buried right in front of it.

Tobias is needed in Bovey Tracey by nine-thirty and has to leave before long, and I manage to head off any inquiries about when he can go back to the chapel as I walk him back to his car by asking him as many questions as I can think of about microcosms and their ritual purposes. It distracts him sufficiently until I've dispatched him over the narrow bridge separating Thornchapel from the rest of the world, and then I decide to ignore his calls and texts for the next few days.

Above all else, I don't want him going back to the chapel right now. Above all else, I don't want him or anyone else catching whatever it is Rebecca has.

Sir James and I walk back to the south lawn, and driven on by an impulse I can't name, I push into the trees, where a narrow path still remains to the chapel. It might be because the path is hard-packed and unfriendly to new growth, but I have this semiconscious, paranoid fear that it's the door's doing. That the door wants us to have a way back to it.

It's a nonsense thought. But what about all of this isn't nonsense right now?

The fog has started to thin—not because of the sun, which is still hidden behind the heavy, hovering clouds—but because of the wind the storm is bringing with it, a restless kind of wind that pulls on the trees and sends gold and scarlet leaves fluttering everywhere as I walk. The roses too suffer the same fate, and wet black petals cover the path like a carpet, muffling my footfalls and sketching out a path to the chapel through the trees.

But I don't go to the chapel.

Instead, I push my way through an opening in the roses, swearing viciously every time the thorns snag on the wool of my coat or the fabric of my trousers, wishing I'd brought my leather gloves to aid with pushing the thorny canes of the roses back. But at last I reach my destination.

At last I reach the River Thorne.

It is the same chirpy, splashing river as always—shallow and stone-filled and flowing fast—and it's also not. Instead of being bordered by the usual trees and ferns and moss, the river's edge is now crowded with rose bushes, which weep dark petals into the water.

Some float and others drown, but they all rush on, on, on down to the village. Down to Thorncombe and the rest of the Thorne Valley.

The other side, however, is blessedly free of roses, and so I cross the petal-strewn river to get to the other bank, where I find the path up to the moors. And from there I make my way to Reavy Hill.

This was a favorite spot of St. Sebastian and me that summer—the perfect mix of convenient and isolated. I stared at his profile set against the sunset here. I used to watch his wine-stained mouth with a hunger that scared me at the time.

For that reason, I've been fond of this place, but there is another inducement to come up here today, and that's because it's the sole vantage that gives an observer a comprehensive look at my ancestral grounds.

I climb onto a rock and sit, the wind whipping at my coat as I take everything in. The chapel, covered in roses, the forest in its vibrant shades of October, its floor black with torn petals. The roses creeping up my lawn, and the exposed graves that lie in their path. The river carrying petals to the village, the valley, the sea.

From here, it's laughably easy to make out the pattern of the cists in the earth. Of course it had seemed familiar to me when I first saw them, of course it did. It was my Thornchapel, standing stones and altar and door, rendered in miniature like one of my models for work.

It was my home.

And so, armed with this new insight, it is only a small sequence of postulations to arrive at a scenario which accounts for the graves. The door came—or whatever form the door took back then—and the roses came with it, blanketing the grounds. Presumably, the people living here also took ill, and they knew enough to connect the door to the disease. Perhaps there was no path through the woods that time, or perhaps they were afraid to approach the door.

Or perhaps they killed the king at the door and then brought him back to be buried with his people.

Whatever the case, they constructed a mirror of their poisoned world, and then they killed a man to make it right again.

What if he'd consented? Does that make it less horrifying? Does it make it more so? I can't imagine renouncing my life, kneeling with a holy person behind me ready to strangle me or cut my throat or smash my head in, I can't imagine it at all.

Until, that is, I remember Rebecca. Then the imagining becomes abruptly clear.

Yes, I would die to save my friend.

I think she would have chosen it. If she felt there was no other way.

That's what Poe said about her mother, and I understand why Poe is so haunted by this now, why it fills her thoughts. It is frightening enough to consider what would drive someone to commit a ritual murder.

But to consider why someone would consent to it…

"You look very handsome like this, brooding in your peacoat," a voice complains from behind me. "It's not fair."

I turn to see St. Sebastian standing below my rock, glaring up at me.

"Not fair to whom?" I reply.

"Everyone except you," he sighs.

I pat the rock next to me. "Fancy a bit of brood with me?"

"I suppose if you're offering."

He climbs easily onto the rock, supple muscles bunching and stretching under his jeans and ubiquitous T-shirt, and despite the roses and the graves and my sick friend back at the house, lust tugs at my groin. I want to lick him everywhere. I want to run my fingernails over his nipples until I give him the goose bumps the cold hasn't. I want to sprawl my legs and watch as he services me with his mouth as he kneels between them.

He settles close to me, cross-legged. Even though we are inches apart, I swear I can feel the heat of him, the energy of him, as viscerally as if he were pressed against me. I feel as if a particularly picky cat has sought me out and decided to sit nearby.

I'm keenly aware that the wrong movement or word might send him sloping away.

With difficulty, I turn my eyes away from him and back to Thornchapel.

"You didn't come from the house," I observe.

I see the lift of his shoulder out of the corner of my eye. "It was bin day in the village, and I had loads of stuff from my mom's office to get rid of. I got up soon after you, I think, and went to go drag my bins out. I decided to come up here after I was done to have my own brooding sesh."

I want to look at him again, but I settle for a small smile, ducking my face into the collar of my coat so he won't see it. "What did you need to brood about?" I ask, after the urge to haul him into my arms has passed. "Rebecca? The door? Bin day?"

"The first two, yes. And very nearly the third thing, because I found out—well, it's the first time I've been back in almost a week because of school, and Auden"—his voice is hesitant now, threaded through with a trepidation I recognize because it so expressly mirrors my own—"there are roses in the village now. Creeping up from the river. And my neighbor is sick. She was being loaded into an ambulance when I got to my house. The EMTs told me she's the third person from Thorncombe to be brought to the hospital this week."

"Oh." My heart thuds and pumps dread everywhere in my body. "Oh God."

"I went down to the newsagent's to ask around. There's a good handful of people who are sick now—fever, bleeding, hallucinations— including Charlie and Gemma."

"The May King and Queen from the village?" I ask. "But they're only teenagers."

"I don't know if age matters when it comes to this, Auden."

I look from the house to my hands, which lay uselessly in my lap. Useless like the rest of me. "Do you think the doctors will be able to help?"

"They weren't able to help Rebecca, were they? It's hard to imagine antibiotics or something not working, but if it doesn't, if it's like it is when it's happened before…"

"Then they will die. Unless the door is closed."

I feel Saint looking at me. "There's got to be another way to close it, Auden. And we'll find it, I know we will."

"That's usually my line."

"Well, you didn't say it, so I had to. I'm worried you're thinking of very stupid things right now."

I shift so I can look at him again. "Me too."

It's the first time he's seen my eyes in the light, and his lips part. "Your eyes."

"I know. I know."

He stares at me with worry, with fascination too, and that's when I notice the moisture on his forehead, the barely-there smudges under his lower eyelids. The dread in my blood is more than dread now—it's panic.

"No," I say, moving onto my knees so I can look at him better. "No."

He looks down, but he lets me touch his face, cradle his jaw.

"You can't be sick," I say fiercely. "I won't allow it."

"It's only been since this morning," he says. "Just a fever. And I saw—I saw the graveyard. You know the one. The headstones and the wall and the tree we sat under when you drew on me. I woke up and they were all in your room."

I press my forehead to his. "Stop it," I plead. "Stop being sick right now."

He huffs out a laugh against my mouth. "Even you can't boss this around, Auden Guest."

"I can try."

"Yes," he says sadly. "You can."

"Will you go to the doctor?"

"Of course. I'm not putting all my health eggs into the magic door basket, I promise."

The relief is minor, but palpable. I relax a little and let my hands fall from his face. "Will you go back to school?"

"No," he says slowly. "I don't think I will. Two of my classes can be managed remotely, I think, but a third I'll need to retake. But I want to stay here."

"I want you here," I say ferociously, and he nods.

"I know you do." He blinks then, and yawns. "I could fall asleep right now, you know, I'm that tired."

I move so I'm sitting again, and then I guide him to lay his head on my lap, which he does without any resistance whatsoever.

"Sleep," I say. "I'll wake you when it's time to go back."

And he nods against my leg, his breathing already slowing. I stroke his hair as the storm rolls over us without breaking, and as the breeze sends leaves and petals dancing everywhere.

He sleeps and I keep my eyes trained on the woods below, on the chapel and door within them, thinking of Estamond's words to me a long time ago.

That is the price, you see.

The price of what?

You will learn.

27

Proserpina

One week before Samhain, I fall asleep in the library as a storm darkens the daylight into lightning-split murk.

Auden's in his office. Rebecca and Saint have both drifted off to nap—they've been feeling a little better the past few days after the doctor prescribed them some strong anti-inflammatories but they still tire easily—and Delphine and Becket, who've also developed fevers this week, are resting in their rooms. As a precaution, Auden's halted the last stages of the old wing's renovation, and he's given Abby paid leave for the next few weeks, too. So aside from the six of us, the house is empty.

And it feels like it. It feels like an empty church in here. Or maybe a passage tomb. Our very own Newgrange, filled with old books, older blankets, and half-empty bottles of Night Nurse.

Exhaustion has been nipping at my heels all day, and so as the fog and clouds resolve themselves into a hearty, thundery rain, I leave my piles of books and notes and find a squashy sofa to lie down on. Even with all the blankets heaped around me, I shiver. And when I look across the library, I see my mother standing by the window, her arms crossed and her expression fixed on the forest outside. She's wearing her favorite type of outfit—practical cargo pants, a sturdy button-down shirt with a tank top underneath, boots meant for hopping in and out of excavation trenches. There's an orange Rite in the Rain notebook dangling from her fingertips and a pencil jabbed through her messy bun, and she looks like she's just strolled into the room from a dig somewhere dusty and blue-skied. But of course she didn't. She didn't because she's dead, so very dead, and this isn't real.

She's not real.

But I still like watching her as I fall asleep anyway.

Sleep comes like a shipwreck. I'm sinking, sputtering, kicking, and then suddenly I'm on the unfamiliar shore of a dream. A new dream—one I haven't had before.

For a moment, I think I might be awake again, and this is a vision, because there is my mother, in more sturdy, sensible clothes, wearing more sturdy, dig-ready boots, but she is also in a coat now, and there's no notebook dangling from her fingertips, only a single piece of paper instead.

Fog drifts everywhere. The trees are dripping leaves of orange and red, and when I look down, I see stray black petals tossing and tumbling around my feet.

I know, with a certainty that goes deeper than logic, that this is Samhain, twelve years ago.

I know that I'm seeing the day she died.

I'm walking with her in the dream, and we're moving fast, so fast I can barely keep up. She's striding from an already-departing cab to Thornchapel's doors and not bothering to knock before she pushes them open. They swing into a silent hall, opening into the grayish darkness of mid-afternoon. Which at this latitude makes the shadows stretch and stretch and stretch—

My mother goes to the library, calling out Ralph's name. Even in her obvious distress and worry, her voice is sunny, bright, assertive. I could listen to her saying Ralph's name over and over again for a hundred years and not get sick of it.

I miss you, I try to say, but it's not that kind of dream. It's the kind of dream where I am less than a ghost, not even a shade. She won't hear me or see me, and I can't change anything, affect anything, undo any tragedies or speak any long-denied declarations. I am a presence only to myself, and I'm bound to her movements, drawn along in her wake as she leaves the library and searches the old wing, calling for Ralph the entire time.

The house is as it was that summer—carpeted in an ugly green, musty in some places, thoroughly decrepit in others. But it's not like that summer in that it seems to be completely empty—there's no sign of the Guests at all. There is only my mother and her increasingly urgent calls.

When she finishes with the inside of the house, she wastes no time going to the south lawn, where the maze still sprawls like something from a storybook. And where, at the very edges of the forest, I can make out the bruise-colored smudges of roses growing between the trees.

In the distance, I see the caretaker with a wheelbarrow—the same one who will later give evidence to the police—but my mother pays him no mind. She walks as fast as she can into the maze, under the reaching arms of Demeter and Persephone, taking the bends and turns with the rushing efficiency of someone who knows the way.

And before long, we are slipping between the splashing fountain and the statue of Adonis and Aphrodite, taking the stairs quickly in the dark, taking the tunnel just as quickly. Very soon, we are in the woods.

The black roses came this time too, although not as thickly it seems. Instead of crowding the forest and climbing eagerly toward the house, they've merely crawled up the trees and settled into the cracks of the stones and boulders along the way. My mother stops to look at them one time only, crouching down and examining a bloom and some dark rose hips dangling nearby, before she resumes her half-jog to the chapel. That paper is still between her fingers, folded into crisp, neat squares.

I think I know what's on that paper.

Actually, I *know* I know what's on that paper.

But as we reach the clearing, I abruptly find that I don't want to know a single thing more. I don't want to see a single thing more. I want to go back to the house and listen to her voice as she calls for her ex-lover, I want to follow her around and watch the light move through her hair. I want to stare at the no-nonsense watch on her wrist and remember all the times I sat in her lap watching the numbers change while she graded papers.

I don't want to see her step into the chapel, I don't want to see if Ralph is there.

I don't want to see her die.

I try to stay in the forest, I do. I bend all of my will toward it. I focus as hard as I can. *Stay. Stay.*

Stay.

Do not go.

But this is a dream, and in a way, it's not even my dream, not truly, and I'm pulled there, I'm pulled closer to where I don't want to be. I don't even lift my feet, and I'm suddenly inside the chapel, inside the crumbling walls covered with the door-roses, listening to my mother argue with Ralph.

She's crying.

He's crying.

I look up to see them talking, shouting, gesturing—her with the paper in her hand—him with an old-fashioned knife in his. He doesn't brandish it at her, he isn't holding it like a man contemplating murder, he's only waving it as he talks, as if he's forgotten he's holding it at all.

The torc gleams around his neck.

"I won't let you," she's saying, and the words are fierce and unwavering despite the tears on her face.

"You should," he chokes.

He looks so much like Auden. The same light brown hair, the same hazel eyes…the same long, elegant nose and wide mouth. He even cries the same way Auden cries, in a quiet, resigned way that's far more powerful than any plangent wailing ever could be. "I meant to tell you that when you called me. That you should let me. That you need to let me. It has to be this way—kings go to the door at Thornchapel. They must. *Convivificat.*"

"I'm telling you," Mom is saying, her voice frantic. "It's not a warning. It's never been a warning, nor a threat—it's not what we thought, Ralph, I swear—"

"It needs death."

"It needs *sacrifice*. They're different—"

"I've already tried symbolic sacrifice, Adelina, it doesn't work!"

"There's another way. We saw it in the stories. Not symbolic at all, but not this either. Not suicide or murder!"

"The stories are too fictionalized, and you know that. You know I can't risk it."

My mother is gesturing now, up to the moors. "It's not just the stories—it's in the archaeology too, only I didn't understand it until now. It's in the gap between the Neolithic and the Saxons—no mass graves, no buried kings. For centuries the people in this valley knew there was another way to live with it, I'm certain of it. And maybe the Kernstows forgot, I don't know, maybe something changed or they became too desperate to trust anything other than death, but there was another way once. There can be another way now!"

Ralph shakes his head. Even with wet eyes and a knife in his hand, he is unbearably handsome. Infused with charisma. Seeing him with the torc around his neck and the very air around him practically burning with his presence, I think I understand a little why our parents loved him. Why my parents in particular loved him.

"Freddie couldn't get through, remember?"

"But he wasn't trying to get *through*, he was trying to close it. Ralph, there is more than one way to sacrifice a life—"

A quiet crack, like the snap of a dry stick, comes from behind us. My mother and Ralph turn toward the sound, Ralph stepping forward with his eyes on the trees.

"Did anyone else come with you?" he asks in a low voice.

"David doesn't know I'm here, and I haven't talked to any of the others. I came alone."

"The caretaker knows not to come here," Ralph says, peering into the trees. The tears are drying on his face now, but there's still desperation written onto every line of his body. My mother sees it too, taking his elbow and turning him toward her. Her eyes dart down to the knife in his hand and then back up to his glassy hazel eyes.

"We have time before night comes," she whispers. "Please believe me. I'll make you believe me. I'll snap my fingers and make you crawl until you believe me."

Ralph shudders at her words, the pulse in his throat beating fast under his torc. "Adelina, don't torment me," he breathes. "I can't take it. I can't take knowing what I'll never have, and I'll never believe you that this is supposed to be a blessing when—"

The cracking noise comes again, and Ralph steps between it and my mother, which is when she lunges for the knife in his hand.

He turns to stop her, to grapple it back, and then someone else is there, clambering over the wall, and just as I look, the world splits open in a flash so bright I'm blinded by it, and I lurch forward to help or to run, I don't know—

And I jolt right into the outstretched arms of Auden Guest. Deafening thunder is still rolling through the library from the lightning strike, and he's holding me like I'm a child in need of comfort, which I am in a way, I am.

"It's just a storm," he says, coming to sit on the couch and pulling me into his lap. He rocks me slowly, slowly, murmuring to me until the adrenaline ebbs away, until my brain is able to process that I'm fine, I'm not in danger, the knife in the chapel isn't real, my mother's pleas aren't real. They happened too long ago to hurt me now.

I look up at Auden, trying to remember what my mother said, needing to tell him.

Not a warning, but a blessing.

A blessing.

But it's hard to speak, it's hard to force the words past my lips, and I'm dangerously close to falling asleep again.

"You're burning up," he says, pressing his wrist against my forehead. "Proserpina…"

The anguish on his face is nearly unbearable to see. It looks so much like his father's that day in the chapel.

"A blessing," I manage to tell him before sliding back into a sleep filled with bright, fever-fed dreams. This time, without my mother.

28

Auden

Four days later, and Poe is out of hospital and back at Thornchapel. Specialist appointments have been lined up; I've brought in a rose cutting so it can be tested for sporotrichosis or something similar; they've scanned all the scans and bled all the blood for an array of tests. Currently she's taking anti-inflammatories like the others, and she's also claiming she's well enough to work in the library, which I allow on the condition that I be in there with her to make sure she's not overtaxing herself.

By her request, we haven't told her father. In fact, no one's parents know—the consensus being that the parents would somehow intuit the connection to Thornchapel and either demand their children leave—or come here themselves and cause an even bigger mess.

As someone who has no parents left to worry over him, I suspect they're making a choice they might regret later, but my protests haven't persuaded them. And in this at least, I've allowed myself to be overruled. For now.

To be honest, I haven't the will to fight them on it. With Saint *and* Poe sick, with Rebecca and the others sick too, I am consumed with a quiet, desperate panic. It is all I think, all I feel.

They cannot die.

They cannot.

In any event, the library has become something of a private hospital this past week. Everyone is able to care for themselves for the most part, able to walk and talk and move and eat, but there is a slowness to them, a languidness that's near to the sultry indolence of summer, but burning with fever and pain rather than lust. And every now and again, their eyes slide to the side, and I know they're seeing their own particular visions. Wrens and tombstones and mothers.

Everyone insists on helping Poe look for answers, especially now that it's all anyone can do. They sit and flip through books, searching for anything that will close the door. Anything that isn't murder.

"This is interesting," Poe says from her chair. Her cheeks are rouged with sickness, but she's more lively tonight than she has been, and I'm trying to modulate my relief. I'm trying to dampen my hope. If she and everyone else can just hang on until... Until what, I don't know, but at least until Samhain. At least until I can try to close the door.

"The locals Reverend Dartham talked about in his journal said that if the door should appear, then the Guests have done their duty and gone to the altar in the woods. But at least for the outbreaks during the Restoration and during King Stephen's reign, there wasn't a Guest in Thornchapel at all."

Rebecca closes her book around a plastered finger. "That *is* interesting."

"In the 1100s, the two Guest brothers of Thornchapel were listed among the knights leaving from Dartmouth for the Second Crusade," says Poe, holding up a slender volume she's been reading. "And during the Restoration, the Guest landowner—Robert Guest—was on the Continent for his Grand Tour. It makes me wonder…"

I know what she's thinking. I'm thinking it too. "There wasn't a Guest here the other times the sickness came."

"It would explain why the sickness spread over the valley at some times, and not others."

The rain has stopped for now, but it's been several days of moody, disconsolate fog, and we've kept the fire going in the library to drive away the damp. A log cracks and slides partway off the grate as we think about this.

"It does seem like the door comes more often than the sickness," Becket agrees from his chair.

"It also explains why Estamond's mother was so emphatic about closing the door," Poe says, her eyes on the crumbling log in the fire. "She knew the illness was coming if Estamond didn't. It makes me think the Kernstows have done it before—shut the door if the Guests couldn't, I mean. The plague during King Stephen's time ended around midwinter, even though the Guest brothers didn't return from the Holy Land for two more years. And the Restoration outbreak stops listing deaths after All Saint's Day, even though Robert Guest was still in Italy at the time."

I get up to stir the fire and add another log. "They must have shut it when it first appeared then. And not waited as we have."

"Yes, but—" Poe sighs and shifts in her chair a little. "I still think there must be another way. In my dream, my mother said that 'it awakens' was meant as a blessing. That the Dumnonii saw it that way—which we now know matches the pollen record Tobias included in the report, because after the cists, there's no record of the roses coming from the chapel until Saxon times. In my dream, my mother said we don't have any evidence of human sacrifice during that era either. No bones. No mass graves or king graves."

"That was the time of the Kernstows," I point out. "At least according to the scant history we have. And if the Kernstows knew another way—a way that wasn't ritual murder—why wouldn't they have told the Guests? Why wouldn't they have remembered later, in Estamond's time, that there was another way?"

"The Kernstows hated the Guests," Poe reminds me. "Is it so hard to imagine them hiding this final secret from them? After they'd taken literally everything else? As for Estamond, she lived thirteen hundred years after Wessex expanded its borders. Is it not possible that the knowledge was lost by then?"

"They remembered enough to watch the door, to close it when they needed to," I counter. "How could they forget something as salient to closing it as *no one needs to die?*"

Her shoulders slump a little. "I don't know. Life was hard on the moors—perhaps one generation died before they could tell the other everything. Perhaps they lost faith in anything other than death, like my mother thought."

Another moment of silence.

"A blessing," St. Sebastian says finally, like he's been bothered by this the whole time. "How could having to sacrifice someone be a blessing?"

"The Thorn King was killed in the woods and his blood fed the land," Becket replies. "That's what Dartham's journal said. Maybe they saw it as essential to renewing not only the land, but any life that was tied to it."

"Or maybe it's a blessing for the king," I say. "If he dies, his blood will protect his people. I suppose that would be the sort of reassurance I would want to hear at the end. The idea that my death would be in service of something good and vital, and—" I stop. I find that I can't say anything more, not without my voice changing. I turn back to the fire and start nudging things with the poker so no one can see my face.

"In my dream, Auden," Poe says slowly, carefully, "your father wasn't threatening my mother. He wasn't acting like someone who'd lured her there to kill her. He was wearing the torc alone in the chapel before she got there…"

I noted this too, when Poe first told me about her dream while I was sitting by her bedside in the hospital. It matches nothing of what I've known about my father, nothing of the manipulative man who wrought destruction and cul-de-sacs wherever he went. But if there was anything he believed in, it was Thornchapel.

It was being a Guest.

And I do believe that he loved Adelina, in his way. He was certainly obsessed with marrying me to her daughter—obsessed in a way that suggested vicarious interest, a desperate sort of do-over with the past.

Of course, if he had murdered her, he might have still felt the same way.

"It's something to think about," I say, adding another log and then standing. The room suddenly feels too close, too intimate, even with the high ceiling and soaring windows. I'm about to offer to get everyone a fresh pot of tea when Delphine speaks up.

"Saint, your mum is in this one!"

We all look over to the book she's flipping through, which is not a book at all, but a volume of bound newspapers. "Well, she wrote this article," Delphine amends.

"Why are you looking at newspapers?" Rebecca asks with some exasperation. "We're meant to be searching through the old stuff."

"I thought," Delphine says, a little primly, "that it would be interesting to read the local papers from when we were here that summer, from when our parents opened the door. We were too young to know what was going on then, weren't we? We wouldn't have known if something important was happening in the valley, and I'm glad I did, because look!" With some effort, she manages to flip the volume around to show us the page she's looking at.

Mysterious Sheep Disease Strikes Valley is the top headline of that day's edition. I step closer so I can make out the date. It's the year our parents opened the door. After Lammas.

"Is there anything about the villagers getting sick later on?" I ask.

"Let's see—Auden, stop hovering, you're in the light and the print on this is so small—here. *Thorncombe Residents Take Ill; Local Officials Urge Farmers to Quarantine Livestock.* It looks like three people were sick when this article was written, and then..." She flips a few more pages. "By the week before Halloween, it was closer to fifteen or twenty residents. Only one had died—a farmer whose farm borders Thornchapel. Everyone else seems to have recovered. Well, except the sheep, the poor dears."

"You're brilliant for thinking to look there," I tell Delphine, and she beams.

"I was rather good at school, you know. Everyone always forgets this because I know how to contour, or something."

"I'll never forget," I promise, dropping a kiss onto her forehead. I can feel her fever burning my lips as I do. "How does a fresh pot of tea sound?" I ask, and then without waiting for an answer, I go to the kitchen.

I am irritated with myself as I go through the familiar ritual of water, kettle, pot. I was going to come in here, collect my thoughts, and then re-emerge with the cool, resolute certainty I've been attempting to exude when I'm with the others. I was going to metabolize my feelings quickly and efficiently, and then get back to the business of saving my friends and my valley.

But I'm not metabolizing, I'm not collecting anything. My thoughts feel like the leaves on the trees outside—flapping, trembling, dangling—and then suddenly torn off and blown away. I can't hold on to a single one of them, much less gather up many and restore some kind of order.

I used to be so sure of things. How was I so sure of the world and its problems and my responsibilities to them? When I knew so little?

How did everything change so fast?

A petal tumbles out of my eye, dropping to the floor as I try to rub away the bleary pain it leaves behind. I throw it in the bin.

The door to the kitchen opens, and Sir James prances over to lick Abby's hand, his tail going in big circles as she reaches down to pet him.

"Abby," I greet, coming in to kiss her cheeks, which are cool from the damp air outside. "I figured you wouldn't even want to think of this place while you were on holiday, much less stop by." I'm very grateful there're no lights on in the kitchen right now, and the shadows can camouflage my rose-colored eyes.

"I left my reading glasses," Abby tells me, returning the kisses. She's much shorter than I am, and she has to raise up on the balls of her feet to do it, even when I'm already bending down. I pull away to see that the fine lines around her eyes and mouth are etched more deeply than usual.

"I'm sure they're in here somewhere," I assure her, turning to help her look. "How has your holiday been?"

"Very poor. I'm sure you've heard about the illness going around—my aunt is in hospital right now, and I'm going up to Exeter tonight to stay with her."

Her glasses are resting on top of an old recipe book still open on the hutch, and I hand them to her. "I'm very sorry to hear that," I say sincerely. "Is there anything I can do to help? You need only say the word."

"I know," she says, managing a watery kind of smile. "You are good like that. I suppose you heard that little Gemma Dawes died?"

I have the disorienting feeling of the floor tilting beneath my feet. "What?"

"Just this morning. Only seventeen years old, you know. My friend Joanie's daughter. Such a damn waste—" She's crying now, waving me off when I step forward to offer a touch or a hug. "I should go. I need to get to the hospital before visiting hours end."

"Please, let me know if you need anything," I tell her, "and don't even think of coming back until your aunt is better. Please."

She gives me a quick, teary shake of her head. "I'm sure it will be quite all right soon," she says, her words full of forced, determined optimism. "Of course they will be." And then with a quick wave, she's gone through the door—undoubtedly because she doesn't want me to see her crying.

I finish with the tea things and set them on a tray. My hands are shaking badly enough that I make myself stop and clench them into fists.

Gemma Dawes.

This year's May Queen. I can see her now, all red hair and shy smiles as she handed Charlie his victor's bouquet after he won the race on May Day. Young and pretty, the quintessential village beauty. Sweet not on the vigorous, football-playing types, but on Charlie, who spent most of his free time in Saint's library reading.

And now she's dead.

I bring in the tea tray and find that everyone is still occupied with research. They seem well enough—all sitting upright, no one looking lost in pain or delusions or both—and so I quietly excuse myself, saying something about needing to work in my office, and leave.

I don't go to my office. Instead, I pull on some lace-up boots and my favorite wool coat and go outside. By myself, since my faithless dog is currently busy entreating bits of biscuit from the others in the library.

I'm not bothered by it, however, not really. It's better that I be alone right now anyway.

The roses have come up to the south terrace now, crawling between the empty graves and over the walls of the walled garden, like a tide of silk and thorns. Tomorrow, I think, they will reach the house. By Halloween, it will be covered with them.

As before, there is a small and winding path which twists through the roses and into the woods, and from there, into the chapel itself. I follow it, not noticing much, barely aware of the thorns as they snag my trousers and coat, my thoughts on red-haired Gemma Dawes and old newspaper articles and Guests going off on boats to join pointless, immoral wars.

On my father, alone in the chapel with a knife, wearing the torc.

Only last week, we wondered if Adelina Markham had consented to her own death, and now I must wonder the same thing about my father. Had he come to the chapel meaning for it to be him?

Had *he* consented?

The fog is thick, thick enough that the trees and roses disappear into it after only a few feet, and the clearing comes almost like a shock, like the rest of the world has fallen away, and it's only me and the roses and the fog left.

The roses have started climbing up the altar again—only along the sides—and when I walk around it, I see that some of the blooms have fallen totally away to reveal berries the same dark color as the flowers themselves.

Hips. The fruit of the rose plant.

I pull myself up on the altar and pluck one. It seems the same as any other rose hip, shiny and round and tendriled with green sepals at the bottom. Rose hips are usually edible, but I don't know what would happen if someone ate these. If they took the fruit inside themselves. Poe said a knight in one of her stories ate rose hips to stay with his fairy queen…I wonder if these would work in the same way. Bind you somehow to the door forever or to the world beyond it.

And if that were true, would it apply to all parts of the rose? The petals, the thorns? Maybe I've been marked for this ever since I pricked my thumb on Midwinter's Day. Like Aurora in the fairy tale, except read in reverse—I was pricked and then I was cursed.

I draw a knee up and drape my arm over it, still holding the small hip in my hand. I roll it between my fingers as I study the door, watching the clearing on the other side. There's no one and nothing. No strange flowers, no dying birds. No shadowed figures moving through the fog.

And here in the chapel, there is nothing either. There's no herd of deer, no Estamond, no vision of my father wearing a torc. No signs.

Maybe that's because I don't need them.

I thought I did, I was hoping for them when I walked out to the chapel. I hoped for some small whisper of magic either so terrible or so wonderful that my choice would be made incontestably clear. I thought it was a decision that could only be made after hours of agony, a decision that had to be yoked with omens and doom.

But I realize now, sitting on the altar and watching the fog drift and curl on the other side of the door, that I didn't come here to decide.

I came here to grieve.

Sometimes choices are like that—lightning instead of thunder, a windfall instead of a harvest.

A puncture instead of a slice.

I thought I would need hours and hours, days and days, and here I am, mind made up with almost no work at all. I've thought longer and harder about where to place a fake tree on an architectural model; I've spent significantly more brainpower on choosing new wrist cuffs for Proserpina while shopping online. But for this, the answer is there like the door is there, like my love for St. Sebastian and Proserpina is there. Eminent and manifest.

I just…know.

Setting the rose hip aside, I pull my legs up onto the altar so they're comfortably crossed, and I push my fingers through my hair as I let the knowing overwhelm me. The choice was fast, maybe, but the knowing still isn't easy. It isn't easy at all—it feels like the hardest thing I've ever done. And it will be the hardest thing I've ever done, right until the moment I have to do the last thing I'll ever do—and that...

That will be the hardest.

I'm scared and I'm lonely and I don't want to do this, no matter how much of a blessing it might be, no matter that people before me have done it too. No matter that Estamond did it and my father tried to. I bury my face in my hands, feeling the tears on my palms before I even realize I'm crying.

I don't want to leave Proserpina and Saint. I don't want to be apart from them. Without them. Even if the gate to death leads to absolutely nothing and everything I am dissolves into everything else, I will somehow still know that I am without my two people, and I can't bear it, I can't bear it.

This the price, though. The price of love. The price of care.

The price of holding people inside your heart.

A true king pays the price. He pays himself.

The afternoon has begun its long stretch into dusk, that October dusk which lasts for hours and hours, and I finally straighten up, my face swollen with crying, my throat hurting like some Druid's already twisting a thrice-knotted cord around my neck. I am dizzy and hollowed out and filled back up with a purpose that feels as alien as it does familiar.

I've known that success must be earned, praise must be earned.

Love and trust and submission must be earned.

And so the necessity of this is a truth I think I've always known, deep in my bones, starting from that wedding in this very chapel when the thorns of possession and love grew through my heart for the very first time.

Yes, this is the truth I've always known, given to me not only by the pagans, but by the Church and my tragic, thorn-crowned god on his cross. The very same truth that Thornchapel was built around.

Life must be earned too.

And there is now so much for me to do before Samhain.

29

Proserpina

I think it's a good plan," Becket says quietly.

We're all in the library, save for Auden, who went to London for an urgent Harcourt + Trask project and still hasn't returned. How funny to think that life goes on, that buildings must be built, and meetings must be had. How funny to think that there is a world where life and death don't dangle from the lintel of a door in the woods.

"I agree," Delphine says. She's clutching a mug of elderflower tea—we read somewhere that it might help with fevers—and when she lifts it to take a drink, I can see the small cuts all over her hands and wrists and forearms, like she fell into a rose bush.

The room smells of roses. We've become a human garden.

"What will we need again?" Rebecca asks, looking over at the blackboard. "Do we have everything already?"

"Lanterns, firewood, fire supplies, the torc, a knife—" I read off the board. "Do you think any knife works? Are there special ones in the cases?"

St. Sebastian pushes out of his chair to go look. His eyes are bright with fever, glittering in the dark. "There are some knives here, pale and old looking—maybe made of bone?"

"At least we wouldn't need to worry about tetanus," remarks Rebecca dryly.

"Do they look sharp enough to cut?" I ask. "They'll need to be sharp enough to cut into the effigy. Which reminds me—we need an effigy."

"I can do it," St. Sebastian says. "Tomorrow. I'll take what I can from the walled garden."

We'd decided that the effigy should be made of Thornchapel—a stick each from ash, beech, birch, elder, oak, rowan, and yew, whatever plants and herbs we could find in the walled garden. We would sprinkle it with someone's blood—Auden's probably—and then it would be crowned with the torc and killed like a king.

"Effigies crop up so often in the sources we've found," Becket says. "This has to work. This has to be the way."

He sounds like he's trying to convince himself. I know the feeling, although I've only half committed to our plan. The doubt burns in me hotter than any fever, and if it doesn't work—

If killing the king-effigy doesn't work, then we need to have an alternative. An alternative that isn't everyone in this room and in the village—and maybe the valley—dying. And while I want to hope that science and medicine will find a cure, they haven't yet, and Samhain is tomorrow. Our chance is tomorrow.

What will a cure matter if it comes too late?

"Do you think the other side of the door is like heaven?" Delphine asks. "Poe said that Estamond saw someone on the other side. Do you think it can be like some kind of afterlife? But then how would that work with the fairy stories of people moving back and forth?"

"I've wondered the same thing," I say, sitting in a chair and wishing I could slip under the surface of consciousness. I've just taken some medicine, and when the medicine pushes the pain away, all I want to do is sleep.

I gesture to the far table, where Becket, Saint, and I have organized all the fairy tales into stacks of subcategories. At the very end of the table, there is a stack that only contains one book. "In almost every story where people go to fairyland and are able to leave again, they are alive when they go through the door. Some are sick, some are dying, but they are still alive. And many of them come back. But in that one"—I nod to the book, *Tale of the Two Sisters and Other Such Stories*—"there's a story where two sisters are quarreling about who will wear a certain necklace to a fairy ball as they're approaching the gate to fairyland. In a rage, one sister kills the other, but immediately regrets what she's done. Hoping a fairy healer can bring her sister back, she carries her sister through the gate and into the fairy realm, where her sister starts breathing once more. The fairy prince rides out from the revel and warns the resurrected sister that she can never go back now, she can never leave fairyland again. But he offers her his hand in marriage, and so the murdering sister is doubly punished—not only will she lose her sister forever if she chooses to return to the mortal world, but then as a princess, her sister is draped in jewels and finery far better than the necklace they'd originally fought over."

"So in that story, the door is more like a one-way ticket?" St. Sebastian asks.

"But she died first," Becket explains. "So in the logic of the story, it's only one way if death is involved."

It needs death.

It needs sacrifice. *They're different.*

"Which is why I've put it in its own category," I say, and then I rub at my forehead. Each blink threatens to send me under, and I can feel the narcolepsy holding me like a Dominant by the back of the neck. "Is there anything else to do tonight? If not, I suggest we rest for tomorrow. It will be a long day." And a hard one, if I have to do what I think I'll have to do, but I don't say that. I don't want to scare them— and I also can't let them know what I'm thinking.

They'll try to stop me.

The others agree, and there is some shuffling around, some grabbing of mugs, dousing of the fire. Everyone filters from the room, except for St. Sebastian. He's tiredly pulling on his boots, as if he's about to leave for his house in the village. He's stayed over a few nights when he absolutely felt too sick to leave, but otherwise he's been refusing to sleep here.

I stand in front of him, catching his chin with my fingers.

He blinks up at me. Even with his fevered gaze and the smudges under his eyes, he is beautiful. Those angular cheeks, that sharp jaw. So much silky hair feathering darkly over his forehead.

"Stay," I say. "It's not good for you to walk home in the cold. I worry."

"I shouldn't..."

"Tomorrow is Samhain." *And I might have to do something terrible and terrifying and I'm scared and I don't want to be alone.*

"Please, Saint. I want you here."

He stares up at me a moment longer, chewing on his lip. "I guess Auden isn't here…"

"He might come back," I say as Saint stands up. "He said he'd be back in time for Samhain."

"So I did," says Auden from the library doors. We both turn and look at him, and even though he's not sick like the rest of us, there's a strange look to him, something sharp and gorgeous and cold and burning all at once. Like he's one of the fairy princes from beyond the door. "And here I am now. And yes, St. Sebastian, you're staying tonight."

There is no question in whose bed St. Sebastian will be sleeping.

When we reach the bedroom, Auden strips off his jumper and shirt, revealing a tightly etched body. St. Sebastian says, in a hoarse, heated voice, "Auden."

Auden looks at him, patient and impatient all at once.

"I'll promise you anything you want," Saint whispers.

Auden shakes his head, his fingers already on his trouser buttons. "Not tonight, St. Sebastian. Tonight is—" A look of powerful sadness passes over his face. "Tonight isn't about that. It's not about the past or the future. It's about the three of us. Right now. Just us."

I look down so he can't see the tears gathering in my eyes. He doesn't know how true those words are, because tomorrow—

No. I'm not going to think about it right now. I have my hopes. I have my fears.

I have my choices.

Let that be enough.

"Okay," Saint whispers. "Just us."

"Are you two well enough…?"

"Yes," St. Sebastian and I rush to say at the same time.

"I can't do big pain right now," I say. "Maybe just small pain. Some bruises. But I can—and want—to fuck."

Auden breathes out slowly. "I don't need your pain, either of you. I only need you. I'm glad you're well enough, because I—" He stops, looking very sad again. Us being sick has taken such a terrible toll on him. I know he's scared and worried and if we died and left him here…

He won't be alone though. I'll make sure of it.

"I know," I say, stepping forward. "We need you too."

Auden is naked now, and wonderful, his strong thighs and his narrow hips framing a silky swirl of hair and his already stiffened organ. He swallows, looking between Saint and me.

"Twelve years," he says. "That's how long ago we were bound together. I can't believe I ever wasted a single second of it."

And then he's over to me, kissing me so hard it steals the breath right from my lungs. He presses his thumbs to the corners of my lips to open my mouth more for him, searching out my tongue and then stroking desperately and hungrily against it. "Clothes off," he says urgently against my lips. "Please."

But I move too slowly, the fever makes me too hazy and languid for him, and I'm swept off my feet to the bed, where Auden undresses me with an eagerness that sets me on fire all over again. Saint has gotten undressed too and is now breathing hard—from the fever or lust or both, I don't know—and then we are all naked in bed together, there is nothing but skin and hands and kisses, and for the first time since Beltane, there is nothing between us. No walls, no ultimatums.

No shadows. It is just us and Auden's hunger, just us and the knowledge that Samhain is coming.

Just this, and what I'll do tomorrow.

But that only stirs me more and more, knowing that this is the last time, the last joining, the last time our hearts will beat together as we kiss and seek and fuck.

"Can you take us both?" Auden asks, tearing away from a kiss to stare down at me. His eyes are completely changed now, that unearthly black-red, and his lips are swollen with kissing. He is all fairy prince again, or maybe vampire, or maybe it's just Thorn King, and I'm nodding yes, because I want it so badly and also because saying yes to him when he's like this is a pleasure on its own, a gift.

"Yes," I say, and he's reaching behind him for something in the end table; he hands it to Saint.

"On your side, hold on to me," Auden instructs. I roll and wrap my arms around him, and then I bury my face in his strong throat while Saint opens the lube bottle behind me.

I sigh as Saint begins anointing me with lube, making me ready for him, and then there is the hot press of him, the wide, flared head pushing against me.

"Breathe," Auden murmurs, and with my lips against his throat, I feel his command reverberating through my very skin. I nod, and then I breathe.

Saint goes slowly but the stretch of him is so wide, so much, and my body reacts with quivers, goose bumps, small noises that I can't control. He groans behind me as he goes in, and then rolls his forehead against the nape of my neck. "I never want to stop doing this," he mumbles, giving me a small thrust that has us both gasping. "Never."

Auden laughs a little, and his laugh tickles my mouth. "Me either," he says. "Me either."

His fingers find my cleft, wet from me and from the trickling lube, and then he carefully moves my thigh to his hip.

He pulls back, red-black eyes glinting. "Yes?"

"Yes, Sir."

He grunts; he likes hearing that, as always. And then he has his penis at my inner folds, and with an inexorable push, he wedges his way inside.

I am so full, I am filled, and it's almost too much to bear, but that's how I like it, how I've always liked it. Pleasure and pain mingling together like water dropped into scotch, mixing and swirling and opening the senses to more and more and more. And to be joined with them like this, tonight, for the last time...

Saint is behind me, kissing the nape of my neck and my hair and my shoulder like I'm a goddess he is servicing, like I am the object of his humble worship. Auden is in front of me, dark-eyed and wild, his fingers leaving bruises on my hips and tits and jaw. Our breathing is ragged, huge, joined—breathing together, moving together, our gasps and sighs and pulses all in one beautiful symphony.

There is more than one way to sacrifice a life.

That's what my mother said, and she was right. Because to walk away from this—to leave it behind—it would be my entire life. Giving them up will bleed me dry.

A blessing, though. It will be a blessing to them.

Auden bends to kiss me, his kisses wicked and snarling and he's feral tonight, like he was on Beltane but even more so, like he's not the one hunting but the one being chased and then he moves to bite my neck, and that's it, that's all the pain and pleasure I can hold without dying, and I come.

Sharp, primal pleasure detonates everywhere in my core—not just behind my clit, but in my cunt, in my womb, in all the low places in my belly. My thighs tense, my toes curl, and my hands are scratching everywhere, everywhere, because I can't handle it, this climax is bigger than me, bigger than my body can hold, and it's the last one—

I'm twisting and whimpering, speared in place by two cocks, and Saint follows me first, crying out against my neck as his organ gives a thick, heavy jolt inside my body and begins to spend.

Auden yanks him into a kiss above my head, and they clash together like not even God himself can keep them apart, and then Auden's coming too, with sharp, filthy grunts as he fucks his orgasm deep into my belly.

He breaks away from his kiss with Saint and then kisses me, and then we're all kissing each other, and there's more then, more of everything. More lube, more positions, more gropes and little bruises and bites and cries into the night. Through it all, Auden pours everything into us, his lust and his focus and his strength, and Saint and I receive it gladly. Though we are fevered, sick, and afraid, with our king, we are only whole. With our king, we are three.

And for tonight, we have joy.

30

In The Hour of My Death Call Me
St. Sebastian

The letter in his back pocket might as well be an ingot of molten iron burning through his clothes.

It was waiting for him on the mat when he walked into his house this morning, and he nearly pounced on it when he saw it, he nearly tore into it with his teeth, that's how much he needed what was inside. But then when he picked it up to open it, he found that his fingers would not cooperate. They wouldn't tear at the corner, they wouldn't slide under the flap. They wouldn't rip the side from top to bottom to retrieve the letter inside.

At first he thought it was because he wanted to savor the anticipation, that it was a sort of paternity Christmas morning, and he needed to enjoy that subtle, electric space between *almost-having* and having. He was justified in waiting until the exact right moment to open this and encounter the knowledge inside.

But then he finished at the house, and he still hadn't opened it. He tore at the roses twining around the semi's front door before he left, and he still hadn't opened it. He went back to Thornchapel, and he still hadn't opened it.

He'd pulled it out; he'd held it up to the light to see if he could read what was inside; he stared at the envelope so long that he practically had the laboratory's address memorized by now...

But he hadn't opened it. He hadn't even tried.

And so, while he gathered the mums and pansies and grass and dying lavender and baby's breath with the envelope tucked into his back pocket, he called himself all sorts of things. Cowardly, craven, weak.

Fickle and inconstant. A disappointment to himself.

It's only as he's finishing the effigy now, hours later, that he recognizes the feeling beneath the relief, beneath the fear. It's a quiet feeling, a steady one, nothing loud or brash like the others, but it's trickling right from the heart of him, cool and clear like water from a spring.

It's certainty.

Not about the letter's contents, but about what they won't change.

He sets the effigy in the courtyard, and then he goes to tuck the letter into the bag of clothes he brought, because he doesn't need to open it to know he's ready to promise Auden anything. Everything.

Forever no matter what.

Rebecca

She wakes as she always does these days. With restlessness, with aching, with the chirps and trills of a wren that doesn't exist. But today she also wakes up with her kitten tucked next to her, and for a moment, before she can talk herself out of it, she thinks maybe it's almost worth it. The fever, the pain, the possibility of death—just to have this. To have Delphine's round bottom tucked sweetly against her hips, to have her entire world be warm skin and tousled hair and the smell of berries and violets.

Sickness has a way of clarifying things, of distilling them down, and last night, Rebecca saw clearly for the first time in months. Here at the very edge of everything they've ever known to be true, Rebecca was tired of pretending her choices were simple or stark. She was tired of ignoring what she wanted in favor of what she *should* want. She was tired of loving Delphine and lying to herself about it.

Her father had been right—love was quantum. Love was multi-dimensional, alchemical, complex, and the alternative was void, the frozen absolute zero of the deepest space. Nothingness.

If vulnerability, if trust and intimacy, brought the risk of pain with it—well. Wasn't that better than a life at zero degrees Kelvin, feeling nothing, loving nothing, unharmed maybe, but unknown and unseen to anyone? Wasn't it better to be known? Better to be seen?

And if Delphine were to get sicker, were to die, Rebecca couldn't bear it if she didn't know. If she didn't know that Rebecca loved her so much that all her nerve endings were seared with it.

They had been loosely sharing a bedroom these past two weeks— at first so Delphine could nurse Rebecca, and then later after Delphine fell ill too, so Rebecca could have her nearby, could more easily assuage the anxious terror that filled her whenever she thought of Delphine slipping into the long sleep of the ancient villagers.

So last night as they readied themselves for bed, Rebecca found Delphine's hands and pulled her close, and then kissed her. Kissed her until their mouths were both plump and wet with it. Kissed her until Delphine sank dazed onto the edge of the bed.

"I'm sorry," Rebecca whispered. "What you said in my office—you were right to. I want more than just to fuck, I want more than friendship. I want us together."

Delphine blinked up at her. "You do? But can you ever forgive—"

"Yes," Rebecca said simply. "I can." She paused. "I have."

And maybe she'd forgiven Delphine a long time ago and was only able to admit to herself now. Or maybe the forgiveness had come right then, spilled into existence like quarks spilling from a smashed atom, waiting only for her to set the forgiveness in motion. Maybe, like love, forgiveness was quantum. Several things at once, visible and invisible, messy and leaving broken rules in its wake.

"Oh, Rebecca," Delphine murmured, eyes shining with tears. "Mistress."

It didn't matter that they were sick—Rebecca was certain even on her deathbed hearing Delphine utter that word would get her wet—and so she'd dragged her pet to bed. And despite the fever, they found several long, quivering releases in the dark. This morning Rebecca can still smell their sex in the air, heady and lingering.

They will have to go to the chapel tonight. They will have to pray their effigy idea works. If it doesn't, then Rebecca isn't sure what they'll do—throw themselves at the baffled mercy of the doctors who still don't understand their disease, she supposes.

But it's not time to walk to the chapel yet. Rebecca pulls

Delphine's backside more tightly against her pelvis and then reaches between Delphine's legs to stroke her awake. Her girlfriend, her sub.

The love of her life and more her destiny than any door ever could be.

Proserpina

Persephone, her sort-of namesake, ate pomegranate seeds, but Proserpina is making do with a tea today. She's sitting on the floor in the Long Gallery, cutting rose hips in half and scooping the seeds into a small bowl. The inner flesh of the hips is redder than the outside, and when she's done, her hands are stained scarlet. She hopes no one notices.

Maybe she can wear gloves.

There is no electricity in the gallery, so she goes downstairs to one of the newly renovated bedrooms to plug in the kettle. While she waits for the water to be ready, she watches the world outside the window. Roses are everywhere, petals kicked up by a melancholy breeze. Fog clings to the forest still, eddying between the trunks and draping the moors with its silvery veil. It feels like Halloween. It feels like a day for graveyards and ghosts.

It feels like a day to step between worlds.

The kettle clicks off, and she starts steeping the hips, cleaning up after herself as she waits. This is really a kitchen activity, but she can't be seen, no one can know until it's too late.

Unfortunately for her, the *too late* part is the only hitch in her plan. There's no manual for this, there's no entry in the *Physician's*

Desk Reference for rose hips from another world. She has no idea how potent the tea will be, how fast it will act. So she needs to wait until she's in the chapel in case it acts quickly. She wonders if the knight in the fairy tale had any second thoughts before he ate the hips. She wonders if he had the second thoughts *after* he ate the hips, when it was too late.

Convivificat is a blessing, she reminds herself. Saving her friends is a blessing. Going to another world is a blessing.

If only she didn't love Saint and Auden so fucking much.

She pours her tea into a flask and then brings everything downstairs, relieved to see the kitchen is empty. She checks her email one last time to make sure the long letter she's written her father is still scheduled to send tomorrow morning.

She tries washing her hands, but it's no use. The skin of her fingers and palms stays as red as the inside of the rose hips. They stay dyed a bright, lurid crimson.

Under the running water, they look like they're covered in blood.

Delphine

Rebecca is determined to answer one last email before they start readying things to take to the chapel, and so Delphine wanders down to the hall, both tired and fevered and also happy, happy, happy. Rebecca loves her, has forgiven her. She can taste her mistress on her lips still, and on her breast is a single bite mark that sings to her every time she moves.

Even though they are all sick, even though this Samhain is dangerous, fraught, and grim, Delphine finds it impossible to be sad. Not when she can still taste Rebecca and feel her teeth on her tit.

Even though she's on a social media hiatus—for personal reasons, according to the statement she wrote on her Notes app, screenshotted and then posted everywhere—and even though she's sick, she's found comfort in the rituals of hair and makeup and clothes, so she's already dressed to go outside in jeans and a slouchy jumper. She steps into a pair of Hunters she keeps here at Thornchapel and goes out to the south terrace, which overlooks a lawn covered in rose bushes. Even the graves have been overtaken by them, and the house—the house is now completely veiled. She turns around to face it, taking a few steps backward so she can see all the way to the end of the Jacobean extension.

Diamond-paned windows glitter from among green thorns and dark blooms. Whenever the breeze moves through the valley, the blossoms wave and tremble and then drip petals into the air, until they fall to the ground like a strange, silky rain.

Delphine lifts her phone and takes a picture, even though she won't post it. She doesn't ever want to forget this. How lovely it is, and how frightening too.

"Beautiful, isn't it?" a quiet voice says from behind her, and it's Auden, he's come from around the other side of the house with Sir James in tow, who is now prancing in circles around Delphine and butting her hand for pets.

"So beautiful," she agrees, stroking Sir James and looking back up at the house. "But in a way that makes me think of ghost stories. It's quite goth."

Auden's mouth quirks. "It is."

"Are you ready for tonight?" she asks him. He looks very handsome today in his crimson jumper and jeans and peacoat, but then again, he's always handsome.

"I am desperate to get it over with," he replies, offering her his arm so they can walk back in together. "I wish I could spur time on like a horse. The waiting is agony."

She knows he's been heavy with worry for all them. She pats his arm as they go inside and Sir James trots off to find someone still abed to snuggle. "The effigy will work. I'm positively certain of it. After all, it's still killing a king, and that's what the door seems to want."

"Yes," he says distantly.

"Auden, I—" She's not sure how to say this, so she just blurts it out. "I want you to know that I'm sorry."

His eyebrows raise—not in sarcasm or disbelief but in genuine surprise. "What on earth for, Delly?"

"For, well, everything, really, but mostly for not ending our engagement sooner, and ending it as abruptly as I did. I love you, you know, and I loved you then, only it was a different sort of love than I first thought. Like it was so natural to love you and then to get engaged that I never stopped to ask myself if it was the right thing to do, and then when I realized it wasn't—when I understood what it was I felt for someone else—it felt like the only remedy was ending things as quickly as I could, setting us both free as soon as possible. Am I making any sense? I'm not, am I?"

"You're making all the sense in the world. I wasn't honest with myself either, you know." He takes her hands, kisses the knuckles on them both. "All is forgiven. All is well. I would have been proud to be your husband, but I'm even prouder to be your friend. To see my two oldest and best friends in love with each other—" When he lifts his head from her knuckles, she can see the smile pulling at his lips. "Remember when you couldn't even be in the same room without fighting?"

"Maybe that should have been my first clue," Delphine says. "Can I kiss you now?"

"Yes," he murmurs. "I would like that."

They've kissed since the engagement ended, of course, mostly at Beltane, but once on the equinox too, but Delphine has forgotten. How firm his lips are, and how warm. How good his mouth tastes, faintly peppery and clean. And when he kisses, he kisses with his fingers in her hair and his thumbs rubbing along her cheeks.

They pull apart after a moment, and Auden's expression is warm when they do.

"I'm glad you are happy," he tells her sincerely. "And knowing I helped in any small way is an honor."

"You're too noble," she replies. "Perhaps that's why you're the king of our little clan."

Something unreadable flits over his face, and he ducks his head. "Perhaps. Have you seen Becket, by any chance?"

"I think he's in the library."

Auden gives her another kiss—a soft touch of their lips—an ex-fiancé's kiss—and then leaves for the library, taking off his coat as he does.

Becket

The zeal greets him when he wakes up and when he starts his day.

It follows him like a storm, like a wind, like a pillar of flame scorching the earth behind him.

He welcomes it.

He used to think that the zeal was an insular gift. One of those blessings that blesses the life of its recipient, but whose ripples are only felt indirectly by everyone else.

But he knows better now.

The zeal will help him today, and therefore it will help everyone.

"Becket," Auden says from the doorway to the library. Becket looks up from the verse he's reading—John 15:13, *greater love hath no man than this, that a man lay down his life for his friends*—to see his friend and Thorn King walking into the room. Auden's eyes are all dark now, all a near-black crimson, and Becket knows his own eyes have changed too. A bright blue like the heart of a flame. The zeal has taken him, just as Thornchapel has taken Auden.

"I was wondering if I could make a confession," says the lord of the manor, sitting in a chair across from Becket. "Before we go out to the chapel tonight."

Suspicion curls through Becket's mind. "In the eyes of the Church, I am no longer allowed to hear confessions, unless someone is at the threshold of death."

Auden blinks. Once. And then he deploys a smile so arrogant and pretty that even underneath the zeal, Becket's body stirs with sweaty, firelit memories. "But you're in the Church of Thornchapel now. Besides, you said all that brilliant stuff about being stamped ontologically or whatever. Surely a little bit of you still feels compelled to pastor me."

"All of me does," admits Becket. Today is a day for confessions, a day for coming clean and for making a pyre of the past. He should be the one begging for confession, really, he should be the one finally, painfully, admitting what he's hidden out of the fear that if the time came—which it has—he wouldn't be allowed near the chapel to atone.

Above all, he must be allowed to atone.

And then he makes his decision. "Yes, I'll hear your confession, Auden. So long as you promise that this request isn't motivated by any future foolishness on your part."

"No, Father Hess," Auden says. "Nothing foolish at all."

Auden

Confessing is hard work. He must drag out all these sins—so many of them—and hurl them into the air. He must pray over them, pray over himself, he must feel remorse. He does for most things. For other things—mostly involving St. Sebastian—the remorse is mixed with too many other feelings to be picked apart and held aloft as evidence of virtue.

But Becket seems to understand.

After they finish, Auden stands to go to his office. His trip to London was busy, but fruitful, and the last of the revised documents has arrived in his email, ready for him to digitally sign and send back. And then it will all be arranged. His townhouse, his money, his Thornchapel—it will all go to them. As it should.

"I'll see you tonight," he tells his priest. "In the chapel."

"Of course," says Becket, but he sounds preoccupied when he says it. His flame-blue eyes are fixed on something Auden can't see.

Auden pats his shoulder and goes upstairs.

It's still morning, and so the trees are still wreathed in fog, and Auden spends a few minutes looking at them from his office window before he opens his laptop and gets to work finalizing all the arrangements. And then Auden pulls out a book he hasn't looked at in a long time—the heavy book of medicinal plants and herbs he'd shoved the rose in all those years ago.

He opens the book and looks at the rose—now dried and mostly flattened—and thinks of Estamond as he cries soft, wet petals down his cheeks.

If it's not done by dusk, it may be too late.

She had told him what would happen, she'd warned him more thoroughly than he ever could have understood then.

That at Thornchapel, the kings walk to the door.

At Thornchapel, all kings must die.

31

St. Sebastian

The house is quiet when I'm done with the effigy, and I can't find Auden anywhere. I'm about to go up to his office to look for him when I find Freddie Dansey of all people coming from the kitchen. I stop short, shocked.

The knowledge of the letter in my bag upstairs burns in my mind.

When Freddie sees me, he gives me a beam of pure relief. "I was worried I missed you! I just spoke with Pickles, and she thought you were in the village, and I didn't have enough time to chase you there."

It takes me a minute to remember that Pickles is what Delphine's parents call her for some unknowable reason. I offer Freddie a tentative smile back. I had Richard Davey of course, and back home in Dallas, I was surrounded by uncles and cousins and a gruffly doting grandfather—I'm not unused to father figures. But for so long, since the graveyard at least, I've resisted letting anyone into my heart, into my life. And then Poe came here and trampled past all my carefully erected walls; then she let Auden in, like a wolf padding in after her. And somehow I ended up friends with Delphine and Rebecca and Becket too—

I have people in my life now, completely accidentally, and now Freddie's one of them. And I like it, even if I'm still not sure how to feel about it, or how to act around him.

"I hope you aren't feeling poorly?" Freddie goes on. "Pickles says she has some kind of flu, but she's on the mend, she thinks. I told her to come home and let me and her mum dote on her, but you know how she is."

I'm relieved that Freddie doesn't know the nature of our illness, and I'm oddly disappointed too. It is something awful about growing up, that your fate is continually in your hands. There's no parent to make it better, to fix it, to do battle for you. No one is going to close the door for us and then tuck us into bed with a good-night story and a teddy bear.

The responsibility of it all feels very, very heavy all of a sudden.

"Are you here about the results?" I ask him.

He blinks a few times, dark blond eyelashes fluttering, and then his beam returns stronger than ever. "Have they come in? I've been away from home this week for work so I haven't had the chance to see my mail—my God. What did they say?"

He sounds so eager, so *happy*, like it would do nothing but chuff him to bits to discover he has an adult son who's an unemployed librarian with an American accent, and I don't even know what to say or do in the presence of such unearned warmth and affection. I've spent so long holding myself in, even from Augie and my adoptive father's family, so certain pain and rejection were waiting for me.

Being confronted with the manifest opposite of rejection is…powerful.

"I haven't opened them yet," I say, softly.

"Oh," Freddie says, looking a little disappointed. But then he brightens. "We could open them now. Together if you like."

I almost say yes. But I have a promise to make first. "I know this will sound strange," I start, not sure how to explain, "but I—I would like to wait. If that's okay with you."

"You'd like to wait?" Freddie repeats. He doesn't sound upset, only surprised. "How long?"

"I don't know." Knowing he deserves an explanation, I search for the right words. "When I found out I was Ralph's son, it changed so much of my life. It changed all my plans, my future."

I don't mention Auden. I think even someone who used to fuck in the chapel might not be ready to hear about that part.

"I'm afraid that I've given it too much control over my life. And I want to choose what I do next on my own, entirely on my own. Without the fear or the relief of the results guiding me."

Freddie's honey-brown eyes are understanding. "I've never bought into that gloria filiorum patres rubbish, and I won't start now, even when I may have a son. I can't say I'm not dying to know the results, St. Sebastian, but I'm content to wait until you're ready."

I let go of the breath I've been holding. "Thank you," I say. "I know it's a lot to ask, but—"

Freddie touches me on the shoulder, a fond, warm pressure. "You can ask anything of me," he says, and the sincerity in his words is matched by the honesty in his expression. "I mean that genuinely. Anything at all."

"I wouldn't mind going on as if we did know," I say in a quiet voice. "And…and getting to know you. And Daisy. If that's okay."

I'm yanked into an embrace. "Yes," Freddie says fervently. "Yes, that's more than okay. I would like that very much. Very, very much."

I return the hug as best I can, and when he steps back, I can see that his eyes are shining. But then he clears his throat and offers me a sheepish smile, like he's embarrassed to have been caught exhibiting such strong feelings.

"Apologies," he says. "I am only so very happy to get to know you."

"No apologies required," I say. "I'm happy to get to know you too, Freddie."

He glances down at his watch, one of those older, well-dinged watches that so clearly signals careless wealth. "I should go," he says regretfully. "I need to be on my way to Plymouth for a late dinner. But I couldn't be this near to you and Delphine without stopping by."

We're walking to the front doors now, and we push them open to find a storm has begun pushing its way over the moors, windy and dark. The fog is blowing away, but the air is tossed with leaves and petals, which whisper and sigh together as they move.

We reach his silver Bentley coupe, and he turns to look back at the house.

"These roses," he says. "They're like nothing I've ever seen before. Has Auden brought them in?"

He must not have seen the village or the south lawn, or he wouldn't ask such a thing. It would have been obvious that no human could be responsible for such an invasion.

"In a way," I answer.

"It's Halloween today. Samhain." Freddie's eyes trace over the rose-covered house, taking it in. "For twelve years, I didn't miss a single Samhain in the chapel. There was a time when I was here for every cross-quarter feast, every ritual. And now—well, I'd forgotten until Daisy mentioned seeing a child in costume at the shop this morning. Isn't that funny? I used to order my entire life around these days, and now I forget them like the name of a school acquaintance."

"You never came back," I guess. "After that Lammas."

Freddie nods, tearing his eyes away from the house to look at the trees crowding the edge of the drive. "I was furious with Ralph, beyond enraged. It was never enough to gather us to him, to have us, to make us play whatever games he dreamed up. He had to have more—he had to have that door. And the minute it appeared and opened, there was no doubt that it needed to be closed. You could feel it in your marrow, the unnaturalness of it. And even after it struck me down when I tried to close it, Ralph still insisted we go back on Samhain, that we try to close it together. But I wanted nothing more to do with it, I wanted Daisy and Delphine far away from it too, and so we left. I didn't come back, I didn't answer Ralph's calls or emails. He was my oldest friend, and I couldn't even bring myself to pick up the phone when he called."

"But you made it up later, right? Your friendship, I mean."

"Years later," Freddie sighs. "And it was never the same after that. There was a new distance between us, and with Adelina's disappearance—with what we thought was a disappearance at the time. He was so haunted by it, so changed, but even that wasn't enough to endear him to me again, for me to give him any sort of trust."

"Why did you trust him in the first place?" I ask. "He seemed *awful*. I mean, for example, he claimed me to Auden and his solicitor, but personally told me nothing and left me nothing. He was cruel and greedy."

Freddie looks to me, his mouth twisted in the bitterest smile I've ever seen on him. "There's no list of adjectives long enough for Ralph. It doesn't surprise me that he left you nothing—not because he was famously miserly, but because he would have known the pain it would cause Auden to work out what to do, and I think he was very angry with Auden by the end, very angry indeed." The bitter smile fades into something more thoughtful. "He was cruel and greedy like you say, but he was so much more—charming and sensual and energetic—he made cruelty and greed feel like gifts when he gave them. And he craved cruelty for himself too—it wasn't as if he was some aggressive god visiting punishments upon his people. He needed pain, periods of being under someone else's control, and that passed for humility—it was a performance of humility that we all believed. Even when we were at Harrow, he'd ask me or Ingram Hess to—" Freddie stops himself and a flush appears along his already ruddy cheekbones.

I think I know what he was going to say.

"It is hard to describe," he says after a moment, "if you've never known a person like him. It's hard to describe how someone can be so magnetic—how they can make you feel so deeply and wonderfully alive—when they also sow such misery inside you."

But I understand. Auden is not Ralph, despite what I've said to him in the past, but he is also a tangle of sensuality and cruelty, possession and charm. He is the monster you want under your bed, the footsteps you want behind you in the dark, and I too have given him my trust and my body, even when I shouldn't.

"I regret that distance between us sometimes. Even knowing now that he caused Adelina's death, I—" Freddie gives a tattered exhale.

"He rang me the night before Samhain, you know, the night before Adelina went missing. I don't think she was there yet, he must have still been alone, and he left me this voicemail…apologizing for everything, saying he'd found a way to close the door and not to worry. He said it had to happen at dusk, when the veil parted, but before anything could come through, and then he asked if I would come down, because he was frightened of doing it alone. Of course, at the time I had no idea he was talking about murdering Adelina, and it didn't matter anyway. I refused to listen to the voicemail for several days, and by the time I did, it was too late." He looks very sad then. "If only I'd put aside my anger for thirty seconds and listened to his message, I could have saved Adelina. It is a terrible thought."

He looks right at me then. "The door has remained shut, hasn't it? There's no sign of it coming back?"

He sounds so hopeful and also so worried, and so the lie comes easily. "No sign at all. Maybe it will never come back."

Freddie gives me a relieved smile. "We can only pray."

I'm given a hearty handshake and then he leaves, off to Plymouth to adjudicate horse law or whatever it is he does. I'm walking back towards the rose-framed door of the house when his words finally catch up with me, or rather the mistaken assumption in them.

I think of Poe's dream of Ralph and her mother in the chapel.

Your father wasn't threatening my mother, Auden.

He was wearing the torc alone in the chapel before she got there…

Ralph hadn't been calling Freddie to tell him he planned to murder Adelina. Ralph had been calling Freddie to tell him he planned to die *himself.*

He was frightened of doing it alone.

All this time, it had been Ralph walking to the door, not luring

Adelina there. I'm not sure how Adelina died, but I don't think it was Ralph's plan to kill her. When the time came to make the choice, he chose to offer himself.

Uneasiness ticks through me. Uneasiness that I can't name at first, not until I get into the house and realize that I haven't seen Auden since lunchtime, when he told me he was taking Sir James on a walk to the village.

Stop, I tell myself. *Stop it.*

Auden is as sensible and grounded as he is arrogant. He's been the one who's been against any kind of sacrifice or violence from the first. He would never leave Poe behind—he would never leave me behind—not after last night. Not after he left me sore and well-ridden, murmuring in my ear that he loved me as he used me over and over…

The uneasiness has cold fingers on my neck, it scratches along the inside of my veins. I start looking for him, in his bedroom, in his office, in the hall. He wouldn't, I know he wouldn't, but I need to make sure. I have to make sure. Because he is not only Auden Guest, pouty, gossipy architect, but he is also the wild god, the horned one, the Stag King. He has eyes like the forest and a heart made of thorns, and if he felt he had to, if he thought it was the only way to keep me and Poe and Becket and Rebecca and Delphine safe…

When I burst into the library, I see Becket kneeling in prayer. I don't care that I'm interrupting him.

"Have you seen Auden?" I ask, my voice hoarse. "I can't find him."

"We're not supposed to meet at the chapel until seven," Rebecca says, coming into the library behind me. "It's barely past four now."

I look outside to where the storm has darkened the world, making a true sunset impossible, bringing on an early dusk.

Rebecca takes in a sharp breath, and I glance over to see her looking at the case of artifacts. "The torc is gone," she says, her voice expressionless.

For a moment, I'm in the chapel on Lammas, collaring Auden's strong throat with my hands and calling it a crown. We were only playacting then. But now…

"Find Poe," I tell the others. "I'm going to the chapel before it's too late."

32

Auden

I'm certain that in days of old, the Thorn Kings were feted and prepared for their sacrifice. I assume there must have been feasting or fasting, sex or sacred abstention, lots of repose or none at all.

Something to mark the person and the day, to mark both of them as holy and apart.

It is not the days of old, however. It is the days of right now. I've written emails, snuck in a confession with a defrocked priest, and dropped Sir James Frazer at Abby's nephew's house, where he'll stay for a few days. I've got an email to the others in my outbox scheduled to be sent tonight, and it includes Abby's phone number and when to retrieve Sir James. It also includes the number of my solicitor, a quick explanation of what to expect from my changed will, the brand of Sir James's favorite dog food, and where I'd like to be buried.

Here, I think.

I want to be buried here.

At any rate, this wild god has finished boarding his dog, and so now it's time to die.

I've gathered all the things I will need earlier today and put them in the poolhouse. I have to shove aside a veritable curtain of thorns and roses to open the door to retrieve them, but soon I'm as ready as I'll ever be. Torc, knife, candles. I've even pulled off the jumper underneath my coat and left it neatly folded on a chair. It's a Brunello Cucinelli, and it's too nice to bleed on.

The air is cool on my bare chest and stomach as I start walking to the chapel, and the wind flaps at the bottom and sides of my peacoat, searching with restless fingers for my ribs and back. Leaves in every shade of autumn float through the air—leaves the color of the sun, of dried blood, of oranges at Christmas—and dark petals float too.

Apples fall off trees like offerings of the forest as I walk, dropping to the thick blanket of petals with ripe thumps, and petals keep catching in my hair, keep fluttering like a lover's fingers against my naked chest. It is like a parade, a procession, my very own Roman triumph. Except instead of citizens, I have trees.

And instead of captives, I have only myself.

There, finally, is my answer. The answer I've been looking for since St. Sebastian left me, the answer I've been searching for since I was twelve. What unites the two halves of me? What joins the teeth in the night to the tenderness, the love, the sacrifice?

It can only be a humble heart.

Love can be bent and stained, can justify all manner of pain and mayhem, and tenderness can be contingent, arbitrary, fleeting—but humility stays true because it can only ever be itself. It tempers arrogance, lust, and possession; it transmutes my roughest, basest urges into something cohesive and whole. I can have all of it—the kink, the love, the possession—all of it in one body and one heart, so long as I see humility as a gift.

I felt like a general when I knelt to pleasure St. Sebastian.

And I feel like a king now when I walk to the door to die for my friends.

There is power in this kind of submission. A power that means every part of me can be used for good—even the parts of me that would eat the world raw if left untrammeled. And maybe that is the lesson of the Year King, of the Babylonian kings who were slapped during Akitu, of monarchs who kneel to be anointed. Power must come with humility.

They cannot be picked apart. They should not.

I will not.

I'm greeted by the faint beating of drums as I walk through the stone row to the altar. In my world, thunder rolls incessantly, a giant celestial drum of my own. Flashes of bright white lightning briefly etch every bloom and dangling hip into stark, unearthly lines.

It's dim enough with the storm and oncoming dusk that I can make out the torchlight flickering from across the threshold of the door. I stare at it a moment before I begin…I wonder if this means someone is on the other side. Fairies or gods or past kings, maybe. Sisters who loved necklaces or peddlers looking for new wares. Loyal knights who chose to stay with their queens.

I also wonder what unlucky quirk of geography or physics or the intersection of the two means that the door has to be here, in my valley, and made heaven or hell or fairyland or an alternate dimension or whatever it fucking is my family's responsibility.

And really, who can ever say if it was luck or if it was fate?

Both of them are cruel enough to have done it.

I brought out lanterns a few days before, and I arrange them now, setting candles inside and lighting them as we did on Imbolc and Beltane. I make a circle which encloses the altar, with the circle's northernmost point against the door, where eerie torches glow and lightning arcs through the sky, just like here.

I say a prayer with each lantern, a short prayer. I should have hunted for a good one, a special one, an invocation that matched the moment, but all I can remember are the prayers of my childhood, of the Rosary and the Chaplet and the Mass. The Anima Christi, which hung on the wall of my boyhood room.

Anima Christi, sanctifica me.

Corpus Christi, salva me.

Sanguis Christi, inebria me.

Soul of Christ, sanctify me. Body of Christ, save me. Blood of Christ, inebriate me.

Et jube me venire ad te,

Ut cum Sanctis tuis laudem te,

In saecula saeculorum.

Bid me come unto Thee, that with Thy saints, I may Praise Thee forever and ever.

It reminds me, oddly but powerfully, of being a boy again, of being that small Auden Guest. Walking the house, dousing flames and stirring ashes.

Making sure no fires were left burning.

And even though I'm striking matches and cupping nascent candle flames instead of killing my mother's forgotten fires, it's the same thing in the end, it's the same thing.

It keeps everyone safe.

The lanterns arranged and lit, I find there's little else to do. There is no priest here to guide me, there is no priestess to anoint me. I am alone, alone, alone.

I don't even have my dog.

And so with dread, and with something almost like relief, I walk to the door.

I've not given this part much thought—I worried the more thought I gave it, the weaker my resolve would become—and so it takes me a minute to decide how I want to do this. I find I'm very particular about how I want to die, and I almost smile thinking of what St. Sebastian would say about the rich boy who's worried about which way his hair will flop when he shuffles off this mortal coil.

But truly, if I have to do this, I would like to be found with romantic hair at least. I have to think God would allow me that.

I ultimately decide Estamond had the right idea, and I move onto the altar, sitting with my legs hanging from the edge while I work the torc under the collar of my peacoat and onto my neck. It is cool and heavy and difficult to bend, and when I settle it around my neck, the terminals at the ends press against my throat. I can feel the deeply etched spirals on them—the same spiral from the Kernstow farmhouse and the carved chamber near the cists.

There. I am a king.

I pull out the knife I took from the artifact case and look at it a moment, although it's hard to judge its edge in this light. I find my glasses in my other pocket and slide them on, squinting down at the weapon and testing its tip against the pad of my finger. It pricks, but only after a good push.

I'll have to be fast and hard with it then. It will be unpleasant.

My eyes burn, and my throat hurts, and my chest is hollow and crushed flat all at once. I think of Proserpina and St. Sebastian. I think of my best friend, my ex-priest, my ex-betrothed. I think of Gemma Dawes and Saint's neighbor and all the people in the village sick with something they didn't ask for and no one else can cure.

What would be more frightening, more horrifying? Me on the altar?

Or me off of it, leaving everyone else to suffer and perish?

What would a humble heart choose?

I already know the answer to that, of course I do. I think I've always known what a good king would do.

Anima Christi, sanctifica me.

I settle onto my back, arranging my peacoat so that it won't wrinkle underneath me.

Corpus Christi, salva me.

I imagine St. Sebastian and Proserpina, smiling, happy, healthy. *Alive.* I lift my wrist.

Sanguis Christi, inebria me.

And I lift the knife.

Hard and fast. I tighten my jaw and close my eyes, braced for pain, which I get. But not on my wrist.

My entire body.

Something big, angry, and beautiful slams into me, rolling me right off the altar and onto the—thankfully—thorn-free ground below. The breath is knocked straight from my lungs—once from the collision and then once again when I hit the ground—and I barely register the soft noise the knife makes as it hits the damp petals below. My glasses tumble off too.

I look up to see St. Sebastian, seething, panicked, eyes wide and breathing hard. "What the *fuck*?" he's yelling at me, his voice carrying over the drums and the thunder. "*What the fuck?*"

I can't breathe to speak and I hold up a hand.

"You unmitigated *asshole*, you absolute *wanker*, you fucking *liar—*"

"I get the idea, St. Sebastian," I say hoarsely.

"I don't think you do. You told all of us to be here at seven with an effigy, and then this whole time you were sneaking out here early to kill yourself. I could *murder* you right now."

"It might save me some effort," I half joke, and St. Sebastian gives something like a roar, like he really is about to throttle me.

"This is the goddamn graveyard all over again," he hisses as I get to one knee, still trying to suck in air. The knife is by his boot.

He hasn't noticed it yet.

I stagger to my feet, wincing a little as my ribs remind me that an angry librarian just tackled me off a stone altar before I could ritualistically sacrifice myself on it.

My year really did take a turn at some point.

"St. Sebastian," I say softly, stepping closer. "You understand why I have to, right? Why it has to be me?"

His eyes glitter from the torchlight spilling from the door. "No."

"We all know the effigy won't work. And if I don't do this, you could die. Proserpina could die. It could spread and spread until we have no choice but to do this anyway, but only after we've lost people we love. It needs to happen now."

"No," he says stubbornly, and fuck, he's so gorgeous like this, restless and angry and framed by lightning and roses. I can't help it—I know I've said my goodbyes, made my peace, all that rubbish, but I need a kiss. Just one more.

I slide my hands up his arms until I can fist my hands in the worn cotton of his T-shirt and yank him close. And then he's grabbing too, seizing the lapels of my coat and pulling, and I'm pulling, and our lips meet in a sear of desperation and heat. I find the back of his head, the taut curve of his backside, needing the pressure, the warm, hard reality of him.

I taste blood, and then it's my turn to growl. I could lick the blood from his kiss for the rest of my life.

Which is admittedly a very short span of time now.

"I'm sorry," I breathe against his mouth.

He blinks at me, totally dazed. "What?"

"I never said it and I should have. I'm so sorry for hiding the letter from you, St. Sebastian. For lying."

His eyes close. "Oh."

"All my life, I've been consumed with the idea of earning. I wanted to earn my career and my friends. I wanted to earn Proserpina and you. But I cheated, you see. I found the thing I wanted more than earning, and that was *you*. I was willing to cozen you out of your love, I lied for it, I swindled you. And all for the cheap reason that I was terrified you'd leave me once you found out."

"Christ, Auden," St. Sebastian says, leaning his forehead against mine. "It wasn't a cheap reason at all. I wish you hadn't lied, and I am grateful for the apology, but...well, it was a very you thing to do. It's understandable."

"I don't want it to be a 'me thing to do,'" I explain, bumping my nose against his. "I'd like to think I've learned some things since then."

Like humility.

"Is that what this is?" he asks, pulling back a little. "Please tell me it's not. That you're not trying to punish yourself or prove that you've overcome your arrogance or—"

I buss my mouth over his. "I will never overcome my arrogance," I inform him ruefully. "But I have learned how to add other qualities to it at least."

He submits to my kisses, his hands flexing on the lapels of my coat. He's holding on too tight for me to move, and with some regret, I realize I'll have to cheat again.

I only hope he can forgive me for it one day.

I unfist his shirt and run my hand down his chest and over the bunched point of his nipple, and then down his firm stomach to his jeans, where a burgeoning erection is pushing against the zipper. I give it a rough stroke—rough enough to make him shudder with pleasure and make me shudder with want—but no, focus, Auden, *focus*—

His hands fall from my coat as he mindlessly shoves his hips against my touch, and then I drop to my knees, lunging for the knife by his boot. My fingers close around the hilt, and an odd sense of victory fills me, but the victory comes too soon. Saint apprehends my purpose immediately, and suddenly I'm shoved to the ground, nearly losing my grip on the knife. Fuck.

I roll to the side, trying to get far enough away that I can just *do this*—I mean, honestly, how is it fair that I have to struggle in order to do something that's already so ghastly anyway—but Saint won't let me, and even though I'm a bit taller, just that little bit more muscled, he is filled with a panic that gives him the strength of three men. Somehow the knife fumbles out of my hand *again,* and we both dive for it at the same time, grappling along the way, wrestling, hands reaching and scrabbling, and I'm so close, so very close, and my God, if I weren't about to human sacrifice myself to close this bloody door, I would belt St. Sebastian's arse for all the trouble he's causing—

A brown lace-up boot comes to rest on the hilt. Leather. Gleaming. Ralph Lauren.

I look up to see Becket crouching down to take the knife. St. Sebastian slumps, rolling flat on his back with his arm flung out, panting up at the stormy sky.

"Thank fuck," he gasps. "Becket, you have incredible timing."

"It seems I do," Becket says. "Otherwise, the wrong person would have died tonight."

I meet his eyes. They are still that unnatural blue.

"No," I tell him.

"Yes," Becket says gravely. "I'm sorry, Auden, but it won't be the king who dies. It's been meant to be me all along."

33

Proserpina

"It should be *me*, if it's fucking anyone," St. Sebastian says as Rebecca, Delphine, and I reach the chapel entrance. "I'm the one named after a martyr after all."

Auden and Becket turn back to each other as if Saint hasn't spoken. "You know it's supposed to me," Auden says. The heavy torc glints around his neck, and sweat sheens along the lines and curves of his naked torso. He is breathing hard. "The *king*, Becket. The king walks to the door. The lord of the manor, the wild god. The Guest walks to the door."

"It's going to be me," Becket says calmly. "I've decided long ago."

"No one is deciding!" St. Sebastian bursts out. "If it's just us deciding, then I decide it's me. There, now how does that feel?"

Auden turns to him, a gentle pity warming his eyes, softening his mouth. "It's no use, St. Sebastian," he says. "It must be me."

"No, it mustn't," Saint says, his voice thick. "I refuse. I refuse and I won't let this fucked-up scene go on a single moment longer. Do you need to hear my safe word to believe me? *May I.* May I, may I, may I."

Auden looks exasperated. "This is bigger than kink."

"Everything with you is kink. Are you trying to tell me this isn't the ultimate power exchange?"

"How did you even know I was here anyway?" Auden says, dodging Saint's question. He looks at Becket and then at all of us. "I thought I had time."

"Freddie stopped by the house today," Saint says tightly. "He said some things about Ralph that made me suspicious. He also mentioned that Ralph had wanted to close the door at dusk, when the veil was thinnest, but before any more of the door's world could leach into ours. I guessed you were following in dear old Dad's footsteps."

Auden pushes a hand into his hair, frustrated, and he looks so very *Auden* in this moment, even bare-chested with a torc around his neck. "It's more…complicated than that."

"How can it be? Jesus, Auden, I'm not letting you do this, and you have to know that. I'll do it myself, if that's what it takes."

"*Nobody* is dying today," Rebecca says sternly as we join them near the altar. "We have a plan. We're following the plan. That's it."

"They have their own plans," Delphine points out softly, her eyes going from boy to boy to boy. She doesn't look at me. But I shove my hands in my coat pockets anyway, so no one can see the stains on my fingers and palms. So no one can ask how I got them.

"There is no *own plan*—this is the plan we all made together, this is what we agreed to do as a group—"

"Well, I lied when I said I agreed," Auden says at the same time

Saint seethes, "He was obviously lying this whole time!"

This is just like my dream, I think, just like that dream I had the night before I returned to Thornchapel. All of us here in the chapel, all of us yelling. All of us very, very aware of the encroaching gloom of dusk.

But in my dream, I was afraid, and I'm not afraid now. I know what's going to happen—until a certain point at least—and I know Auden and Saint and Becket won't have the chance to hurt themselves. I know the others will be safe.

We are in a sort of circle now, in front of the altar. Rebecca is nearly in the middle of it, trying to talk sense into the men. They're arguing with her and with themselves, and Delphine is lambasting all three boys with curse words I've never even heard of, and Auden is eyeing the knife in Becket's hand like he's about to go for it at any moment, and so no one notices me step sideways out of the circle. From there it's only a few steps to the altar, and then to the door.

The flickering glow of torches or fires comes from the other side, and there, like here, there is a dark ceiling of clouds, their bellies flickering with lightning. Wind tosses the trees on the other side and I can hear it, I can hear that world's thunder along with my world's thunder, and there are drums too, and I forget all my doubts for a moment. There is only this beautiful, terrifying evening. There is only the gorgeous danger of the unknown.

I want to take it with both hands, I want to bite into it. For years, I've chased my curiosity through codices and palimpsests and folios, indulging my appetite for the little secrets and stories history has forgotten. And now here I am, with a forgotten story so big it could swallow entire lives—and already has.

Here I am, with my mother's last and final secret.

Of course this moment is meant for me. It was meant for me all along.

I dig the flask out of my coat and unscrew the lid. I'm not sure what it will taste like or how long it will take. I'm also not sure it will work at all—but I'm not admitting entrance to any doubt right now.

It has to work.

I put it to my lips, already smelling its heady, floral scent. Like mortal roses, but earthier, spicier.

"Poe?" Becket asks, interrupting the bickering and turning toward me. "Poe, what are you doing?" For the first time today, he sounds afraid. "Step away from the door."

Auden looks away from Sant, and he goes pale. "Proserpina," he says. "Come here."

The altar is between me and the others. A barrier. A buffer. It would give me the time I need to do what needs to be done.

"No one has to die," I tell them. "That's what my mother figured out. That's what the Kernstows figured out years ago. No one has to die. They only have to be sacrificed—or sacrifice themselves."

"Whatever etymological differences exist between *die* and *sacrifice* are flattened here," Auden says impatiently. "At Thornchapel, a sacrifice *is* a death."

"It has been for a long time," I agree. "But it doesn't have to be that way. The stories—"

"Are just fairy tales," Auden cuts in, and then his face gentles. "Please come away from the door, Proserpina. We'll talk about this, I promise, just—let's talk about this away from the door."

"Freddie couldn't go through because he didn't want to go through," I continue, taking a small step backward. Saint notices, his eyes flaring, but Becket is the one who steps forward first. I hold up a hand to stop him. "Please. I promise I'm not going to hurt myself. I'm just trying to explain. Freddie couldn't go through because he wanted to stay here, he wanted to protect his life here. But what if someone was willing to leave their life behind? What if someone was willing to *pay* their life, not by dying but by crossing over and staying? Not a suicide or a murder, but more like…like a one-way trip to Mars."

I scan their faces fervently, desperately. "This is what we've been missing. We've assumed this whole time that a life paid has to be paid with destruction, but what if it can be paid with consecration instead, with transference, with movement?"

"We can't use fairy tales for this," Becket says. "They're not reliable enough sources—"

"And our other sources *are*? My dreams? A collection of cists we've only just found?"

"—*and*," Becket continues over me, "the people in the fairy tales seem like they were planning on coming back, not staying over there forever. The peddler. The sisters."

"We don't know if they closed the door by crossing over as—I don't know, tourists—but we do know the door did close for the people who thought they could never return. The abducted woman had to wait for it to reopen. The knight who pledged his life to the fairy queen knew that the gate was closing behind him and chose to stay with his queen forever anyway."

"Estamond didn't know," Auden says.

"It had thirteen hundred years to be forgotten," Rebecca says after a minute. She is looking at me appraisingly. "Knowledge this esoteric has been lost in a far shorter time."

"The Eleusinian mysteries were lost in less, and hundreds and hundreds of people did those, rather than just one family," Delphine agrees. "So I understand Estamond not knowing. But if the fairy tales were inspired by real stories, wouldn't the people who returned from the door have told other people? Wouldn't they have told the Guests?"

Auden makes a face. "I don't know that my ancestors would have listened. If they were anything like my father. They would have thought they already knew the best way to handle the door."

"I don't know that other people would have listened either," Rebecca says. "These experiences are recounted as fairy tales, not as a legitimate record."

"It's always possible some Guests listened though," I say. "We can't know that they didn't. We only know that the knowledge was lost by the time Randolph Guest lived, and then it died completely with the Kernstows. Everything else is a guess."

"Exactly," Becket says. "Which is why you shouldn't do this on the basis of a guess."

"Do what? Prevent someone from killing themselves? No one has to die this way," I say, desperate for them to understand. "Don't you see? The worst that will happen to me is that I'll be in a new place."

"We don't know this new place, Poe," Saint says. "We don't know what it's like. Say this works and you're able to walk through it. What happens to you when you get there? There's no guarantee of your safety or your future—"

"That's the same in any world," I say softly. "That's part of the deal when it comes to life. There's no promises."

"But the wren," Saint says. "Rebecca's wren—"

"Yes!" Auden cuts in and gives Rebecca a pleading look. "Rebecca, remind her of what you saw, remind her of what the door showed you!"

Rebecca is still giving me that appraising look, her eyes narrowed and her lips pressed together in thought. She doesn't answer right away, and Saint explodes with, "How can you be standing there *agreeing* with her when you saw that wren die—"

"I'm *not* agreeing," Rebecca counters sharply. "I'm listening." She pauses, and then adds, with less sharpness and more hesitation, "Becket said we might have been wrong about the wren, remember? That it wasn't a threat or a warning, but something else. What if I was wrong? What if the door is safer than we thought?"

Auden turns away from Rebecca with wild eyes and a frustrated stab of his hair with his fingers—like she's a defecting general and now he has to salvage an entire battle on his own.

"If you go and you can't come back, then St. Sebastian and I will never see you again," Auden says to me. His voice has a hoarse, urgent edge.

My throat hurts and there's a hot stinging in my nose. "I know," I whisper. "It has to be a sacrifice, remember?" I try to give him a reassuring smile. "And you'll have each other."

"We're meant to be a three," he argues.

Tears spill from my lids and I push them off my cheeks with one hand, the other hand still clutching the flask. "You were planning on leaving Saint and me here," I point out.

"That's different," he says, voice pained. "It's my job to give everything to you."

"Poe," Saint says, stepping forward. Becket mirrors Saint's step and I start to feel like a castled king on a chessboard. "What's in that flask?"

"Poe—your *hands*," Delphine exclaims.

I take a step backward, holding the flask tighter with my crimson-stained hands, refusing to answer. I'm very close to the door now.

"Enough of this," interrupts Becket. "I am going to close the door today, not Poe, and that's all there is to it. I've known this was coming for me since I was a teenager. This is my destiny."

"Firstly," Auden says, turning to the ex-priest and sounding miffed, "this is *my* destiny. Secondly, only I'm allowed to be dramatic here, on the grounds that I *am* the king, and also I've always been the dramatic one."

"I'm not being dramatic," Becket says. "I deserve to die."

"*You* deserve to die?" Saint echoes in disbelief.

Becket turns to me. In the twilight, his eyes are a shade of indigo that belongs on the other side of the door. "I was the one who killed your mother, Proserpina," he says. The words come out cleanly, simply, as if he's rehearsed them many, many times. "Twelve years ago. It was me."

The words slice through my mind like the lightning above us. Bright, hot. Branched into jagged sprigs that seek the earth.

I'm already shaking my head, already saying, "No, Becket, no, you didn't. Remember? You saw Ralph burying her. You told me he killed her—you *said* that he killed her."

"I lied," Becket says. His eyes are burning into mine. "I lied because I had to stay close to the chapel, near to the door. It's why I came back to England in the first place—I needed to be here in case it opened so I could be the one to close it. I owe your mother that, Poe, and I owe God that too. If I'd told you what happened, you wouldn't have allowed me near you, or near here, so the lie was unfortunate but necessary if I were to atone."

The drums roll through the chapel still, as does the thunder, but the rest is quiet, hushed. I stare at Becket, handsome, brilliant Becket, who I've let inside my body, who I've cried for and worried over and trusted with my proximity and my friendship.

Nothing is making any kind of sense. Becket doesn't lie. Becket doesn't kill. Becket charms old church ladies and fucks like it's his singular goal in life. Becket prays and prays and prays.

He can't have done this.

He can't have done this.

My mind is buzzing with static now, my thoughts breaking into pieces and hissing into nothing before I can properly think them to myself. "You're a priest," I whisper. "You're holy. You're righteous. You wouldn't have."

"Maybe I'm holy and righteous because I did an evil thing once," he says softly. "Maybe I've been trying to atone my entire life, trying to smother the guilt with good deeds."

"No," I say, because I know that much isn't true. "You love God like no one else I've ever known. You would have always been a priest. No matter what your past held."

He gives me a sad smile. "Perhaps. I don't deserve that kindness from you. But thank you for it anyway."

"I don't understand," Auden says, stabbing his fingers through his hair. "You killed Adelina Markham? But why? How? You would have been, what, fourteen? Why would you have killed her? And..." He trails off, looking at the space between me and Becket. Maybe wondering how safe I am right now.

It's a question that flits through my mind too. If he killed my mother, is he capable of killing me? But I'm too deeply stamped with our friendship, I suppose, because I'm still stunned, I'm still in a place of disbelief, and my trust in him remains.

"All my life," Becket says, "I've been tormented by this...ardor. Ardor for the divine. Zealousness. As a child, my priest told me it would temper with time; as a seminarian, my mentor told me to tie it up and starve it. When it's with me, I feel God very deeply. And I feel everything else less. My body, for example, I don't notice if it's hungry or if it's tired. Or the space I'm in, I'm not aware if it's hot or if it's cold. When I'm in the zeal, sometimes it's difficult to perceive...clearly."

"Is that what happened twelve years ago?" Auden asks, his voice soft.

I look at Becket, and I remember the dream. "You were outside the chapel," I realize. "They heard you. But then my mother tried to get the knife away from Ralph..."

"I thought they were fighting," Becket says miserably. "I thought he was trying to hurt her. I couldn't hear everything they were saying, and I thought—I thought if I didn't help..."

There's torment etched into his face now, clinging to his brow and his mouth. "Like I said, the zeal makes things cloudy sometimes. If I hadn't been—if I'd been clearer—then I think I would have understood. Or I would have done something differently. As it was, I charged out of the trees and over the wall. I was trying to tackle him, pin him to the ground so she could run away, but I slammed into them both. We all fell to the ground together." He closes his eyes. "She fell on the knife."

I'm crying again, but I don't know who I'm crying for.

Myself twelve years ago, or myself now.

My mother, flying across an ocean to save an ex-lover from doing the unthinkable, only to die herself. Ralph, who walked into the chapel to die and instead buried the woman he loved.

Becket. Young and reckless, hazed with a mysticism I'll never understand.

"The noise she made then." Becket exhales, opens his eyes. "I knew. We rolled her over, Ralph tried to staunch the bleeding, but the knife must have struck somewhere vital. There was so much blood. And she managed to say, at the last…" He sucks in a breath. "She said *it's okay.*"

He lifts his gaze to mine. "*It's okay.* I don't know whom she was saying it to. Both of us maybe."

That would be so like my mother. Trying to comfort someone, trying to make something as sunny as possible, even when there is no light to be found at all.

"She had something in her hand—a note—and she was trying to lift it up, trying to wave it maybe, but her hand dropped to the ground. I remember taking the note because it seemed like that's what she wanted, but before I could read it, Ralph let loose this howl like…like his soul had been ripped out of his body and I was responsible." Becket looks at the ground now. The same ground he killed my mother on. "I *was* responsible. I knew it even then. Instinct made me run anyway. I hid in the woods, and the rest of what I told you that day in the church is true, Poe, because I did watch him bury her from the trees by the light of the fire. I did wait hours and hours until he was done to leave. I was terrified that he'd kill me if he found me, that he'd hurt my parents instead of me. Above all, I was terrified that I'd never be able to stop the wrong person from dying at the door again. Every choice I've made—every truth I've hidden—has been to that end. So I can be here. So it can be me when the times comes."

I'm not ready to absolve him of murder *or* lying. But I have to be fair; in fact, I find I want to be fair. Because he is dear to me and a good person, and sometimes there is tragedy without sin, even here at Thornchapel.

"It's okay," I tell Becket now, echoing my mother's words. "It's okay. It was a mistake. You were trying to help."

He shakes his head. "I wasn't good enough or smart enough, and I wasn't even needed. And then later, I was such a coward, hiding in the trees and clutching that note like it would undo what I had done."

I blow out a breath. "The note. You sent it to me."

"I mailed it hoping you would come. I had dreams that you would, that you were here again. But I also mailed it knowing you deserved to have it. Whatever it meant, it was vital to her, so vital that she came back to the chapel. If anyone should inherit it, it's you. Not the stupid boy who killed her." This last part he says with such self-hatred that it scalds everyone in the chapel.

"So you see," he says heavily, "why I won't let anyone else suffer. I owe it to you, Poe, for what I've taken from your life. I owe it to your mother."

I'm very, very aware that he's still holding the knife, that it would take nothing for him to use it on himself. That we are so deep in the moor that it would take a very long time for an ambulance to arrive. If he hurts himself, there might be no saving him, no reversing it.

I can't let that happen.

We all take a collective inhale as he presses the point of the knife against his neck, and a very thin trickle of blood starts streaming down his throat. It catches the bevel of his clavicle under his button-down shirt. Auden surges forward at the same time Saint and Rebecca do. Startled, Becket lowers the knife the tiniest amount.

I seize the moment. I might not get another.

I tip the flask to my lips and I drink long and deep of the contents inside. It's remarkably easy to drink. Spicy and rose-flavored. A little sweet.

I finish and then take a long breath.

I feel exactly the same. Not at all like I'm somehow bound to another world.

Becket has staggered back from the others, still holding the knife, but no longer holding it at his throat. The bleeding on his neck has already slowed, although blood still gleams along the edge of the knife. It drips onto the ground.

"This is hard enough," he's pleading with the others. "I only need a moment. You don't have to watch."

"How fucking magnanimous of you," Saint retorts. "We'd only have to clean up your body later and somehow explain to your parents and the police that you killed yourself for a magic door."

"Not to mention that we'd have to live without our friend. Our priest." Auden steps forward, hands outstretched, palms up. "Give the knife to me."

"No, give it to me instead," Saint cuts in. "We can't trust Auden with it."

"I'm not trusting any of you with it," Rebecca says shortly. "Give *me* the knife."

"Everyone," I say. I mean to speak it loud, to shout it, but it comes out like a wisp of a word, like a whisper. The tea is finally working.

"Stop. *Stop.*"

Delphine is the first to hear. Her gold-brown eyes flick from my face to the flask and then back up again. "Poe," she breathes. "What did you do?"

The others turn to me with equally horrified expressions. Auden looks stunned in a way I've never seen before. What was it Becket said about Ralph when my mother died?

Like his soul had been ripped out of his body and I was responsible.

That's what Auden looks like right now.

"The roses," I say faintly, trying to hold the flask up. The ends of my fingers are numb now. My arm is weak. "Like in the fairy stories. I had to be certain, you see. I had to make it so I really couldn't come back. I was worried if I didn't—if there was a part of me that hoped to return—then it wouldn't be a sacrifice. Not really."

I'm so dizzy now. I feel my knees give, I feel the moment my balance slips like a wineglass on an unsteady tray, and I think, *the door, I have to make it to the door.* If I don't, then I might die for real.

I *could* die for real.

I don't want to die. But if I do, at least I will have spared the others, saved them...

I step to the door, close enough to touch it now, but I stumble sideways, and somehow that stumble takes me to the ground, and then the air in my lungs is gone, gone like it was never there to begin with. I struggle to breathe and breathe, and I realize all this has happened in an instant, in only a second, and that the others are yelling, screaming, rushing toward me.

On the other side of the door, I see a figure step into the torchlight. A narrow, utilitarian watch gleams from its wrist.

Torchlight glints off the buttons of cargo pockets.

I see green eyes and a smile like the sun.

I'm so close to her, but I can't breathe, I can't think, but all I want is to reach her, to tell her I know why she left and why she never came back and that I love her. I try to crawl, but I can't, and everyone is still screaming, and I think maybe she will come to me. Maybe she will step out of the door and hug me so hard it hurts, and suddenly it will be twelve years ago, and she'll be alive still, and I will have my whole life ahead of me, and everything will go right this time. I'll find Saint again and Auden, and we will spend all our years in a tangle of kink and a bramble of love, and when we die, we'll be old and gray and so full of each other that we'll be like cups overflowing with wine, love sloshing out with every movement, and it won't feel like a burden at all to die, not then, not when every atom of ours has been baptized with the draught of a full and spirited life.

Maybe it could happen. Maybe she's just about to step over the threshold and take me in her arms. Maybe the clock is about to turn back, and all this chapel's wrongs will be righted, and Saint and I can live inside the cruel affection of our wild god for decades and decades more, the three of us with one beating heart, for all the years we deserve.

Maybe.

Everything is possible, after all.

34

Auden

Her eyes are glassy and staring at nothing, her red-stained hands limp on the petals covering the ground. Her lips are parted in the small, slack yawn of death.

Becket was the closest when she fell, and so he has her in his arms already, he's standing as I'm shoving myself past the corner of the altar with St. Sebastian on my heels. He's cradling her in his arms. Right in front of the door.

Our eyes meet, and suddenly I know. I know what he's about to do.

"Just like the sisters," he says to me.

"No!" St. Sebastian shouts, but it's too late, Becket has stepped through, is setting Poe down on the ground on the other side. He kneels next to her and brushes her hair away from her face.

Becket's gaze finds mine again, across the threshold of the door. "Join us," he whispers to me over the noise of the drums. "Join us when you can."

Petals begin tearing free of the roses, flying into a storm of flowers, and they are everywhere, like confetti, like rain, thick and fluttering, and the drums are so very loud now, and so is the thunder cracking through the valley over and over again, and so is the wind, whipping the trees until the branches groan and shriek and there's leaves everywhere to join the petals, everywhere, everywhere. The chapel rumbles and shakes, and through all the petals, I see the door begin to swing shut.

Seized with a sudden panic, a desperate intuition, I lurch forward, but it's too late, the door is already almost closed and I can't make it, I won't make it through to my little bride, my wonderful Poe, my heart's curious, summery half.

I'm too late.

But.

But.

The last thing I see before the door closes is a miracle.

The last thing I see is Proserpina Markham blink herself awake.

Like she's just woken from a long and violent dream, like she's done so many times before, usually in my arms as the morning sunlight shafts in through the windows and Sir James snores on the floor.

She turns her head toward me and Saint, and she gives us a happy, sleepy smile, emerald eyes sparkling with curiosity and love. She opens her mouth as if to speak and—

The door slams shut before she can. It slams shut, and she is gone.

Lost to us.

And the minute the door closes, it has vanished altogether. There is nothing door-like left at all, no lintel, no jambs, no frame. No architrave or weathered wood.

It is gone like it never existed in the first place. There is only crumbling stone left where it stood. There is only a ruin where there was once my Proserpina.

Dark petals flutter everywhere.

I press my hand to the stone, and then my forehead. Saint's arms come around me, and he is weeping into my shoulder, just as I'm now weeping against the stone.

She is gone and we are left.

We are left.

She is gone.

"Auden," Delphine is saying, "Auden. Listen. Auden."

I can't move my face from the stone. I don't want to. I want to spend the rest of my miserable life here, remembering her, missing her. I want to starve here, I want to freeze here. I want to die here.

"Auden, she's alive on the other side," Delphine says. "You saw. She is *alive*. Do you remember what she said? About the blessing?"

I blink my wet eyelashes against the stone.

"She said the convivificat is a blessing," Saint says, slowly.

"Exactly," Delphine says. "We wondered how it could be, because it sounded so much like a warning. But 'it awakens' sounds a lot more like a blessing now, doesn't it? It stirs, it comes back. The door will return, Auden, and when it does, you can follow her. It's a promise."

"Oh," Saint says, pressing his face into my shoulder. "Oh."

We stay there for a long time, the magnitude of Delphine's words sinking in. The door will come back, because the door always comes back. And when it comes back, it will be a gift, because it will be the way back to the one we love.

I'm not sure how long we've been there, when we finally straighten up, spent of tears and sobs. It is full dark now, but the clouds have broken to reveal a heavy orange moon.

I touch my hand to the wall. "Convivificat," I murmur throatily to it, hoping she knows. Hoping she knows we understand the blessing and one day we will join her.

Convivificat.

I turn and take St. Sebastian's hand, feeling it warm and strong against my own. His piercing glints in the moonlight. There are still petals everywhere.

"Let's go then," I say. And together the four of us walk back to the house.

Epilogue

Bid Me Come Unto Thee
Eighteen years later

He starts the day as he usually does, by tying his husband to the bed and fucking him. He relishes it even more today, because St. Sebastian is still limp and well-pleasured from the night before, when Auden wrung climax after climax from him by the light of the Lammas fire.

Auden makes him come again now, even though Saint pleads and pleads that he's too sore from last night, that his cock aches too much to bear any kind of touch, but there is no safe word uttered at any point during the complaining, so Auden does it anyway. Caressing Saint's erection with teasing touches as his husband twists and squirms in his bonds, trying to escape the pleasure, and then later with a lubed but otherwise merciless fist until Saint's back bows and he releases all over his belly with a half-miserable, half-grateful whimper.

Then Auden climbs on top of him, relishing the feel of Saint's muscular, hair-dusted thighs on the inside of his own, loving how utterly limp and pliant his martyr is right now. He positions his hard organ against Saint's slowly softening one, and with Saint's seed slicking the way, Auden fucks, his cock trapped between their stomachs, their balls pressed together, their chests heaving as one.

He could come at any moment, but he forces himself to make it last. He always wants it to last after a night by the fire, where everything is blurry and carnal and urgent. He wants it slow, deliberate, his senses crackling with awareness. Less wild god and more greedy, affectionate man.

Finally, his cock swells and then pulses his seed between them. There's not much left after last night, but it's enough to make them even stickier, even messier. Sated, Auden drops a kiss on Saint's mouth, licking the small scar where his piercing used to be.

Saint had to remove it after taking his first supervisory position with the library, and now that he's the manager of the county's flagship branch, there's no question of it ever going back in. Auden misses it, and he thinks Saint does too, given how often he catches Saint sucking on his lower lip. But Auden knows exactly where the scar is and worships it often, biting it and kissing it and pressing on it with fingers and thumbs.

Things will change, but sometimes the memory can be enough.

Not always.

But sometimes.

He roots against Saint's temple, pressing soft kisses to the scattered threads of silver there.

"Don't uncuff me," Saint whispers. "I want to stay like this a while longer."

"You have to get to Exeter for your meeting," Auden says, although he doesn't stop nuzzling Saint's face and neck. "And I have a call with Isla in an hour."

"Why do we have jobs again?" Saint complains, turning his head to kiss Auden's jaw. "Or rather, why isn't my job being tied to your bed?"

"I ask myself this question every time you leave," Auden says, amused and serious at the same time. These moments sustain them both, when the power is naked between them, when the vulnerabilities and the cruelties are fed by trust and rewarded with the same.

It is the *only* thing that sustains him, he thinks sometimes, when the gaping hole in his chest seems to grow bigger and bloodier by the day. The unhealable wound left by Proserpina Markham. By her absence.

"Besides, I need to let Hilda Davidson out," Auden says, reluctantly pulling away from his lover and sliding off the bed to get a wet flannel.

"You know that dog would sleep until noon if you let it," Saint calls after Auden, as if *that dog* isn't the same dog Saint spoils rotten. However, Saint has a point about Hilda Davidson's disposition. Unlike Sir James Frazer and his successor, a cheerful corgi named Joseph Campbell, Hilda isn't rambunctious or energetic in the least. Even when she was a puppy, she'd trot halfway to a toy and then throw herself on the ground for a nap. And as Auden steps over the dog to get to the en suite now, Hilda's ears don't even twitch.

"God help us if we were beset upon by robbers or thieves," Auden says, stepping back over the lump of snoring bulldog, flannel in hand. "She'd be the last to know." He climbs onto the bed and carefully cleans Saint's stomach and groin, taking his time. When he's done, he tosses the rag to the side and uncuffs his husband, massaging each wrist and ankle after he works the padded leather free.

Saint sighs in pleasure and closes his eyes, but Auden watches and watches, not wanting to miss a single flutter of his eyelashes or contented part of his lips.

Eventually the room becomes too bright to ignore, and they both get dressed for work. St. Sebastian has long ago given up his collection of T-shirts and ripped jeans—at least during the week—and has allowed Auden to furnish him with proper work clothes, not the cheap trousers and ill-fitting button-downs he had before. This has backfired somewhat, as it means before he leaves the house, Auden is confronted with Saint looking like a magazine editorial for broody, dark-eyed men in expensive clothes. St. Sebastian is very often almost late for work, since Auden has trouble keeping his hands off him after he's dressed.

"Auden Guest," Saint says now, exasperated. They're at the kitchen counter waiting for the kettle, and Auden has been sliding his hands under Saint's jacket and over the taut curve of his arse.

"St. Sebastian Martinez-Guest," Auden teases back.

"We've just spent the last twenty-four hours fucking like we were twenty-five again."

"Mm," Auden hums, skating his palm over the fresh erection in Saint's virgin wool trousers. He can't imagine how sore his husband's poor organ must be right now. He wonders if he could get St. Sebastian to cry even as he climaxed. The mere thought has Auden so stiff he can barely breathe for the throbbing in his cock.

"So surely you leave me unmolested for a few hours while I go to work?"

SIERRA SIMONE

Auden thinks about this for a moment and then resumes his groping. "No."

Saint huffs. "You're only like this because I'm in all this expensive shit."

"Demonstrably false," Auden purrs, shoving a hand right into the front of Saint's trousers now. Despite his earlier protests, Saint pushes his penis into Auden's touch. "I like you on the weekends in your boots and jeans too. Especially with eyeliner."

"I'm too old for eyeliner," Saint says faintly, his pelvis rocking back and forth, back and forth.

"But you wear it for me anyway, because you know how wild it makes me. Do you remember last weekend?"

"Yes," Saint groans, his pelvis rocking faster. They went to the supermarket to get ingredients for a cake, but on the way back home, Auden looked over to see Saint in his ripped jeans and eyeliner, head resting against the window as he sang along with the song on the radio, and he suddenly couldn't take it. He cranked the Land Rover into a hedge-lined turnoff and had Saint in the back of the car in a matter of seconds. They went at it like young men, even with silver at their temples and fine lines beginning to branch around their eyes, even with wedding rings and years of marriage behind them, and Auden sucked Saint off like they were young men too, with accidental teeth and fumbling fingers and Saint's jeans only just barely shoved out of the way.

Auden pulls his hand free of Saint's trousers now and thoroughly enjoys the panicked whimpering that ensues.

"You can't leave me like this," Saint whines, turning to face his Sir.

"Oh but I can," says Auden with dark glee. "Just think of how needy you'll be all day, how difficult it'll be to sit through your meeting knowing I'll be waiting for you at home."

The knot of Saint's Adam's apple bobs up and then down. "You're a sadist."

Auden straightens Saint's clothes and flashes him his wickedest grin. "You like it."

"No," Saint sighs. "I love it." He looks down at his wedding ring, which is none other than the Guest family ring, the crest faintly visible in the morning light of the kitchen. "She loved it too."

She. Proserpina.

Their ghost, their grief.

Auden often wishes she were a ghost; he wishes she would haunt them. He wishes he'd walk into the chapel one day and find her like he found Estamond. He wishes he could dream her, hallucinate her, summon her. Because life without her…

It is difficult.

"Yes," he says, the bloody hole in his chest widening a little bit more. "Yes, she did."

The first few years were the hardest.

Waiting on a knife's edge of heartache—hoping, lamenting, praying, enduring. Day after day, week after week. Year after year. They went into the chapel on every cross-quarter feast, every solstice, every equinox. Every time, thinking this could be it—this could be the day. This could be the day the door opened, and Saint and Auden would step through and have her in their arms once again.

But feast after feast, the wall behind the altar remained stubbornly a *wall*. There was no flicker of wood or metal, no glimpse of bruise-colored roses, there was only stone and blackthorn and the usual dog roses, red and white and pink.

The door didn't come; the door never came.

And each time it didn't come, each feast where they built fires and ate cakes and prayed prayers, was a fresh blow, a new wound.

It was like losing her all over again.

It felt like losing themselves all over again.

Auden was very, very aware that there was a time between Estamond and his father when the door never came at all. More than a century.

Too long for anyone to wait.

At first, St. Sebastian didn't want to marry without Proserpina there. It felt wrong, he said, when they'd always envisioned a future with the three of them. It felt like giving up.

Auden agreed with the emotional dimension of his argument, but he also couldn't tolerate the possibility that something could happen to him and Saint would be faced with byzantine legal or medical struggles. And also he just...*wanted* it. He wanted rings, he wanted a wedding night, he wanted to show off Saint at pretentious work events—the whole thing. If they couldn't have Poe, then this felt like something they could have while they waited. Maybe it was only a part instead of the whole, but it was at least a *part*.

But Auden didn't seduce him into it, he didn't cajole or push. He waited as patiently as he was able, he reminded Saint that he was Saint's no matter what. Even if they never married, even if they were never affianced, all of Auden's forevers belonged to Saint, and that would never change.

And finally, one night as Saint was sitting at Auden's feet in the library, both of them reading while an arthritic Sir James Frazer napped by the fire, Saint looked up at Auden and said, simply, "Okay."

There was no question what he was agreeing to. Auden felt like he couldn't breathe. "Yes?"

Saint nodded and then rested his head against Auden's knee. "Yes."

Auden had tackled him right to the rug then, kissing him so deeply that they'd both been gasping for air when they finished, but smiling too.

"You won't regret it," Auden vowed fiercely.

"Oh, Auden," Saint sighed. "I know."

They were married a few months later, at Thornchapel, the ceremony small and private but no less lavish for its intimate size. Auden would only get married once in this world, and so he spared no expense when it came to flowers and food and marquees and music. (And with Delphine Dansey planning it, no expense would have been spared anyway.)

It was indulgent on the order of a king—a wedding fit for the lord of the manor.

And so they married, and so the years circled on, a giant wheel which ground from despair whenever the door failed to appear to the ordinary joys and toils of life.

St. Sebastian took a supervisory position at the library and helped his uncle Augie sell his business and finally retire. He and Auden visit the family in Texas every year, and Thornchapel is often filled with visiting grandparents and cousins and aunts and uncles with brand new anoraks and selfie sticks. He talks often about finally cataloging Thornchapel's library, but he never starts and Auden never pushes him to. Neither of them can bear to pick up where Proserpina left off.

Samson Quartey also retired, earlier than anyone expected, and passed the reins of Quartey Workshop to Rebecca. He then moved to America, where he lives with David Markham to this day, both of them teaching at the university and adopting more dogs than their house can hold. After he left, Rebecca expanded Quartey Workshop into one of the largest and busiest landscape architecture firms in Europe, building on the foundation he laid.

Delphine founded a line of lipsticks, which turned into a full-fledged beauty brand. A handful of years ago, she expanded into clothing—plus-size lingerie and formalwear, and then sportswear a few years after. She has Freddie's knack for accidentally making money she doesn't need.

She and Rebecca married at Thornchapel too, two years after St. Sebastian and Auden. A wedding so big that it was featured in every possible society rag and was attended by several minor celebrities and even a princess.

They live here whenever they're not in London.

As for Auden, Harcourt + Trask is now Harcourt + Guest, after Trask retired and sold his share of the business to Auden. They've won some RIBA awards, been in the right magazines, appeared on television a few times. He still loves the work, the vision, the marriage of the ephemeral mind to things like glulam and steel, but the loss of Poe changed him in a way that is difficult to articulate.

He finds that he loves architecture in a distant, disassociated sort of way now, as if he's playing an architect for television rather than being one in real life. The things he really loves—his husband, his friends, sitting in the woods with a notebook and pencils and sketching whatever comes to mind—call to him more and more. He's finally earned the success he craved as a be-scarfed, be-satcheled young man, and the irony is that now he really couldn't care less. He just wants to make love to his Saint and laugh with his friends and draw when the light is good.

He often draws her. He tries to capture the way her lips would crease from their own fullness, or the way her brow would pucker while she scoured books for the metadata she needed.

But it's been so many long, full years. And so he finds that he's beginning to lose these tiny quirks, these little singularities that made up Poe Markham. He knows she isn't dead, he believes that as much as he believes anything. But forgetting her feels like death. It feels like finality. It feels like something closing in on him, a loss even the Thorn King can't outrun.

And again the wheel of the year turns.

Midwinter, Imbolc, equinox.

Beltane, midsummer, Lammas.

Equinox and Samhain and then midwinter again, on and on and on.

Dogs are adopted, trips are taken, small fights are fought and then resolved. Sex is had, kisses are stolen in the morning and at night before sleep sets in. Sometimes Auden has to go run through the woods alone. Sometimes St. Sebastian disappears to wander the hills by himself. Sometimes they find each other crying. It is a lesson they have to continually relearn, that it is better to cry together than alone.

Auden's eyes remain hazel, as they have since that night, when the dark crimson bled out of his irises just as the life bled out of the invading roses. By the time All Saint's Day dawned, the canes and bushes had crumbled into a fine dust, which would be completely blown away before the end of the week. The petals lingered longer, shriveling into dry, dark husks that skittered over the drive and gathered in the crevices around the cists, a fragrant dredge of dead blooms that drifted around the estate until the snows came and they finally rotted back into the earth.

The trees still move when he's sad or restless; storms come when he wants them. Rebecca still grows flowers when she presses her hands to the earth. Sometimes they grow under her bare feet as she walks, small and tender, springing up under her footsteps.

These things follow them elsewhere, but they are strongest at Thornchapel, and the strength of them fades the farther away they get from it. And with the resonance between the valley and the door in a kind of stasis, there is no reaction to Rebecca growing flowers…other than there being flowers everywhere.

Auden hasn't cried a single rose petal since that Samhain.

The feasts are celebrated still, although hope becomes a ghost, an imprint of itself. A photo-negative now only recognizable by its absence. The anguish of this absence is potent. They mourn the death of hope now too.

They miss her. They miss her. They miss her.

The wheel turns and turns again. Their bodies change, the missing piece of their hearts doesn't. They cling to each other like Paul the Apostle clinging to pieces of his ship after a shipwreck.

Upstairs, tucked into Jennifer Martinez's Bible, is a letter from a lab, containing test results. Auden doesn't know if it's ever been opened, and Saint never says. But sometimes Auden finds him staring down at the Guest ring on his left hand, as if expecting it to speak to him. As if expecting a different kind of answer than alleles can give.

Whatever the results say, Freddie has thoroughly adopted Saint as his son, and they have a warm, if more fraternal than paternal, relationship.

The official records still list Richard Davey as Saint's father.

The one time Auden asks Saint about it, just after Saint's thirtieth birthday, Saint presses his left hand to Auden's exposed chest, hard enough that Auden can feel Saint's wedding ring against his skin. "I'm a Guest now anyway," he says softly.

Auden covers Saint's hand with his own, knowing that's all the answer he'll get. But he's never really cared about the answer, only about St. Sebastian. "You're mine now."

"I always was. I wouldn't have it any other way, Auden, just so you know. I'm here to stay."

That's all that Auden needs to know.

And the wheel turns.

And turns again.

After Saint leaves for work, still grumbling about his thwarted orgasm, Auden goes up and starts his call. He's in the middle of discussing the benefits of a sod roof for an Icelandic modern arts centre when he sees Rebecca through one of his office windows. Coming up the lawn past the labyrinth she finally built; running not walking.

From the direction of the chapel.

Instinct surges through him, clear and sharp. Instinct—and something he hasn't felt in so long that he's afraid to name it to himself.

Auden turns off the camera on his call and sends a quick private message to Isla that something urgent has popped up and he'll be back when he can. And then he runs down the steps to the ground floor, practically vaulting over Hilda Davidson snoozing on the landing.

He meets his friend just as she's coming to the terrace steps, her brown eyes bright and pinning him with exigent joy. Behind her, the low turf of the labyrinth gleams with dew, and the tombs incorporated into the switchbacks and circuits of the path are still wet from a pre-dawn shower. At the center of the labyrinth is the now-empty king's grave and the rose-carved chamber.

In a way now, anybody can walk to the door.

"I thought you and Delphine were still asleep," Auden says. "I didn't realize you were awake—"

"It's back," she interrupts him, breathlessly. "Auden. It's *back*. The door is here. It's open again."

The door is back.

Just like eighteen years ago, it is a thing of old wood and dull metal, and just like eighteen years ago, it looks out onto a clearing that seems cloned from the one outside the chapel.

There is no sign of Proserpina or Becket.

"Will you go through it?" Rebecca asks. She and Auden stand shoulder to shoulder in front of it, watching the breeze play over the grass on the other side. "You could go tonight, Auden. You and Saint could be with her tonight."

Auden lets out a long breath. The idea is tempting—beyond tempting. To think that he could see her, hold her, smell her, kiss her.

That the three of them could finally share a heartbeat once again.

But.

"There are things that must be done first," he says, forcing himself to think rationally. "We'll do it at Samhain."

"And if the roses come?"

"We will pray that they don't."

Rebecca is convinced the door has something to do with entropy and thermodynamics, with ordering and transformation. If this is the case—and if this is what causes the sickness in the valley when it comes—then Auden is not sure there will ever be a cure as such for the sickness, other than moving people out of the valley. He and Rebecca have talked about the various different ways to do that, if the time comes.

Gemma Dawes still weighs heavily on his mind.

"It's strange," Rebecca says after a moment, her eyes on a vine-wrapped tree in the door-world's clearing. "If I hadn't watched the wren die that night, everything would be different now. I wouldn't have felt the need to protect Delphine, to keep her close while she was here. I wouldn't have realized how powerfully I still felt for her or that I still thought of her as mine. Without that wren's death, I could very well be alone and miserable, with a trail of wasted years behind me."

She turns and gives Auden a small, sad smile. "I wish Becket were here so I could tell him so. He'd want to know that the wren was a blessing too."

That night, when he tells St. Sebastian that the door has returned, his husband starts crying. There is hope and terror both in his face. "What if it doesn't work?" he asks Auden. "What if this is when we find out that we truly are separated forever?"

"Shh," Auden says, kissing him, pushing him back onto the bed and kissing him more. "Shh now. We cannot know until we try."

"What if something's happened to her over there?" Saint whispers. "What if we can cross over, but when we get there, she's dead or moved on?"

Auden has thought of this too. "Then you and I will be together still, only over there," he says firmly. "We will have each other, just as we do here and now."

"Are you"—Saint's lips twitch in a small smile against Auden's mouth—"Are you saying going through a magic door is a lateral move for us?"

Auden laughs a little. "Yes. I suppose I am."

"And if we do find her? Will things be as they were?"

Auden kisses St. Sebastian again. "I doubt they will be the same, because we are not the same. But I have to believe she's held on to us as we've held on to her. Perhaps even more than we have…she was the one who recognized what the three of us were, remember. The first one who spoke it aloud."

How foolish he'd been then, how young and prideful, obsessed with all the ways he felt he'd been hurt.

Saint seems to be thinking along the same lines. "Nothing will be wasted ever again. Not this time."

"We won't waste a moment," agrees Auden. "Not a single moment."

Auden's prayers have been partly answered, and while the roses return, they bloom only in the clearing, climbing up chapel walls and snaking around standing stones. Rebecca postulates that the double sacrifice of Poe and Becket has dissipated a good store of whatever energy the door seems to bring with it when it appears. There had been no pollen record of the roses when the Kernstows were in charge, after all. Maybe something about the Kernstow style of sacrifice creates a positive feedback loop, making the door easier and easier to live with.

Whatever the reason, Auden is grateful. No one sickens this time, not even the sheep. No one has to be peremptorily displaced from their homes for their own safety. He hopes the combined sacrifice of him and Saint walking through the door today will be enough to keep any illness at bay for a very long time.

As for what happens after they walk through: while Auden insisted the door remain a secret until it returned because he couldn't abide the possibility that its discovery by the wider world might compromise his chance to get back to Poe, Thornchapel is now officially and legally the property of Rebecca Quartey and Delphine Dansey to do with whatever they will. Auden can't say what will happen then, but hopefully it will be the beginning of something new for Thornchapel, something new for its secrets. It has been in its own world long enough.

The legalities have been arranged, jobs gracefully resigned. Saint spends a last few weeks in Texas, and then makes his farewells with Freddie.

Auden asks David Markham, who—along with the other parents—was told the full truth of Poe's disappearance after it happened, if he'd like to come through the door with him and Saint. Auden already knows that the answer will be no.

And it is no. Not because he doesn't desperately miss his daughter, but because he has a life on this side, a new life with Samson.

Auden tells him he understands. And he offers to bring a letter to Poe when he crosses over, which is an offer David gratefully accepts.

And then...

And then they are ready.

Samhain comes with a glittering frost.

When dusk encroaches, the four of them walk through the eerie chill to the chapel. Unlike that night eighteen years ago, no clouds darken the sky. A sunset of red and orange is fading below the hills, and purplish shadows are creeping between the trees.

They have no lanterns this time, no cakes and ale. There is no agenda, no schedule or order of events, nothing to propitiate the spirits of the place. The only thing Saint and Auden carry are small bags. Auden has David Markham's letter to Poe tucked safely inside his, along with a letter from the Hesses, who also chose to stay here—although not without plenty of struggle and doubt.

Rebecca, Delphine, Saint, and Auden process down the stone row and into the chapel, where darkness has already pooled in the corners and around the altar. Dry leaves rustle from all around the chapel walls.

Through the door, Auden sees torchlight.

"Make sure Hilda gets a walk every day," Auden tells Delphine. She and Rebecca are adopting her, which Rebecca pretends to grumble about, even though she is the worst about sneaking Hilda bites from her plate during dinner. "She won't want to do it, but she needs it."

"Of course," Delphine says. They are very close to the door now. He pulls her into a tight hug, gives her a soft kiss on the lips.

"Take care, Delly," he whispers. "And take care of Rebecca for me. Force her on holiday now and then."

"I heard that," Rebecca says sharply, stepping forward for her own hug. She and Auden also kiss, firm and quick. "*You* take care, please. I can't help from over here if anything goes wrong."

"I know, Quartey." Auden runs his knuckles along her jaw. "And I have something for you." He reaches into the pocket of his coat and then presses something cool and heavy into her hand.

She looks down. Gold glints in the crepuscular light. "The torc."

"You're the king now, the wild god."

Emotion trembles in her mouth. "Auden…"

"I couldn't be leaving Thornchapel in better hands," he assures her.

"Even though I'm the first owner in fifteen hundred years who's not a Guest?"

Auden grins. "*Especially* because you're the first owner in fifteen hundred years who's not a Guest."

She smiles, and then with a flash of her eyes, she fits the torc around her slender neck. Auden feels a final weight lift from his shoulders—though it means nothing to the outside world, and to the outside world, this was sealed weeks ago with signatures and deeds— in the argot of this place, Thornchapel is now really, really hers.

And he is free to leave it.

St. Sebastian makes his farewells with Delphine and Rebecca too, and then there is nothing left to wait for, nothing holding them back. They step closer to the door, which is framed with full, fragrant blooms, and adjust the bags on their shoulders.

"Are you sure you don't need to eat or drink anything, like Poe did?" Delphine asks.

Auden shakes his head. "Poe drank that tea so she'd have a reason she could never come back. But we already have our reason."

"You do?"

"She's our reason," Saint says. "It's her."

Auden finds Saint's hand, laces his fingers through Saint's fingers, and then looks back to see Rebecca and Delphine on the other side of the altar, Delphine tucked under Rebecca's arm. They are both crying, Rebecca only a little, swallowing and swallowing to keep her tears back, and Delphine quite a lot, her entire body shaking.

"Are you sure you don't want to come with us?" Auden asks a final time.

He already knows the answer before Rebecca shakes her head, smiling under her tears. "Someone has to set this place to rights." And then she shakes her head again, as if she realizes that's not quite the answer she means. "I *want* to set this place to rights. And life here is…" She looks down at her wife. "Life here is beautiful too," she finishes softly.

Auden nods. He didn't expect anything different, but it does hurt, to say goodbye. It does feel wrong in the sense that goodbyes often feel wrong. Especially permanent ones.

"I love you," he tells them both.

"We love you back," Rebecca says, the words a little wavery. But then they firm up. "Now *go*. Delphine is getting cold."

He's already turning back to the door when he hears Delphine gasp. He inhales too, when he sees. Poe is at the door, just on the other side.

"Proserpina," he whispers.

"Auden," she says. "St. Sebastian."

They can hear each other across the threshold, and see each other too. The veil is completely parted now.

She isn't wearing fairy clothes, nor some heavenly robe nor the garb of the ancients. She's not in the clothes she crossed over in, the clingy jeans and the wool coat. She's wearing a short, flared skirt with a shirt and cardigan, with thick tights and Oxford shoes. She's wearing the kind of thing she loved to wear on this side of the door.

She also hasn't aged, not at all that Auden can tell. She still looks twenty-two, still dark-haired and soft-skinned and young, and for a moment, Auden is worried. Worried that she will see the gray flecking their temples or the lines around their eyes and mouths and dislike it.

But instead her expressive eyes rake over them, and then flare with something Auden recognizes immediately, even after eighteen years.

Lust.

The rejoining arousal kicks him hard in the groin, and then there's a surge of need beyond lust, a need of power and connection. The loose braid over her shoulder should be in his fist. Those creased lips should be pressed to the top of his foot. Those eyes should be looking at him from inside the circle of his arms.

"We've come to join you," Auden says. "Can we?"

Tears shine in her eyes.

"Yes," she says, voice breaking. "It's so wonderful here, and Becket and I have been so happy, but without the two of you, I—" She wipes the tears off her face and gives Auden and Saint a helpless kind of smile.

"We know," Saint murmurs. "We know exactly what you mean."

With a subtle flex of his fingers, Auden asks Saint if he's ready. Saint's hand twitches in his own. And then, with a final smile tossed to Rebecca and Delphine, Auden leads St. Sebastian across the threshold and into the clearing on the other side.

It doesn't feel like anything, leaving their world behind. It doesn't feel like death or transformation or anything other than stepping through a door.

It's still chilly. Moors still frown down at them, and the forest still sways. The air still smells like October—smoke and cold wet leaves—and the stars above them are the same.

He looks over at Saint, who looks back at him, a rare smile pulling at his pretty mouth. They both turn to Poe, who is fully crying now and smiling too, and she flings herself into both their arms, smelling of sunshine and books, her warm, curvy body sandwiched between theirs.

A great gust of wind comes rushing through, and the drums pound louder, louder. Auden lifts his face from Poe's hair and looks over his shoulder to see a chapel much like the one he just left, only whole and complete, with light blazing from windows still paned in stained glass.

"The door," says Saint, looking too. They turn enough so that they can watch, although they stay in each other's arms, Poe caught between them.

The door is closing.

They lift their hands to Rebecca and Delphine on the other side, and Rebecca and Delphine lift their hands too, and for a moment, it really does feel that there's only a few mundane yards between them, that all the years have fallen away and they are young together in the chapel once more, ready to light a fire and kiss each other senseless.

"Goodbye," he whispers.

The last thing he sees before the door shuts is the torc, glinting faintly around Rebecca's neck. Then, with a dull thud as ordinary as anything, the door closes. The dead leaves in the trees rattle as the drums cease.

And the door is gone.

It's done.

Auden pulls Proserpina close, pulls Saint in close too, so that they are all pressed, all tight together. "I'm so glad you're here," she says, and her hands are restless now, seeking their hips, their necks, their hair.

"You don't mind that we took our time?" Saint asks dryly.

"It hasn't been as much time here, I think," she says, her fingers straying over the silver in Saint's hair. "Not as much as it's been for you."

"You truly don't mind?" Saint asks, something vulnerable in his voice. Not due to his age, Auden thinks, but from the worry that there could be any remaining barriers between them and Poe.

A hot look flickers under her tears. "I don't mind," she says throatily. "You can feel for yourself how much, if you'd like."

Auden can't wait. He knows they've just left their entire lives behind, they're in a world that's not their own, they haven't seen this girl for eighteen years. And still he snakes his arm around her waist and shoves his hand up her skirt.

Underneath her tights, she's as slick as he's ever felt her.

He is nearly torn apart by the need clawing inside him, then, and Saint appears just as undone.

"I will take you at any age," she murmurs as Auden pushes a finger inside. "But I did always have a thing for older lovers…"

"Can we?" Auden asks. Saint is already dropping his bag to the cold grass at their feet. "Here?"

"Yes," she says, arching her throat as Auden explores her more thoroughly. "Here."

He pulls her down to the ground—him sitting and her straddling—and Saint follows, coming to kneel behind her. A hole is ripped in her tights, his trousers torn open, and then he's piercing up into her living heat for the first time in eighteen years. Wet, silky warmth envelops his length, slick and squeezing, and his mouth is on hers while Saint savages her neck with eager sucks. Auden can hear Saint pulling at his jeans, and then Auden is abruptly exposed to the chilly air as Saint thrusts into Poe from behind.

"Fuck," Saint mumbles, his head dropping forward. "I forgot."

Auden had too. Not only what it felt like to have her body against his, around his, but what it felt like to have the three of them together. Saint's eyes like ink in the night, Proserpina's soft cries like music.

Auden pulls her back onto him, and then they continue like this, with turns, with wet, hungry kisses, with hands shoved under shirts and feral grunts, and she comes first, fast and hard enough to make her thighs shake around Auden's hips, and Saint follows her, rutting under her skirt like every single day of these eighteen years apart is eating at his soul, and then when he slumps back, Auden takes his turn, fucking until she's crying out against his shoulder and he's emptying himself into her hard enough to make his hips lift off the ground.

He stays like that a minute, knowing they need to move, knowing he needs to spend the next eighteen years making up for every day they've lost, but wanting to feel her just a moment longer. Wanting to meet Saint's gaze and take in the wondering, wonderful bliss on his husband's face.

"Where's Becket?" Auden asks in a murmur, stroking Poe's hair.

"In the chapel," she says dozily. "He's a priest again. Here."

Saint trails a line of kisses from her neck down to her shoulder. Auden watches Saint's fingers roll a stiff nipple under her shirt. Happiness spikes his blood like a good whisky.

"I need to fuck you again soon," says Auden bluntly. "Saint does too."

"You better," Poe says. And then she is grinning, dimpled and wild, and Saint is smiling too, a big, unabashed smile that even Auden has only seen a few times. Auden hardens as much at that smile as at the renewed friction against his organ as Poe shifts in his lap.

"What happens next?" Saint asks, sifting his fingers through Poe's hair. His other hand is idly stroking Auden's thigh. Auden's heart—that wild and thorny thing—is burning with grateful possession, with contentment, with hunger and with joy. He flexes cruel fingers on Proserpina and Saint's thighs, hard enough to hurt, shivering ever so slightly as he witnesses their twin gasps, the way their lips part with a yearning that so perfectly fits his own.

"I don't know," he says, a slow smile curling his lips. "Little bride?"

She leans in to kiss him, pulling Saint's mouth to theirs too, and as the torches in the clearing gutter in the wind and leaves of crimson and gold flutter and swirl around them, they share a long, hard kiss.

A kiss that promises eternity.

"Next," she says, her breath tickling their lips, "we go home."

And then they are up and moving, grinning as they fix their clothes and the chilly breeze catches their intimate flesh, hardly able to stop touching each other as they set themselves to rights and Poe leads them into the moonlit forest, laughing as Auden hauls her up into his arms and refuses to put her down.

As they go into the trees, Auden hears singing from the chapel.

Something like a hymn, old and Latin and beautiful. A benediction, maybe.

Or a blessing.

Convivificat.

Afterword

When I was ten or eleven, I found a book in the tiny YA section of my local library called *The China Garden*. I can't remember why I picked it up—it definitely wasn't the cover—but I do remember that I read it two or three times on its first checkout. And then I checked it out again. And again. And again, until I convinced my mom to buy me a copy at Barnes and Noble for me to love on forever.

What I loved about *The China Garden* was how it swirled things together into a unique and seamless whole: the gothic settings of a cloistered village and an old manor house, some hints of ancient Celtic rituals, sulky boys with motorcycles...

What I *also* loved is how the book made me feel. (Which was, as my friend Jean says, 'creeped out and comforted all at the same time.') I imprinted on that feeling as much as I imprinted on the book itself,

I think, especially on the way the setting itself could evoke that feeling. And so when I started writing longer stories at that age, the *creepy but wonderful* vibe was the one I was always trying to chase.

Fast forward to 2007, when I was a baby creative writing student wearing big black boots and smoking clove cigarettes outside douchey literary events. I went to a thing co-hosted by PostSecret and Found Magazine—which only matters to this story because I was just creative-writing-major-y enough to buy a random CD off a folding table in the lobby.

The act was called The Poem Adept and the CD was called *The Sight of Any Bird,* and while the whole album was great ("Bus or Beer" is still a total anthem), there was a song on there called "Commons" which I listened to on repeat for a decade. I had no idea what had inspired the song or what it meant—only that it was about a dead friend—but the *feeling* of it, the idea that murdering someone close to you could be necessary and awful and haunting and maybe the worst thing you've ever done and maybe you'd still do it again—it stayed with me. It sank into my storytelling bones.

Fast forward to 2017, when I finally caved to the eighty-seven different recommendations that had flown my way over the years and cracked open *The Secret History* by Donna Tartt, and at the very first line, I realized I'd found the inspiration for "Commons". So after a decade of being obsessed with a song about this book, I finally had the chance to obsess over the actual book now too, *which I did.* Because the idea that a group of friends could grow so fascinated with ritual, with ancient belief and a forgotten way of life, that they could commit murder—it terrified me.

It terrified me so much that the terror felt like fascination instead. Now, finally, we get to early 2018. I was on a plane to Australia for a signing, and having just turned in a book, I was determined to use the long journey to noodle over some of the stories I needed to work on next. The next book in the *Priest* series maybe, or that Mark, Tristan, and Isolde thing I'd been talking about. But when I laid back in my seat and turned on my music, all that was moving through my mind was *The Secret History* and how it made me feel...which reminded me so much of how Primordial Sierra had felt reading *The China Garden.*

Add in my fascination with the origins of myth and human sacrifice, Robert MacFarlane's *Landmarks,* some stuff on the Simone Scale I was dying to write, and my ongoing recovery from VC Andrews—(not to mention my forever love of broody, kinky boys)—and I had a pretty wild mix circling on the old Sierra Thought Carousel.

I was, in short, primed to dream up Thornchapel. A series that made no commercial or career sense to write. A series that didn't really match *Priest* or *New Camelot,* a series that was maybe, ah, *less* than mainstream, we could say.

A series I couldn't stop thinking about.

It had a gravity, this idea. Forbidden romance. Gothic setting. Old books. Older secrets. A king learning how to be a king. A sacrifice that can't be avoided. The feeling that the world is so much bigger, creepier, and sexier than we give it credit for.

As Peter Rothbart of The Poem Adept sings in "Commons," "It's the beautiful in life that's so alarming" and yes, that's the feeling, that's the gravity. It's creepy *and* comforting. It's beautiful *and* alarming. It's good and bad, and life and death, together and alone.

It's Thornchapel.

And thank you for going there with me.

xoxo,
Sierra Simone
Olathe, KS 2020

Author's Note

While this series is shameless fanfic of *The China Garden* and *The Secret History*—along with *Strange Grace* by Tessa Gratton, which I read the year I started *A Lesson in Thorns*—I was inspired by several works of non-fiction as well, especially the works of H.R. Ellis Davidson, Catherine Bell, Karen Armstrong, and Robert MacFarlane. (And obviously Sir James Frazer's *The Golden Bough*, but I'd use the term 'non-fiction' a little loosely there.)

All of the cross-quarter feasts and their attendant rituals have been *very* liberally interpreted by me, as I thought would best suit the narrative and also allow for the most angst (or the most sex). My forever thanks to Robin Murphy, Tessa Gratton, and Natalie Parker for letting me bug them with alllll the questions, and also to Robin for the stacks of books lent from her personal library, which helped immensely.

Additionally, I've taken great liberties with the archaeology of Dartmoor, which is extremely archaeologically rich, but not rife with evidence of neolithic plagues and ritual murder, like I make it sound. I owe a great debt to legendarydartmoor.co.uk/ for filling in the gaps left by the broader works on ancient British history.

If you're interested, you can find a complete Thornchapel bibliography here: thornchapel.com/bibliography.

Not Ready to Leave Thornchapel?

Is your heart still at the door with our friends? Check out all the Thornchapel playlists here: www.thornchapel.com/the-music.

Tipple thematically with these Thornchapel-inspired cocktails: www.thornchapel.com/thornchapelcocktails

Check out how it all began (and get a taste of the next MMF series I'll write) with *American Squire!*

Former presidential aide Ryan Belvedere has been drifting in a fog of misery, but he reluctantly agrees to do a favor for a friend—fetching a rare book from a crumbling manor house in England.

There he meets Sidney Blount—cold, sophisticated, Dominant—who's at the same house to appraise the family art.

It doesn't take Sidney long to appraise Ryan too, and decide exactly what Ryan needs. Which just so happens to be the one thing Sidney wants to give…

And finally, if you must leave Thornchapel, might I recommend a healthy dose of kinky MMF deliciousness with my New Camelot series? Start with *American Queen!*

"…a delicious fantasy, a filthy fairytale…rich in texture, intensely emotional, and highly erotic, with a perfect hint of magic."

— Meredith Wild, #1 New York Times bestselling author

Acknowledgments

This series has taken me two years, multiple crises of psychic pain, and many afternoons of lying facedown on the floor…and I simply could not have done it without all the wonderful people in my real life and publishing life. Especially this year, of all years, I've found there's simply no way to carry on without the love and support of family, friends, and team.

Firstly, I owe a profound debt to my editor, Erica Russikoff. Erica not only talked me through many authorial meltdowns and offered compassionate encouragement and clear-eyed calm, she also shepherded this story with her observations, insights and thoughtful questions. From keeping mysteries tallied and accounted for, to personally emailing the CMoS for information on enabling my em dash abuse, she's both the doula and the midwife for this entire series.

I'd also like to thank Nana Malone, Julie Murphy, and Vanessa

Reyes for their notes, ideas, and insights about Rebecca, Delphine and St. Sebastian over the course of the series. Furthermore, this series couldn't have come to be if Robin Murphy hadn't let me corner her in her pool from time to time to ask her every question I could think of about ritual practice and contemporary pagan culture. Karen Cundy has been a compassionate and indispensable resource for cultural accuracy and lexicon, and I am extremely grateful.

I'm also grateful to Michele Ficht, for her eagle eye; to Ashley Lindemann, newsletter maven and website asskicker; to Candi Kane, PR wizard and author life manager; to Serena McDonald, Facebook wizard and all around fun-time girl; Melissa Gaston, organizational guru and social media whiz. I'm additionally grateful for my agents, Rebecca Friedman at RF Literary, and Meire Dias and Flavia Viotti at Bookcase, for all their support and acumen.

I rely heavily—I mean, *heavily*—on my friends to talk through plot, inspiration, research, and also for help getting off my floor when the book has sent me there. Ashley Lindemann, Julie Murphy, Nana Malone, Tess Gratton, Natalie Parker, Kennedy Ryan, Kyla Linde, Becca Mysoor, Jean Siska, Kayti McGee, Kenya Goree-Bell, the authors of the *Naughty Brits* anthology, the authors of the *Duke I'd Like to F...*anthology, and the women in the 2019 RITA Writer's Room have been sources of wisdom, encouragement, laughter, and ideas all through this series.

I also have to thank Kenya Goree-Bell, LaQuette, Christi Caldwell, and Naima Simone for those afternoon and vampire-hour sprints—this book wouldn't have happened without them!

Most importantly (and most cheesily, I know, I know), I have to thank my husband. He is deeply supportive in all ways big and small; he's encouraging, generous, and genuinely excited for my highs and ready to be a safety net for my lows. He is like a weighted blanket, aged scotch, and sunny day in the form of a person, and whenever I've thought about what bravery and loyalty look like on a practical level, I've come back to him as a model. (There's a reason my heroes recycle and are concerned with fire safety, haha.) Thank you, Mr. Simone, for everything.

Finally, I have to thank *you*. Thank you for letting me write something unexpected and weird and taboo. Thank you for letting me write rich boy/poor boy angst and doors in the woods and all the gothic fever-dreamy things I love so much. Thank you for indulging me, and thank you for walking to the door with our characters. I wrote this series in part because I wanted to explore what it meant to be a king—and a good one—and the answer I found is the same answer that underpins any writer's life, reality, and career.

Humility.

I wouldn't be able to do this job without you, and I'm humbled by the time, energy, and emotion you're willing to give my kinky, thorny words.

Thank you.

About the Author

Sierra Simone is a *USA Today* bestselling former librarian who spent too much time reading romance novels at the information desk. She lives with her husband and family in Kansas City.

Sign up for her newsletter to be notified of releases, books going on sale, events, and other news!

www.thesierrasimone.com

Also by Sierra Simone

Thornchapel:
A Lesson in Thorns
Feast of Sparks
Harvest of Sighs
Door of Bruises

Misadventures:
Misadventures with a Professor
Misadventures of a Curvy Girl
Misadventures in Blue

New Camelot:
American Queen
American Prince
American King
The Moon (Merlin's Novella)
American Squire (A *Thornchapel* and *New Camelot* Crossover)

The Priest Collection:
Priest
Midnight Mass: A Priest Novella
Sinner